matters familiar

e. g. fabricant

ISBN: 0615727042
ISBN-13: 9780615727042

Library of Congress Control Number: 2011917205

Cover designed by E. G. Fabricant

Cover photograph property of E. G. Fabricant

Printed in the United States of America

DEDICATION

For Frank and Betty, for the gifts of life and love—theirs, mine, and ours—and

For M. A.; BeeEss; Tomiss; Jerome; J. L.; Fuffy; and The Brat, for helping me fill in the blanks.

.

CONTENTS

1 Ashley Alert

ಬಿಂಚಿ

She pushed her ginger curls away from her ear and laid it carefully against the door and listened. *All right!* She clapped her hands and squealed, thought better of it and almost as quickly shushed herself. She sailed into the room and onto her trundle bed, one knee aboard and a straight leg trailing. She glimpsed the lacy blouse, pinafore, and Mary Janes on her image in the mirror and frowned. *I hate me! Why do I have to be so girly all the time?* Out came the tongue. *Oh, well...* Pushing her round, black eyeglass frames up her nose brought a hint of a smile. *Very* Harry Potter. Daddy'd won that one, liking them over those wiry things Mommy picked out.

She reached behind all the "educational" stuff on her bookshelf and brought out her latest guilty pleasure. She gladdened as she traced the image of the wild-haired girl on the cover, airborne in vapors and gaily pinching her nostrils. *Betty has red pants with green polka dots—and yellow socks! I could be her, 'cause our hair's almost the same color.* Looking up again, she frowned at the pastel clasps holding her locks.

No barrettes for Betty! She tore at them, flung them aside, and shook her head fiercely. Freedom was pleasing.

Settling in cross-legged, she cracked the book and laid it reverently across her thighs. Page One—again; there he was, in all his blue-eyed, dirty-sheep splendor. She turned the page and read softly to herself, savoring every word:

> "Mother walked in and said, 'He still smells awful.'
>
> And that's when they got the first clue. The tell-tale bubbles in the water.
>
> 'He's probably just a little nervous,' said Mother, hopefully. 'His stomach must be upset.'
>
> But Walter's stomach wasn't upset. Walter's stomach was fine. He felt perfectly normal. He just far—"[1]

The door cracked. A laundry basket. Her Mother.

"Come *on*, Ashley! It's the second Wednesday—you know that. We're late for your play date at Ryan's and there's tap class, after that." Rosemary Butterworth looked up and saw her panicky, slack-jawed daughter hugging a book to her bosom. She shoved the basket onto the toy chest and put her hands on her hips. "What're you reading?"

Ashley's eyes fell, as did the book. "Nothing..."

Rosemary took it. "'*Walter the Farting Dog*?!' Where did you get this?"

Ashley pushed her lower lip out and her dark eyes blazed. "Found it."

Rosemary scowled and tucked the book under her arm. "We'll talk about this later. Get your sweater and your shoes."

ℰℭ

     Alex Butterworth nudged the front door open with his briefcase, juggling his keys and the daily mail in his other hand. He slid inside, shoved the door closed with his heel, and pitched the keys onto the hall table. Dropping the case by the banister, he stretched, sighed, and scratched his scalp. *Another day in the particular Paradise that is the San Bernardino Unified School District.* He'd barely begun shuffling paper when the door burst open behind him. Ashley grazed him behind the knees and hit the stairs hard.

     "Hey, half-pint! How 'bout some love?" Alex's voice trailed off as she ascended; she turned, briefly, her face wreathed in anger. The *thump-thump-thump* of her footfalls receded until replaced by the echo of her door slamming. He turned back to see Rosemary standing in the doorway, clutching Ashley's wrap, book bag, and dance regalia. She wasn't a lot happier. "We need to talk," she said as she climbed the stairs.

     Oh, boy. Alex calculated he could weather the gathering storm a little better with some nourishment, so he made for the kitchen and stuck his head in the refrigerator. As he took inventory he tried to guess the basis for this complication *du jour.* He shrugged and settled on string cheese and a low-carb beer. Leaning against the counter, he took a couple swallows and paused when he detected his wife's low, insistent monotone leaching through the ceiling. At that, he drained the bottle and went after another. He chose the back route to the family room and planted himself in his recliner. He had both the TV remote and the second beer under control and on target when Rosemary steamed in from the dining room. She marched up and pushed the book in his face.

     "What is the meaning of *this*?"

     Alex's suspended arms fell. "It's a *book*."

     "It's *inappropriate*, is what it is!"

"*What* 'inappropriate?' It's a prize-winning kid's book about overlooking imperfection and finding value."

"It's about *farting.*"

"That's just a bonus. Farting is *funny*, especially to kids. What's the big deal? *Everybody* farts; that's the point!"

"I'm sorry. I don't get it."

Alex spoke toward his shirt. "Maybe if you'd had a brother—or a full-time father..."

Rosemary worked her jaw muscles and turned away. "I'll ignore that—and I'm not going to belabor this, either. Except to say that this is the kind of thing that'll take away every advantage she gained by going to that expensive pre-school *I* got her into."

"Which she *hated.*"

"Alex, she's barely six years old. She doesn't have a clue what's good for her."

"And neither do I, apparently," he snapped.

"Oh, honey; let's not argue." She reached for his arm. "All I want is what's best for Ashley."

Alex jerked away. "Whether she or I like it or not, is that it?"

Rosemary grew chilly. "And I suppose you'd be happy if she fell behind and had to be home-schooled?"

"Look—I'm a tenured middle-school teacher in a public school district. That's not gonna happen—any more than she's going to a private school. We can't afford it anyway, not since you decided to stop working to ride herd on her full-time."

That wounded Rosemary. "At least one of us wants to make sure she gets everything she needs."

"Oh, *bullshit!*" Alex wasn't going to relent; not this time. "And, besides, what is it she's going to 'fall behind' in? Dance? Music lessons? Karate? Or 'structured play' with those other little robots?"

"That's not fair!" She crossed her arms and turned up the volume. "*Every* activity *I* have her in has demonstrable pre-collegiate value—unlike 'soc-*cer*.'"

"Oh, yeah. Pointless for a little kid to run around, kicking and screaming, with a bunch of scruffy little renegades, especially after a full workweek of 'structure.' Don't you see, honey? All this false urgency and fear of underachievement does is rob a lot of these kids of the best parts of their childhoods—playing, imagining, discovering...*thinking*. For themselves. By the time I get them in Science classes, they're defeated. They wouldn't dream of touching anything that isn't preprogrammed and pre-approved by adults."

"So, I guess what you're saying," she sniffed, "is, all the time I spend with Ashley doesn't count for anything?"

Alex rolled his eyes. "Melodrama aside, what I *am* saying is that you're not spending her time *with* her, you're spending it *for* her. She's a human being. She has more than needs; she has *feelings*. All you're doing, I fear, is making her resentful and rebellious. Is that what you want, for Ashley to grow to *hate* you?"

Before Rosemary could respond, Ashley appeared in the doorway, making fists of her tiny fingers, her alabaster face in knots. "*Mommy!* Gimme my book back. *Now!*"

"Ashley!" Alex came halfway out of his chair. Rosemary set her jaw and bound the book tighter to herself. Ashley burst into sobs and fled. Rosemary wasn't far behind.

"I can't talk to *either* of you anymore!" she said in the direction of the chandelier.

Alex fell back into the cushions. "I'll talk to her, later," he said weakly.

ᔪᕲ

Rosemary sat, watching Ashley and Ryan test each other with flashcards. After dunking and draining her teabag, she sipped carefully and reached for a cookie.

"They do seem to get along, don't they?"

"Looks like it. Better, since we got rid of that little monster, Tyler!" Across the table, Ryan's mother, Jennifer, laughed. Rosemary didn't. Jennifer squinted at her. "You okay? You look distracted."

"Oh, Alex and I are hammer-and-tong about Ashley, as usual." Rosemary searched her neighbor's face. "Do you think we push these kids too hard?"

"Who knows? Sometimes it feels like it, but things are so much different from how they used to be. Everybody has to work; everything's so expensive. There's so much to do; there's no time. There's more to learn and less time to learn it. I dunno. My father said in the Sixties the hippies on campus would laugh at 'straights' like him and say, 'Work, study, get ahead, KILL!' Makes you wonder; how on Earth do you suppose our grandparents dealt with a Depression and World War?"

"Well, thanks for answering my question!" They giggled. Rosemary dropped her chin into her hands. "I mean, I suppose I can see Alex's point. My Dad was away a lot, so it was Mom and I most of the time. She saw to me, but wasn't really available emotionally—"

"Whose parents were?"

"—But, yeah, did it matter all that much, really? I'm okay; I want for Ashley and me to be close and all that, but everything I read and see on TV frightens me. I want her to be *prepared*. Like, did you see that thing last night about the registered sex offender? Living right on a street full of kids!"

"Oh, honey; come on—that was 20 miles and two freeways away!"

"I know, but they said there were more calls on the Megan's Law hotline and more hits on the web site from this county than anywhere else in the state. Doesn't that *bother* you?"

Jennifer munched and gulped. "I don't even want to *think* about things like that. Let's just get these kids through school and into a good college, okay?" The silence made them both restless, so Jennifer changed subjects. "So—where are you and Alex on the subject, again?"

"We've agreed I can go back to work in a couple months, when Ashley starts first grade. He's determined to put her in public school and, as long as there's only one income, he can say we can't afford anything else. If I work, he loses that hedge and we can keep our options open. Anyway, I'll have more flexibility than he does, so I can make sure Ashley keeps up. You'll still be available for exercises after school, right?"

In the academy, silliness broke out. Ryan and Ashley had taken an impromptu palm-slapping game to the next level: laughing and rolling around on the floor.

"Ashley!" Rosemary stood, pointing two fingers at her eyeballs. "*Focus.*"

೫೦೮

Bracing his patellae against a cabinet door, Alex scratched a gluteus absently through his plaid flannel boxers and massaged his stubble with the other hand. None of this, not even his steady gaze, hastened the brewing process. Still, he stared. *Must be why it's called 'automatic drip.'*

Rosemary cupped her mug, inhaling chamomile and eyeing her husband. "You came in late."

"'In-service.' My choice was six hours yesterday after school or all day today."

"Was that all?"

"Had a burger and a couple beers with Harry." He didn't look at her.

"You could have called."

"Did." He groped for a large mug. "Your cell was busy."

She focused on the tawny liquid. "Didn't leave a message."

Alex pushed the newspapers aside and set his vessel down. He leaned on a hand, engaged her, and pointed at the freehand calendar on the melamine board behind her head. "What's that say?"

She swiveled and flushed a little. "'Friday;' '16;' 'In-service.'"

He looked down the hallway. "Where's Ashley?" He'd already heard the harsh singsong of an animated, synthesized musical score, so he didn't have to ask but he needed to, anyway.

"Watching TV..."

Mock horror wreathed his face. "Is that *allowed*?"

Rosemary sighed and pushed herself up gamely. "Look, I'm sorry, Alex. I haven't been sleeping as well since I started working again."

Alex gulped at his caffeine. "Mondays, Wednesdays, and Fridays too much for you?"

"It's not just that." She sounded truly weary, which caused him to thaw some. She used his waistband to pull him near and nestled into his side. "I've had to rejigger Ashley's schedule, since St. Ignatius is so rigid about pickups..."

"Ah, yes—St. Ignatius. Pity we aren't really Catholics; that'd be worth a healthy tuition break." His lack of hostility allowed her to relax a little, which led to shudders of emotion. He tipped her back and saw her streaked face.

She raised her eyes. "It's just—it seems like I worry all the time."

"About what?"

"Ashley."

"Why?"

"I want so *much* for her. I want her to be all right."

He stroked the down under her chin with a fingertip. "She will, darlin'. You just have to trust it—to trust *her*. Let her wander; let her *breathe*. Kids have a capacity to surprise that's boundless."

She wiped her nose. "You make it sound so easy. I

want it to be easy. Mostly, I'm just...terrified."

He looked at her a little harder. "Of what?"

She clasped her hands. "We were happy last night, just the two of us; I put her to bed and listened to her prayers. She drifted off and she was my baby girl again. I turned on the news and there were stories. Two possible abductions yesterday, just in California. Registered sex offenders."

Alex's chin jutted out as he bit his lip. "Oh, Jesus, Rosemary. Why do you watch that crap, anyway?" He reached down and flipped open the *Press Enterprise* and the *County Sun*. "If you have to torture yourself, use these; at least you can pick your poison and there's some semblance of perspective."

She pushed away. "What are you saying—that they're lying?"

"Not lying; more like distortion. What they choose as 'news' bears no relation to real life and its priorities. Murders; fires; celebrities; and ratings tie-ins. What does any of that have to do with us?"

"So, you don't think times are more dangerous?"

"Than what? Come on, Rosie. I teach rudimentary statistics and probability to 12-year-olds. We're a nation of 300 million people that built a 50-state child-abduction alert system on what, 112 cases? And most abductors are close relatives in the first place. Violent crime has dropped steadily since 1981—except among people who don't look like us, and whom we hardly ever see. Entire political careers have been built on 'Three Strikes' and 'Megan's Law.' We turn off our TVs, buy more guns, and cower behind our doors. In the safest nation on the planet!"

Rosemary shook her head. "Oh, Alex. I wish I had your...confidence."

He reeled her in again and touched his nose to hers. "All you gotta do is *believe*."

Her eyes were wells of uncertainty. "In what?"

"Something. Anything. *Every*thing." He hooked her

neck in the crook of his arm, kissed the top of head, and saw his watch. "And now, *I* believe I'll join my daughter in some *Looney Tunes*."

"Damn it, Alex." Her inhibitions closed on her like a shroud. "Can't you be serious?"

"As a heart attack," he said as he backed out, pointing at her with a flourish. "Made me what I am today. *Bee-*lieve it."

ℰℭℜ

Ryan pulled his finger from deep within his nostril, raked his umber hair back, and pushed the numbered manila card at Ashley.

"Eeewwww," Ashley said, grimacing.

"Shuuutuuup; I was only scratching." Ryan turned and looked into the dining room. At the table, his Mother looked away from Rosemary momentarily and nodded, satisfied. "SIX TIMES SIX EQUALS?" He leaned forward furtively, his voice lowered to a whisper. "Did you get *Walter* back yet?"

"No." Ashley scowled. "Mommy won't give him back; Daddy even tried. I HATE her!"

"SHH!"

They stole a glance in unison.

"THIRTY-SIX!"

Ryan flipped the card mechanically to reveal the answer. "Crap. I wanted to read it, too. SIX TIMES SEVEN EQUALS?"

"FORTY-TWO! She never lets me do anything I want to—never, never, NEVER!"

"SHH!" Ryan shrugged. "What you gonna do? We're six. SIX TIMES EIGHT EQUALS? Maybe your Daddy can buy another one..."

"Nuh-uh. FORTY-EIGHT! I'll just get caught again and we'll both get in trouble. Again." She pursed her lips.

"I guess you're totally busted. SIX TIMES NINE

EQUALS?"

She lowered her brow and darkened. "I'll figure it out. I'm gonna find some books *I* like and a place to read them, too—without anybody bothering me! FIFTY-FOUR!"

"How? SIX TIMES TEN EQUALS? We can't leave the yard without a police escort." Another secretive glimpse sideward.

"Dunno. SIXTY!" Ashley brightened some. "Mommy works Fridays—you know: 'free Fridays?' Like, 'no fixed drills Friday?'"

"But—SIX TIMES ELEVEN EQUALS?—you're still *here* on Fridays."

"Yes. SIXTY-SIX! But I don't *have* to be."

"Uh-oh. SIX TIMES TWELVE EQUALS?" Ryan's forehead furrowed. "I don't think I want to hear any more..."

"Don't worry—I wouldn't tell *you* anyway. SEVENTY-TWO! You're *weak*." She made claws of her fingers between them. "You might be *captured—*" Ashley scratched the cards from Ryan's grasp to the floor. "—And *tortured!*" She made for his armpits and they collapsed, a heap of hilarity.

The chorus swooped in from the other room like Valkyries.

"ASHLEY!"

"RYAN!"

೫೦೦೩

The minivan was barely curbside, still moving, when the pair burst out of their harnesses and attacked the sliding door, impatient to begin their brief parole. Jennifer scrambled out the passenger side to get the front door, where Ashley and Ryan stood already, on one foot and the other. Rosemary shut it down and sprang onto the door sill, popping up over the roofline like a stern and vigilant rodent. "Kids! Fractions! Ten minutes! I'm serious."

Jennifer waited on the front walk. As Rosemary circled the car, Ryan's warden peered up the street. "Well—look at that, willya."

"What?"

"Somebody's moving in up the street."

Rosemary craned, searching among the suburban rides. "Where?"

"The first house on the cul-de-sac, on your side. See that Wee-Haul panel with the doors open?"

"Oh, yeah. Huh. I didn't realize it was vacant. I didn't ever see a sign, did you?"

"Nope. Who do you suppose it is?"

"Are you kidding? I barely recognize the couple next door, much less anybody five doors away."

"Right. Where are we going to see anyone around here unless they have kids?"

"Well, I hope whoever it is has kids close in age to ours; the old car pool could stand some new blood, what with the price of gas."

"Not likely, with that little bit of stuff."

"Yeah, guess so. Wonder if there was anything left behind?"

Jennifer touched Rosemary and folded her arms. "This is positively engrossing; I could stand out here the rest of the afternoon."

"Okay. You win. Back to the rug rats, eh?"

಼ಂಓ

Ashley stood in the doorway, burnished into silhouette by the afternoon sun. She looked over her shoulder, irritated. "You coming or not?"

Rosemary rummaged her keys out of her handbag. "I'm right behind you."

"I *can* walk myself across the street, you know."

"Look, kiddo," Rosemary said, pulling her knuckles gently down the side of her daughter's face and pushing her curls back. "I know you get irritated with me, but the world you're living in is so much different from mine when I was your age. When you're older, you'll understand—and you'll thank me. I promise."

Ashley looked straight into her eyes with heat but had neither the energy nor inclination for another confrontation. She seized her mother's hand and pulled her over the threshold. "Let's just get it over with, okay?" she muttered.

They walked in silence. Jennifer opened the door, smiling, and Rosemary guided her through the opening from behind. Jennifer watched her slip past and raised her eyebrows at her neighbor.

"You good for about an hour? I've got...something I've got to do. Okay?"

Jennifer looked her up and down. "Whatever; we'll be here."

Rosemary watched the door close, pivoted, and looked at her watch. She sprinted home and let herself back in hurriedly. She ran into the living room and vaulted into the sofa on her knees. Braced against its back cushions, she parted the sheers and pressed her cocked forehead against the picture window. *Eleven o'clock—c'mon.* She made out the pane-distorted figure leaving the house five doors up. *Right on schedule.* She squinted at the figure taking halting steps toward the driveway. *Gray hair, crappy jacket, Denim shirt and pants, crepe-soled walking shoes. Can't see his face...* He guided the old, oxidized cobalt Buick into the street and headed toward her. As he passed, she saw his lined, haggard face turn. His wild mane filled the window and heavy horn-rimmed spectacles magnified his piercing, pale green eyes. He seemed to look right at her. Rosemary lurched backward and dropped the filmy curtain; it was several seconds before she dared to breathe. She backed onto her feet, went to the kitchen and retrieved the covered casserole she'd left on the counter. Clutching it, she left the house and tripped the deadbolt. She hesitated ever so slightly at the head of their walk, and turned right. *Be cool.* She feigned nonchalance as she strode along, her peripheral vision working to assure her that no one in between was as vigilant as she had been.

Rosemary reached the tract home, distinguished from those flanking it only by its creeping neglect. The calf-height juniper hedges that edged the walk were yellowing pathetically and losing fullness. A parched, cracking crust was visible under the drooping fescue. The covered concrete porch along the front façade was devoid of any comfort or adornment, its dark paint flecking. An aluminum screen door stood ajar, its hydraulic piston hanging like a severed tendon. She pushed it open; lacking resistance, it shuddered and banged the siding. She caught it and glanced around. Squaring herself with mock expectancy, she pushed the doorbell. No sound. She knocked officiously. *Make it a good show, just in case.*

"Hellooo? 'Welcome Wagon.' Anybody home?"

Rosemary knocked rhythmically and paused for effect. She closed the screen door and stepped to the bay window to peer through the canted blinds. A battered living room suite, tasteless enough to disgrace any economy motel, lay about, interrupting an otherwise bare front room architecturally identical to the Butterworth's. A pile of clothes and a dozen or so unopened book boxes, their contents awaiting tenancy on the built-ins, completed the furnishings. Palming the casserole, she turned into the sunlight and looked both ways. She took a half step backward and reached into the mailbox. Removing the contents gingerly, she

scanned the yellow forwarding sticker on a Number 10 envelope:

John W Harding

She took mental note, her mouth moving and her upper lip moist, and shoved the sheaf back where it belonged. "Maybe next time," she announced, and headed south and east. Her pace quickened the last 50 feet, in spite of herself. She fumbled her way through the door and abandoned the casserole on the hallway table with a clatter. She bounded up the stairs and turned on the computer. *C'mon*, she urged, her leg bouncing. She hit the bookmark for the Attorney General's site and clicked on the frame labeled "Megan's Law Mapping." She scrolled straight to the bottom of the page, checked "I have read the disclaimer and agree to these terms and conditions" and "Continue." At the mapping page, she hit "Search by → County" and typed in "San Bernardino" feverishly. She clicked "View Map" and used the "Zoom In" control to hone in on their region. Her eyes landed on the blue button near the west end of Periwinkle Court. She moved the cursor over it and pressed the left mouse button deliberately. A data window jumped at her.

"Oh, my God." A hand flew to her mouth, and then clasped the other on her scalp, flattening her hair. "Oh, my God..."

🙢🙠

Alex lowered the paper as Rosemary swept into the kitchen, dropping her bag on the table en route to the counter. She grabbed her covered "go" mug and splashed coffee and creamer into it simultaneously. Flinging open the overhead cabinet, she searched it impatiently.

"Where the Hell are the protein bars?"

"What's the matter with you? Lately, you've been jumpier than a long-tailed cat in a room full of rockers."

"Nothing—I'm late. Oh, and nice metaphor," she said icily.

"Hey—I do have four periods of American Lit a week.

Seriously—why are you up so early?"

Rosemary searched out the Power Puff Girls lunchbox—flinching yet again in the face of her husband's creeping cartoon influence—and busied herself making Ashley's lunch. "I asked for flex-time. If I start at seven and take a short lunch, I can pick Ashley up at school myself on workdays. Take some of the load off Jennifer."

Their daughter doddered in, fully dressed, yawning and rubbing her eyes. She looked at her mother's back balefully. "What time is it?"

"Get yourself some cereal, Honey—quick, like a bunny."

Alex watched Ashley's foraging sleepwalk for a moment, finally setting his cup down forcefully. "When did 'we' decide this?"

Rosemary turned her head enough to speak quietly out of the side of her mouth. "If we could ever have a civil conversation about this..."

"Answer me." He equaled her in both quietude and conviction.

She responded by bisecting the sandwich she'd made, wrapping and stowing it carefully.

Alex appeared at her side, glancing at Ashley struggling bravely with the outsized milk jug before he whispered. "Look; this is so unfair—to her, at least. You do what you want. Why should she have to get up an hour earlier three out of five days a week? For what?"

"I want to pick her up *myself*," she said, setting her jaw.

"Why, for God's sake? You or Jennifer—what's the difference? God forbid she should go the four miles on the bus, where she might be exposed to some other human beings."

"Don't start *that* again. You don't understand." Her eyes flashed resentment. "You never have."

Alex threw up his hands, catching Ashley's groggy attention in mid-gulp. He quelled himself and assured her with a fleeting smile, and touched his wife. "Okay. Let's try this. If you're determined to get up at the crack of dawn, go ahead, but let the kid sleep. I'll drop her myself Mondays, Wednesdays, and Fridays from now on. Nothing else changes—except I'll get her after school Friday."

"How can—?"

"I can, and I will. I'll work it out."

"But—what will you *do* with her?"

"I'll drop her at Jennifer's, take her back with me, find her something to do—whatever. Don't worry about it."

She folded her arms. "You always say that—'Don't worry.' How can I not?"

"I can't answer that," he said wearily. "Listen to me. It's three hours once a week, 'max,' and all three—four—of us could use the break. I insist."

Rosemary dropped her arms and slid the plastic box in Ashley's direction. In motion, she snatched up her coat and bag, halting at the doorway. "You want to be responsible? Okay. Be responsible. Whatever happens is on you. Do what you want." She eyed both of them and left.

Alex sat down again. "Well, we will—won't we, Punkin?"

Ashley's eyes cleared some and she grinned, unfazed by the concussion made by the front door.

෨൙

Rosemary hustled up the flagstones and pounded on the door. Jennifer answered, wide-eyed. "Rosemary, it's barely after three. What are you doing here? Did you go back to flex-time on Fridays?"

"No—I just, just got worried about Ashley. Is she okay?"

"Well, I don't know; she's not here."

Rosemary's mouth hung open. "What do you mean?"

"I mean, she's not here. She hasn't been here Fridays in weeks."

"I—I don't understand." She shifted on her feet, her eyes darting. "Alex said she was busy, close by; I just assumed he meant here."

Jennifer frowned. "I'm sorry, Honey, I don't know what—"

Rosemary was already halfway toward the street, speed-dialing Alex on her cell phone.

"'Lo?"

"*Where's* Ashley?"

"Rosemary?"

"Where *is* she?"

"Rosie, calm down. She's—"

Anger and panic welled up in her. "If anything's happened to her, I swear..." She pulled the phone from her ear and clutched it before her face; sobs came. She dropped Alex and dialed 9-1-1.

"This is San Bernardino Rapid Response. What is your emergency?"

"Hello? My daughter is six and she's missing. There's a Registered Sex Offender in our neighborhood, and I'm afraid he has her!"

"What is your name, Ma'am?"

"What?"

"Your name, please, Ma'am?"

"Uh—Butterworth. Rosemary Butterworth. My daughter's name is Ashley."

"Fine. What is your location, Ma'am?"

"Periwinkle Court; Seventeen Thirty-four. Oh, God. Please hurry—she's just a *baby*!"

"We'll send Sheriff's Deputies right away, Ma'am. Stay calm; is there a number where you can be reached?"

She gave the operator her cell number and signed off. A beep told her she'd missed a call from Alex; another signaled that he'd left her a voice message. She dropped the unit into her bag and paced, her eyes fixed on the open end of the street. Within minutes, a white cruiser emblazoned with a seven-pointed gold star and chevron rounded the corner and slid to a stop near her. Two deputies in pressed khakis—a beefy, flat-topped Anglo and a remorseless-looking Latina--dismounted, reflexively sliding their batons into their service-belt retaining rings. He spoke.

"'Afternoon, Miz—" He flipped up his shades and consulted a notepad. "—Butterworth? I'm Deputy Parker and this is Deputy Valencia. Your daughter is missing, correct?"

"Yes! Oh, God—I know he's got her. We've got to hurry..."

Deputy Parker flipped a page and clicked his ballpoint. "Now, Ma'am; first I need to ask you a few..."

Rosemary had broken away from them, sprinting west. They traded glances, then galloped after her, each steadying a holstered Glock and making metallic music as they ran. They caught her on the porch.

"Ma'am, Miz Butterworth," Parker wheezed, "first we've got to—"

"You've got to *do* something!" Rosemary looked in. In the dim light, through a narrow gap in the slats, she saw the tousled old man sat with Ashley stretched beside him, her head in his lap.

"She's *in* there! Something's happening!" Tears streaked her drawn face, her arms rigid by her sides like hammers.

Valencia stepped over and took her by the shoulders as Parker pushed the bell.

"It doesn't *work*!"

Parker studied her. "What's his name?"

"Harding—John W. Harding!"

Parker pounded on the door. "John Harding! San Bernardino County Sheriff's! Open up, sir!"

No answer.

He tried the knob; the latch gave. Valencia took his back; they nodded, unholstered their weapons, and hit the hallway. Parker swung left, lowered himself into the room, and shifted right, leveling his nine-millimeter with both hands at the forms on the sofa. Valencia leaned into the left side of the arch, training her pistol in the same general direction.

"Sheriff's! Don't move!" Parker barked.

The noise started Ashley awake and the old man closed his arms around her instinctively. She bolted upright and gripped his arm as confusion and fear came over them both.

"Sir! Let go of the girl! Now!"

The old man remained frozen, clutching the girl and searching the dimness by cocking his head at odd angles. Parker's nerve endings danced at the failure to comply; he took a deep breath and snapped on a lamp. Startled, the man raised an arm at him and relaxed his hold; the big Deputy grabbed it. Valencia darted in and pulled Ashley down the sofa. Parker levered the man forward to his knees; deftly, he cuffed that wrist and seized the other arm as the suspect rotated. He pitched over, hit the floor hard, and yelped in pain. Parker cleared sweat from his eyes and, sensing no struggle, merely held him down and came to a knee.

"John W. Harding?"

"Yes, sir," Harding said weakly, muffled by carpet.

It was only then that Parker saw the hearing aids and thick eyeglasses on the end table.

Ashley erupted, her little face crimson with anger. "Stop it! You're *hurting* him!" She bit Valencia's wrist and wriggled onto her feet. She coursed toward where Parker knelt and kicked him squarely on his shin. "Leave him alone! He's my *friend*!"

Parker corralled her, flailing and shrieking, with his offside arm and clenched his teeth until the throbbing subsided. "Let's everybody just calm down now, okay? Until we get this sorted out?"

Rosemary stood in the archway. In the light, the room was somehow different from what she remembered. Sure, there was the sad but still obnoxious plaid Herculon, but an overstuffed leather wing chair, ottoman, and Tiffany reading lamp took up a corner. The shelves were fully stocked with handsome volumes, still others occupying nearly every horizontal surface. Framed fine art enlivened a couple walls and more lined the baseboards, waiting to be hung.

"Mrs. Butterworth?" It was Valencia; she had relieved Parker of Ashley, who was rigid but quiet, and guided her toward her.

Rosemary knelt and opened her arms. Ashley recoiled, balling her hands into pale fists before her grotesque vermilion face. "I'm *staying*. Professor *talks* to me; he *listens* to me. We *dance* and we *play*—and I get to read what *I* want, *when* I want to!" Motionless, mother and daughter stared across the void between them, and bawled.

"What's going on?"

Alex strode in, past his family, past Valencia, and knelt beside Harding. He pushed a hand under the frail man's chest to raise him. Hesitating, he looked at Parker. "Okay?" Parker nodded and fished for his handcuffs' key. Gently, Alex pushed Harding into a sitting position, back against the sofa's front stile. His color compromised by shoulder pain, Harding eyed his benefactor, myopically.

"Alexander? Is that you?"

"Yes, John. Just rest a moment." Alex reached for the sexagenarian's appliances and installed them. "There. That better?"

"Oh, my, yes." Harding surveyed the room as if he'd just arrived. "My stars—this is something of a Gordian knot, what?"

Alex saw puzzlement deepen on both Parker and Valencia. "Another time, Deputies." Overcome by fatigue, Ashley shuffled over and fell into her father's lap.

Rosemary's tongue loosened. "You—you *know* him?"

Alex extended a hand for introduction. "Ladies and gentleman, meet John W. Harding, Retired Professor of Classics and Literature. Had him for English Lit at Fullerton. Thought I really loved the written word, until I met this guy. Had no idea."

Harding adjusted his glasses and cleared his throat. "Apparently, I didn't emphasize enough that all sentences should have subjects."

"But, he's on the Internet," Rosemary said, still pleading. "In the database of Registered Sex Offenders!"

"That would be John *Wesley* Harding, my elder brother by five years. I, alas, am John *Watson* Harding. Our father was a man of faith and of letters, and somewhat prescient at christening, if lacking in imagination. Strong family resemblance, between Wes and me; regrettably, I am neither quarry nor sleuth, but merely a bystander, a chronicler."

Parker narrowed his eyes. "What did he just say?"

Alex smiled. "Case of mistaken identity."

"Oh."

"Rosie," Alex said quietly, "I didn't tell you because *I* was afraid—of further conflict and, even more, rejection. I hadn't seen John since sophomore year; ran—I mean—I ran into him in the supermarket three months ago. He told me the whole story; helping his brother after his arrest and conviction wore him and his marriage out. He set him up in this house after he was paroled; along came Megan's Law, he disappeared—for his younger brother's sake. A pension, his books, and this place are all he has. He loves books, Ashley loves books; I hired John as a tutor, one day a week. If anybody can stoke her literary fires, it's John *Watson* Harding!"

"And, I presume you, young woman"—Harding really did see Rosemary this time—"are she who believes that learning occurs best by rote and prescription. On the contrary; unlike any other muscle or organ, the mind profits more from a casual, reflective stroll into the unknown than from brisk exercise and rest in the riskless familiar."

Outside, in the street, children laughed.

ഇ൫

2 **Boys Will Be Men**

ᏕᎧᏣ

"Can Mommy come live with us again?"

Chad Wilcomb's shoulders sagged as he switched off the coffeemaker. He turned. His six-year-old's eyes shimmered above his cereal bowl like tiny blue Christmas balls. "Chuckie, we've been over this a million times in the last three years. No; Mommy's not going to live with us anymore."

Chuckie frowned into his milk. "I don't like two houses and Mrs. Sherwatter—she smells funny. Mommy has day care; she doesn't need no babysitter at night."

"'*Any*'—'*any*' babysitter," Chad said. "Daddy and Mommy have different jobs. Sometimes Daddy has to work late or go away. Finish your Lucky Charms. I gotta drop you and get to the office." As he swiped up his keys from the hallway table, the phone rang. "Hello?"

"Hi, dear." It was the "ex"—Lana Margo McCarthy. "I'm glad I caught you. Don't forget Chuckie's appointment at Dr. DiPassini's at four; I'm pretty sure he's got a cavity. All that sugar weekend mornings, no doubt."

"Shit."

Silence.

"I forgot. Look, can you cover it? I got a full day today."

"Goddamn it, Chad. I've run through almost all of my sick leave as it is." She paused, and sighed. "Listen. Did Chuckie bring up getting back together again?"

Chad turned toward the wall as Chuckie emerged from his bedroom, struggling with a backpack strap. "Yeah. He said something this morning."

"Did you talk to him about it, Chad?"

"Yeah—sorta."

A longer pause and deeper sigh. "Do you ever really *hear* that kid?"

"Gotta go," Chad mumbled, and hung up. *A woman who uses all three names—I should have known better.*

››

"Why me?"

Chad sat and propped his feet on Tim Ireland's desk—he, the *Sacramento Independent Review's* News Editor and his boss.

"What I got from his mother's letter was that he saw the piece you did on the temple bombers and decided you were fair." Tim grinned. "Go figure. Maybe he used to be a 'subscriber.'"

"Okay—so Charlie Don Morton, convicted local rapist and murderer, wants to give our little lefty rag an exclusive before he gets put to sleep at San Quentin in three months. That about it?"

"Not entirely. Two conditions."

"Oh?"

"One, he wants the piece to be 'first person' — you know, 'Charlie Don Speaks.' Your ruminations and purple prose in sidebars only. Two, he wants you as a media witness."

Chad used his best Ted Baxter voice. "Won't giving a felon an 'open forum' besmirch our journalistic integrity?"

"Listen, wise-ass. This is a no-brainer, a *coup,* if we can pull it off. Set all your other stuff aside. I've already gotten the Department of Corrections' new guidelines. You work on whatever phone calls you need and a visitation request, and I'll get started on getting us into the media pool. There's one slot for a weekly and Morton's local, so we should have a shot. A guy I used to play racquetball with works in CDC's legislative office, which might help."

Any lingering *bonhomie* evaporated.

"Get *on* it, Chad," Tim said.

∞⌾

Chad leaned into Tim's doorway. "Here it is. Under the Department's media policies, non-'random,' face-to-face interviews and recording devices of any kind are prohibited. Inmates can make outgoing, recordable collect calls 'according to their privilege group'—Death Row being the most restricted. I can visit only after I get CDC Form 106, 'Visiting Questionnaire,' from Morton, return it, and wait for the prison to approve it. Realistically, that'll take four to six weeks—just on their end."

"I should write him immediately," Chad continued, "since their search of a Number 10 envelope and a one-page letter for 'contraband' also can take four to six weeks. I'll give him the *Review's* number, and you'll authorize all charges. I'll ask him to try to call me at least three weeks in a row, since each call will be monitored and restricted to 15 minutes, and I'll ask his permission to record the calls. A pal of mine teaches speech at Sac City. He's willing to send Morton a blind syllabus on public speaking—Chad glanced down—'Tell Them About Yourself: Organizing Your Thoughts into Words.' I'm hoping he takes the hint and works on what he wants to say ahead of time. Okay?"

Tim shrugged. "Hey—with any kind of luck, we

might wind up a test case. Go for it."

ℬℭ

Sitting in the visiting area, waiting for the condemned man to be brought down, Chad's annoyance at the prosaically absurd visitation rules and the going-on two hours of intake and boredom had given way to idle review. He paged through his mental photocopies of research and notes. (He'd had the foresight to ask for and get his prison-issue paper and pencil already, before he started to sound too much like a reporter.) *Four hundred twenty-seventh of 601 sentenced to die in California since 1978. One of 595 on Death Row, of 578 men at San Quentin. First scheduled execution since Robert Lee Massie, March, 2001. Convicted November 1988 for the murder and mutilation of a prostitute in North Highlands the Christmas before. Time on Death Row, 13 years, one month—slightly above average.*

He'd spent the drive to San Rafael replaying the 40-plus minutes of Morton's taped telephone calls. Turned out Charlie Don really had just wanted to tell his story—coherently, unemotionally, and without much prompting. Born and raised, Antelope, CA. Only child; single, working-poor mother; absent father. Few friends, but friends. Slight, but apparently witty enough to deflect bullies. Undistinguished but untroubled academic history, through high-school graduation. Stab at community college, then unremarkable succession of mid-wage jobs. No overt romantic entanglements, until his gift of holiday intimacy to himself went wrong. He recounted the crime sadly as her obituary, not his life-episode. Perfunctory appeals he endured passively and finally shook off as so much bad investment advice. Lastly, he was sorry she was dead because of him. End of story.

Each review reinforced Chad's core impressions. No overt physical or emotional abuse, in-home or out. No standout 'turning point'—too old for Judas Priest, the Trench Coat Mafia, or any other 'fill-in-your-own' crackpot theory. No white sheets, no swastikas. No addictions other than nicotine; drug of choice was fermented. No 'Up the System.' No priors; no protestations of innocence. No Kafkaesque 'Death Row Chronicles.' Remorse. What the Hell are we going to talk about?

As the interior door clanked open and the "Grade A" East Block tenants shuffled in, Chad amused himself with the uneasy arrogance of his final thought: *My Pulitzer hangs on the answer to one question: 'Why?'*

"You Chad Wilcomb?"

Chad was nonplussed. Charlie Don Morton's file footage and disembodied voice had failed to prepare Chad for how unimposing he really was. *Thin, sandy-haired...ordinary. Good thing they didn't have to pick him out of a lineup.* Only one feature captured his attention: Steel-gray eyes, pale and clear.

"That's me, Charlie. So—what's the most memorable thing about life on E-Block?" *Great ice-breaker, Wilcomb. Profound!*

Charlie smiled. "The smell." He lit a cigarette and exhaled. The smoke coiled upward over him like a departing soul.

"Those things will kill you, you know."

Charlie laughed gaily at Chad's nervous, half-intentional joke. "So will potassium chloride."

Chad scrambled for higher ground—and control. "What's your opinion of lethal injection as a method of execution?"

"Too clinical. But, that's the point, isn't it? One of the guys on the Row says the jurors who sentence us should be required to beat us to death with clubs."

"Right." Chad was aggressive. "Look, Charlie, I don't usually do business this way. This environment doesn't exactly promote frank discussion. And you pretty much covered four of the five 'Ws' in your calls. What do *you* want to talk about?"

"How old are you?"

"Uh—29. But what—

"Same age as me when I did it. Brothers or sisters?"

"Nope. Just me."

"Is 'Chad' your real name, or short for something else?"

"No—it's 'Charles David Wilcomb, Junior.'"

"Me, too—'Charles Donald Morton, Junior.'" Charlie rotated a thumbnail under a front tooth. "He around much?"

"Who?"

"Your old man."

"Not really—outside salesman."

"They divorced?"

"My parents? No, but they might as well be." Chad looked beyond the wall behind Charlie's head. "Dad was on the road most of the time, I guess. My Mom's been emotionally alone since the honeymoon, except for me. She's more married to Jack Daniels than him." Here— in this place—Chad startled himself with his candor.

"Yeah—mine just split. Left me and the bills to the old lady. My Mom cut the knot but remarried her two jobs. Oh, he called a couple times—birthdays, I think. Didn't ever have much to say, one way or another." Charlie chortled.

"What's funny?"

"Weird thought. 'Home-schooled.' Always makes me think of 'jumbo shrimp.'"

"How's that?"

"The whole concept. Parents get pissed 'cause schoolteachers say it ain't their job to teach values, so they yank 'em out of school and teach 'em subjects at home—assuming the values are there and worth a damn. Me, I didn't learn anything either place. Nobody told me shit I could really use!"

Charlie rocked onto his propped elbows. "Here's how I break it down. From the beginning, there's no open connection. You're an obstacle, not a support. He's gone, so you become her biggest problem. The only way you connect is through conflict. Forget emotional nourishment—you just have a problem, a question. 'Ask your teacher.' 'Go see the counselor.' 'Talk to the minister.' It's like we're all particles with opposing charges. Jiggle. Bump. Deflect. Repeat. After a while, you live inside yourself, full-time. 'Ask nothing, expect nothing.' Conversation becomes a car alarm; either annoys people or scares 'em off. Problem is,"—a wistful pause—"the need never dies."

Chad searched for something to ask—or say. The distant scrape of chairs signaled that the delay-truncated encounter was nearly over.

Charlie saw Chad's dilemma. "Well, Hell. At least they gave us their names, huh? Got any family of your own?"

"Divorced. Got a boy, Chuckie—six," Chad stammered.

Charlie had formed a response, but was defeated by the order to rise and file out. Halfway out of his chair, he said, "You didn't ask me."

"What?"

"Why I did it."

"Okay. Why?

"I told her I loved her. She laughed."

ഇരു

Chad kicked his apartment door shut and pitched his keys at the table. Another drive home replaying Charlie's tapes still hadn't provided a meaningful frame of reference for what he'd heard that morning. Two pints of dry Irish stout hadn't helped, either. His jacket was just past his elbows when the phone rang.

"Chad?"

Just what I need. "H'lo, Dad."

"Just finished my last call, headed to a client dinner.

Wanted to see how everything was. How's work?"

"Swamped. Doing a piece on a guy on Death Row."

"Great. How's my favorite grandson?"

"The one you haven't talked to in a year? He's great, Dad—Oh, and I'm fine, too. Thanks for asking."

Muffled cries from another room—Chuckie's nightmares, again.

"Is he crying?"

"'Let him cry.' Never hurt me—right, Dad?"

"Son, I don't know why you have to be this way. Maybe if you and Lana had stayed together—"

"Like you and Mom? There's a sterling example: Ozzie and fucking Harriet!"

Chad thought he heard sniffling at the other end.

"Um. Oh—there's my dinner date. Well, gotta go. You take care, Son. G'Bye."

Why am I always waiting to hear words he's probably never used together in a sentence his whole life? Chad thought as he hung up.

&)(&

Tim's good, Chad thought as he and 16 other scribes followed "12 reputable citizens" into the Witness Area, joining others anointed by occupation and the Penal Code to watch Charlie Don Morton die.

The viewers gathered on a pair of dark-shellacked risers, like some macabre glee club, arranged in an "L" on either side of the entrance. A stand-up desk the same shade of wood was between them, as though a celestial clerk would enter and scratch Charlie's name from the Book of Life. Chad did a quick nose-count to himself. *We're seven short—that'd be 'Inmate family/friends: five (if requested)' and 'Inmate spiritual advisor: two (if requested).' Dear God. Did he not ask his parents to come? Could he even find them? Or did they turn him down?*

The room represented a failed compromise between

industrial convention and horror. The converted cyanide chamber was painted with a color described by Fifties motel and kitchen decorators as "Sea Green." Its five windows were shrouded with same-vintage eggshell drapes that mirrored the color of the naked walls. The *faux*-marble linoleum squares also matched, chromatically and in taste.

The curtains parted. There lay Charlie, sealed in and strapped flat on a padded gurney, his right arm connected to a saline IV line 10 minutes before ("slow rate of flow"), and his left arm by his side. (The obvious if profane imagery wasn't lost on CDC; Chad fantasized momentarily about the left arm swinging up and Roman soldiers appearing, with nails.) A "secondary location" line also awaited, "in case of malfunction or blockage."

At the Warden's command, five grams of diluted sodium pentothal was pushed anonymously through the line into Charlie's veins, soon to render him unconscious, to be followed by 50 cubic centimeters each of pancuronium bromide and potassium chloride, to stop his lungs and heart.

Dean Carter is right, Chad mused. The only way to make this less personal is to bomb him from 30,000 feet.

Charlie craned to find Chad's face through the window. He slowly and repeatedly mouthed two words that Chad finally deciphered, with difficulty, before Morton's eyes closed.

'Love me?'

ഇരു

Near dawn, Chad had just turned the deadbolt after another two hours in the car. He was more exhausted from this trip than the last, but just as perplexed. He saw the note. *Hm. Mrs. Sherwatter bailed after Chuckie tucked in—emergency.*

Soft whimpers floated from the second bedroom. Noiselessly, Chad bent over Chuckie's bed. Struggling under a veil of thin sleep, he lay on his back, his straight right arm thrust out over the edge of the bed. A length of lamp cord lay carelessly over his forearm. Suddenly, his crystalline eyes were wide open and he cried out:

"Love me, Daddy!"

Chad snatched up his son, crushing him to his chest and bathing him in his tears.

"It's okay, Chuckie. Daddy loves you. Daddy will always love you."

Pressing his son's head against his neck, Chad stepped out and dialed the phone.

"Lana? It's Chad. Can we talk—soon?"

Chad's urgency blasted her awake. "Is it about Chuckie?"

"Mostly. Maybe us, too." Chad exhaled, hard. "I *did* love you."

He hit the "Flash" key and dialed Tim, at home.

"Tim? It's Chad."

"Jesus Christ! What time is it?"

"I need some time off. Starting now."

☙ℭ☙

3 Chosen

৯৩

The teenaged Volvo, a kaleidoscope of rust, gray primer, and gloss red, wheezed into a ground-floor space in the Twelfth Street garage. Marie Kohlfeldt snapped off the ignition and glared.

"For Christ's sake, Don—Do you have to do that with the kid in the car? And today, of all days?"

Her husband of nine months pinched the roach delicately and sucked the last life out of its glowing coal. "Jesus, honey, cut me some slack. Ronald Reagan's been in charge for five months and the band hasn't played so much as a toilet in six weeks. I'm having enough trouble dealing with another Catholic in the house."

Marie sighed, climbed out, and forced the rear door open. She leaned into the back seat and lifted the baby into his christening blanket. "If we get through this, it'll be the first promise to me you've kept since our wedding day!"

Don's ponytail trembled lazily while he held in the last of the smoke. He exhaled with more force than necessary. "Go ahead—I'll be along." Marie tried to kick the door shut but it stopped halfway with a rusty croak. She slumped into it until it latched. *Good thing there'll be godparents and sponsors, she thought. Otherwise, I'd have to confess to breaking the Fifth Commandment.* Cooing and bubbling saliva brought her out of it. She smiled at the tiny, swaddled face as she emerged from the garage's darkness and headed up the alley toward the Cathedral's front steps. The bluff of its doeskin-colored stone protected the momentary peace.

Still absorbed as she made the corner, her vague sense of a physical presence was confirmed by sharp odors and a near-collision. She saw his boots first, shoulder-width apart—buckles and smooth, black leather up the calf; early aviator, maybe, but for the moldy cracks and dilapidation. His trousers featured sidelong stripes of hand-applied yellow material. For the effect, they might have been cavalry jodhpurs, rather than black Slim-fit jeans long ago consigned to thrift. The filthy fatigue jacket was anonymous. Its name-and-rank identifiers had been torn away and replaced with an amalgam of patches, pins, and bric-a-brac that added up to a busted-back and grounded starship commander from a nearby galaxy. A Jamaican-flag, knit cap, and greasy dreadlocks framed a stubbled face, inches from hers, that revealed nothing but wear. The eyes were masked by heavy wraparounds. The utter calm in the sound that emerged from between his uncharacteristically sturdy teeth banked her shock and fear.

"What's his name?"

"Halston."

A dirty index finger touched the infant's downy cheek. "Beautiful."

With that, he spun around and took the handlebars of an old bicycle festooned with street flotsam—improvised reflectors, foil-and-hanger antennae, and miscellaneous logos—and draped with makeshift saddlebags crammed with repossessions. He guided its flaccid tires away from her, up the K Street Mall.

Don loped up behind her. "What was that all about?"

"Nothing—I guess," she said, as she watched the figure recede.

Inside, Marie pulled the blanket away from the infant, which roused him enough to mewl a little. The priest nodded toward her. "And what name do you give this child?"

"Halston."

The priest winced slightly. "Halston...?"

"Just Halston," she said, beaming into the little pink face. "Halston Kohlfeldt."

೮ාଓୠ

Perched on the edge of his desk, Brother Ambrose folded his arms and furrowed his brow at the question. He frowned. "Mr. Kohlfeldt, *The Celestine Prophecy* is not on the study list for sophomore religion here at Christian Brothers. Your search for spiritual meaning will be guided by Scripture and acceptable theology—just like everyone else's. What you read outside class is your business."

RING!

Halston sighed, slung his backpack, and headed for the door, dogged by the usual exchanges of nudges and murmurs. Adrianna Wong caught him by the elbow in the hallway. "Hey, Aristotle! Gonna pick up from last year and start the fall semester of '97 as the designated deep-thinker of the Class of '99?"

His wan smile breached the embarrassment. "Yeah—I guess."

"So," she said as they merged into the stream of hallway bodies. "Will I see you at 'Christians in Action' tonight?"

"Dunno," he said hesitantly. "I'm kinda leaning toward Philosophy Club this year."

She covered her disappointment some with playfulness. "Oh, I get it. A big talker, but not much at putting beliefs into action."

"It's hard when they're not fully formed yet." He looked a little wounded, and Adrianna was sorry. He was oblivious. "You wanna get some coffee or something after school? I don't start at Jasper's 'til next week."

"Can't," she said. "I've got Band and Chorus all afternoon, then piano practice. Back here for CIA, then dinner late and homework. Ugh."

"Is Rich going to do Chorus again this year?"

"That's what he says. He's also thinking about Debate and Chess Club. Wants to"—she posted digital quotation marks in the air—"'round out his vocal skills and network more.'"

"Wow—he's becoming quite the resumé-builder. His future as a freak is in serious jeopardy. Okay, tonight's out. What about lunch? I'll see if I can round up Rich and Eugenio."

She fondled his arm and made him look at her. "I'll be there."

₧

The first meeting of the Philosophy Club ran long. Opinions were loose and immoderate, pushed along by general ignorance and the usual adolescent hormones and insecurities. Brother Ambrose presided, tolerantly and ineffectively. Halston was lucky to catch Rich after Chorus and bartered the price of a coffee for a ride to New Helvetia, in mid-town. (A rehabilitated firehouse, its bakery, caffeine, and conversation attracted the post-elementary demographic city-wide, as well as neighbors who had graduated and acquired sufficient possessions to be full-fledged metrosexuals.) It wasn't exactly an easy freeway exit between Oak Park and the Pocket, but it was only five blocks from the upstairs apartment Halston shared with his mother. He ran in, paid for two large French Roasts, and delivered one to Rich at the curb, bidding him good-bye. He looked at his watch.

Shit—It's after seven, he thought. *Mom will be waiting dinner.* Pulling out his paperback copy of *The Celestine Prophecy,* he combined reading and sipping as he strode south on 19th Street in the failing light.

Sodium vapor was sputtering awake in places as he stepped off the curb into N Street, absorbed by the text. Suddenly, a black Explorer was his universe. Time tolled as he processed the cell phone, the raised eyes, and the bright, blue grille medallion. Its legibility indicated that panicked braking had barely begun. The blackout Halston anticipated was overwhelmed by a force, cold but brighter than burning magnesium, that struck him in the back, enveloped him, and propelled him to the opposite curb. It loosened its grip and he fell. Halston had no sense of how long he lay there, just of sequence. He stared upward, heard the SUV's wailing tires, and saw a face floating over his.

"Buddy? BUDDY! You okay? Jesus Christ! Where'd you come from? Where's your board?"

"Huh?"

"Your *board,* man. Hell of a move, to get out of my way like that. You hurt?"

"Don't know...Don't think so."

"Can you move?"

Halston signaled his extremities and they replied. He sat up.

"Wow. Good," said his assailant, who came out of his crouch and started back-pedaling as he looked nervously around. "Look—if you're all right, I'll just...I'm late, okay?" He bounded away and was gone.

In the deepening dark, Halston looked at his feet. The white toecaps of his Chuck Taylor sneakers were striated with dark abrasions. Nothing else on him was so much as marked. His backpack was in place and his book and half-consumed coffee were at his side. He snagged them after struggling to his feet, and looked around. A block east on N, he detected a figure, barely revealed by surrounding shadows. It seemed to watch him, then pivoted slowly, throwing a glint of reflected light from dark eyeglasses. He watched it move away, pushing something with wheels.

℠℧

"Mom?"

Halston dropped his things on the kitchen table.

"In the bedroom, Hal. I'm getting in the shower. Check the meat in a few minutes, will you?"

"Yeah—okay." He studied his stuff, wanting her to help him understand what had just happened. *Not now, I guess,* he thought. He shrugged, straddled one of the mismatched vinyl dinette chairs, and retreated into his book.

"Honey, I've got to cover Gina's shift tonight, so—"

Marie arrived in the kitchen, in her second waitress's uniform and drying her hair, just about the time that smoke began to curl from the oven. "God*damn it!*" She raced to it and tore the door open. Smoke billowed out. Impulsively, she barehanded the pan onto the counter. It clattered a foot or two while she cursed and fanned her hands. She wheeled, hands now on hips, to find Halston still in his seat, gaping. "Halston Kohlfeldt, I swear to God—sometimes you're as useless as that ex-husband of mine!" She saw she'd stunned and hurt him, and softened. "Aw, Christ, honey—I'm sorry. I didn't mean it. Really. Here..." She reached into the freezer and dropped a frozen entrée onto the counter. "Heat this up, then clean up and get on that homework." She crossed to him, hugged his head to her abdomen and kissed his cowlick. "Don't wait up, okay?"

Halston nodded without looking at her. He heard her receding footfalls, her key cycling the distant deadbolt—then nothing.

℠℧

Its baccalaureate over, the Christian Brothers Class

of 1999 spilled from the Cathedral onto its paving-stone plaza. Whoops filled the air, half-open royal-blue gowns billowed, and matching mortarboards flew into the bright, midday sky from all directions.

Halston found Adrianna first and kissed her longingly. She reciprocated.

"Get a room, you cheap—!"

Eugenio and Rich skipped over, arms draped over shoulders. They all traded hugs and high-fives.

"WHOOOO!" shrieked Rich. "Four down and two to go!" He pointed his fingers like six-guns at his friends. "I'm off to Sac City College. Who's coming with me?"

Adrianna was perplexed. "YOU? Community college? With your father's money and influence? Me, I mean, I'm poor..."

"It's the grades, stupid," Rich replied. "And there's the character-building factor. I guess Pops wants to assure himself I won't be as big a fuck-off in the second four-year increment as the first. How about you, Eugenio?"

"Yup—me, too. My grades and scores were okay but being the class clown didn't leave a lot of time for anything else. Besides, my folks are still paying tuition for three behind me."

The trio looked at Halston. "Me? Yeah, all of the above. I'll be there in the fall, I guess."

Rich shook his head and raised his right arm, palm out.

"Musketeers!"

They all leaned in, grinning, and wrapped their upraised hands around his. "All for us—and nothing for anyone else!" they bellowed.

Rich's intonations mocked solemnity. "Here's to a wasted Summer and a mindless future!"

They all bunny-hopped and chanted. "A WASTED Summer! A MINDLESS future!"

They broke and scattered to find their families—all but Halston. His Mom had to work.

—•—

It was a perfect, late-Spring Saturday. A mustachioed Halston lounged on a bench at Sutter's Fort, reading William Dembski's *Intelligent Design*. He yawned, stretched, and checked the time.

Twelve forty-five—Shit! Late again!

He jammed the book into the back pocket of his cutoffs and covered the eight blocks at a dead run, though scrupulously deliberate at each intersection. He pulled up at New Helvetia a little before one. After hunching over briefly to recover his breath, he opened the front door, dodging departing patrons. The edge was coming off the mid-day rush. His eyes adjusting, he found a table of four with a chair empty. Rich, Eugenio, and Adrianna were finishing lunch.

Rich, angry, spotted him first. "About damned time! YO! HAL!"

Halston approached. "You ordered for me, right? Tall, double, half-caf latte, no foam, chocolate, and an apple-cinnamon scone?" It was a lousy attempt at ingratiation. He stiffly seated himself. Rich picked it up.

"You're late, as usual. So, no—we didn't order for you. As usual."

Adrianna, for the defense. "Ease up, Rich, okay? Let's make it a low-stress day."

The *barista* wandered by, so Halston snagged an order. Rich persisted. "Right—what is it this time? Nose in a book or just daydreaming?"

Hal stammered. "I, uh—"

Knock him off-track, thought Eugenio. "I don't know about you, but I'm totally booked, myself. I've got six quarters on "Dry" at Fluff'N'Fold across the street."

"Geen-O—ever the comedian." Adrianna laughed and, facing Hal, exercised her official-announcement diction. "'Nice to see you again, Hal.'"

Halston relaxed a little. "Thanks, babe. Guilty, Rich, to the first count." He produced the book. "I'm still wrestling with this 'Creator of Us All' theory."

Rich rolled his eyes. "Aww, Jeez—"

"No—his Father," Halston said.

"Isn't there a bird in there somewhere, too?" Eugenio added.

Adrianna narrowed her eyes at Rich. "It wouldn't kill you to take a few moments out of your crushing schedule to ponder your place in the universe, Material Boy!"

Rich volleyed. "Hey, I know exactly where I am— three credits short of a UC transfer, business degree, and Baghdad-by-the-Bay. Big bucks. Beemer. Babes. End of story."

"Dude! I wish I was that confident about my Computer Science degree and the health of Silicon Valley right now," said Eugenio. "Even from Sac State, C++ and Visual Basic were a free pass out of here a year ago. The way things are, I might be eating cat food before my parents!"

Rich stayed with Adrianna. "How 'bout you, Ms. Liberal Arts? Gonna parlay that high-school fiddling award and that Fine Arts degree into a killer career?"

"I might." She was frosty. "If I do or don't, at least it'll be my choice — and not my father's!"

Uh-oh, thought Eugenio. "Reminds me—glad I got my old man to cosign on my student loans."

Rich grew hotter. "Butt out, Geeno—no cavalry to the rescue this time." He focused again on Halston. "At least there's an old man still in the picture, and I'm helping part-time, unlike Book-Boy here!" He closed in and increased the volume, as though Halston's hearing had waned. "What's up, Hal? Still letting your Moms support your 35-bucks-a-credit habit on her waitressing wages, huh?!" He kicked back his chair and aimed for the door. "If you're gonna have a voyage of self-discovery, Dude, you ought to at least be able to chip in for the ticket. Oh—and you might want to figure out where you're landing before you shove off!"

Eugenio got up. "I'd love to stay and monitor the

oxygen, but I'm folding and Rich is driving." He shrugged helplessly and followed.

Halston and Adrianna floated in the heavy silence. Halston's order came. Adrianna shooed the server away with a tepid smile and reached for Halston's hand. "Hal, he doesn't mean to be so hurtful, really..." Her voice trailed off, then continued, more to herself. "I just don't understand why it always seems to end this way."

"Naw—it's okay, " Halston said, studying their laced fingers. "He's right. I'm totally adrift. Don't have the first clue where I belong. It's unfair—to Mom, the guys..." Halston finally met her eyes. "...And to you."

Adrianna lowered her gaze and flushed. She pulled away and resolutely gathered her belongings, making a show of adding her own to the bills left by Rich and Eugenio. After re-pocketing his book, Halston self-consciously wrapped his pastry in a napkin, dropped it into his backpack, and snapped a plastic lid on his coffee cup. She stared; he avoided. She leaped up and bolted for the door.

Setting his cup on a newspaper vending machine outside, he caught her by her trailing hand. His beseeching look thawed her a little. She relented and, throwing her free hand casually across his hip, placed her head softly on his chest. "You know, Hal, things could be like they were between us Senior year." She scarcely breathed. "That door's still open—

"Oh, God..."

"—And it can stay open until you close it."

Hal was momentarily paralyzed. Then, he braced her upper arms, distancing her a little. "I can't, Adrianna. I'm past that, but I'm still in-between, you know? You're so *there* already, with so much to give. I don't even know where—or who—I am yet." He broke away, retrieved the cup, and strode off, head down. Adrianna watched him go, then bowed toward her purse and fumbled for her keys. Hot tears dropped onto the back of her hand.

Halston retraced his route to Sutter's Fort in a fog.

He found the bench, set down the cup, and unshouldered his backpack. He slouched, punctuating his preoccupied stare with gulps of coffee until it was gone. He pivoted his face upward toward the sun, hoping for some kind of simple purification. When it didn't come, he resumed reading.

A commotion roused him. Ten yards away, a gang-banger had set upon one of the neighborhood's homeless. The gaunt, dark-skinned habitué was known in midtown as Bicycle Man, owing to his solitary, two-wheeled companion—which no one had ever seen him ride. (Not that it was a real option; its rusty rims and airless fragments of tire were held together by black electrical tape.) For him, it was less transportation than pack mule to his prospector of recyclables, and a mobile in the artistic sense. He seemed prideful of the inexplicable, fastidiously applied decorations on its frame and spokes. This was reasonable conjecture at best, though, since Bicycle Man shunned most contact and never uttered more than a handful of words at any given time. At least, that anybody knew.

The thug had straddled the front wheel to pursue his bored intimidation. His knitted Yankees cap and matching bandana bobbed and the arms of his Michelin-Man Raiders parka windmilled as he gestured and shouted. "Yo! What you doing on my sidewalk? Got a bike; should be in the street, man. Wazzup? Too crazy to talk to me? Maybe I should loosen your tongue a little bit!"

This can't end well, Halston thought. He stowed the book and fished out the scone. He struggled upward, suddenly afflicted by a strange, debilitating disease. Crossing his eyes, he gimped absurdly toward the pair, his voice a mangled screech. "UNCLE BUNNY! IS THAT YOU? I GOT YOUR LUNCH!"

The hoodlum's eyes jerked onto Halston. Surprise silenced him, and confusion caused his jaw to unclench slightly. He backed off a little and loosened his grip on the handlebars as Halston stumbled into him and regarded him with insane amblyopia. "OH—HULLO! ARE YOU THE WARDEN? BECAUSE BUNNY'S OUT, YOU KNOW? SORRY! I GOT NO LUNCH FOR YOU TODAY—ONLY UNCLE BUNNY!" Halston screamed, showering his target liberally with spittle.

The punk stepped back and found his jacket pockets. Halston continued in vigorous mime to breach the tension. A couple more steps and it seemed that Xenophobia and uncertainty had blunted the "disrespect" reflex just enough. "WAY too crazy for me!" The gangster pointed and retreated. "Later for you, Homes!" He turned and swaggered away.

"RIGHT-O—SORRY! G'BYE, THEN!" Halston remained in character briefly, not daring to look at Bicycle Man. Finally, he turned, finding nothing on the expressionless face or from behind the opaque wraparounds. He extended his hand, nervously.

"Hey. Want an apple-cinnamon scone?"

Deliberately, the denizen took the scone and placed it in the bike's basket. He picked up his bike, flipped it around, and wheeled away. Halston stood there, dumbly, until the figure was halfway across the property. He called after it. "Coffee's all gone. Sorry..."

℘℃ℜ

Halston reflected as he stood near the Cathedral's Chancery entrance on K Street, waiting. *It's been at least a month since I've seen any of those guys. I wonder how they are.* The lapse had been eventful. Marie's mother had taken ill, requiring a move to Portland to find a job up there and care for her. Halston had been reluctant to go, wanting to finish the semester. She left, and he got fired, so there went school and the apartment. Eugenio put him up for a while, but that soon stretched even his good humor, what with his big family. That left the green hotel and the kindness of strangers.

Father Jack emerged with a folded bill and a used paper copy of *Summa Theologica* in his hand. "Here's 20 bucks, Hal. And, now that you're past the neo-creationists, try this on for size. See if you can't finish "Part I" on God. You'll find ol' Tom Aquinas relatively uncluttered, if quaint."

"Thanks, Father. I'll give it a shot."

"Good," said the amiable priest. "See you next time."

True to form, Halston threw himself into the "Foreword" and wandered east toward 12th Street. Rounding the corner, he walked blindly into a body. He looked up. Yankees' cap. Bandana. Raiders' jacket. They recoiled in mutual recognition.

"Hey—I KNOW you, man!"

Panicked, Halston burst by him and two confederates, up 12th Street. He banked left and pounded blindly down the alley. He was abreast of the garage entrance when they caught him. Their tallest and swiftest pinned his arms while his antagonist and the other one sauntered up.

"Take him in there."

The orderlings grabbed Halston, dragged him across the blacktop, and pinned his back against a concrete pillar. *El Jefe* braced his feet 18 inches from Halston's and raised a blade between their faces. "Not too crazy today, eh, Homes? You dissed me a long time ago, but I remember. I told you I'd see you later. Maybe I cut you open and find some respect, huh?" He shifted backward onto his right foot; Halston moved his head slightly and gritted his teeth in anticipation.

Bicycle Man materialized in the garage entrance, backlit harshly by the sulphurous lemon-lime of sodium vapor. He lowered his wraparounds and his eyes flared like cobalt-blue star sapphires. The stars erupted into blinding, jagged bolts of cold energy that arced toward the gangsters, immobilizing them and suspending their every function. Their electric cocoon slid noiselessly past Bicycle Man and disappeared.

The sheer force had knocked Halston to the asphalt. He opened his eyes. Bicycle Man loomed over him, hand extended. "You okay? Name's Will."

"Yeah—I guess. What happened? Where are those guys?"

"Back where they were when you met."

"But—"

"Don't worry; they won't remember." Will pulled him up. His eyes glinted an unholy blue but were quiet. "Your search is over, if you want it to be."

"Who—who are you?"

"Not 'who; 'what.'" A conductor. One of many assigned to keep the train from jumping the tracks."

Halston brushed the dirt and blacktop pebbles away. "Are you ...*God*?"

Will chuckled. "Ain't we a curious lot? Humans, I mean. Got to have a picture of an animal to justify bite marks. Let me put it this way: If "God" is the Old Watchmaker, I'm a timekeeper. 'Night watchman of the Soul.'"

"Then—you're mortal?"

"Just a pile of meat, closing in on ashes and dust—with one Helluva secret weapon.

Halston's mind raced. "Okay. Was Jesus—

"One of us? Yep. And Krishna. And Buddha. And Mohammad. Maybe Sai Baba and Maitreya, too, for all I know. We don't have cosmic e-mail." Will crouched and twirled his shades. "Those guys were special cases; sometimes the situation calls you outside yourself. Every team produces the occasional Hall-of-Fame quarterback. Mostly, we're mere blockers and tacklers."

"Is there another 'team'?"

"Army of Darkness? No. I refer you to the prophet, Pogo: 'We have met the enemy and he is us.'"

"So, evil's just IN us?"

"Along with good. It's a matter of maintaining some balance. We're the 'referees'—here to keep the fight fair."

"Why not just leave it to the battle of wills? You know—winner take all."

"It's about human nature and perfectibility. Look—when confronted with a moral choice, which bottle do most folks reach for first? Whoever started this didn't want it to end in a draw."

"Well, what about the Holocaust, then? How'd that happen?"

"Organized evil creates its own luck. A lot of us got swept into the camps. We can't aggregate our powers. Sometimes our cover's blown and we become outright targets. Think Salem. That's why we're partial to anonymity. Once in a while, the ball just gets dropped, on a greater or lesser scale. We're only human." He grinned.

"Miracles?"

"Eye candy. Keeps folks interested."

"Religion?"

"Structure. Not everybody's cut out to sleep under the stars. Some folks need a tent. Others need a roof. It's for the civilians, though; got nothing to do with us."

"One more question?"

Will laughed. "Well, Glory Be! I can't guess."

"Why me?"

"I'm past sixty, tired, and can't break the chain. I've got to recruit a replacement, and you're qualified. Rootless, searching, few commitments. Oh—a random act of rescue is usually a pretty good indicator." Will rose wearily and made for his bicycle. "Anyway, you've got to volunteer. Give it a day or two and meet me for lunch at Loaves and Fishes on Saturday. Then, you decide."

§∞⌀

Halston dodged cars across upper 12th Street and came upon Sacramento's premiere homeless shelter and soup kitchen. It was late morning and 600-odd souls—loners and families of every potential description—were queued up for the midday meal. Halston picked his way around, warily, and found Will in line, leaning against his bicycle. His eyes darting, Halston whispered.

"Why here?"

Will smiled. "Like I said: 'Anonymity preferred.' Know anybody more faceless that a homeless person?"

"Are you all homeless?"

"'You'? Don't you mean 'we'?"

"I'm—My situation's just temporary?"

Will shook his head. "Sure it is. Anyway, depends on the culture—level of potential distraction. In other countries, where they're more attentive to the needs of the displaced, the cloak of mental illness is a workable disguise. In any case, you have to keep your eyes open." Halston sensed that Will's eyes were twinkling—if that was possible. "Monk's robe or a clerical collar is a good front, too—long as you don't get too big." They shuffled through the door. Will parked his bicycle near the wall at the head of the serving line. They took their food trays to a table in the back corner and sat. Will tossed his head before lowering it to eat.

"Go ahead. Look around."

Halston spun around on his seat. For the first time, he noticed that a smattering of the throng—two dozen, maybe—were wearing sunglasses. He honed in on a few of them. As they met his gaze, they glanced briefly at Will and opened their collars. Each revealed an amulet, all identical. Some opened nearby children's collars, showing the same thing. Halston returned to Will. "The kids, without the sunglasses. What are they?"

"Apprentices. Some are born"—Will lowered his shades slightly, looking directly into Halston—"some are made."

Halston assayed the dining room again. Nobody looked back. He turned to Will again. Hanging before him from Will's hands were his wraparounds and amulet.

"You in, or not?"

෯෦෬

It was a gloomy day as Adrianna Wong made her way east along the K Street Mall. She was so absorbed that she nearly fell over the homeless man sitting cross-legged on the ground near the light-rail stop across from the Cathedral. His incoherent babbling brought her out of it.   She studied the soiled, bearded figure in wraparounds, shaking a Styrofoam cup. One of her hands pressed at her lips; the other reached for him. "Hal? Is that you?!"

The man stopped babbling and motioned her downward. "Alley. Two minutes," he hissed.

She hesitated, quizzically. He jerked his head and resumed the gibberish. She backed away and darted across the tracks. She walked the half-block to the alley quickly and waited by the Dumpster. Halston made the corner and seized her by the shoulders. "Adrianna? How ARE you?" He waited a moment, allowing her shock and natural fear to subside.

"Oh, okay..." Her eyes fell and her shoulders sagged. "My life has pretty much fallen apart. My folks went ballistic when I dropped music for art and philosophy, so I had to quit school. Still part-time at Kinko's—I'm probably one lame-excuse sick day from being fired." She sniffled and her eyes brimmed over. "Other than that—" Now the sobs came.

He touched her cheek, gently. Look." Halston lowered his wraparounds slightly and his eyes flashed blue sparks. He fished into his shirt and dangled his amulet from his fingers.

"Can I interest you in some jewelry?"

෯෦෬

4 Gemini

ೞೞ

Flowers, candles, incense. Context is everything.

The thought promoted itself from vagrant to insight as Jim traced the outline of his oxblood brogans against the dull, gray veins of the cathedral's marble floor. Altar-boyhood artifacts that transubstantiated into adult talismans of sensual carnality became the stuff of Gothic nightmares again, as he stood there. Smoke curled lazily out of the thurifer being dangled by a somnambulant acolyte. *Christ. Twenty years of smoking and that crap still makes me dizzy.*

"What do you think he's going to *say*?" she hissed.

Jim looked at Laura, the baby, as his little brother, Cary—all six-and-a-half feet of him—embraced the rostrum. The meadow of blue, gray, and oddly strawberry heads that had known them all as children stirred slightly, as if anticipating a chilly gust—fed, no doubt, each by their own recollections of the rocky history between mother and son. Laura's chrome-blue eyes summarized her, and their, concern. So did her fingers, tamping her notes to her silk-covered thigh. Jim's were already pocketed, him having led the tribute. Candle flames jumped and bowed spastically at the corners of his vision.

"Not a goddamned clue," he whispered.

Cary had no notes. He stood, feet apart, and stared hard at thedull silver casket under the floral sprays—his Superman to her Lex Luthor—to satisfy himself she was truly vanquished, and her Kryptonite of passive aggression entombed with her.

"Good-bye, Mother."

಼ಲ

There they stood together, again, at the edge of what was weakly called a wake by such as themselves, two generations removed from the authentic. The lack of a propped-up stiff with coins on the eyes was a bargain, maybe even a blessing. Even a medium-watt look from the old girl while alive could etch glass at a considerable distance. Cary had bailed and planted his glass and elbows in front of the bartender, expiating the boredom he was loudly inflicting with clumsy gropes between pocket and tip jar. Jim and Laura had pretty much worked the room, getting their cheeks pinched ambiguously by Alzheimer's candidates as they flashed the mordant wit she'd passed to them to mollify those peers who retained some clarity.

Father John, the nephew canonized as her favorite by dint of his vocation and distance, drifted by, basking in his Jameson's. "Nice touch, you two. She'd have been proud."

She watched him leave to resume the cheerful falsehoods of ignorant comfort. "I need air. C'mon."

They repaired to the stunted ballroom's balcony. Jim lipped a cigarette and flicked at a balky flint.

"Gimme one."

He withdrew another, lit it, and handed it over. "When did you start smoking?"

"Tobacco? Never."

Even half-hidden under her lids, her irises were huge. Lesser men had slipped into those pools and drowned desperately, like non-swimmers. Until Jon. In low heels, she was his equal. *Six feet tall; blonde, gorgeous. My little sister, The Man-Eater.* He entertained the phenomenon of magnetism between weak men and strong women again and almost as quickly dismissed it, still unresolved. She caught the quiver at the corner of his mouth opposite the butt.

"What?"

"Nothing."

She exhaled, her blue vapor creating a vortex in his. "Ever think of quitting?"

"Constantly. Should be a no-brainer. The old man croaks from lung cancer—not young, but not old. The grandkids nag her into quitting, so she lives another 20 years, then dies from emphysema. I was the athlete, and the only one who took it up." He reflected, then pointed the tiny ember at her. "See, this is why my therapist's Benz is never more than three years old."

She laughed. Her head cycled up methodically, like an observatory's telescope, measuring the winking constellations. "Did they really love each other?"

Pathos and guilt radiated in him like gin. *Eight years old when Dad died. She missed so much*, he thought. "Oh, yeah."

"How do you know?"

"I'd catch 'em."

"Ick. Do I want to hear this?"

He realized, and waved the specter away. "No, I mean touching and kissing and stuff. It was weird; they tried not to fight in front of us, but the same restriction applied to PDAs. Like there's a rule that emotional neutrality equals stability."

"Speaking of stability, and therapy..." Laura studiously crushed the low-tar menthol on the railing. "Do you think he'll ever snap out of it?"

"Cary?"

She nodded at bigger brother, hopefully. Jim pursed his lips. "After this? I wish I could say. Shit, for that matter, I wish I could say *something*."

They stood, hips touching and hanging onto each other's waists, looking out at nothing in particular.

ಇಾಂ

Everyone had since pushed away from the decimated bird and congealing side dishes and collapsed in gluttonous disrepair around the house. That, football, and the mostly temporary gender *détente* of shared tasks made it Thanksgiving. Balmy from equal parts Chardonnay and the pleasant anesthesia of shared company and comfort food, Jim and Teri started shifting the carnage from dining room to kitchen. Entertaining taught them that a decent interval before dessert and coffee seemed less like piling on. Today, it made a serviceable excuse to let the charge in the air die away. Rhett, their 14-year-old, wandered in.

"Things calmed down any out there?"

"Yeah, Dad. Uncle Cary's working Rory over pretty good right now. Something about the ratio of malt and hops to barley in most microbrews."

"Just what every 11-year-old jock needs to know. Was he all over your new Strat and your CD collection?"

Rhett stiff-armed a countertop, raising his feet off the floor. "Uh-huh. That, and the lecture about the role of live music in bringing balance to a working man's life." He watched the heels of his hands go white. "He's gonna take me blues-clubbing in the city when I'm old enough." He smiled slyly. "Maybe before."

"Peachy—as long as you're old enough to drive, because you'll wind up having to."

Rhett's stepmother circled behind him, balancing half-bowls of potatoes and dressing, and matter-of-factly blew at the thick hair fraying the nape of his neck. Surprised, he dropped and slapped away a spasm of pleasure. Jim took it all in, with satisfaction. Teri left for another round-trip. Rhett found a green bean and dipped it into a nearby glob of cold Durkee's onion pudding. He munched, seriously; Jim shuddered.

"Dad, can I ask you something?"

"Of course."

"Why do you and he always get into it?"

Jim stopped slicing, released the turkey medallions onto the foil, and tapped the carving knife's tang on the cutting board, softly. "You know, son, I have no answer. Lots of working theories."

"Like?"

"How about, 'because we're brothers?'"

Jim grinned. Rhett couldn't separate his father's congenital gift for sarcasm from defensiveness. It wasn't material. Either way, good or bad, it was usually about deflection. "Oh, I get it—like Rory and me?"

"Approximately."

"But you two are *old,* so testosterone and immaturity are no longer issues. Right?"

"So, you're saying Theory Number One is bogus?"

"Duh."

"Well, then—there's genes. History. Presence. Absence. Admiration. Jealousy. Theories Two through Seven—in no particular order."

Rhett frowned. "Explain, please."

Jim draped an arm around the boy's shoulders. "Remember what Gramma—my Mother—was like when she lived here?"

"Yeah. Pissed!"

"In a word—exactly. So, we've both got that going for us. But she wasn't always like that—at least, for me."

"How so?"

"She was barely 40 when my Dad died. Cary was 12. They both really needed him around then, in spite of themselves, and neither ever forgave him for leaving them."

"How was it different for you?"

"When I was younger and Cary and Laura weren't much more than babies, she wasn't like that. There was at least as much sunshine as lightning. My Dad and I grew close, starting when I was about your age. Thinking back, Mom was menopausal or depressed, or both, and I was old enough to be emotionally available. Anyway, she'd get crazy and he'd run interference for the three of us." He gave Rhett the once-over. "'Paging Doctor Freud!' Aren't you bored yet?"

Rhett swallowed. "No."

"Damn it! Well, Dad was diagnosed when I was 18 and away at college—end of my freshman year. Wasted away in under six weeks. Mom was nuts the whole time. I remember standing by his bed, that last day. He and I made our peace, alone, before the delirium set in, so I was more or less a bystander by then. Little Laura couldn't really process any of it. Cary, though—bright, sensitive Cary—was aware enough to be panicked. When Dad went, he blurted out something like, 'Well, that's it!' Mom just went black, and turned on him."

"Wow. What did you do?"

"Nothing. Everything after that is a blur. I was still stupidly adolescent enough that my grief came out selfishly, as anger. I had a summer job lined up, so I made tracks. Finished college and law school; got married. Left those two alone. With her."

Jim took to messing with the spikes of hair at the top of his son's forehead. Rhett pushed Jim's jaw down with his index finger so he could connect with him.

"Don't worry, Dad. When I run away, I'll take Rory with me."

"You'd better."

They hugged, then separated at the sound of escalating voices from the living room. Jim rounded the corner in time to see Cary snatch his jacket from the extended arms of Mimi, his common-law girlfriend, and hurl it to the floor. He was unsteady and loud. Teri, Rory, and the host couple's friends were all either rooted to their chairs or in some stage of thwarted assistance.

"God*DAMN* it, woman!" he roared. "I'll decide when

it's time to go home, and not one minute before!" He cast a bleary eye at Jim. "And *you*. I suppose you have something to add. As usual."

"Always," Jim said, calmly. "I am an Irish Catholic lawyer, after all." He picked up the jacket and clapped his brother on the back. "We should probably go to bed, anyway, on account of being much older than the two of you. No more action here tonight, but I'm fairly certain there's a club or two in full tilt closer to home. What do you say, Meem?"

She looked back, her face blending embarrassment and relief. They both knew that he'd be snoring 10 minutes into the trip. Cary softened and stuck his arms into the jacket without a word, like a child being dressed for school. He turned, tossed off a small wave and half-glance, and ducked out the doorway. Mimi took her wrap and bag from Teri and hugged everyone, especially Jim.

"Good night, and thanks. For everything."

"'Night, Meem," Jim said. "Be careful, and call when you get there."

From the doorway, he watched her bend Cary's long levers into her roadster. She was in, the concealed headlights bobbed up, and they were gone. Jim closed and latched the door, and turned into the room.

"Another holiday train wreck, recorded for posterity," he announced, mostly to himself.

Teri overheard him, and punched his shoulder playfully. "Hey, cheer up, 'Little Engine.' It's just the one car that jumped the tracks." She closed in and fingered the points of his collar. "You pulled the rest of the train into the station safely, just as you always do."

Jim folded his hands in the small of her back. "It's more like the scriptural sheep-shepherd thing," he said. "I wonder how long I'll have to leave the 99 to chase that one?'

"Break it up, you two," called Rory. "Where's dessert?"

ՏՅՇՅ

"Whaaaaa..."

Jim's shoulder shook, violently. It was Teri, gruffly semi-conscious. "Doorbell!"

She rolled away, taking covers with her. A minor curse of their marriage was that he slept deeply and neither of them was attractive and wakeful at the same time.

The amber display read One-Colon-Four-Three. He sensed the flap and whine of awnings and spatters on glass. He snagged his flannel robe, wrapping and tying as he stumbled downstairs. The chimes cycled under a persistent finger and guttural growls crackled through the intercom speakers.

Jim hit the porch light and peered through the beveled panes, but saw no one. He turned the deadbolt and knob, and the door leaped away. In tumbled Cary, drenched from the downpour.

"*JEEZus!*" Cary! How did you get here?"

"Cab. Train. Walked. No coin." He was drunk, underdressed, trembling, and bluish—and not due to the poor light.

"From *HAYWARD*? That's two hours, by car! Can you stand?" Jim propped and pushed, but it was as futile as wrestling a giant, soggy Pillsbury Doughboy. "I'll get towels—don't move!" Cary coughed and gurgled, amused.

Jim returned, dragged Cary fully inside and bolted the door. He yanked off his sneakers and socks and peeled his soaked windbreaker and sweat pants over his lanky extremities in membrane-like sections, leaving his underwear. He mopped and rubbed, drying and warming. Cary came around some and found an elbow.

"Mimi...bitch..." he said and repeated, as he tried to find purchase on the floor with his heel. He failed, but Jim managed his head into the new arm-crook and squat-thrust them both to approximate vertical. He steadied them, with difficulty, and explored movement enough to learn that Cary might participate. Jim launched the maneuver toward the guest room and Cary joined in, splitting his foot-contact time equally between Jim's shins and insteps, and the floor. Balancing Cary momentarily on his own feet, Jim swatted the shams off the bed and drew back the spread and linens. He released and pushed slightly, and Cary spun onto the mattress on his back. Jim pulled off his briefs and undershirt, tucked in his legs, and covered him. For an instant, his brother's hairy body disappeared; Jim was 10, and Cary was four and feverish with flu. His hazel eyes were bright and calm in his snug little face.

Thank you, Jim remembered.

Suddenly, Cary was old and sepulchral. His eyes were dull and sad, but smoldering a bit—and colder than his sallow skin.

"Leave me. Alone."

Cary closed his eyes and Jim retreated.

ℬℛ

Jim slid off the last step finishing his post-dawn rites—yawning, scratching, and adjusting, of the type that put women off televised baseball. Recollection made him peer at the closed bedroom door. Concern propelled him a half step in that direction. Experience stopped him. He meandered into the kitchen, where Teri had already begun filling his mug. She regarded him with that look found on the man-boy, love-pity continuum, reserved exclusively for the one who finished his sentences. They hadn't spoken, but she knew. The only unique thing this time was that Cary had taken his act on the road.

"Coffee, up. Cereal? Hemlock?"

"Ha-ha." He made a face at the tiny, packing-material jewels in the Lucky Charms set out in Tupperware for Rory. "I swear to God; that kid has pure glucose in his veins."

"He never stops," Teri said, sipping. "Four thousand calories a day, minimum."

Pop-Tarts were laid out for Rhett. Jim reached for his box. *All-Bran: Manna to the Atherosclerotic.* Here they came, like the circus parade rounding the first corner at the head of Main Street—galumphing, jostling, and laughing, all cymbals and calliope. Jim backed reflexively to the counter farthest from the breakfast bar. Now raptors, they swooped and kited, snatching up their processed prey. Rhett pocketed the pastry and trained his eyes on Jim. "Tonight. Tattoo. Talk?"

"Terrific," Jim said, rolling his.

"Homework! Shit—uh—Darn!" Rhett wheeled and coursed back up the stairs. Rory had applied the milk, snapped the top, and packed away the bowl and plastic spoon without coming to rest. "Late. Bus." Out he went.

Jim gaped. "Did Bud Bernanke declare an active verb shortage?"

The door at the other end opened. Teri heard the hinges and rinsed her cup. "Nursing home—meeting about Mom." She was gone.

Jim spread his arms in exasperation. "Can I get a complete sentence here?"

Cary materialized, an apparition in air-dried underwear closer to parchment than cotton. He was still pallid but his size, wild hair, and presence defeated the ghostliness. His shield of aggression was firmly affixed and powered up, even in the face of—maybe reinforced by—last night's debacle. From practice, Jim could tell. "Coffee?"

"Unh-hnh."

"Anything to eat?"

"Don't think I could keep it down."

Jim slid the mug under his brother's face and used casual artifice to brush his cheek. It was hot, so Jim palmed Cary's forehead. He recoiled. "Don't start."

"Cary, you're burning up."

"I'll be fine; just need to organize my shit a little."

"What happened this time?"

Cary looked up. "What do you care, really?"

Pushing buttons; don't go there, Jim thought. "Wouldn't ask if I didn't."

Cary paused, as if shuffling details. "Same old stuff. Had a few beers after work, came home. She cooked; it got cold. How was I supposed to know? So we get into it, she freaks, and starts throwing my shit out the door. I go after it, and she locks me out. I yell; I pound on the door. She called the cops, she says, so I take off."

"Why did you come all the way up here?"

Jim watched labored nonchalance force the pleas out of Cary's eyes. "Couldn't think. Didn't have my truck keys."

"What can I do to help?"

"Nothing, really. Just needed a place to crash. Thanks." Jim couldn't tell which embarrassed him more—last night or the required courtesy. "Maybe spot me thirty bucks to get home?"

"To what?"

"Oh. That. She'll take me back; always does."

Jim folded his arms. "What is Mimi, Cary? 'Serious relationship' number three?"

Cary stiffened. "Don't even go there, 'bro'." He aimed a finger. "None of your goddamned business."

Jim laughed bitterly. "You're sitting in my kitchen, half-naked, sick, and broke!"

Cary knocked the chair backward, making his body into a high wall. "I should have known better—you gave up on me a long time ago!"

Jim's emotional turf trembled, so he retaliated. "*Who's* given up on you? Look at yourself!"

"Oh, yeah," Cary parried. "I may be a lot of things, but at least I'm not a mortgaged-up, corporate toady like you!"

Jim hardened. "Ah, Mister Proletariat speaks, once again defending the masses against the cold creep of commitment and responsibility!" He stopped himself, working his fingers through his hair into his scalp. "Jesus. Who do we sound like?"

Cary got it, and backed down. Jim approached and laid on a hand; it wasn't welcomed but it wasn't rejected, either. "At least stay on to see a doctor."

"Can't. Can't afford to leave this job and go back on rotation at the hall."

Jim sighed. "I'm going to get ready for work. Your clothes are in the dryer. I'll drop you at the station." He pressed his fingers into Cary's shoulder and hesitated; whatever it was that seemed to be caught in his brother's throat stayed there.

℘ℛ

"Hiya, Honey!"

Jim chortled. Laura's stock, Alice Kramden-Lucy Ricardo telephone greeting always did that. "Hello, brat. What's new in the Sandwich Islands?"

"*Nada.* I just spent an hour on the phone with Mimi. She call you?"

"You know they *never* call me. Who gets to play 'Twenty Questions' when Cary wants to know anything about me?"

"I do."

"I rest my case. Anyway, back to Mimi."

It's not really about Meem. It's Cary..."

"Now *there's* a fuckin' surprise."

"Hey. Anyway, she has to stick him in the hospital."

Jim holstered the attitude. "What's wrong?"

"Walking pneumonia, they think. The last course of antibiotics didn't clear him up."

"Poor Meem. How long, do they think?"

"A week—maybe longer. They want to do tests, as well."

"For what?"

"They don't know; just to rule stuff out, I guess." She

paused; Jim could hear the odd cacophony of exotic birds and chickens—one of Hawaii's bouquet of splendid paradoxes. He thought he also heard partially formed words bumping against her lips.

"What are you going to do?" she asked.

"What do you mean?"

"About Cary—and Mimi. I think she's pretty close to the edge."

He switched ears and leaned heavily against the bar. "My best instinct is to stay out of it. You know the first thing out of my mouth always amounts to a declaration of war. Pointless conflict is probably the last thing she needs right now."

Laura began flexing her fingers against her handset, producing plastic noises that fell harshly on Jim's ear. Though small things like that annoyed him more than most, he did his best to overlook it. She heard his choppy breathing and stopped.

"I don't know. It's not like the motorcycle accident in high school, where he acted like his pulling through was worthwhile because it would disappoint the old lady. I'm scared he wants to give up."

"Now, that's truly weird."

"Maybe, but for him I think her death was like pulling the cooling rods out of a nuclear reactor. All that anger is purposeless now; instead of being bled off on an external object, it's trapped inside and is melting the core."

His chosen profession to the contrary, he was powerless to disagree, so he did the next-best thing. "I'll give it some thought."

"Well. *Somebody* has to be the grownup."

"Fine. Tell Meem she can call me anytime. How's Jon?"

Laura exhaled, petulantly. "He's fine. We're fine. Everybody's fine. Whatever."

ℰℚ

Teri twirled her fork between her fingers, watching the neglected food's warmth vaporize—once again the victim of the inconsequential rhetoric and crude foolishness that only young, hormonal males and their fathers can bring to an evening meal. Jim caught her glare and broke off, sheepishly. The boys desisted; Rhett cast his crooked grin at her. "Go on, Teri," he said. "Say it, and get it over with."

"I *hate* boys." She felt her snit melting and heard snickering. The phone rang, enabling her escape. Jim and his sons were still savoring the rout when Teri returned, holding the cordless like a bomb dismantler.

"Jim, it's Mimi. She's crying."

A firing-squad pall fell on the room. The boys focused on their entrees. Jim cupped Teri's hand for an instant, then removed the phone and took it into the kitchen. "Meem—it's Jim. What's wrong?"

The filtered snuffling subsided. "Cary needs an operation. They found something."

"What did they find?"

"They did a CAT scan and some kind of biopsy, and found spots on his lungs—something about non-small cell cancer. Early stage, I think. I didn't understand much of it. Cary signed the papers."

"When are they going in?"

"Tomorrow morning."

"Are you at the hospital now?"

"No." The sobs resumed. "Cary sent me home—said I'd just be in the way. Jim, I'm frightened."

Jim swallowed. "I'm on my way. You try to rest; I'll call you on my cell once I've seen Cary."

"O-Okay."

Jim felt Teri's hands creep over his clavicles and turned. "Cary's shut down again. I'd better go."

She nodded and softly kissed his cheek. The wisp of warm breath propelled from her nostrils into his ear barely diluted the dread building in his breast.

℘℧

"Cary Ellison, please?" This prompted that look of detached authoritarianism from the desk nurse in Surgery East, so Jim anticipated the question. "I'm his brother."

"Forty-two-ten-B. Visiting hours are over at 10."

"It's 8:30."

"He might be sleeping."

"Tomorrow, he might be dead." He turned and started away; mercifully, that was the end of it. He found the door already cracked, so he pushed it into the fluorescent-fed twilight. Cary dozed in the second bed; the first was vacant. *Good.* Jim quietly lowered the near side rail and pushed the meal tray over Cary's heaving chest. He retrieved a portable DVD player from his briefcase, opened it, and gently placed its attached earphones onto Cary, working around the oxygen tubing. Cary stirred. Jim held in his breath, pushed "Play" and stepped to the headboard.

Cary awoke to the familiar "Yah-YAH-yah-YAH-yah-yah-yah-YAH" overture, and The Three Stooges in "Whoops, I'm an Indian." He rolled his eyes back toward Jim for an instant, then became transfixed for 18 minutes, erupting occasionally with belly laughs mitigated by coughs. Jim winced. The strategy was to find neutral ground and he remembered them lolling on the carpet at home, laughing helplessly at the endless slapping, poking, and tweaking and ignoring the impatient, maternal radiation warnings. It worked, but he hadn't anticipated the side effects.

As the disc spun down, Cary doffed the earphones and wiped his eyes and mouth. "Great idea," he said. "Cough up a lung and shorten the surgery!"

"I was going to bring 'Dizzy Doctors,' but I thought that cut a little too deep."

"Good call—and decent word play. 'Pardon My Scotch' was my all-time favorite." Cary darkened a little.

"So. What are you doing here?"

Jim shifted his feet. "You know—the brotherly thing."

"Better late than never, I guess."

The elder seized Cary's left hand and held it tight until he stopped tugging. "Okay. For present purposes, let's assume that you've just listed all the things I've ever done that piss you off, and I've apologized for each and every one—so there's nothing left for us to hold against each other. Deal?"

"It doesn't work that way."

"I *know* it doesn't, but why can't it?"

"Because, man—it wouldn't be right."

"What's right about being angry and depressed all the time? Who did we both know, like that?"

A nerve was struck. Cary jerked his hand away and made a fist. "Don't you *dare* compare me to her!"

Jim sat and gingerly caressed Cary's thigh through the covers. "Look, it's not about that any more, Cary. She's *dead*. Why can't you just bury it all with her?"

Cary reeled a little from the rhetorical round-house but quickly regained familiar emotional footing. "But—but she was so *bad* to me. She—she never *listened* to me. She never really loved—"

"Stop," Jim said behind his raised hand. "She loved you; she loved all of us—especially Dad. Why do you think she freaked like she did? One day, he's the center of her existence; the next, he's gone. 'Now what do I do?' Her terror turned to rage, with no one available to help her through it."

"But she was mad a lot way before Dad died..."

"Yes, she was. That was the only way she could manage her feelings. 'Absorb. Internalize. Explode. Repeat, as necessary.' Dad was the buffer. My first year away at college, she would write these horrible letters. Every time, without fail, another letter from him would come behind it, a perfect antidote. It seemed almost instinctive."

"Why was she like that?"

"Don't know; don't think I want to. Her oldest sister was like that. The rest just escaped or became alcoholics, or both. She talked about her father in a way that left almost everything important out—you know, human-being stuff—that always made me wonder what he was *really* like."

Cary sat up and folded his arms over his knees. "Jesus."

"Yes."

"But, it seemed like she blamed *me*. It wasn't *my* fault."

"Of course not. She didn't blame you; you were just in the line of fire, and a constant reminder of what she'd lost. She probably saw herself in Laura, at least until she was older."

"Well, what the Hell did she expect *me* to do about it?"

"She didn't. You set that expectation for yourself."

Cary searched Jim's face for definition. He scratched it, self-consciously. "You've made your views on psychotherapy well-known, but the help I got when my first marriage was breaking up was a godsend." Cary's skepticism was apparent, but a little curiosity bled around its edges. "The guy made it pretty clear that I was treating Julie like my mother and she expected me to behave like her father—making us both resentful and argumentative, because that's the last thing either of us wanted. He told me; he said, 'Jim, you're what we call a 'rescuer.' You feel responsible for the happiness of everyone in your orbit; if anyone isn't, you're failing. Well, guess what? Some people are determined to be unhappy and there isn't a damned thing you can do about it.' At that moment, I felt like an anvil had been lifted off me. I understood so much."

"Like?"

"Like…" Jim suddenly took an interest in his cuticles. "Like, why I bugged out on you and the brat." His eyes came up to meet Cary's, and they shone. "Without Dad, she'd be even unhappier, and I'd be a bigger failure. So, off I went."

Cary smiled, oddly. "According to her, compared to you, *I* was the failure!"

Jim wagged his open hands. "Hey—don't lay that on *me!*"

Moments slipped silently between them as they stared just a bit away from one another. Cary broke in. "So, I just...'lay my burden down, boy'?"

"That's it, exactly."

"I don't know. Where do I start?"

"Anger is like a contagion. First, you just make up your mind to get over it. Then, you inoculate yourself against it."

"How's that?"

"For what's passed, abandon what's bad—seek forgiveness, if you need to—and hold on to what's good. What it was like when Dad was alive, for example. Little things. For today and tomorrow, open yourself up, especially to those who care most about you. Let them nourish you with their love and make you strong."

Cary was pensive. "I miss Daddy. I want to remember..." He choked up. Jim leaned in and clasped his neck with one hand. "...but most times I struggle just to see his face." Hot tears slid randomly away from the corners of his eyes.

"I've got pictures, and most of his stuff. Come, look; we'll talk. Laura and I do it, every chance we get. Bring Mimi."

Cary's eyes widened. He pitched forward into Jim's embrace, convulsed. "Jimmy—I'm...so...fucking...scared." Jim felt his brother's body herk and jerk with rasping sobs and stroked his back until they relented. He lay Cary back onto his pillows, adjusted the soft, glassine tubes snaking around his ears, and brushed the unruly hair away. Cary pulled Jim's hands together and clasped them desperately between his own.

"Don't leave me. Okay?"

Jim startled then reassured him with a satisfied laugh. "Not hardly—I just got you back!"

🙟🙞

His shoes were glossy black this time. The marble was veined and neutral, but a much cheerier rouge—making a nice contrast, as did their boutonnieres, with the striped pants, morning coats, and cravats. Jim sized Cary up and adjusted his neckwear. Cary nodded and they both returned to that ridiculous, "football coach" pose—hands clasped over groin, feet apart—that men fall into, in conspicuous situations. They waited at the railing with the priest as the rest of the wedding party began its stiff, inexorable march.

"Never did I think I'd be in a friggin' church again," whispered Cary. "Well, vertically, at least."

"That's what you get for taking up with a Catholic girl. Meem will back off again, until you have kids."

"Yeah? Well, thanks for standing up with me." Cary touched his face tentatively. "At least you're getting a better deal than *I* did when *you* got hitched the first time."

"Whaddya gonna do? Jerry was my best friend and my college roommate. Beer's thicker than blood when you're 21—you know that."

Cary cleared his throat. "That was great, looking at Dad's stuff Thursday night. I had no idea about all that work and other stuff he was into."

"Amazing guy, really, but a man of a few words. Unlike today—" Jim glared, comically "—when you can never shut anyone up. We'll go through the pictures again, soon, and you can take what you want."

They refocused up the aisle. Laura was a gorgeous Maid of Honor—no surprise there. Mimi was a gossamer and taffeta vision. Teri was a credible Mother of the Groom, installed in the first pew in beige, with her mouth firmly and uncomfortably closed.

"This is gonna sound perverse..."

Jim rotated his head a little, waiting for the rest of the announcement out of the little corner speaker Cary had made of his lips.

"In a certain way, I almost wish the old lady was here."

"For her, or for you?"

"For her *and* for me."

"Correct answer. They really did the best they could. Look at us: we're the golden fruit. The rest is husk. Hang on to that."

Jim was happy. There was no incense, and he really didn't crave a cigarette all that much.

ଛଔ

5 Intentional Walk

ഇ൚ങ

"'Won't you be my luh-ver (yeah)/
I'll treat you ri-ight (uh)/
I know you hear your friends when they say
you might...'"

The nascent 16-year-olds rocked and bumped hips under the earnest, two-dimensional eyes of their favorite boy-band, crooning along into their hairbrushes.

"LeLe!" her mother cried from below. "Turn that racket down!"

They froze and eyed each other. "Uh-oh—Busted!" They embraced in mock terror and collapsed onto LeLe's bed in peals of laughter.

"You two are supposed to be studying!"

LeLe rolled her eyes. "Yesssssss, Mu-THER." On reflex, she reclaimed an abandoned book, browsed, and listened for disengagement. "So, Tif; you ready to crank it tomorrow?"

Her best friend in the 10th grade world and starting pitcher for the Scottsdale Copperheads made a face. "Whatever—regionals and all. At least we're at home; travel-ball so, like, totally *sucks*."

This took the shortstop/leadoff hitter by surprise. "It's all still fun, right?"

"Oh, yeah." Tiffany waved the concern away like a minor odor. "*Playing* is so *cool*. When the hitter's dug in, you're all down behind me, and Tonya's glove goes up, it's like I'm in charge of this big, powerful *machine*. Everyone is tense, straining, and nothing happens until I make it. I kick to the plate—*BOOM!*" She slapped,her hands together, startling LeLe a little. "Everything, something, or nothing. Then I do it again!"

"Yeah, gurrrrl!" They clasped hands, holding it just long enough to allow the sensation to course through them both. Tiffany's soaring eyes returned to earth. "It's all the other stuff I can do without."

"Like?"

"Drills. Camps. Videos. Special coaching. The rants. 'Trophy, Tiffany. ' 'Scholarship, Tiffany.' 'The Olympics, Tiffany.' It's not bad enough that we play half the year..." She drifted away, lost in her laced fingers.

LeLe bounced into her, trapping her thick, blond French braid against her neck inside the crook of her elbow. "Hey—we're 15. What *else* are we gonna do?"

Evil Tiffany rolled her eyes up to meet LeLe's. "Boys?"

They tumbled backward, smothering giggles and kicking their feet. Again, quiet descended. Tiffany stared at the ceiling. "What if I'm not that *good*? I mean, like they all want? What then?"

LeLe took her hand firmly. "My Dad has this favorite Zen saying: 'Wherever you are, be there.'"

Tiffany smirked. "That's deep, Le. What in Hell does that mean?"

"It means, you're spending all of today worrying about tomorrow. You've got the ball *now*. Live in that as long as you can before you have to find something else. Softball ends—for all of us."

Tiffany was pensive. "Do Buddhists play ball?"

"No, but Christians do." LeLe jerked Tiffany toward the computer. "We'd better check Arnie's web site. You *know* there'll be a quiz in the dugout." They logged on, bringing up "Arnold Jeffries' First Calvary Chevrolet—Proud Sponsor of the Scottsdale Copperheads," and clicked on "Today's Inspiration." They read, aloud:

> *The Lord is my light and my salvation; whom should I fear?*
> *The Lord is my life's refuge; of whom should I be afraid?*
> *When evildoers come at me to devour my flesh,*
> *My foes and my enemies themselves stumble and fall.*
> --PSALMS 27:2

Tiffany screwed up her face. "I wonder if he has a clue what a goober we all think he is."

"Dunno." LeLe chewed a thumbnail. "Four sets of uniforms for us, and the 14Us and 12Us, plus equipment and fees. That's got to run into serious money."

"Yeah, but it's not like he *owns* us. And why do we get the same Old Testament 'vanquish mine enemies' rap all the time?" Tiffany was up again, hands on hips. "Jesus is about love and forgiveness, right? What do fear and hatred have to do with competition, anyway?"

∫ↂ

WhirrrrrrRRRTINK! The dimpled rubber sphere leaped off the aluminum barrel and ploughed a blurred canary trench into the upper netting, then stalled and sloughed harmlessly into the back of the cage.

Outside, Tiffany pulled her gloved fingers out of the chain-link and clapped. "Good contact, Le—keep it up!"

LeLe striped the last five pitches methodically into almost the same location. As the machine whined to a stop, she squatted and peeled her batting gloves into her teal-and-copper helmet—marking the end of their Saturday, pre-game warm-up ritual. She wiped her face on her jersey and looked up into the cross-hatched glare as a shadow fell over the half of her not already covered by Tiffany's.

"Hey, 'Britney.'"

Jarred, Tiffany peered over her Ray-Bans at the profile a half-head above her own. She might have been an Aztec princess, with her strong bronze features and her thick headdress of black ringlets, offset by a gold earring.

LeLe stood and shaded her eyes, circling her bat handle lazily around its head planted on the concrete. "Hey, 'Queen Latifah.'" She picked up her gear and made for the gate.

The stranger turned to Tiffany, looked right into her, and stuck out a hand. Tiffany examined it, momentarily. It was muscular, a little rough, but its umber depth was set off by dainty pink nails. Its owner revealed a mouthful of strong, flawless teeth.

"Marisella Rivas."

"Uh—Tiffany Queensberry." They shook hands.

LeLe arrived and Marisella enfolded her. "What's up, home-girl?"

"Same-same. Playin' ball. What're you doing way over here?"

"Cage time—and regionals." She eyed LeLe's bag. "You a Copperhead now, huh?" LeLe nodded.

Tiffany conveyed her puzzlement. LeLe saw and pushed gently away. "Oh—me and Marisella played

12Us together on the West side, before we moved over here. Tif here's my best friend, and our starting pitcher."

"All *right!*" Marisella extended a low palm toward Tiffany, who slapped it tentatively. "Me, too!" The big girl's mirthful eyes narrowed on LeLe again. "She any good?"

LeLe pinkie-pointed back. "You get past the Bombers this afternoon, you'll find out tomorrow!"

Tiffany finally understood. "Oh. You pitch for the Strikers!"

Marisella opened her jacket. "One and the same!"

"Marisella! You're up! Let's go!"

She wheeled and waved at a husky Latino in a ball cap matching hers. "'Kay, Coach! Well, gotta go. Get your ya-yas out, Sistahs!"

LeLe caught her arm. "Good luck."

"What's luck got to do with it?" They stared at her; she laughed. "You, too, now. See you later—I hope!" She loped away.

Tiffany watched her quads and glutes ripple in retreat. All she could manage was a low whistle. LeLe seized her shoulders and got up in her face. "You two are going to be *awesome*, tomorrow. I can't *wait!*"

✥

"Bring it in, ladies!"

Pete Lopez—auto parts distributor, retired semi-pro infielder, and die-hard diamond tactician—had coached the Copperheads from 12Us up after taking his granddaughter, Letitia, to their first meeting and impulsively sticking up his hand. His love for her and for the game took care of the rest.

"All right, Copperheads. Coach Young—"Pete nodded toward Ronnie Young, his lanky assistant sucked in with daughter LeLe the meeting after that—"has the book on the Sting. Their pitching is decent but nothing you haven't already seen. Relief is weak when coming from behind. Defense is adequate but inexperienced, so they tend to short the field and press when leaned on. We're faster, so let's get on them early. We're away—LeLe, you can expect to lay it down to test the first baseman and how they cover, so pay attention to Pops over at first, for a change." LeLe and her father traded grins. "Tif, I'm moving you to the two-hole. I need you to work a walk, so pick her up as quick as you can. We might try to move Le over before then, depending how sharp she is. Sierra? You move from seven to three; be ready to punch it into the alleys. And Tonya, you're cleanup for Tif today. I want those bases cleaned and all those Sting shorts dirty, so gimme that Tonya glare." Their massive catcher smiled and slid her face into a passable Shaquille O'Neill glower. She couldn't sustain it, though, and delicately covered her mouth as laughter and playful punches rained in on her. Pete mused just long enough, then raised his hands. "Okay, people. Everybody else check with me before I give the card to the ump. Otherwise, Plan A. Tif, I might rest you if we're up early to let Brie get good and loose before tomorrow." Tiffany the competitor suppressed a frown. "Hey," Pete said. "You're my leader, and I'm going to need every bit of that rotator cuff if we get the Strikers tomorrow." He chucked her chin to bring her back. "How's it feel, by the way?"

She melted a little. "Good to go."

"That's my girl," he said, and turned. "Anything else, Coach Young?"

Ronnie watched his Nike trace an arc in the dirt below his folded arms and poked at the smokeless behind his lower lip with his tongue. He husbanded a smile. *This guy is so good*, he thought. *Short, sweet, complete. You can almost smell the focus on these girls.* "No, Coach Lopez."

"Any questions?" He glanced around, satisfied. He thrust a fist out, waist high; 14 hands landed on it.

"One, two, three—COPPERHEADS!"

They broke. The players busied themselves with bench positions, managing the nervous excitement with low trash talk. Pete detected a prominent Adam's apple in his peripheral vision.

"Coach?"

Pete stifled his pique out of sheer habit. "Oh. Hi, Arnie. A little late today, aren't we?"

"RV sale—what can I say?" The sponsor flashed that car-closer grillwork—all the enamel, with most of the pink tissue thrown in. "Lord's work is never done."

Pete rubbed his face to erase any evidence of true feelings. "Ladies, bring it back in for Arnie, please?" He shifted backward a little to allow the reluctant semicircle to form and to find his own shelter. A couple of throats were cleared; Arnie closed his eyes and abruptly raised his arms to the Jesus-over-Rio position. Brie ducked, successfully.

"Our Dear Lord Jesus, guide us on Thy path and make our bats to be true as we lay Thine enemies low, as Samson slew the Philistines with the jawbone of an Ass…"

"Amen!" Tiffany cried. Heads were bent in practiced piety; yea, many were buried in backs, and it was good. The blasphemer gave LeLe such a baleful look that she almost swallowed her fist. Arnie rambled to a close and a proper chorus of "Amens." Pete crossed himself deliberately, knowing that it made Arnie uncomfortable, and commanders and warriors resumed their girding.

Marc Queensberry appeared behind the wire— ever the buttoned-down lawyer, even in the hot afternoon sun. His gaze slid by Pete's and landed on his daughter. "Step out, Tiffany." She balked listlessly but complied. Father and daughter moved a few rows up the bleachers, near Missy—trophy wife and stepmother—and he questioned his daughter in a low voice. Pete ignored the ritual just as poorly as he always had. He spied that she was as tortured and defensive as she always was. She returned wordlessly, her Ray-Bans firmly in place to mask her self-inflicted verdict of personal treason. Marc was in her wake.

"Coach, may I see you for a minute, please?"

"I haven't finished the lineup card."

"Won't take long." Marc was already headed up the third-base line. Pete met him near the coach's box.

"Tiffany tells me you've moved her up the order and might pull her early. Is that true?"

"Look, Marc; this opener is likely to be a laugher and I'm going to need her fresh against the Strikers."

"I'm afraid you can't do that."

Pete sighed. *Here we go.* "And why's that, Marc?"

"Two reasons. First, I've got a Wildcat assistant coming today and tomorrow, and I want maximum exposure, including Tiffany in the four-hole. Second, there aren't going to be any Strikers—tomorrow, or the rest of the season."

Pete mistrusted his ears. "I'm sorry. What?"

"The Strikers. There'll be a forfeit today and they're out. We'll face the Crush. It's taken care of."

"A forfeit, huh?"

"You know that big pitcher of theirs, that Rivas girl? Well, a little *too* overpowering for my taste. Turns out her parents are illegals and she was born out of the country, or at least on the way over. Won't be able to produce a proper birth certificate."

Pete folded his arms slowly, to contain himself. "Why are you doing this?"

"I don't want Tiffany to risk any kind of

embarrassment, under the circumstances." Marc was maddeningly nonchalant.

"You can afford to buy that kid *eight* years in the Ivy League. What's the point?"

"The point is, I'm in a position to help my daughter succeed and I'm going to take full advantage of it."

Pete seethed. "And if I don't go along?"

"You've done your job very well, Coach Lopez. These kids have practiced and played together long enough to excel almost without supervision. Ronnie could step in for another month, easily. Then we could take the fall to recruit a new coach—maybe even a more cooperative one."

Pete shook his head and laughed bitterly. "You know, Queensberry—it's guys like you saw to it that somebody like me never had an even shot at the Show. You're so blinded by...whatever that you don't see you're hurting your own flesh and blood a lot worse than the other girl." He leveled a finger at Marc as he pivoted away from him. "You're going to regret this, and a lot sooner than you think."

Ronnie had seen the drill before and was practiced at diverting the girls' attention from it—except for Tiffany, of course. Even so, he was vaguely uneasier about this one. When he saw Pete stalking toward the dugout, he legged out to meet him halfway.

"What is it, this time?"

"Let's just get through it. Stay close today. We've got to talk to the team after—just you and me."

"Want to talk about it?"

"Can't. Not now." Pete brushed by. Ronnie had never seen him so rigid. The head coach was pounding his palms together fiercely as he made the dugout. "*Andelé*, my little *niñas*—let's get *busy!*" Ronnie saw him plant his feet, jam his hands in his back pockets, and pretend to watch the Sting finish infield warm-ups. *Uh-oh*, thought Ronnie. *He's blown off the obligatory sermon on parental sportsmanship. This must be bad!*

Pete felt a noiseless uncertainty growing behind him. Without looking he pulled out the lineup card and handed it to Ronnie. "Give that to Turk, will you?" Slowly turning, he met each pair of eyes in succession. They softened him. "How do we feel today, ladies? Ernie Banks used to say, 'Let's play two.' What he meant was, it's a privilege to step inside these lines. The ball is round, the grass is green, and the sky is clear. Let's have some fun." The girls erupted in chatter and activity. All was right again.

Things developed as planned. LeLe dragged a dead bunt up the right field line. The Sting's catcher nearly collided with her pitcher and overthrew first, yielding second to LeLe. Pete felt Marc's hot stare burning into him as Tiffany stepped in second. She drew a walk, but not before taking a monster cut at 2-0 to get LeLe into third easily. A clean single by Sierra into the right-center gap scored LeLe, then Tonya boomed a double over the center fielder's head to bring Tiffany and Sierra in. Another base on balls, a single, and two more errors pushed the score to 6-0 before the Sting scratched up the third out. Tiffany was spectacular; her control was flawless and her location spot-on. She yoked her head and heart and drove them together, inspiring her defense to rise behind her. Through three, she had five strikeouts, no walks and nothing hit out of the infield. Two hits, a run, and an error tested her in the fourth, and she came off shaking her right arm. Pete picked his way to her as she pulled the jacket half-on and sagged onto the bench. He cupped each shoulder with a hand.

"Tif—you okay?"

She nodded, unpersuasively.

"How's the arm?"

Tiffany dropped her head.

"It's your call, kiddo. I can leave it out here. You have to go home to it."

"I *am* a little sore, Coach." A wisp of gratitude flashed through her verdant eyes before the coming ordeal of the post-game debriefing reclaimed her.

"Okay." He glanced up into the bleachers; Marc was absorbed with the Arizona scout, who appeared a little bored. Pete shouted down the bench. "Crystal—start warming up Brie." Marc snapped his head toward the dugout. The scout got up to leave. Marc followed, alternating gestures and excuses. Pete took it in discreetly, with satisfaction.

Brie was game. She booked the save, suffering one unearned run. Pete cleared the bench and worked his tactical magic, assuring that every Copperhead got at least one at-bat. Tiffany rode the bench alone, her jacket collar up around her cheeks as she contemplated her fate. Her teammates interrupted her only with supportive taps and slaps as they passed by. The final was 7-2, Copperheads. Ronnie saw two bright spots in the margin: it hadn't been close enough to generate serious umpire-abuse issues, and Pete and he would be less occupied at defending themselves against charges of favoritism over playing time.

Pete browsed the scorebook as the girls snaked through the post-game sportsmanship rite. When they returned to the dugout to pack up, he raised his hands. "Team meeting, Copperheads. Follow me." He strode out and headed for center field. His charges followed, murmuring and visibly anxious over this cryptic break from routine. Families laden with coolers and lawn chairs fell in behind, as always. Pete caught them out of the corner of his eye and stopped. "Players only, please. Won't take long." The firmness inside his courtesy couldn't be missed. They froze, puzzled. The caravan ended in a circle at the fence, near the stark, red-white-and-blue signboard identifying "The Queensberry Law Firm, LLC" as a "proud supporter of ASA-Arizona Softball."

"Take a knee, ladies." Pete shifted his feet and rubbed the back of his neck. "First, let me say what a privilege it has been for me to guide and to teach you these past three years. At your age, your love for this simple but bottomless game is pure, as it deserves. It thrives in you and you in it because you respect it— when you're allowed to." Pete took a deep breath. "I've been informed that the Strikers had to forfeit their opener today and are disqualified from the tournament. I disagree with this decision and my conscience will not allow me to continue as your coach, under these circumstances."

Ronnie's mouth dropped open. LeLe sundered the stunned silence. "What happened, Coach?"

"One of their players is in technical violation of the eligibility rules, through no fault of her own." Pete brushed at his eyes. "I'm turning things over to Coach Young, if he's willing, and you can decide what to do about tomorrow. All I ask is that whatever you do, you do as a team. I love each and every one of you, as my own—" He pulled the bill of his cap down, shielding his face; hot tears mottled his dusty black cleats. The Copperheads were mired in disbelief. He held out his arm. "Come, Letitia. Let's get you home." They came together and trudged toward the parking lot.

Still, no one spoke. Tiffany leaped to her feet and charged her father. She threw her glove and ran full into him, sobbing and pummeling his chest with her fists. "YOU did this! I *hate* you!" She swatted at Missy's lamely outstretched arms and bolted toward the main gate. A crimson-faced Marc picked up the glove and dragged Missy after his daughter.

The rest turned their attention to Ronnie. He wanted to hide. "Listen—this is just as big a shock to me as it is to you. Our next game, against the Crush, isn't until two tomorrow. I'll go tell your parents. We'll sleep on it and see how things are in the morning. That's about all we can do for now."

Wordlessly, the girls rose and drifted away. LeLe looped her arm around her father's waist and they glumly walked toward the backstop. He pried himself away reluctantly to confront the clot of mothers, fathers, and relatives behind the dugout.

LeLe continued, frowning and turning her glove over and over in her hands. A royal-blue figure moving behind the mesh startled her. They converged at the corner and its shadow swallowed her. "Marisella!"

The Striker's star shoved her hands into her jacket pockets. Her pristine uniform and steady gaze made LeLe uneasy. "Just came over to say 'Hey' before I left."

"Coach just told us you forfeited. What happened?"

"It's on me. My parents came to this country illegally. I was born in Sonoita at my aunt's house, who's a midwife, so I don't have a birth certificate. All my folks have is a Bible with our family tree in Spanish."

LeLe's face burned. "I'm so, so sorry."

Marisella offered a crooked smile. "I saw you."

"Huh?"

"The Copperheads. I watched you all play today. You're good—real good. Little *Anglo* girl swings a big stick."

LeLe laughed in spite of herself.

"Too bad, too bad." Marisella spread her jacket panels like wings. "The 'field of dreams'—the one place I thought I could get respect, just for what I can do. Where the same rules apply to everyone. Where I'm just a ballplayer—not a spic or a wetback or a beaner." Her eyes brimmed and she dragged a sleeve around her face. "Guess not. Well, I'm goin'. See you sometime...out in the world."

Helplessness paralyzed LeLe. Finally, she shook free and fled to her Mom and Dad.

౸ロౚ

LeLe pushed a radish aimlessly around her salad plate as Fawn, her mother, pulled the jerk chicken from the oven. "Ow!" The tea towel failed as a potholder, so the baking dish clattered to the table, blasting both her husband and daughter out of their troubled reveries. "Sorry..." She repositioned the Pyrex after sucking her smarting fingers, and served. She pretended to be unconcerned. "So. Anybody know what's going to happen tomorrow yet?"

LeLe took a swig of iced tea and swallowed carefully. "Daddy, what do you think we should do?"

Ronnie bought time. "By 'we,' do you mean 'you-and-me—we,' 'you-and-us—we,' 'or 'you-and-somebody-else—we'?"

"I mean, the *team*. Should we play the Crush?"

"I'm not playing—you are. What do you think you should do?"

"I *hate* what Mr. Queensberry did."

"So do I, but rules are rules. Right?"

"But what he did was so *wrong*!"

"Was it?"

LeLe banged her fist on the table. "I *also* hate it when you do *this*!"

"Hey, hey," Fawn said. "Let's keep this civil, okay?'

Ronnie touched his mate's arm to comply. "LeLe, would you rather I made your decisions for you, like Tiffany's Dad does?"

LeLe deliberated. "Dad, you remember when Marisella and I went to elementary school, right? Her birthday party was always the month after mine, in March. It's not like she's *trying* to cheat!"

"That's true; but isn't it possible that she's older than you?"

"But her family has a Bible with her birthday written down. Why would they fake that?"

"I didn't know that. Well—what if they made an exception for Marisella? Wouldn't they have to take the word of anyone who didn't have a birth certificate?"

"Dad." LeLe's blue eyes darkened. "What if Marisella was White or not as good as Tiffany? Would the rules have even been brought up?"

Ronnie pursed his lips. "I don't have an answer for that." He paused. "How do you feel about what Coach Lopez did?"

"I think he did what he thought was right."

"Did he let the team down?"

"No. He is—*was*—our leader in softball, not our conscience. He didn't try to force us to agree with him. He left that up to us. *Us*—each and all."

"That's also true. Well, I'm done. What are you going to do?

"What do *you* think I should do?"

Ronnie wasn't grateful for the irony but he acknowledged it with a chuckle. "Honey," he said, taking her hand in seriousness, "One of the best things about this game is that you can play it with all your heart, but you have to keep your head, because how you react affects the outcome. If you're open to its lessons, it trusts you to find that balance, for yourself and with your teammates. So, I think you should follow your heart and use your head."

LeLe winced. "Thanks for clearing that up for me!"

He stroked her flaxen hair. "What I'm saying is, Pete was dead right about one thing. It's not up to him, or to me. It's up to you and the rest of the Copperheads to decide what's best. Find the balance in what feels right—for you, your friends, the game itself—then act on it. I wouldn't be much of a coach, or a father, if I couldn't live with that."

LeLe stood, hugged his neck, and kissed his cheek. "Thanks, Pops." She glanced at her mother. "May I be excused? I have some calls to make."

"You may," Fawn said, quietly. "Your Dad and I will handle the dishes." LeLe left the dining room soberly and went upstairs. They sat, waiting for the air to stop stirring. Fawn spoke first. "What would you do?"

Ronnie laced his fingers behind his head and studied the ceiling. "Honestly? I don't know—and I'm just a grownup still in love with a kid's game. She's a 16-year-old girl who's really good at it. I can hardly imagine the weight."

৪০৫৪

"LeLe? Sweetie? You in there? It's almost 11..." Fawn rapped softly and waited. Nothing. She pushed the door open. LeLe's room was in typical disarray, littered with everything but a tenant. "Ronnie! LeLe isn't here."

Ronnie came in from the master bath, drying his hands. "Where is she?"

"Not *here*, obviously." Fawn moved to her daughter's desk and picked up a notebook. "Here— Seen this?" They studied a Copperhead roster, in LeLe's hand, complete with names, addresses, positions, and phone numbers. All of the entries had been worked over. Some had been lined through, then restored. Some had "Xs," some had "Os," and some had pluses and minuses next to them. A few had all those legends. Ultimately, it appeared, they all had check marks in ink.

"Doesn't appear to be a snap decision—whatever it is," Ronnie said.

"Hardly!" Fawn scoffed. "She was on the phone at least four hours last night."

"She came down and borrowed my cell at 10:30."

"Did she take it with her?"

"No, it's back in the charger. What's that?" Ronnie pointed.

Fawn followed his line over to LeLe's inkjet printer. She retrieved the lone page lying in the tray. "It's the Sunday bus schedule for Valley Metro Transit. Wait—this is 'Page 2 of 2.'"

Ronnie clicked LeLe's PC out of "Sleep" mode and opened the browser. "What's the URL? Bottom left corner." He entered as she read. The page opened and Ronnie studied the screen. "Hello, Watson!"

"What did you find?"

"I've got an idea where they might've gone. I'll see if I can raise Pete on his cell, to find out if he's heard anything. Get your stuff together."

ℬℛ

Pete wheeled his middle-aged wagon into the lot behind Southeast High's ball fields. He recognized the girls easily, though distant on the lone, down-at-the-heels softball field. He pulled the gear bag out of the back seat and made the trek over bare spots and wanton crabgrass. As he arrived, the coach in him noticed the infield's unforgiving, pebble-strewn condition. Tiffany bounded up.

"Hey, Coach—"

Pete raised a finger. "Not any more. Not today, anyway. We agreed."

"Understood—but you'll never be "Mister" or "Pete" to me. Not good enough. You'll be 'Coach' to me as long as I live." She smiled. "Which may not be too much longer. I see you brought the balls, bases, and old stuff?"

"As ordered."

"Excellent! Come meet Coach Aparicio."

"I'll join you in a minute. I need to speak to my daughter first." Pete dropped the equipment and found Letitia. He took her aside. "Thank you for leaving the note, but you missed Mass with us."

"I know, *Abuelo*; I'm sorry. I'll go with *Tía* Guadalupe tonight; I promise."

"Okay. Priorities, remember? God; family; everything else." He kissed her forehead. "Now I find out how much trouble I'm *really* in, eh?" He crossed in front of the scarred backstop to where the Strikers chatted with their leader and Tiffany. He thrust out his hand. "I'm Pete Lopez."

The thickly-built 20-something wrapped it in his, warmly. "Lupé Aparicio, *Señor*."

"I want you to know that I had nothing to do with what happened yesterday," Pete said gravely.

"No need. My Pop used to take me to see you play. Best infield glove I ever saw."

"*Dé véras?* And my bat?"

Luis hesitated. "Gotta go with Tony Gwynn."

"*Qué?* What about Clemente?"

"Never saw him hit." Sparkles danced around Luis's irises.

Pete affected a sulk. "At least he's not Anglo." Sensing that his satisfaction was hidden poorly, though, he desisted. "*Gracias, verdaderamente.* I am humbled."

"Coach, it's my honor to be here with you, today—regardless."

Tiffany came between them. "Break it up, you two. Honestly—Latinos. So emotional!" They tipped their heads her way without rotating them; up went their eyebrows. She giggled. "What do you say—half a game each at umpire?"

"Who's in charge?" Pete asked.

"Nobody."

Pete stroked his chin, smiling, and turned to Luis.

"Want to see if these babies have learned anything?"

"I'll go you one better. Let's both umpire; switch home and second each inning. Let 'em play until they're sick of each other."

"Hell of an idea. That okay with you, Tif?"

"Works for me. I'll run it by Marisella." She peeled away.

Pete's cell went off. "Excuse me. Hello?...Hey, Ronnie. Guess where I am, and guess who else is here?...How'd you know?...Yeah, come on over—this should be interesting. Better call their folks, so they won't worry...Who? Nah—let *him* sweat; Tiffany will appreciate it...Arnie? I wouldn't, but I'm retired. Your call...Yeah, Okay...'Bye. Sorry, Luis. Your bunch ready to play?"

"I think they all want to change first."

Pete surveyed the area. "Where?"

"I've got gym keys. Why don't you anchor the bases while I go let them in?"

"You got it." Pete set to work while Luis rounded up the girls and led them off in a noisy, festive gaggle. Once the bags were set, Pete sat himself on the third-base bench, threw his head back and enjoyed the rare midday breeze. In time, he heard the rustle of cleated feet through dry grass. He threw a leg over the venerable plank and shaded his eyes. Under the flaring sun came two columns, the Strikers in their royal-and-black and the Copperheads—well, they weren't the Copperheads today. Pete's former charges were an assemblage of plain red tops, black shorts, and white socks. There were a few red hair ribbons. Each of them bore her sponsor's parti-colored uniform, neatly folded, like a burnt offering. The columns reached the backstop and halted. LeLe came forward with an empty Copperhead equipment bag, opened it and laid her uniform inside. As she held it, her teammates passed in turn and did the same. That bag and another filled with Copperhead gear were abandoned there. The columns split and moved onto the foul lines. As one, the players pivoted to face home plate and waited. Distant buzzing of tree-topping male cicadas and the more localized whir of winged insects in the thick, arid stillness harmonized into a natural anthem. Pete formed an image of medieval knights-errant at the lists that scarcely equaled the solemn dignity he saw. He felt proud and blessed, himself.

Pete fished out his worn mask and chest protector and met Luis at home plate. "Captains, please."

Tiffany, LeLe, Marisella, and LaWanda, her catcher, strode up and shook hands all around.

"All right, Strikers and, uh—"

"Reds," LeLe offered.

Pete repeated the moniker. "How do you want to handle first 'ups', ladies? Coin flip?"

"No need—already decided," Tiffany said firmly. "Strikers are at home."

"Okay. Everything else by the book, then?"

"Uh-huh," Marisella replied.

"Well, then—let's play some ball!"

Palm slaps and good wishes followed. Tiffany offered her pitching knuckles to Marisella. "Good luck."

Marisella bumped them with hers and showed that 300-watt grin. "You already know how I feel about *luck*." They parted and the banter began as the Reds took their bench and the Strikers, the field.

By now, Ronnie, Fawn and a few other parents had settled in behind their girls. Finishing a practice cut, LeLe saw them and came to the wire. She laced her Franklins into it and let her eyes wander around them. "Sorry I didn't leave a note or something."

Ronnie spit. "The clues you left behind worked fine. How did you all get here?"

"Bus. Sierra was going to make two trips in the mini-van, but we wanted to come as a team. She took us all to the stop."

"How'd she get out?"

"Told her folks she was taking us to the mall."

"The mall?" Ronnie grimaced.

"It wasn't a total lie. The stop is only a half a block away—and she parked there!" LeLe rehearsed a pout, in case. "You mad at me?"

"Did you cook this up all by yourself?"

"Naw—me and Tif. We decided we'd only do it if everyone agreed. Took a little while, but..." She loosened a hand and swept it behind her grandly, like a game-show appliance model.

Ronnie let his face fall forward to hide the smile. He took Fawn's hand and went to the wire. LeLe examined the laces on her shifting shoes.

"Look at us." She did. Her parents' eyes shone.

Ronnie: "Any regrets?"

"Nope."

Fawn: "We're very proud, Le."

"Play well, little girl. Oh—and, have fun."

"No worries!" LeLe reclaimed her bat and jammed on her helmet. She slapped its side, hard, and pointed at them.

"Play ball!" Pete ordered. LeLe bounced to the plate and dug herself in. Marisella pawed the rubber, checked her defense, and settled. A wicked expression flashed across her face.

"Don't blink, 'Britney.' Here she comes!"

LeLe straightened up, licked her fingers, swung her weapon full-circle, and crouched deep. "Bring it, 'Queen!'" The wild-haired colossus kicked, spun high and extended. LeLe strode in just behind the fastball, rocketing a magnificent foul up the right side. The Strikers came down off their toes and pounded their gloves. The Reds breathed and elbowed each other. She made contact again, into the upper backstop, and shrank the strike zone to work the count even before Marisella set her down with a changeup. Sierra and

Tonya didn't do that well; Marisella rang them up with nothing but heat.   She took LaWanda's gratuitous throw, faked a spike, and laid the ball gently on the rubber. As she ambled to the bench, she found Tiffany's stare over her shoulder.

Tiffany pulled her Ray-Bans into position. "Let's go, defense!" She sprinted to the mound and warmed up furiously as her infield took grounders behind her. "Balls in!" cried Luis from behind second. Tiffany concluded her personal wiping and mound-keeping rituals and peered in at Tonya. A black SUV tore up, its front doors flinging wide like a hooded viper. It still rocked and died while Marc and Arnie discharged themselves. Marc accelerated into a trot in his Bruno Magli shoes. More accustomed to moral than physical aggression, Arnie caught a toe and planted his face in the dusty sod. Delight flashed around the diamond. Missy followed at a deliberate distance.

"Tiffany!   Get over here!"   Marc's color had scarcely changed in 24 hours.

Pete stood up and wheeled slowly, peeling off the mask. He touched his fingers to each shoulder point. "My time." Marc came at him with raw gestures.

"This is your doing, isn't it?"

"Nope—I was invited. How about you?"

Marc was nonplussed. "I'll deal with you later!" He focused on the mound. "Tiffany!" Now!"

His daughter gloved the ball and cradled them on her hip. She stood her ground.

"I said—NOW!"   Marc was going to vermilion, cords breaking out of his neck.

Tiffany shook her head, absolutely calm. "No, Dad. Whatever you have to say to me, you can say to the team."

Her father advanced on her, and Pete stepped between them.

"Unless this is a pitching change, you don't belong

out here."

Marc brandished his fist at the chest protector. "I ought to—!"

Pete was cold-rolled steel. "Touching me would be your second-biggest mistake today, my friend." Luis moved in to investigate.

"Who's the *pendéjo*?"

"Here's your forfeit—on the hoof."

"Ah—the Great White Sportsman." Luis was about as stony-faced and welcoming as a repainted lawn jockey. "Welcome to the West Side." The combination of his age and apparent athleticism, and his elder's resolve, shook Marc loose. He ignored them in favor of his progeny.

"You are going to get in that car, young lady, and the Copperheads are going to play the Crush in an hour, as planned. Do you understand me?" Arnie had finished brushing himself off and mourning his abandoned largesse. He stood by the backstop, nodding lamely.

Tiffany raised her sunglasses and fixed on Marc. "The Copperheads are dead, Dad. You killed them." The steady maturity in her voice riveted everyone it reached. "This is *our* team now, *our* game." She huffed, as though expelling a demon. "This is the first time *I've* decided what *I'm* going to do—and, guess what? It feels pretty good. Today may be the last day I pick up a softball; maybe not. Who knows? The point is, Dad, I'm not afraid of you any more."

Marc started for her, bringing Pete and Luis to the balls of their feet. A finely-manicured hand caught the sleeve of his Ralph Lauren Polo knit.

"Back off, Marc."

He spun, mouth agape, to find Missy right there, her arms folded and her sharp green eyes flaring. "I've held my peace for almost three years. You're on the edge of blowing any chance at having a relationship with your only child."

His flush became blush. "What—what do *you* know about it?"

"She talks to me, Marc. I listen; I try to *hear*. So should you."

"I see," he sputtered. "You're *both* against me!"

"Oh, grow up, Marc! I love you and so does Tif— when you're not being a self-indulgent, emotional bully. Now, are you willing to work at this, or—?"

"Or *what*?

"How do double alimony and a shot at a third marriage sound?"

Stung, both by Missy and the indifference his ocular pleas for support were getting, Marc stomped off and slammed himself into the SUV. Missy paused, then reached toward Tiffany, haltingly.

"He's a good man, Tif—worth the effort. Really." She grimaced. "He's just *selectively* crazy."

Tiffany smirked back. "We'll see."

Missy headed for the car. Pete watched them leave, then picked up his mask. "Ready to go, Tiffany?"

The Bolsheviks' leader wiped her nose with her glove. "Oh, yeah."

Arnie couldn't help himself. "How about one last prayer together?"

Pete's shoulders slumped a little and he approached. "Arnie, you believe, as I do, that God is everywhere?"

"Well...of course."

"Okay. When God's children are at play in His great, green cathedral, He's making something *pure*. If you'd shut up for five minutes, for Christ's sake, you could *feel* it!"

The salesman's jaw dropped. He staggered a little, and sat.

"Batter up!"

Tiffany fired back—a weak grounder to the left side and two quick punch-outs. As the drama unfolded, an unexpected paradox developed. An eerie silence prevailed outside the lines as parents, loved ones, and friends saw their girls in a larger dimension. A joyful noise built among these combatants, now in exclusive control of what was to be gained or lost. They battled fiercely, without stress, and respect grew freely among them, unfettered by adult guile. Pete's and Luis's decisions were swift and just, and they never stopped smiling— suspended with their pupils in this eye of perfect competition. Unencumbered by signs and tactics, Ronnie was mesmerized. At this age these demigoddesses, sinew straining under moist, burnished skin, might have been Delphic priestesses or dark virginal royalty, in other times and places. Their delicate sensuality clung like tender buds to the vines of their physical power. *Yep,* Ronnie thought. *There they are—'the weaker sex.'*" He felt a brief pang of pity for the gangly boys who would soon start appearing at his door to waste their clumsy venerations on his princess, his worthy heir.

It ended as any decent Greek drama should. Marisella and Tiffany pushed each other up a level at each appearance. Scoreless through six-and-a-half innings, the Strikers came alive in their last at-bat. Tiffany opened with a strikeout. She jammed Marisella on a full count, who fisted a seeing-eye single into right. Tonya guessed right and pitched Terésa out; she couldn't dig the ball out, though, so Marisella took second standing up. The hit-and-run moved her to third. Everyone saw the suicide squeeze coming, so it had to be perfect. It was. LaWanda's bunt had enough topspin to make it jump crazily up the first-base line and Marisella didn't waste a heartbeat breaking for home. Tonya raced after the ball, which flirted with the chalk enough to provoke the tiniest hesitation in her. Tiffany covered the plate. Sensing her loss, Tonya bare-handed it and flipped it blindly, straight behind her. Tiffany captured it smoothly, planted her leading foot and contorted into a low, backward lunge toward third, sweeping her right arm wide. Pete backpedaled, ejecting the mask. Marisella kicked her right leg out and flattened into a quartering hook slide. She saw the glove and jerked her head away. Tiffany missed her ear by a lace.

"Safe! Safe!" Pete yelled, scissoring the rising billows with his outstretched arms. Tiffany collapsed heavily onto Marisella and rolled off. They eyed each other for an instant, then embraced in hysterics. Within seconds, a blur of bodies melded into a pyre of odd, animated parts, like someone had overturned a bucket of giant, spastic bait on the spot. Delirium reigned and no one wanted it to end—least of all Pete, Luis, or Ronnie, standing by. "Look at that," Pete said. "And not even a damned trophy at risk!"

"Hey, Luis!"

Up came a burly redhead in redneck casual, flip-flops, and Sun Devil ball cap. "What? You called me away from the La-Z-Boy and the Sunday *Republic* to watch a scrimmage?"

Luis grabbed his hand. "Coach, I'd like you to meet a friend of mine, 'Stooge' Powell."

Pete shook hands. "'Stooge?'"

Stooge rolled his eyes and doffed his cap. Advancing hair loss had pushed him to start shaving his head as a younger man. Pete saw the resemblance to Curly Howard.

"Stooge is—was—a catcher," Luis said. "First-rate baseball mind. We banged around the Indian organization together. All the way to Triple-A."

"I'd a traded a lot of brain cells for healthier knees, I'll tell ya," Stooge mused

Luis jumped in. "Not that you had many to begin with.

"What are you doing for the good of the game

these days?" Pete asked.

"Oh, I ride herd on the ladies over at A-State. Luis here thought I might want to waste my day off on a couple bodacious pitchers." Still giddy but seated nearby, Marisella and Tiffany overheard and stopped chatting. Stooge bent, hands on knees. "How 'bout it, ladies? Think you could perform like that if it mattered?"

Tiffany hung her sunglasses on her collar. "Today mattered more to me than any game I've played before; maybe ever."

Stooge turned slightly to Marisella. "And you?"

"Oh, I'm gonna pitch somewhere, someday—maybe for Coach Aparicio at Glendale—

Luis gave his star a thumbs-up and nudged Stooge.

"—But this girl is right about *today*." The new comrades clasped wrists.

Stooge regarded Luis slyly. "You sure these women are only 16?" His friend treated the question as rhetorical, which it was, so he returned to them. "Something to think about, anyway. Coach Aparicio knows where to find me." He waddled off.

The pair internalized their happy amazement together. Tiffany wrinkled her nose. "I dunno, Mare. I might want to be a pilot."

"Or a rock star!" Marisella shrieked. They fell back in the grass and roared.

LeLe wandered over. "Hey. Wanna do it again?"

Marisella leaped up. "Ones and twos!"

Tiffany: "What's that?"

Marisella dragged her to her feet. "Line everybody up and count off, by twos. Ones versus the twos."

"What about positions?"

"Who cares? Strikers!" Marisella bellowed. "Y'all get over here!"

"Bring it in, Cop—I mean, Reds!" added Tiffany.

They assembled quickly, all eyes on Pete. LeLe

spoke.

"Coach?"

"Yeah," Pete said. "Let's play two.

෨෨ඥ

6 **The Jewel of Genoa**

It started like any other Friday at Maranatha Senior Residence.

Just give it a few more hours, she told herself.

Pearl O. Mutter gathered up her purse, gloves, and hat. *Oops—Almost forgot.* She stepped over to her freshly-made bed and retrieved the balled-up napkin she'd carried back from dinner last night and secreted under her pillow—a ritual begun at each meal, years ago. She opened the linen carefully and picked out the tiny, peach-colored oval. *Huh. Xōnoft. Get on it, like Fern, you don't give a shit. Get off it, you can't stop. If that pill-peddler Delroy hired ever saw me, he'd know I don't need it. Old Doc Morgan never would have stood for this. Oh, well—it'll come in handy today.*

She added the dose to the dozen others she'd squirreled away, in rotation, in an old breath-mint tin. She smiled at its more-pregnant slogan—'Curiously Strong!'—and returned it to the bottom of her purse. She walked around the other, vacant bed and stood behind the half-closed door, finding herself in the full-length mirror. Even after all this time, she still couldn't believe her eyes. In another glass she'd seen a strong, brown woman with auburn locks, eyes that danced over a nose that drew more breath awake and alive than asleep, and a grin-prone mouth. Sturdy frame in a faded denim shirt, Levi's, and rough-out boots. A woman more familiar with the essences of lime, sweat, and just-singed cowhide than with those of Paris. Sinewy forearms and gnarled hands with the veins, knots, and calluses standard on the wife of a working cattle feeder.All she could find now were the eyes, if she allowed it, and the hands, which she couldn't help. *Where did she go?* Pearl asked herself. *Well, I'm going t' find her again, and the lookin' starts now.*

The door parted slightly and another, dark-haired woman with brown skin appeared—the nurse-assistant. "Señora Mutter, are you ready? You must hurry or you will miss the bus!"

Pearl looked grave and took the attendant's hands gently into hers. "Marisōl, you've been real good to me for a long, long time. Made life in this place almost bearable—almost. I'm goin' to miss you the most."

Marisól Contréres patted Pearl's hands, puzzled. "But, Señora; you are only going overnight to the South Shore, like you do every four months." Her eyes flashed. "Maybe even to gamble a little, yes?"

"Whoop-tee-do," Pearl said. "If Miss Goody Two Shoes takes her eyes off us for five minutes." She dropped her hands and her eyes. "Anyway—Goodbye, Marisól." She sidled past her and pushed her octogenarian's bones determinedly down the dim hallway toward the lobby.

໒ⓒ২

"Attention, 'Sprightly Seniors!'"

Anna Mae McDonald, Maranatha's Director of Recreational Services and Spiritual Development (although not necessarily in that order), stood beside the steps of the ancient, converted Blue Bird school bus and tapped her pencil on her clipboard. It was an uphill effort, quieting the gaggle of 20-odd residents queued up to escape, if only for 36 hours.

"Give me your attention, please, so I can review the slate of exciting activities we've planned for all of you!"

We're going to the playpen of the Sierra Nevada over a Friday night, thought Pearl, *to go to church. Is this a great goddamned country, or what?*

Anna Mae was warmed up. "We'll be meeting Reverend Alston at the First Church of the Evangelist, as usual, for a spirited afternoon of Holy Land slides. Then, a *yummy* early buffet at the Royal Plate—"

"Aw, fer Chrissakes, Anna Mae," complained Barney Rasmussen. "It's the same dern trip every time. Give us a little credit, willya? All the droolers are stayin' home, anyway!" His Adam's apple bobbed over a turquoise bolo tie and under a hat that would have made Roy Rogers jealous.

"There'll be no cursing on this bus, Barney Rasmussen," she scolded. "Remember: 'To say is to pray; to curse is worse.' Now, if I may continue ..." As she resumed her sing-song prattle, Pearl relived the parade of outrages that helped her crystallize her plan, beginning with getting dropped in this Bible-thumping Purgatory and culminating in the loss of her old friend. She'd known Hattie Gardner for 70 years on the outside. When Hattie's husband died of emphysema 12 years ago, Pearl had bargained with her son, on condition of good behavior, to move Hattie over from Minden. A third-generation Nevadan, Hattie Churchill had helped Pearl over most of her country-girl innocence before she herself got in a family way with Abner Gardner. After that, they opened up the Silver Rowel, where she cooked and tended bar weekdays and sang Friday through Sunday nights. For 40 years she harbored more secrets and solved more social problems than a hatful of clergy and social workers. Not the least of these was seeing to it that Pearl Opal Veneman and Earl Ludwig Mutter were in the same place at the same time often enough to give in and make it a habit.

Having Hattie's daily company again had become salve for the running sore that Pearl saw her Maranatha existence to be—as was the full case of Seagram's that rode in with her, swaddled in bed linens in her second suitcase. (That stream never dried up, either, thanks to a Douglas County liquor distributor with local contacts. Seems Hattie had talked the deed to his house off the poker table and back into his pocket in Abner's private clubroom in the rear, some years back. Being retired from the saloon business had its perquisites.) At any rate, most nights the girlish giggles started after dinner in Room 219 when the meds were flushed away. ("Buried at sea," Hattie called it.) They became full-throated laughs after the shift change, when the shrinking staff lured the liquid courage out from behind the empty suitcases on the closet floor. The crude "Seven-and-sevens" they fashioned with lukewarm, six-ounce Sprites purloined from the dining room weren't essential to their reminiscences, but they seemed to help loosen their memories as well as their tongues.

A month ago, Hattie had taken a header in the day room. She insisted she was only bruised and embarrassed, but the home seized on the occasion to rotate her out for hospital tests long enough to bleed off a little Medicare cash at both ends. The powers-that-be found no fractures but decided she needed a walker—meaning that she was no longer fully "ambulatory" and would be transferred from "independent" to "assisted living." So, exactly two weeks ago, Maranatha won a higher daily rate for Hattie and freed up a bed, while Pearl lost her roommate. She'd tried to visit Hattie on the other side whenever she could, but it broke her heart that she was so miserable. A woman who'd never opened an eye on purpose before 10 A.M. after baby Johnny could find his own milk was suddenly required to present herself for breakfast in the dining room by eight. Worse, a woman who could mesmerize royalty in sentence and song was assigned to take all daily meals with the same three tablemates, all of whom were either deaf or demented.

This just ain't right, Pearl remembered thinking. That's when she made up her mind. She looked down at her friend, hanging on her elbow and moving with her toward the steps.

"Now, Hattie, you just stay quiet 'til Bea and I get you past Anna Mae and to the seat in the back. Okay?"

Hattie nodded, just about halfway between anticipation and fright.

Pearl looked across at Beatrice Knudsen. "Bea, if you would just help me get Hattie up the steps, I'd appreciate it. Just wait 'til Hector goes into his little act." Beatrice winked and caught Hattie at the other elbow.

Pearl tapped Hector Alvarez on the shoulder. "Hector, you ready?" Hector turned and smiled furtively. He played out most of the slack in his oxygen line into large loops. As he drew abreast of Anna Mae he tripped into her magnificently. He grabbed for her upper arms after thrusting the loops over her forearms. She reacted by stepping backward and jerking her arms violently upward, which drew Hector, the lines, the little green cylinder, and its trolley to her—tightly. She struggled and shrieked.

Pearl and Beatrice hustled Hattie onto the bus. Bertha pulled up to block the aisle while Pearl herded Hattie to the last seat on the left. "Duck down, dear, while I find Lindell." Pearl spread her arms to unlatch and lower the top half of their window. She peered out, searching for her inside confederate. *Clockwork.* Around the end of the building came an imposing orderly, with two suitcases. He muscled the grips adroitly through the window. "Thank you, Lindell," whispered Pearl. "Hattie and I—"

"Uh-UH!" Lindell drew his arms quickly to his sides, palms down and fingers spread, striking his best 'Whachoo lookin' at?!' pose. "I got a Spalding leather basketball signed by Chris Webber and a half-case of Seagram's. That's *all* I need to *know!*" Still, he cocked an eyebrow. "Where'd you *get* that basketball?"

"Gift from my son, Delroy," Pearl replied. "Just the thing for an 83-year-old cowgirl, don't you agree?"

Lindell approximated half a wave as he strode away, his stern expression barely masking his amusement.

Pearl stashed the cases beneath their seat. She and Hattie donned their best innocence as the shortish bus filled up. Pearl leaned over. "You ready, hon?"

Hattie opened her shoulder bag. Pearl could just make them out, between the Preparation H and the Fig Newtons: A nickel-plated, pearl-handled, .32-caliber semi-automatic pistol with a nine-shot magazine, and a box of cartridges.

"Ready to fornicate, fight, or flee," grinned Hattie.

Pearl smiled. "Let's just stick with the 'flee' part, for now."

℘℧

Due to their late start, some heavy-duty whining, and Pearl's representation that she was good for it, Anna Mae was persuaded to depart from the usual plan, which was to stop briefly for coffee and relief at Lenny's in Placerville, then drive straight into South Lake Tahoe for a late lunch of equivalent elegance. Instead, they motored straight to the Heidelberg Inn, between Pollock Pines and Kyburz, for heavy German food. (Besides the cuisine's enhanced post-prandial impact, Pearl also hoped that some of the more excitable members of the troupe might be thirsty enough to sneak 12 or more ounces of some fine Teutonic anesthetic to help things along. She did advise her co-conspirators to "stay sharp," however, since she knew they were already bent in that direction.)

Pearl got back on the bus and summoned Hattie back to a sitting position, placing a Styrofoam "go" box on her lap. "I'm sorry I had to leave you out here, dear, but I couldn't risk Anna Mae finding out that you weren't on her list. You know Anna Mae and her goddamned head-count."

"Are you still worried that Ellie Hathaway might snitch on me?"

"I was, but not so much anymore. You've only been gone from independent living a couple weeks, so I don't think she's even noticed. You know how busybodies like her are—so taken up lookin' out the side window to catch the neighbors at somethin' that she doesn't see her husband goin' over the back fence."

"So, did you get 'em into her?"

"The Xōnoft? Yup. It didn't come to me until we were all inside that this place probably didn't have any fish dishes, so I got a little worried since I'd made up my mind that tuna salad would've been perfect. Anna Mae was a failed Catholic before she went fundamental, you know, so that 'Fish on Friday' habit dies hard—especially since it still had Hell attached to it when she was a girl. I regrouped and told her I'd order for her, since Earl's folks were German and it was my treat. I snatched up her menu and studied it hard until she went to the Ladies'. Then I grabbed a waiter and ordered the Szegediner Goulasch with Spaetzle for both of us. It's pork, but I convinced her it was swordfish stew. I was going to put the doses in the noodles but the gravy was a little too thin."

"Then, how'd you do it?"

"I told Anna Mae she really needed to have some of their famous Strudel with her coffee. Even an old blue-nose like her has a weakness, and her sweet tooth is it. I distracted her by telling her that Mira Bridges needed to ask her about the 'Eggs 'n' Scripture' breakfast tomorrow. While she was up, I stuffed 'em in the pastry."

"How many?"

"Three."

"You think that's enough?"

"Well, she finished it up. Hell, Hattie—we just want to relax her a little, not kill her! Now go on, hon, and eat your lunch; the rest of 'em will be out soon. I'm sorry I couldn't get you a drink. They wouldn't let me take any beer outside."

"That's all right, Pearl." Hattie opened the box and stared at the thick, shiny Knackwurst lying between the two boiled red potatoes.

"You know, dear, I still miss Abner—a lot."

ℴℴ

Pearl watched with amusement as Anna Mae's chirpy recapitulation of all the imminent soul-building activity began to suffer in its clarity and cadence. She was content about replacing their leader's most obvious tic—jerking her head slightly from side to side and cocking it occasionally at odd angles, like a white Leghorn eyeing a grub—with a languorous, swiveling bob that seemed immune from the bus's frequent lurches. The rest of Anna Mae's captives were glad for the break in convention, accepting her new attitude without apparent question. Ellie Hathaway might have had her suspicions, but she had never been one to assume command until the battle was over.

They chugged through Little Norway and around the Echo Summit hairpin, revealing the breathtaking panorama of the sculpted Tahoe basin. *This is it,* Pearl thought. *The border; not just between California and Nevada, but between two worlds. Over there, where Hattie and I come from, people are more caught up in life and each other than in themselves. Over there, the price of self-sufficiency is knowing from the get-go that it just doesn't happen without others. No such thing as 'my life.' If it works out right, someone else is always involved. Over here, the idea of 'independence' is all jumbled up with isolation. Being alone with your toys is the most accepted definition of being free. At some point, after a life of ducking risk and sneaking around conflict, you have to come to terms with the strangers you've shared a lot of air and space with.*

℘℘

By the time they'd turned right from Emerald Bay Road onto Lake Tahoe Boulevard, Anna Mae was babbling through a throat full of molasses and could barely sustain a sitting position. Mr. Rosca, the Filipino driver, was clearly alarmed but not blessed with any kind of authority.

Pearl got to her feet. "*Carpe Diem,* Hattie. C'mon, and bring your bag." Hattie crawled around her and made her way forward, attaching herself to the pole behind the driver's seat.

Pearl followed. Once she'd braced Anna Mae and her odd, slack-jawed smile in her seat against the outer wall, she watched intently as they entered Casino Row. She ordered Mr. Rosca to pull over at the stoplight in front of Harrah's, and stood again.

"Now, folks, there's been a slight change in plans. We're all going to take a little detour up over Route 207 and down into the valley, into Minden. Hattie and I will be leaving you there and—if everything works out right—you'll be back to the First Church of the Warehoused and Waiting to Die before dark. Mr. Rasmussen, would you escort Miss McDonald into the casino and leave her where a Good Samaritan might eventually take pity on her, please?"

Barney Rasmussen leaped up. "It would be my pleasure!" he whooped, throwing Anna Mae's arm around his neck and whisking her down the steps. She looked as comfortable as anybody present remembered.

Mr. Rosca rose and began to speak. Hattie fished into her bag, produced her weapon, and pointed it at his neck. "*We mean business,*" she hissed. Mr. Rosca sank back into his seat.

Good old Hattie, mused Pearl. *Even if her flair for the dramatic outruns her good sense every once in a while.*

Now Ellie Hathaway was up. "Pearl Mutter and Hattie Gardner, you are both going to burn in Hell *forever!*"

Pearl glowered. "Ellie Hathaway, if you don't sit down and keep a lid on it, I swear to Christ you'll have to trade that gold cane for a white one!" Ellie fell back.

Barney bounded back up the steps, only a little out of breath but fanning himself with his hat. "Mission accomplished, Pearl."

"Good work, Barney. Mr. Rosca, if you'll put it in gear, we'll be making a right turn about—

"No."

Pearl and Hattie looked at each other. Mr. Rosca looked at them both, pleadingly.

"I don't have a 'Class A' license. If I get caught, I lose my job!"

"Uh, oh, Pearl," Hattie said. "Looks like we've got a kink here."

Pearl weighed her options. *Here we have a man who beat alcohol the old-fashioned way—bypassed the '12 Steps' for the '3-D' method. 'Drunk; Dried out; Devout.' He probably deserves a break; besides, he might be capable of anything.*

"Barney, didn't you used to drive a bus?"

Barney brightened again. "Yes, Ma'am. Trailways; 32 years."

"Think you can handle a Blue Bird?"

"Just like riding a bike!"

"Mr. Rosca, if you'll take a seat over here next to me, Mr. Rasmussen will spell you for a while. Hattie, come sit behind us. Barney, you'll want to go north about a mile and bear right onto Route 207, then—"

"Know it like the back of my hand," said Barney as he slid eagerly into the driver's position.

Pearl glanced over at Mr. Rosca. He appeared more relieved that frightened, even though his peripheral vision picked up the occasional flash of nickel behind his left ear. "Hattie, is that safety on? You know—in case of a bump. Or Parkinson's. Or something."

℘℣

The Maranatha Express labored up toward Daggett Pass and the Kingsbury Grade beyond. Barney had been briefed. He was to turn north on Foothill Road, take Muller Lane over to 395 and head on into Minden, where he could drop the escapees and head back to South Shore. It was a short hop out to the old place, and Pearl figured she could bulldoze Charlie Nye, Ned's boy and the current tenant, into putting her and Hattie up. There, she could figure the best way to beat back the legal onslaught sure to follow, once Delroy found out.

Ellie Hathaway had plucked up her courage and taken to reading Old Testament passages aloud, pausing to emphasize those that featured the fiery retributions of a just and vengeful God. A handful of fellow true believers muttered prayers. Hattie, Barney, and Hector shared the mien of a young, fit bridge crew aboard a hurtling starship, awaiting the order to battle stations. The rest were mostly over the shock of the break in routine and found themselves daring to hope for—they weren't certain what, exactly, but it didn't really matter that much. There was nowhere else pressing they needed to be.

Pearl looked back through the window of the emergency exit and picked up the shimmer of the lake just beyond the Nevada Beach campgrounds. Suddenly, she was 18 again.

℘℣

July 4, 1936—a Saturday, if she remembered right. She and Earl met at midday at Abner's place in Minden, which was closed for the holiday celebration. Hattie had planned a drive to Nevada Beach for sun, swimming, and a picnic supper. Dark would bring fireworks from both ends of the lake. Hattie and Abner had been married a year and her mother had baby Johnny for the night. They took Abner's Model 'A' over, with Earl and Pearl in the rumble seat. The bright heat and the wind made normal conversation impossible. During the ride Pearl saw Hattie's eyes flashing at her, a tacit admission that she had fixed it so the new couple had 90 minutes to get comfortable physically, before anything potentially awkward could be said.

The afternoon was spectacular. They piled their clothes on an old khaki blanket and ran, swam, wrestled, and lounged. They fell into the roles of creatures with which they were familiar. Abner and Earl preened, snorted, and athletically circled the females, seated together—now teasing, now feigning indifference. Up to then, Pearl had been a journeyman flirter in town, thanks to Hattie, and perfectly happy with it. Once in a while a shirt might come off a boy there, but the most flesh she'd routinely seen was the crimson neck under the brim of a hat or a brown arm crooked out a truck window.

The oddness of Earl's alabaster chest, trunk and legs against his tanned face, neck, and forearms gave way to a delicious curiosity about both the parts and the whole of his ranch-hardened body. Their random physicality had accelerated her education. The wiry hair that sprouted between his chestnut nipples, under his arms, and that snaked into both sides of his trunks from his navel and the small of his back was remarkably soft. The smoothness of the skin under his arms and high on the back of his thighs was in sharp contrast to his cracked and callused hands. Pearl surprised herself when her swimsuit raked her own nipples or tugged against her pubic mound, sending sharp currents of pleasure racing through her.

They talked and laughed easily. Easier for Pearl was looking into Earl's face and eyes. No boundaries or fences, and she could see for miles, without so much as a cloud. They chased the fried chicken with lemonade; bathtub gin followed the pie and a thermos of coffee thereafter. At dark, Abner built a fire and the couples huddled under blankets and talked. Earl spoke shyly but earnestly into the lake about his plans; Pearl listened and watched the strong lines of his profile and his jaw. Abner and Hattie disappeared.

Earl was in mid-sentence—something about the number of acres in graze versus feed—when the staccato crackle and rockets' red glare interrupted him. Pearl laughed at his surprise and impulsively pulled herself to him. His leathery scent—witch hazel, tobacco, and sweat—filled her nostrils and inflamed her. He flushed and kissed her, hard. Everything that followed was natural, warm, and right to her. The pain Hattie had warned her about was brief. Though seized by passion as they pressed and gasped and slid into and around each other, she marveled at the cool unity of their drenched flesh—as though they'd been anointed for a divine ritual. Earl, then she, and then the sky behind them exploded. *Glory be to God,* Pearl thought. *Real fireworks, my first time.*

Earl held her close and called her his "jewel of Genoa," after her hometown. For Pearl, from that moment until Earl died, nothing was guaranteed, everything was up for grabs, and anything seemed possible.

℘ℭ

"Uh-oh. Pearl!"

The alarm in Barney's voice ended her reverie. He'd managed the route professionally and was about a half-mile from where Muller Road ran into Route 395 when he heard the sirens. They were now within sight of the intersection.

"Barney, pull onto that gravel drive behind the stand of trees and stop, will you, please?"

Pearl alighted, walked to the edge of the trees and squinted. The Dopplered wail of two highway patrol cruisers peaked as they flashed past, headed south toward Minden. *H'm,* Pearl thought. *Maybe Anna Mae has more grit than I gave her credit for.* She reboarded. "Mr. Rosca, I know you have one of those cellulite phones. I need to borrow it a minute, please. Barney, turn it around; I'll guide you as we go."

Barney had doubled back to Foothill, turned north again, and mostly covered the two-plus miles to Genoa, while Pearl alternated between instructions to him and her telephone business. Pearl snapped Mr. Rosca's phone shut, returned it, and watched out the windshield.

"There, Barney—Agnew Street! Turn right, please. And...stop!"

Pearl let herself down and took it in. Same yellow clapboard, same white trim. Magnificent, three-sided porch that never saw a summer night it couldn't lengthen and magnify.

"Pearl! Pearl Opal Mutter!" A lean, 50-ish man burst through the screen door, vaulted down the steps, hoisted her above his head, and twirled her aloft, joyously.

"Easy, youngster. The only knife's ever been waved at me was in the Silver Rowel, and I'd like to keep it that way!"

He set her down and she braced his upper arms, his face shining down on hers.

"Is that *really you,* Bobby Sangiacomo?"

"Yes, Ma'am!" A mock frown. "But, please; it's 'Bob.' I'm a businessman now." He swept his arm grandly toward the sign. "That is—when I'm not coaching and recruiting for U.N.R."

"'Genoa Home Inn Bed and Breakfast,'" Pearl read.

"God knows it was home to me and half the town when your grandparents lived here."

"Just like your place was to me that summer I hired on to buck bales. Made a man and a better football player out of me—eventually."

Pearl was pensive. "That was a harder year than I bargained for." She reclaimed his hand. "You were more than a help to us, Bobby; you were a good friend to Delroy—when he needed one."

"How is Delroy?"

"We don't talk much." Pearl swept aside the uneasiness. "Is the hardware store still thriving?"

"No. Dad closed it and retired 10 years ago. Between Wal-Mart and the growth in Carson City, he took a beating."

"How are Robert and Linda?"

"Dad died seven years ago and Mom, right after that."

"Oh, Bobby, I'm *so* sorry."

"No, Pearl, *I'm* sorry. Mister Mutter was buried 19 years ago and I was on the road with the team. I didn't ever get to say a proper good-bye to either of you."

"That's life, these days. Everybody's on their way somewhere else. Oh, what the Hell, Bobby—no need, where I'm concerned. I'm *back*."

"So you told me, and you need a ride?"

"Please—if it isn't any trouble."

"Not a bit." Bob looked up at the branch full of owls in the bus. "Is it just you, or am I gonna have to make several trips?"

Pearl laughed. "Give me a minute to figure this out; originally, it was just me and Hattie. What do you have in the way of wheels?"

"The Inn has a nine-passenger van, mostly for fetching guests from Reno or Carson. It also has tinted windows," Bobby said slyly, "if that's a consideration."

Pearl folder her arms and paced. *Let's see. Barney and Hector are into this pretty deep, and we're gonna need a bargaining chip in case anything else jumps up.*

She sensed someone behind her.

"I'll make a better hostage."

Pearl jerked around and down, into steady green eyes carried a little below Hattie's level.

"Why, Bertha Sue Hanks! The new girl who doesn't say five words a month at Maranatha!" Pearl was merry. "Well—what are your qualifications?"

"Ain't as big a pain in the butt as Ellie Hathaway, for starters."

Woman read my mind, Pearl thought.

"I am—used to be—an actress; pretty good one, too, "said Bertha Sue. "My youngest is a big-time lawyer back in Sacramento, with political ambitions. Complete horse's patoot. He'll do anything to avoid bad publicity—or, failing that, turn *any* publicity onto him."

Pearl tried her hand at appearing serious. "What's in it for you?"

"Publicity'd do me good," grinned Bertha Sue. "Might get some character work again—look at Gloria Stewart! Besides, if my grandkids think I'm famous, maybe they'll tear themselves away from their PlayStations more often."

"I guess you're hired!"

Pearl and Bertha Sue got back on the bus.

"Good news, Ellie," Pearl said. "We're back on track. You and your faithful will be back in Jesus' arms by sundown. Hattie, get our things. Anybody else want to remain fugitives?" Barney and Hector were both up, looking like two school kids afraid of being picked last at recess.

"That's what I thought. Come on, boys. Mr. Rosca, you can find your way back to South Shore, can't you? I wouldn't worry too much; the only thing more boring than driving the Kingsbury Grade is patrolling it. They won't be expecting you from this direction, anyway."

The five disembarked. The boys waved stupidly, as if they'd just been left at camp. Pearl thought she saw a hint of a smile as Mr. Rosca closed the door and turned the engine over. As they crept away, Ellie glared back as she launched a spirited chorus of 'Shall We Gather at the River?'"

"Ready, Pearl?" Bob had pulled the van up.

"Just one more favor, Bobby. May I use your phone?"

"You bet. Right inside the door, in the hallway."

Pearl hustled up the steps and into the house.

"Hello, information? Carson City or Mound House. I need the number of the Rabbit Ranch, please."

໖ငຊ

The Rabbit Ranch is one of a half-dozen legal brothels seven miles east of Nevada's capital city and 41 minutes from Reno-Tahoe International Airport. Dropped anywhere else, its cluster of low manufactured buildings might easily be mistaken for a nondescript trailer park. Except for the tawdry signs ("Hot'n'Nasty sex, 300 ft.") and the security. Never mind the high-desert desolation; inside the white, welded-steel fence and motorized gate, tattooed biceps and neck chains make perfect sense. You didn't need neon and floor shows to be reminded that entertainment was serious business. Indulging the appetites of others for profit required close and careful supervision.

Pearl marveled at the gatekeeper who waved the van through. He looked a little like that Mr. T. on cable, had he been born 20 years later and gone directly into the WWE. *Six o' him,* she thought, *and Earl and I wouldn't have needed horses and ropes to brand cattle.* She was equally impressed—in the other direction—by the sight of the bloatish apparition who threw open her door and poised himself to deliver a bear hug. She was fairly certain it was Caswell P. "Pete" Collier, the last hand hired by Earl before his heart gave out and she'd kept on, until Delroy uprooted her.

"Miz Mutter? God*DAMN!*"

"Is that *you,* Pete Collier?" She had to be certain

before she broke free and corrected his choice of language with a lady.

"You bet it is, Ma'am; best calf-roper this side o' Lovelock. Wull," he backtracked sheepishly. "Used t'be." He angled his fleshy, slick-haired head downward and tried to find his Italian shoes under the paunchy outcrop. "Still eat like a hand, but the hardest thing I ride these days is a desk chair." He sheltered the office side of his mouth behind his hand. "These days, I'm Cashwell P. FoXXX—three capital 'Xs'—C.E.O. of Happy Hare Enterprises, Inc. Show business—film, publishing, and . . . pleasure."

"You *own* all this?" Pearl was skeptical. Pete had a habit of finding everything he owned but his saddle in the pot, most Saturday nights back when.

"No, that would be our Chairman."

"Who's he?"

"Dunno," he shrugged. "Some dude in New Jersey."

Pearl was about to tell Pete he looked like he'd been rode hard and put up wet, but reconsidered. Even under these conditions, she was grateful for the loyalty and the sanctuary. "Thanks, Pete; I truly appreciate it."

"Least I could do for the best and prettiest ranch cook in five counties."

Hattie, Bertha Sue, and the boys had already made the parlor entrance. Hattie had the bearing of a diplomat come home after a long foreign posting. Bertha Sue was already in character, manifesting anxiety. "I'm being kept against my will, you know," she told Mr. Stone-Cold T, who had offered his considerable arm. The boys were absorbing it all, eyes wide. Barney was simply transfixed, like a child just given a toy-store spending spree at Christmas. Hector began studying the "hostesses'" glamour photos intently.

"It's nearly five, so I'm expecting our Friday-night regulars pretty soon," Pete said. "There's a new suite just delivered for our fall expansion that has three bedrooms and its own bath. It ain't been decorated for business yet, but the essentials are in there. Sorry, ladies. I guess two of you will have to double up, unless the gentlemen are willing to make up the dinette. Cook'll whip up whatever you want when you're hungry."

Barney was about to be chivalrous but Pearl spoke first. "Hattie and I'll be fine together, thank you. Bertha Sue will need her own room, being under 'house arrest' and all, so you boys can take the third. We'll take meals when the others do. If you'll just show us the way, Pete, we can put away our things."

"Is 'Marine Corps Marla' working tonight?"

Everyone looked at Hector. He returned their quizzical looks by tapping an envelope through his shirt pocket. "Eagle flew this week, folks. I was goin' to sneak out and risk a little Social Security on the slots after Anna Mae was asleep, like usual. Change of plans; gotta make do. Guess my nephew might have to work a little harder next summer to meet college expenses."

Pete's concern was obvious, so Hector continued. "Don't worry, Mr. Cashwell. Look." He pushed up a sleeve, revealing a faded, "Birdie-on-the-Ball"/*Semper Fi* tattoo. "Japs couldn't kill me on Guadalcanal or Iwo Jima; I doubt Marla'll be able to."

Pete laughed. "Don't you want to inspect the goods first? Every customer's entitled, you know."

"One Gyrene always trusts another to get the job done," Hector answered.

"Sure you're up to it, Hector?" Hattie asked, elbowing Pearl.

"I'm 77 next week, Hattie—never find out any younger. Besides," he said over his shoulder as he followed Pete out, "just because I can't ride the elephant doesn't mean I won't enjoy the circus."

An hour later, Barney switched on the monitor in their quarters' sitting area, after the ladies had dropped their grips, mopped their faces, and Bertha Sue had been welcomed to borrow any necessaries.

"Oh, boy—premium cable. Wonder if they have 'Pay-per-View?'" Barney paused and admired his little joke.

"Find some news, Barney," Pearl said.

Barney began flipping.

"Wait—there! Turn it up!"

One of Carson's local anchors was doing a lead-in, with a graphic of Maranatha's bus over her left shoulder. The smirk in her voice annoyed them. Up popped tape of a network feed of a goggle-eyed Anna Mae, recounting as much as she could remember, then the casino guard who found her. The perky newsreader voiced over it:

"...ALLEGEDLY DRUGGED-*blah-blah-blah*-INCOHERENT-*blah-blah-blah*-FORMER NEVADA RESIDENT-*blah-blah-blah*-APPARENTLY HIJACKED-*blah-blah-blah*-WHEREABOUTS UNKNOWN-*blah-blah-blah*-FAMILIES CONCERNED-*blah-blah-blah*-AUTHORITIES LOOKING-*blah-blah-blah*-ANYONE WITH INFORMATION..."

Good, thought Pearl. *Looks like Mr. Rosca got them back into town and over to the church undetected. That'll give me the night to think, before all Hell breaks loose.*

❧❦

Hector was not only all right but all smiles at breakfast. Whether they'd wanted to or not, they learned that he'd not only hit the beach, but—with a little expert help—he'd also remembered how to plant the flag. For dessert, Hector treated them all to the Marine Corps Hymn. *A cappella,* all three verses.

Pearl pushed away her scraps of scrambled eggs—good, and made better by the absence of Bible recitation—and made her way to the front. She found that the dominos had fallen just as she expected. Ellie

Hathaway had squealed to Reverend Alston, who'd tried to retrieve Anna Mae from the casino. Finding her sobering up to her newfound notoriety in a welter of newshounds, he retreated, opting to let her make her own way there if and when she truly came to her senses. He phoned the authorities and the home. Before nightfall, Bobby Sangiacomo had confessed (just as he'd been instructed) to Douglas County Sheriff's deputies that he'd been forced at gunpoint to transport the fugitives to the Rabbit Ranch. The highway patrol was notified and dispatched a hostage team overnight, joining the county inter-jurisdictional task force already on-site. It wasn't long after that the sharks of the Fourth Estate began to circle, drawn by the chum of tips from unnamed sources and intercepted police-scanner transmissions.

Pete had managed to get most of his early-weekend regulars out unnoticed, before the hordes descended. The adventuresome few who ordered *a la carte* were allowed to stay where they were and focus on what to tell whoever was most likely to find them missing. The stress on the manager was telling already. "Pearl, I hope we can wrap this up before I lose the whole weekend. It is the slack season, but my East Coast associates get all worked up about unexpected cash-flow problems."

"You're not thinking clearly, Pete," said Pearl. "What with the publicity and all, I do believe the extra attention will pay off come September, when things pick up anyway."

Pete seemed thankful that Mrs. Mutter was still capable of seeing through to the end of things and went outside to find The Man in Charge.

Captain Steve Hutchinson, the headquarters watch commander, lounged against the half-open door of his unmarked cruiser with the small antennas and rear-shelf, colored lights that bespeak rank and authority. A Carson City police unit and a half-dozen sheriff's cars from Douglas and Lyon Counties, with occupants, made up the balance of the uniformed detail. A large, windowless van was the only hint that things might take a paramilitary turn. Every other available inch unclaimed by sagebrush was occupied by print and broadcast media. Only the muscle on both sides of the fence kept them at bay, so they occupied their time with loud, ceremonious bouts over territory and pecking order. Elements of the First Amendment Air Force whirled by occasionally, low enough to kick up dust and complaints. These scenes—of which he'd already seen too many, even by Silver State standards—always put Capt. Hutchinson in mind of that ubiquitous Western poster, on which one buzzard, perched in a tree over a waning, prostrate prospector, says to the second: "Wait, Hell! I'm gonna kill me somethin'!"

Pete hailed him from the gate. "Captain, I believe our fugitives want to pow-wow." Breaking a trail through the thicket of lenses and microphones, Capt. Hutchinson slipped through the gate and followed Pete into the parlor. He removed his hat and sunglasses and allowed his eyes to adjust. The first figure he encountered was a small, white-haired one who had struggled to her feet and was patting her breast excitedly.

"My land! Is that *you*, Stevie Hutchinson?" asked Hattie.

He scratched his head in pleased and embarrassed recognition. "I guess it is, Miz Gardner."

She doddered forward and hugged his waist, tearfully. She pushed herself back and looked him over. "My stars and garters, look at all that collar and shoulder hardware. I don't guess you're still pushing a cruiser full-time any more, huh?"

"No, Ma'am. I've managed to get promoted way past my usefulness."

"Still single?" Hattie narrowed her eyes and widened her smile.

"Sorry—Lana Gaynor ran me down and saddled me

with twins. Abner and Hattie."

Hattie was obviously pleased, but asked anyway. "Where on Earth did you come up with those names?"

He rested his arm on her shoulder and looked down into her. "After this crazy old saloonkeeper and his wife, who let me do homework at the bar and sent me home with beer and smokes, so the old man wouldn't hit me quite so hard." His voice was thicker, but gentler. "Who finally convinced me I wasn't a waste of space and gave me the guts at 16 to pack up my sisters and move to my aunt's in Reno. Who came to my high school graduation. Who made a couple calls to friends at the University and pointed me toward a degree in criminology."

He brushed at his eyes and scanned the room. He traded introductions, saving Pearl for last. "So, Miz Mutter. I hear you're the mastermind of this criminal conspiracy."

"Well, Stevie—uh, Captain, Hattie and I were just lookin' to get on back home, and things got a little complicated."

"Complicated?" Hutchinson cleared his throat. "Something on the order of assault and battery, kidnapping, and interstate flight, is all. Spoke to Delroy this morning; his drawers were in a serious knot."

"Hmph. Just like Delroy to call the law without talkin' to me. He's the reason Hattie and I wound up in that place to begin with. Earl wasn't hardly in the ground before I found myself sittin' on a bed in a strange place, staring at a white-bread print o' the Lord. And folks tryin' to push drugs into me. It's been near 20 years, now."

The captain's fingers crept around his hatband. "Could've chalked it up to a family squabble, Miz Mutter, but you inconvenienced your chaperone and dragged three other people along." Hector and Barney grinned like retrievers. Bertha Sue looked at Pearl, pleading for direction. Hutchinson shook his head. "Feds have made a lot of hay out of joyriding and this 'crossing state lines' stuff. Another 48 hours and they'll probably be real interested."

"What do I need to do so nobody but me's at any real risk, Captain?"

"Tell you what. You give up a 'hostage' or two—

"I ain't no 'hostage,' and I ain't givin' up!" exclaimed Barney, setting his few lower teeth and bridge against his upper plate.

Hector was studious. "I'll go. My people are a little sensitive about putting it on the street, and"—he smiled slyly—"my work here is done."

"You'll need someone with you who can handle the press," said Bertha Sue, who'd already gotten the nod from Pearl.

The captain came back to Barney. "Mister Rasmussen, you got any close family living?"

"Nossir."

"Okay. That's a good start," Hutchinson said, turning to Pearl. "How about you try your best to work something out with Delroy? I'll get these two started back home and tell those scavengers outside that you're protesting the state of nursing home care today and working up a list of demands. That'll keep everybody busy for a while. What do you think?"

Pearl was mollified, except for the Delroy part. She mooned. "Do I have to call him?"

"All but the French believe that whoever takes the table first has the upper hand." He winked.

The trooper escorted Bertha Sue and Hector through the gate and into the maelstrom of surging cameras and shouting manikins. Pearl watched, amused. Hector slid into the back seat as Bertha Sue drew all fire with her fanning, gesturing, and remonstrating. Pearl regretted she couldn't be in the room when Bertha Sue's son turned on his television that day. Capt. Hutchinson delivered an oral memorandum more stylish and subtle than "No comment," but scarcely more enlightening. He referred further inquiries to a thunderstruck deputy standing nearby and climbed behind the wheel.

Hattie took Pearl's hand by the window and they watched their friends disappear in the dust.

"I'm goin' to go lie down for a while, Pearl."

℘∞

"Yes, operator, I'll accept the charges."

Delroy A. Mutter, attorney-at-law, sighed as he switched the cordless to his other ear and collapsed into an Adirondack chair on his Mill Valley deck.

"Hello? Delroy?"

"Mother, what in the Hell is the matter with you? I'm missing a pretrial strategy conference at the office because of all this nonsense!"

"Why, I'm fine, son. And you? What did you with the manners your Daddy and I taught you, anyway?"

Here we go, he thought. "All sarcasm aside. What is it this time—not enough red meat in the Maranatha diet?"

"Don't patronize me, Delroy. It is what's it's always been. You put me in that place against my will. I was still weak from Earl's death. You know that. I've lost every bit of the only life I knew, except Hattie."

"I thought we agreed that a structured environment was what you needed after Dad died."

"*We* didn't agree on anything. I was lost and confused; half my life was torn away, just like that. I *had* a structured environment. What else would you call 50 acres, with half that in hay and 200 head of feeder cattle?"

Delroy pinched his temples with his free hand. "Okay—for the sake of argument, Bitsy and I thought the Maranatha situation was best-suited for someone in your situation at the time."

"What—dropping me in the middle of a bunch of Holy Rollers, so in love with life that they spend all their wakin' hours jostlin' for position at the Pearly Gates?" Pearl snorted. "And, a lot that dried-up, social X-ray wife of yours knows about anything. The only time she's ever gotten dirt under her fingernails is applying a mud pack. She's plain ashamed of me—too country."

"We just thought you might benefit from the opportunity to form a more personal relationship with God."

"Hah! It doesn't get much more personal than takin' hay to cattle on the high desert in the dead of winter. Show me anybody that won't turn to prayer in a wet blizzard at 40 below! Fine talk comin' from you, down in the front row at the Church of the Almighty Dollar."

"I've earned every penny I've ever made," he hissed. "I never asked you and Dad for anything."

"You never wanted for a thing as a boy, Delroy. Had your college all paid for, if you'd wanted it; Earl and I saw to that. The dramatic, personal 'declaration of independence' on your 18th birthday was your idea."

"Give me a break. Dad didn't want me around. He couldn't stand the sight of me after—"

Pearl interrupted, softer. "Son, you've got to get past your sister's death. You and Bobby were 10, just kids; it couldn't have been helped. Opal was always walking on the edge. After she broke her neck in swimmin' at Topaz Lake, Earl lost a big piece of his heart that he never got back. I'd probably have gone the same direction, if anything like that had ever happened to you. You know how it is—father-daughter, mother-son. But he never blamed you for a single minute. He just wasn't one who found it easy to put his feelings into words. Truth be told, your havin' nothing to do with him afterwards hurt him more than even Opal's dyin'."

Delroy swallowed. "Ma, I don't want to talk about this anymore right now. What do you want to do about this?"

"I want my life back. I want to live the rest of my life *in* my life. I want to sit on the porch with my friends and look out on what your father and I made, together. I want to fall asleep in the room I shared with him for 46 years, with his scent in my nostrils and him in my head."

"You can't live in the past, Ma."

"Torn away from it, Delroy, I'm not *me*. Without it, I have no present, nor future. Don't you *see*? Just because you can't go back there doesn't mean it's wrong for me."

"What if something happens to you?"

"Son, I don't mean to hurt you, but you haven't seen me more than twice a year in the last 20. I'm 83 and I have my share of aches and pains, most of which my pills will handle until I stop breathin'. I can get 'em just as easy through the mail as in a little cardboard cup every day, and a damned site cheaper, too. There's nothin' that's goin' to happen to me that you could do anything about anyway, bein' two hours away. But—to answer your question—I'll lie down and die in the bed that my children were born in. Seems fittin', doesn't it?

"How will you manage?"

"I'll do fine. Charley's holdin' out okay, though I might need to take a hard look at some of the hands he's hired lately. The house is plenty big enough for the both of us, and it's on the half of the place that Earl left to me."

"But, Ma, the whole of Carson Valley is going the other way. Ascuaga is selling off three of his four ranches right now."

"Delroy, as long as people eat beef there'll be a place for the 'Diamond M.' Why are you in such a damned rush to subdivide and sell, yourself? You're a big-time San Francisco lawyer and Nevada's only goin' to grow."

"Wouldn't you rather have your share of the purchase money now, Ma?"

"And do what with it, Delroy? Take it back to the home, where I'm not allowed to do *anything*, much less illegal, immoral, or fattening? Buy a house? I *have* a house. For someone trained in logic, you're not making much sense. Plus, I don't think you've heard a word I've said."

"All right, Mother," Delroy said as he studied his feet, "you win. It's clear to me that we're not getting anywhere this way. I'll move things around and drive up there—"

"You can point that German four-wheeler this way if you want to, Delroy," Pearl said crisply. "I won't see you. Hattie and I are going home from here and we don't need you to get us there. And you know I'm not crazy, so as long as I'm alive and clear-headed there's nothing legal you can do to stop me."

Delroy stood up and leaned hard on the deck rail. "Is there *anyone* that could come up and talk sense to you?"

Pearl waited a bit. "You could send my granddaughter."

"Staci?!" *My 19-year-old screw-up?* Delroy thought in disbelief.

"Yes. Goodbye, Delroy."

As Pearl hung up, she was filled with melancholy over how long and how far her son had run in 42 years to escape what he'd always carry with him. Money and marryin' up hadn't changed anything. He was still blind to it all.

She turned in her chair. There was Barney. He looked stricken."Pearl," he said, trying to find someplace for his hands. "It's—It's Hattie."

Be strong, girl, she thought, as panic pulled her down the hallway and into their bedroom. Barney tumbled in behind her. She blanched herself when she saw her old friend. Her face was as white as her hair and the sham on which it lay. The rims of her eyes almost matched the pillow's crimson legend: "Foxy Lady!'" She raised her hand weakly but decisively, as a marshal halts a parade. "Now, before anybody else goes to pieces, the bar is open. Pearl, fetch that Seagram's out of my bag. Barney, rustle us up some glasses and 7-Up or Sprite; either will do—long as it ain't diet!"

Barney buttled out toward the kitchen. Pearl set the bottle on the nightstand and herself at Hattie's side on the bed. Pearl stroked her companion's hair, her eyes brimming with tears.

"I'm not goin' to tell you, 'No tears,' Pearl. A good cry does a girl a world o' good every now and again. Nobody knows that better than me, Minden's answer to Sarah Bernhardt. Just remember—I'm more'n two years older than you and had a lot less wick to burn, anyway. Abner and I worked hard, just like you and Earl, but the light was bad and the air was considerably worse. And Land, girl—you know how I liked to stay up and holler, most nights!"

Pearl choked on her own sobs. "Oh, Hattie, dearest. We're so close, now. You've *got* to go home with me. Can't you stay with me, just another day or two?"

Hattie pressed Pearl's hands to her breast. Her own eyes shone with tears. "You know I've always said that the Good Book had it backwards: 'The spirit is willing, but the flesh is firm.'"

Pearl began weeping openly and fell beside Hattie. "I don't want you to go," she cried.

"Don't you worry, my old, sweet friend. You never know—those Jesus freaks we ran away from might be on to something. Whatever waits over there, waits for both of us —win, lose, or draw. I'll save you a seat right in front of the best-lookin' dealer, and I won't double-down 'til you're beside me again. I promise..."

Hattie rolled her eyes up and closed them.

Pearl pushed herself up when she felt Hattie's chest stop heaving. Everything rushed away from her as she watched that withered little rosebud of a mouth, hoping desperately for another note or two to come.

Slowly, she removed her glasses and looked toward the door. Barney had returned with highball glasses and the sodas. Quietly, Pearl motioned him over and poured out three fingers of whiskey and lemon-lime for each of them. She raised hers and waited for his.

"Here's to Hortense Atticus Churchill Gardner, the best damned friend any mortal soul could hope for. May Gabriel get her a harp directly, so she can start right in, singin' for Abner again."

"To Hattie," Barney echoed.

They sipped in silent tribute; at last, Pearl put down her drink. "Barney, can you leave us alone for a minute or two? Please, dear?"

℘℃℞

When Pearl had pulled herself together enough to function, she rummaged through Hattie's small document file and found her interment papers. She called the Geer-Waite Douglas County Mortuary in Minden about having the body picked up. They told her that the earliest they could manage was late that evening. That was fine, she said. At that point it seemed profane to her that Hattie was there at all.

Outside, a brittle ennui had set in. Hutchinson hadn't returned and nothing had changed there, so cameras and sound booms had been replaced with decks of cards, Game-Boys, and sundry other diversions. Blazers were doffed and ties loosened as much of the on-air talent retreated to their stations' SUVs and vans to spare their coiffures the midday sun. Most everybody but Dick Prince, KORN-TV7's correspondent. He kept his post near the gate fully presented, with his cameraman right behind. Prince was in the autumn of a regional broadcasting career that had thus far failed to catch fire, a situation he wrote off to "politics." He had never connected his fortunes in any way to his lack of scruples, even by pack standards, and a humorlessness unleavened by any real sensitivity. Lately, his routine aggressiveness gave off a whiff of desperation. Prince was known behind his back as "Road-kill," both for his toupee and the state in which his interview subjects were left.

Pete strode to the gate. "Miz Mutter's friend, Miz Hattie Gardner, has passed away," he announced, "and Mrs. Mutter wants to talk to somebody about it."

Vehicle doors had scarcely cracked and crossed legs unbent before Prince, spouting his superior qualifications to no one in particular, had wormed through the gap in the opening gate, pulling his cameraman in his wake. Pete nodded and Mr. Stone Cold T toggled the barrier closed again. The wave of noisy bodies that followed threatened to break over it, until the bodyguard stoically patted the bulge under his vest where the lines of his shoulder holster merged. The swell receded, replaced by an oscillation of whining and veiled threats.

Pearl watched them approach. *It's just not right, to end like this*, she thought. *Folks need to know about my Hattie and how much she meant to folks in Carson Valley.*

Prince's spontaneous charge had foreclosed the possibility of a live feed, so his overarching objective was to get an interview on tape and head north as soon as possible. This cut deeply into whatever limited courtesies he was normally capable of.

"Miz Mutter, I'm Dick Prince, KORN-TV7 News, Reno. If you'll just remain standing, when Ralph turns the light on I'll ask you some questions. Don't be nervous. Ready?" Pearl halfway nodded, while being pushed into best-lighting position by the cameraman. He lurched back and switched on. "'Thanks, Rob and Cheryl. This is Dick Prince, with an exclusive interview with Pearl O. Mutter, former Minden-area resident and go-go Grandma, whose alleged daring, daylight escape from her Sacramento nursing home has her facing possible federal kidnapping charges. Tell our viewers, Pearl, is it true that you drugged an employee to make your getaway?'"

"Well, yes; I—"

"'And isn't it true that until just this morning you held

three other residents hostage?'"

Pearl stopped squinting and quickened. "No! Now that's just not—"

"'And the death of your best friend from Minden, Hattie Gardner, may have been caused by all this excitement?'"

"Now just you stop—"

"'How does that make you fee'—huuhhhnnnNNNHHH!" All of Prince's breath leaped out of his lungs and a shock wave of pain radiated from his groin as Pearl's right foot penetrated his trousers. His head recoiled so violently before he crumpled to the floor that his hairpiece was torn from its front moorings and fluttered, belly-up, at the back of his head. In an oddly clinical way he looked like he'd just been scalped. Ralph pointed his camera down at him, still rolling.

Pearl stood over Prince. "Beat a rapist that way in '38. Funny; I don't remember feelin' quite as violated at the time." She examined her stocking foot in her open-toed sandals. "Had a boot on then, though. Hope I don't lose a nail over this." She fixed her gaze on Ralph, who had powered down and was almost beside himself.

"You're not plannin' on doin' anything with that, are you?"

"I'll erase the tape just as soon as everyone back at the station's seen it, Ma'am. I swear."

"Well, all right, then."

Mr. Stone Cold T impassively dragged the groaning, purple-faced Prince outside and toward the gate. Ralph followed, switching shoulders so the recorder shielded his expression from his subject.

₰ℂ

As the afternoon shadows lengthened, a slender, leggy figure clad in a midriff top, skinny jeans, and UGGs pulled her battered Toyota as close to the gate as she could manage. She emerged, snapped on a carrier and packed a squirming bundle into it. Slinging another bag onto her shoulder, she blew the stark bangs fronting her otherwise streaked, short-cropped hair off her forehead and strode up to the gate. Any journalist's notion that she might be somehow involved was quashed immediately by the cynical assumption that she was an employee. She spoke uncertainly to Mr. Stone Cold T. "Hi. I'm Staci Mutter. My Dad said that my grandmother wanted to talk to me?" The sentinel carried the message to Pete, who admitted her before she became the center of another frenzy. Inside, she strained to see Pearl fully, who was laboring herself out of her chair.

"Gran!" Staci was happy to see Pearl on mostly her own terms.

They hugged, with a little difficulty.

"Staci Opal Mutter! How's my favorite granddaughter?"

"Great, Gran, but if you were serious about flattering me, you'd say, 'grandchild.' That'd at least put me ahead of Thad."

"How is your little brother?"

"Thriving under close supervision, apparently. Maybe he won't crack, like I did."

"So, 'child.' Who's your friend, here?"

"This is your first great-grandbaby—Joshua Earl." Staci peeled back the tiny hood.

Pearl gaped; her heart was pierced when she saw him. "You passed your Grampa's eyes along to him, I see." Her face and eyes shone. "Who's his Daddy?"

"Not important right now—believe me."

"Oh, my. Sit a minute and let's talk about it, dear." Pearl switched to the sofa and helped Staci make herself and Josh comfortable beside her. She decided to give the woman a shorter hill to climb.

"I see that you're not one o' them 'Gothics' any more, girl."

Staci laughed. "No, Gran. It's just not acceptable to

waitress and 'temp' in Marin County looking like a figment of Anne Rice's imagination. It may be just across the Golden Gate but, in many ways, it's still a world away from 'The City.'"

"Who's Anne Rice?"

"She's—never mind."

"What're you now—19?"

"Yep. Be 20 in a couple weeks."

"Did you ever get out of high school—one way or the other?

"Finally. I went back for a G.E.D. nights after I got out of Juvie." Josh cooed at her and she smiled. "That's where I met Josh's father." Staci raised her eyes. "He's kind of a loser—still working some shit out. Sorry."

"I'm sure he'll come along, in time," Pearl said. "Most important thing right now is that Josh's Mama loves him—and his Gramma, too. May I hold him a minute?"

Staci surrendered her charge and clasped her arm around Pearl's shoulders. "I wish other people heard me the way you do, Gran. You've always been the one I could talk to. I hate it that you're so far away."

Pearl dangled her index finger, thubbing Josh's tiny lower lip and delighting him. "What happened this time?"

Staci clouded over. "I thought things might improve after I flunked out and did my stretch for dealing pot. Getting a day job and taking classes evenings was my idea—Dad wanted me to intern at the firm, towards something permanent. I just couldn't stand the idea of being ignored all day *and* all night. Stuff was tolerable 'til Dad found out I was pregnant. I refused to give up Josh's father, so he kicked me out and cut me off after Josh was born. 'Tough love,' he called it. Said he was sick of the arguing, paying for therapy—"

Pearl sniffed. "Only therapy I ever needed at your age was a long, hot bath at Walley's." She was going to add "with Earl," but she thought the better of it.

"—And the shame, his first grandchild born out of

wedlock."

Pearl stared out ahead. "It's a pity your Daddy gets so full of himself most o' the time. His sister wasn't exactly born *out* of it, but she wasn't made *in* it, either. Delroy never did the math, I guess."

Staci's mouth fell open. "Gran?!"

"That's right. Your late aunt, Opal Ursula—after Earl's mother—was born April 14, 1937. Earl and I married on September 5, 1936. Opal came to us on the Fourth of July. I'm certain of it."

"So you and Grampa *had* to--?"

"Not *had to,* child. "*Did.* Held my breath a little when I told him, but I wasn't afraid. He'd already proposed. If my folks or his were ashamed, they had the grace and the sense not to say so. I was lucky, and so was your aunt."

"I know so little about her; Dad never even mentions her. All I ever really got is what I could guess from a few pictures. What was she like?"

Pearl touched her granddaughter's chin. "Pretty, headstrong, a handful. Like you. You favor her, in a lot of ways; maybe that comes up between Delroy and you. See, he never got over Opal's death. He thought it was his fault because he was young and he was there. On top of the normal, brother-sister things at that age—well, it was too much for him."

"Did Grampa blame Daddy for it?"

"No, child; I told Delroy that again, just this morning. Earl bore it as best he could by takin' it inside himself for good, which the boy took for shuttin' him out. Earl was just a creature of his time. Things are more complicated now, I guess. You have to find a different name for every kind of feelin' right about somethin' and takin' the risk of doin' it. Then, you have pay somebody to lie down and talk about it. What's it called? 'Paralysis through analysis'?'"

Staci frowned. "There's just so much I always wanted to say to Dad and Mom—about me, my fears, my dreams. Seems like that's what they were most afraid of, hearing that I was as fragile and vulnerable as they are in spite of my 'advantages.' The worst part is feeling like I'm disappointing them, without every really knowing why."

"I know, dear, I know. Lord knows Hattie and I were wild enough at your age. I can't say what's changed. Watching yearlings run, buck, and kick for no apparent reason and then just grow out of it must've been some comfort. Know it was for me, anyway."

Josh began to fuss. Staci took him back and pushed him under her top. Pearl watched them until he was fed, burped, and asleep on Staci's lap. They sat, wordlessly, for a time, deep in their own thoughts but touching each other in random, needful ways. Light from the western parlor windows seeped across the floor until it bathed their feet. Pearl caught a breath halfway out and pursed her lips. "Staci, how are you gettin' on, right now?"

"Like I said, Gran, waiting tables and temporary office work."

"No—I mean, how are you living?"

"Oh. I have two pretty good roommates; one actually has a little boy. We kinda look out for each other."

"That's good; that's real good," said Pearl. She resumed her meditation.

Pete came through the door. "Pearl; 'scuse me. The man from the mortuary is here."

Will Waite came in behind him, wearing the standard-issue dark suit, starched white shirt and nondescript tie. He crossed to Pearl and took her hands out of her lap.

"H'lo, Miz Mutter. I'm so sorry for your loss."

"Thank you, Will. How's the senior partner these days?"

"Oh, Ralph passed on three years ago. Had a real nice service—" he interrupted himself, ever so slightly chagrined—"If I do say so, myself. Circumstances aside, Miz Mutter, I'd be lyin' if I said I wasn't glad you and

Hattie are back home again."

"*Home,*" Pearl repeated slowly. Suddenly, she was standing and making an effort to pull Staci up. Staci was willing but had to keep an arm back to cradle a startled Josh.

"Granddaughter, how'd you like to take a little ride down the road with me?"

"Gran?"

Pearl didn't wait. "Will, what'd you bring today—van or hearse?"

"I've got the panel truck, Pearl. We save the hearse for burials."

"Does it have windows?"

"Only in the back doors, but they're heavily tinted."

"Got room in the back for anybody besides Hattie?"

"Not to sit, but there's leftover floor space, once the gurney's in. Why?"

Pearl, to Pete: "Think Will can get his wagon close enough so's Hattie can get in there privately?"

"Not through the parlor," replied Pete. "We could get him around the side to the break between Buildings A and B, though."

Pearl squeezed Staci's hand. "Anything in that car out there you can't part with?"

"I—I guess not..." Staci paused, then straightened herself. "Matter of fact, not one goddamned thing!" Her hand fluttered to her mouth in surprise until she saw her grandmother's grin.

"Well, then hitch Josh up; we've got a lot to talk about. Barney, get our bags from the bedroom, please?" *Barney!* "Barney, did you want to come—"

"Naw, Pearl—but thanks just the same. Me'n Pete been talkin'. He says he can use a driver to run errands and such, for room and board. I'm old enough to handle a car but too old to handle the girls." He smiled. "Pete says it'd be like ancient times, havin' a *Eunice* around to tend the harem. Best thing is, I wouldn't be a burden to the God-fearin' nor the Medi-Cal anymore."

Pearl spun Barney gaily around. "Barney Rasmussen, you're the best goddamned wheel man I've ever seen—and a true friend. I get in a scrape again, I'll know right where to turn!" He blushed with pleasure.

Pearl turned and kissed Pete on the neck. "Caswell P. Collier, you're a wonder, and I'm grateful. If I was a 25-year-old man I'd spend every other paycheck up here. Now go on and clear out any judges or politicians you got left back there before Capt. Hutchinson gets back. And, you can tell him for me that if anybody still wants to press charges, he knows where I live."

Cashwell P. FoXXX, flesh merchant, found himself a little choked up. "Will do, Pearl."

Arm in arm, Pearl and Staci walked the hallway toward where the van was.

"What do you want to be when you grow up, girl?"

"Artist, I think—though Daddy always thought that idea frivolous."

"Huh! Feels the same way about runnin' steers, even though it fed *him* pretty well. How about waitress or maybe cowgirl for a little while, just to hold the ends together? Lived in or sold, I'll bet my half of the 'Diamond M' will be worth a lot of paint and brushes one day."

Staci stopped, clasped her hands behind Pearl's neck and kissed her forehead. "We're a pair, ain't we, Gran?"

Pearl pinched her granddaughter's cheeks. "Not yet, honey—but we will be!"

&⊃○&

7 **Medalists**

He noticed her first while on the Stairmaster in the hotel's fitness room. (In truth, she may have noticed him then, too—or before. Selfish indifference and no eye contact were strict guidelines in these preliminaries.)

She staked herself to a treadmill and removed her Reebok Hipster warm-ups. *Nice*, he thought. *Champion JogBra, Chickabiddy Retro Boardshorts, Nike cross-trainers; athletically stylish. Jewelry. Eye and lip liner. A player.*

He'd claimed the spa when she emerged again, after changing. As she busied herself with a deliberate deck shower, he updated the inventory. *Black mesh, high-cut Polo tank—Caesarian? Stretch marks? No breast cups; outstanding nipples. Quality salon tan, no lines. Subtle—therefore, expensive—surgical enhancements: nose, lips, gluteals. Breasts? Can't tell; good contours. Why leave the weaker jaw line? Interesting. Above-average manicure and pedicure.*

He feigned interest in the pool rules as she lowered herself into the sanitized froth. Their heads and eyes moved in non-synchronous orbits. *Wait. Wait. Now.* Discreetly, he tucked in his TYR Heatwaves Male Racers to accentuate his genitals. He stood, grasped the

---

handrail and climbed, hesitating on the top step. Slowly, his eyes moved to her fingertips, lingered at her tennis bracelet, and glided up her arm into her pupils. *Violet—real, or lenses?*

"Cartier?"

She smiled, holding his gaze, but did not reply. *My contact. Your move.*

හිෆ

She was already there, conducting business, when he met his own clients that evening. He'd confirmed the sighting by doing a men's room fly-by, two tables away. *Evening Business Utility: DKNY separates; DvF fragrance; pearl choker and matching bracelet. Gucci sling-backs. Coach briefcase.* She feigned interest in her dinner partner's tabletop electronics.

No further intelligence to be gathered through the meal, since their table was out of his seated line of sight. He disguised his slight alcohol intake with accustomed ease. His own commerce concluded with light, conversational cuddling to take the edge off the deal making. He called an end to it, got up, and walked his *confreres* out toward the valet desk, leaving his paraphernalia behind. He loitered politely, bid them away, and turned to see her disappearing into an elevator. Withholding judgment, he went back into the restaurant and over to his table. There it was, under his Dunhill cigarillos—a magnetic key-card, with a room number in neat cursive applied to it. *Mont Blanc Meisterstuck Classique Rollerball, fine,* he guessed. *Game on.*

To give her time to prepare the home field, he lingered in his room over his own physical pre-routine. He reviewed the relevant data in the elevator on the way up, before devising his own strategy. *Thirty-one, tops— eight, 10-year difference. Five-four, in the 108-112 range. Thirty on the treadmill this morning, then a full circuit. High rep-to-resistance ratio. No cocktails and no wine on the table, that I could see.*

Before knocking, he laid an ear on the door. Silence. No TV, no tinny clock radio, no imported background. He rapped twice, slid the key-card through the reader, and entered. In the half-light cast through the open bathroom door, a balmy breeze billowed the sheers away from the half-open slider. He could make out two snifters, each with an inch of Esteve Très Vieux, on the nearer night table. The only other illumination came from a desk lamp in the sitting half of the suite. He swept his eyes toward it.

She was at the Queen Anne desk, just hanging up. She regarded him briefly over her Armani readers before sliding the Mont Blanc slowly from her encircling lips and laying it on the notepad. The spectacles followed.

Ah, the old "business-to-pleasure" lead-in. Grrl Power!

She pushed back and tossed her freckle-dusted leg over the chair's arm, dangling a Gucci off her stocking-less toes. The hip-length, crimson kimono she wore retreated, revealing a neat, rust-colored pubic triangle.

I'll be damned—a real redhead!

She arose, languidly, and the kimono's tie slipped away, baring her abdomen.

No   scars   or   stretch   marks,   after   all. Understatement—I like that.

The wrap slid to her elbows. Her breasts were displayed in a Cosmetic Blush Bali Enchantress—just enough lace over mesh to reveal her wide areolas and, again, those magnificent, caramel nipples.

Just a soupçon of fantasy. Nice touch.

She approached, hands on hips.

"Your call."

"Oh—you mean rules?"

"Yes; you opened, so you get to call it. Domestic or international?"

He searched her face in vain for any hint of

predisposition. "Domestic."

There it was. No meditative Tantric preliminaries, no Kama Sutra contortioning. Regulation foreplay—give or take—and straight-up coitus. Strength and stamina over sensitivity.

She retrieved the cognac and handed him one.

"A toast," she said. "To the contest."

"The contest."

Hers disappeared in a gulp, as if a challenge. He stared, took a healthy draught, and set the snifters down.

Still expressionless, she knelt on the bed, unhooked and shed her bra, and pivoted, hands on thighs. He fished for a condom and threw it on the night table, then stripped to his RIPS Coutoure Mesh Briefs (black only), a bit too snug for everyday wear. He faced her.

She lunged.

Oh, no you don't! Deftly, he gripped behind her knees and flipped her on her back. Before she could react, he elevated her hips, clamped his fingers on her buttocks and buried his face in her pubic mound. Once secured, he slid his hands up her sides and began caressing her breasts and teasing her nipples with his fingertips, as he lapped furiously at her labia and clitoris. She writhed and clawed at losing the advantage but couldn't reach him. He worked methodically, driving a wedge of pleasure into her resolve. When he sensed that her pelvic cycling had taken firmer hold of her, he moved around her thigh so he could massage her G-spot and rectum while continuing his lingual stimulation. At that, she hooked a thumb in his garment and tore it away. "You're not the biggest, are you?" she gasped. "And circumcised!"

I thought so. First, the direct approach—no acute visual or mental stimulation. Then alcohol. Now insults. He'd constructed a theory that she had tried to arrange things to make him last longer than he otherwise would—maybe to use him as a mere tune-up, for a showdown with a younger competitor. Now she was behind, and panicky.

"Time out!" He tore open the packet and sheathed his weapon. *Time to reverse field.*

He surprised her again by rolling onto his back and pulling her onto him, which forced her on the offensive. She oscillated slowly, almost reluctantly, and rode forward on him to reduce her stimulation level. *Delay of game!* Bracing her hips, he rocked upward until he felt his feet hit the floor. He whirled, dropped her on her back and clamped her thighs tight against his chest. He leaned onto her to assure maximum glans and shaft contact, grinding and thrusting confidently. He watched her eyes widen, then saw a final determination take over her face. She set her jaw and Kegeled him fiercely.

WOW! Now, for an instant, he was taken aback—and impressed. *The Abyssinian Milkmaid Maneuver. Good thing I remembered the de-sensitizing cream. Age and treachery beat youth and inexperience every time, baby!*

It wasn't working for her, and the pace of her breathing told him she was close.

He's at the 15... the 10...the 5...

She grasped at the sheets and shrieked.

Touchdown!

He was gracious. He dropped into the Missionary and she obliged him by rocking along until he finished. He rolled off and dressed quickly while she got up and completed the scorecard. She hurried through the checks and scratches and held it out to him.

"Hmmm—9.4. Generous, but you didn't factor in the age handicap. That would take me up around, oh, 9.65?"

Impassively, she rechecked, re-totaled, and handed it back. He took it and stuck out his right hand, smiling.

"Good game."

℘∞℘

The flight back was unremarkable. The valet delivered the Jaguar XK8 and stowed his cases in the boot. A generous tip, then the drive home.

"Daddy!"

Dashiell and Lillian, his perfect twins, hugged his legs.

"Hi, kids. Now, go find Nanny."

The Swede appeared. He pecked at her.

"Astrid—sweetheart."

"Welcome home, darling."

Consuéla's Southwestern offering was satisfying. He crawled onto their California King and lay naked, enjoying it as Astrid dried herself gracefully. She finished her preparations and slipped under the sheet from her side.

He mused. *Old girl's held up pretty damned well, considering. Pity she's not in the game.* He felt momentary guilt for taking her as a Procreator.

"How rude of me," he said. "How was your day?"

She lay away from him a little, on her side. "Home-theater-installer—huge, but unschooled. 9.8."

"Congratulations. Personal best, right?"

"Yes. G'Night."

He took in the darkening ceiling and drowsed.

What a life...

8 **Meridian**

ഇരു

Light came over him, slow, dappled, and indistinct.

It was the gauze that bordered his eyes thickly, along with a single layer draped loosely over them, which accounted for the lack of luminary definition. It seemed the strongest source was to his left. He turned in that direction; hot pain shot from his trapezoids through the cords in his neck to his temples. Its shock tensed him and the exertion, combined with his drugged and weakened state, relaxed him just as abruptly.

"Brace own yuh nehck."

Startled, he tried to focus on the area from which the words had bolted, somewhere just above and beyond his feet. His pupils fought with the cotton web, laboring to make out the high-contrast details of the figure seated against the wall. *Hat?* As he groped for more data within the "thing-on-top-of-human" concept, he catalogued its details. Construction: textured substance, dark lines cross-hatched against general gray; protuberance above...*face?* Its rear half was encircled by a loose flap tied up into the top-center. Below the face, a garment similar in coloration but less severely textured covered the upper limbs; the center torso was interrupted by a dark, heavy panel supported by metal clasps and thin straps of the same fabric as the panel. Some kind of framed-glass object was partially hidden by a stitched-on enclosure. The bed rail behind his feet masked everything below there. His attention drifted upward. Wide dark eyes shone beneath full, angled brows as light as the gauze framing them, against darker, deeply lined leather. Thegrizzle of high contrast mustache and stubble and a halo of thick hair hugging the head under the hat completed the picture. The lips parted and a tongue wagged out of the darkness between rows of brilliant ivory.

"Thet aron thang keep yuh head fum toinin' round. Much payn?"

I...don't...understand. He signaled an extremity and a...*hand*?...appeared before his face. He turned it slowly, wiggling its fleshy digits arrythmically. *Left?* Through them he saw the figure glance in that direction and rise abruptly. Pressed into its thick middle was a zippered bag, its dual handles looped around hands and wrists for...*why?* He tried to track the movement but another stab of pain put his lights out.

The sensations of warm breath and cool taps against the gauze at his temples revived him. His eyelids fluttered. He started and recoiled slightly until he managed to focus on a pair of rich umber irises and black pupils; they receded, joined by soft angular facial bones and a full smile.

"Don't pay him no mind; he's crazy." She arose from his side, dark hair falling away from her bosom. The starched cap distracted him until she straightened fully; he traced her from her shimmering hairline to her slender waist. Ganglia came to pleasing life in the center of his body, giving him confidence that at least one piece had been added back to his puzzle.

"Can you talk yet?"

Talk?

She touched his barely exposed lips gently. That sensation activated another sector and he heard himself rasping. She tapped his lips again and wagged a finger. He stopped.

"That's all right; let's not rush it. I know you're in a lot of pain." He watched her turn a translucent dial on a snake of tubing above his head. She smiled broadly again and a warmth bathed his sharpened present. *Hopeful?*

"You rest now." She placed two fingers against his wrist and looked at the metallic object on her own. She turned and he followed the rhythm of gluteals undulating beneath her uniform skirt; his pubic nerve endings fired again. After she was gone, he turned away and wallowed in this state of satisfied confusion until the edges bled away into narcotized slumber.

ℰℭ

Another specter came into his focus—different. The effect was startling, since it became apparent to him that the gauze had been removed. Her hair was shiny black too, but there was no cap and her face, while pleasant enough, was broader with flatter features. He felt her rough, strong fingers creep past his cheekbones and down the sides of his neck. Her palms slid across his shoulders, their warmth penetrating the gown; she monitored his eyes and facial muscles for sensation. She seemed satisfied. She arose and receded toward his feet, gently uncovering them. He lifted his head slightly to watch and was surprised, happily—no pain. His range of motion told him that the metal appliance was gone, too. He felt himself smiling as he caught her thrusting a thumb and forefinger at his left heel pad. An electric charge shot up his leg and flashed hot in his frontal lobes.

She studied him. "You felt that? Good."

Good?! Shit—OW!

She played off his scowl. "What I mean is, you have feeling in your extremities. No paralysis. That's good.

Doctor wasn't sure; said your spinal cord was pretty bruised." She noted his uncertainty and came to his side again. Her upper thigh made contact with his, warming it as she sat. Smiling, she lifted his hand and pulled its digits gently; his registration made her smile broadly. "I'm Coretta, the physical therapist—leastways, what passes for one around here. We're going to work together to try to get you back on your feet." She squeezed his other hand. "Do you remember anything about the accident?"

Accident?

A jumble of partially-assembled images played nonsense in his head, nothing amounting to a full concept. He saw—*Coretta?*—reach above him for the valve and within moments those indistinct structures melted away like a child's unfinished sand castle in surf.

80CR

"John?"

He stirred. *John? Who's John?*

It was Apparition Number Two. He was pleased. "Hi—I'm Rosa. How are you feeling?"

"Am—" The throaty fullness of the word brought him up short. "Am I, 'John?'"

Her laugh was what music must be, he thought. She covered her mouth momentarily, embarrassed at the breach in her professionalism. "No; that's just what we call you, or anyone else that we can't identify: 'John Doe.' Do you know what your name is?"

"John" shook his head, gravely.

"Let's try something." Rosa reached into the nightstand drawer and produced a framed object. She pushed it toward him until her face was edged out by the reflected growth of another. Aside from the freakish sutures that snaked around his forehead and across the bridge of his nose and an eye socket the color of an eggplant, he found himself drawn to what he saw. Light, mottled skin, close-cropped hair, and pale-bright eyes were visible there. John watched them cloud as any association he'd expected failed him. She lowered the mirror and the sight of his disappointment defeated her expectation as well.

"Worth a try," she said softly as she laid the glass aside. "You talked a lot in your sleep last night. Do you remember?"

"N-No. What did I say?"

"Nothing worth repeating."

He studied the room as if for the first time. "How long have I been here?"

"Six days."

"How did I get here? That other girl said 'accident.'"

"Ambulance brought you. Your car slipped off the highway in the rain last Saturday evening, dozen or so miles north of here, and rolled over. This was the closest place, given your condition." She looked again for any glimmer. He shrugged.

"Good afternoon, Mr.—?" A tall, white-coated man appeared in the doorway and glanced at Rosa, his eyebrows raised. She shook her head. "—Doe. How are we feeling today?" Close dark hair salted with gray framed his head, as did the mustache surrounding another expansive smile with strong teeth.

Terminally confused—and you?

"I'm Doctor Dunbar. Stitched you up last weekend, up to the limits of a General Surgeon's abilities. Since then, we've just watched and waited to see what Nature brings." Glancing at the parti-colored digits and squiggles on the vitals monitor, he unpocketed a fluoroscope and peered into John's eyes and ears. Seizing his hands, he drew John's arms parallel in front of him and manipulated them like jump ropes. He moved down the bed and tapped the cartilages below his patient's kneecaps until they jerked. He pulled back the sheet and knifed John's arches with the edge of his hand. John felt the concussions dart from the brow of his skull back toward his ears.

"Well, sir; I'd say we're about ready to get you on your feet, if you're up to it. I'm going to ask Nurse Scott here to dial down the painkillers a bit so's you can get a better idea how you really feel. I'll check in tomorrow."

"What happened to my face?"

"Hit that air bag pretty hard, you did. Lacerations—cuts—accounted for by partial roof collapse and flying glass in the rollovers. Other than that, you were pretty lucky. That seatbelt held you in tight; bruised clavicle and pelvis was the worst you got from that." Dr. Dunbar leaned in a little and modulated his voice. "Truth is, that nippin' flask he—they—found under the seat helped keep you relaxed. Good thing it was late and that passerby wasn't the law." He winked.

John grinned a little, not fully understanding why. "What about my memory?"

Dr. Dunbar scratched his head. "How long you been here?"

"Six days; but what—?"

"See, you've got short-term retention and that's good. What it is, is traumatic amnesia—total memory loss caused by sudden shock and physical injury. I could explain it better if I was a brain doctor. Best we can do is get you clear-headed and moving around some and see what develops after that. Could be that some association might trigger a longer-term memory function. Give it three or four weeks; if there's no improvement by then I'll make some calls down south to see about a neurological consult. Meantime, you just focus on getting better."

"What is this place?"

"Convalescent center," the doctor said. "Ambulance took you to Jeff Anderson. I was on call and had you transferred here when you stabilized."

"Where?"

"Meridian." Dr. Dunbar paused. "Mississippi. Accident happened partway up 19 near Okatibbee

Lake." Another pause; he and the nurse traded glances. "You were headed here from Philadelphia, apparently."

"Oh." John blanked.

Dunbar motioned at Rosa with his head and they adjourned to the open doorway, whispering.

"I've directed Nurse Scott to leave that drip open enough to give you one more good night of knockout sleep." Doctor and nurse departed; over his shoulder he said, "Courage, Mr. Doe. Time is on our side."

₧ℂ

John sagged at his armpits over the parallel bars, panting and aching from every pore; the area between his hip sockets and slippers was jelly.

"C'mon, John; two more steps and we'll call it a day." Coretta stood at the end, beckoning him with both hands.

"Oh, Jesus, Coretta—it hurts so bad..."

Coretta flushed and straightened up. "If you'd call His name in a helpful rather than a hurtful way, you'd be dancin' by Friday night, I guarantee."

"Who?"

Coretta's lacquered nails flashed against her white hips. "Our Lord Jesus Christ, is who!"

"I'm sorry, Coretta," John said, puzzled. "I don't..."

She thrust her arms skyward, then out, moving toward him. "Of course you don't, honey, and I am powerfully sorry." She pushed herself between the bars and clasped her muscular forearms around his upper back. As she started to lurch him to his wheelchair and he tried gamely to shuffle, John looked into her unblinking eyes. He couldn't name what he saw but it was bottomless and unflinching. They reached the chair and paused, breathing hard and leaning into each other; Coretta recovered and set the wheel brakes. John fell back into the webbing. Still fighting for oxygen, his eyes wandered around her middle edge. There, peering into the PT room from the darker hallway, was Apparition Number One—hat; teeth; coveralls; and gym bag, still clutched to his sagging midsection by gnarled, bony fingers. John pushed with both arms against the side rails and raised himself on the chair's foot pegs, at which point he weakened and tipped himself and the chair toward Coretta. She caught him in mid-crouch and battled his dead weight back into the vehicle. John strained to see around her.

"Who *is* that?"

Coretta patted his thighs to assure herself that he was stable, then turned around. "I don't see nobody."

"An old man—with a bag; I saw him when I woke up."

"Oh, him." Coretta chuckled and waved dismissively. "That's just ol' Freddy Dee. Don't pay him no mind; he crazy."

℘℘℘

John frowned at the tray on the bed table bridging his legs—not because the appearance and smells were unpleasant but because he had no names for two of the items.

"What's the matter, John? Lunch taste bad?" Rosa had come noiselessly to his side again; he was no longer taken aback when she materialized.

"Naw—especially since I still got no frame of reference, mostly. Meat's good. Greens are okay." He tapped the shimmering cube on its own plate with his spoon. "What's this called?"

"Jell-O." Rosa smiled. "Inpatient facilities are famous for it."

"'Inpatient?'"

"Like hospitals and this place—where you have to stay overnight and can't go home until you're better." Rosa covered her mouth.

Home. At this stage, hearing the word put John beyond wistfulness, on a progressive scale toward anger.

He abandoned the Jell-O and raked his fork through a glutinous pile next to the Salisbury steak. "And this?"

"Now, John." Rosa wagged her finger playfully and with purpose. "You're a son of the South. How can you not know what *that* is?"

John gave her a hard look. "I'd guess, if I had any options."

"You're right; I'm sorry. It's grits. Stone-ground corn—usually hybrid white, or sometime hominy—water-soaked and pan-fried. Some folks like 'em with just butter; others like gravy or syrup. You tried 'em yet?"

He drew in a forkful-plus with his lips. It leveled out in his mouth, bathing his taste buds and salivary glands. John cocked his head in anticipation, then grappled for the spoon as a rivulet coursed out the corner of his mouth and down his chin. He found Rosa and spoke gamely around the gob as he fought to swallow. "Shoot—guess I'm a Southerner, all right!"

Rosa laughed gaily, seized his face in her hands, and kissed his cheek with no hesitation. He felt the lubricious warmth irradiate his jaw and, as she drew back—trapped between pleasure and shock—John pushed an index finger through the glossy smudge and touched his own lips.

"Dee-licious."

෩

John decided to strike out, instead of waiting for Coretta after breakfast, like always. He felt good and the combination of close supervision, isolation, and the static landscape of the courtyard outside his window had made him restless. He slid his feet into his slippers and headed for the hook where his robe was. As he closed it and tied the sash, he studied the wheelchair; he was walking with increasing confidence but Coretta still required him to use it as an aid. *Screw the chair.* He opened his door quietly and stuck an eye just past the jamb. It was still too early for meal service, so the long spoke of a hallway stretching away from his outward end toward the staff hub was quiet and lifeless. He stepped out, turned, and started through the antiseptic dimness toward the dull fluorescence ahead of him—keeping his outstretched left arm just a hand's width from the waist-high coving, in case. Unlike when Coretta was along, the doors of the rooms he passed were ajar and every one he looked into was vacant. That surprised him; he'd assumed that behind every closed door was another like him, searching for that which had been lost or taken by accident. His shuffling startled a janitor backing out of a closet and steering a mop bucket. He looked John up and down but said nothing, opting to study in succession the keys that jangled on the ring tethered to his belt.

"Does this place have a name?"

The young custodian's eyes seemed sad beyond his years to John. "Yup. Chaney."

"Is—or was—that a person?"

"Guess so."

"Who was he, or she?"

"Don't rightly know; before my time. 'S'cuse me; got work to do." With that, he showed John his back and made for one of the other hallways.

John shrugged and continued. He edged a little closer to the wall to get the maximum angle on peering into the nurse's station without being detected. *Good.* The front counter was uncovered; the door to the rear office was open and the light was on but he heard no noise or conversation. He edged by, his eyes fixed on the station.

"Mornin'."

Jesus Christ! Even in Coretta's absence, John was glad he didn't blurt it out this time. He relaxed a little and looked into the face of a rangy stranger, also in sleepwear. Huge smile; sturdy teeth.

"Cain't sleep. You?"

"Guess not. Beginning to think I was the only inmate here."

"Naw; they's a mess a folks on my wing. Full, I reckon. You all by yo'self?"

"Well—not anymore."

"Breakfus' ain't for another hour. You want to come over to our day room and listen to the teevee? Maybe get some news—no trouble ef I keep it down low."

John was perplexed. "'Tee-Vee?'"

Baritone laughter boiled out of his new acquaintance. "You serious? They got you locked up down there, boy?"

"Mr. Doe!" They turned to see a rotund nurse charging out from behind the counter. "Doctor doesn't want you out of your room without supervision." She hooked John by the arm and pointed at the other man. "Ephraim, you go on back to your own room; we'll talk directly about whether you forgot your meds again last night. Go on, now." She shooed him away with her free hand; the old man bade John *adieu* with his eyes and backed away, muttering.

The duty nurse hustled John back down into exile, relieved him of his robe and slippers, and stood guard as he stretched himself out on the bed. "I'll let Nurse Scott know you've been up and around," she said with some foreboding, and left.

John sat up, brooding. *Tee-Vee. Tee-Vee?* Not a glimmer.

Rosa appeared. "Hey, Ulysses. Find what you were after?"

"You—who?"

"Never mind, for now. Are you all right?"

"What's 'Tee-Vee?'"

Rosa sighed. "Television. Visual entertainment—and information, if you're determined or lucky. Doctor Dunbar doesn't want to risk overstimulating you until he's satisfied you're physically recovered. Like he said, could be a matter of weeks or more."

John clenched his jaw. "But, I'm—"

"Bored?"

"If that means nervous and fitful inside, yes."

"Doctor had a suggestion for when you reached this stage. Wait here." She rounded the corner.

"'Wait here,'" John sulked. "Good one, Miss Rosa."

She returned with a thick paperbound volume in her hand and gently placed it in his. "Here."

He tested its heft. "What's this?"

"A book for you to read; a novel." She anticipated his response. "A long, made-up story. *The Adventures of Tom Sawyer*, it's called."

"What's it about?"

"Life, long ago and not so far away. Some folks call it a children's book. You can read it and tell me what *you* think."

છ૦ભ

Rosa helped John into his jacket and zipped hers. Hands on hips, she surveyed him with satisfaction. "You make a dashing figure in jeans and boots, sir."

John swiveled, arms out, like he was trying to locate a flying parasite. "Are these my clothes?"

"They are, now!"

"But—I mean..."

"Oh. No; those were cut away in the emergency room."

"Does anyone still have them?"

"Don't know."

"Were there any, you know..."

"Personal effects? Not that I know of—they might have been left in the car or the ambulance."

He looked at her, disparaged.

"I know, John; it's very frustrating for you. I'll see if I can find out, all right?"

He nodded toward the floor.

She cleared her throat. "Ready?"

"Won't know until I'm in it, I guess."

Rosa clutched at his arm. "Come on. The car's right outside the front door."

She hustled him down the hall, through the hub, and toward the harsh security-lamp glow in front. John peered into the dim light behind the closed double doors masking the other hallways. "Is there anyone here besides the staff, that other fella, and me?"

She tugged at him, scanning behind her nervously. "It's late, John...curfew. The other patients are in their rooms. Please. We have to go now—or not at all."

"But...the doors. I didn't see..."

They careened into the night. John looked up and around. "I don't understand why we couldn't go in the daytime."

"John!" she hissed, holding the passenger door open and shaking her keys. "We're—I'm not supposed to be doing this *at all*. I'm trying to help you; I could lose my job."

"Okay. Okay."

John admired the stars, shimmering and barely distinct through the windshield, as they wheeled through darkened neighborhoods. The spaced punctuation of street lights forced his attention out the side windows. "I see lights on but nobody's out. Why?"

Rosa focused ahead of her. "It's nearing 10 PM on a Sunday night—a school night. This is a small town, John. Church-goin' folks are in with their kids, reading bed-time stories and hearing prayers."

"No 'Tee-Vee?'"

She relented and smiled a crack. "Oh, yeah. I suppose 'Tee-Vee.' Lots of 'Tee-Vee.'"

"Why don't I get it? Ephraim said he does."

The crack closed. "We've been all over this. Ephraim has his memory, mostly. You don't, yet. Confusion causes stress, which could make things worse for you."

They continued in silence until Rosa hit Route 19 and turned northwest. John scratched his face and dug into his breast pocket, producing the paperback. "Speaking of children..."

Rosa eyed it and him. "So, you finished it?"

"Yes." He set it on his thigh and tapped it deliberately. "Tom, Becky, and Huck. Which one do you think I was like, at their age?"

"Not Becky, I hope..."

John roared; she joined him, perforating the tension.

"No. What I meant was, *that* girl was a serious pain; I don't know what Tom saw in her." Her eyes glistened at him in oncoming headlights. "I'd reckon you were more like Huck."

"What—like less thoughtful and more impulsive than Tom?"

"Uh-huh."

"How long ago did this take place?"

"Hundred fifty years, give or take."

"Was it really like that?"

"You mean, life in general? Oh, yeah." She nodded to herself. "Too many things ain't changed enough, matter of fact."

"What? I didn't get that last..."

"Nothin'." She concentrated up the highway.

John rolled his tongue around in his mouth, thinking. "What's a 'nigger?'"

She turned. "It's—was a term that some folks used to refer to other folks." Rosa stared, waiting.

"Were they different from the folks who used the word?"

"In some ways—mostly not; just in status and regard."

"Were they royalty?"

"The 'niggers?!'" Rosa screeched with laughter, startling John. "Why do you think that?"

"Well..." He hunted for a dog-eared page. "Tom talks about them like they're wise and true and Huck thinks they're liable to be liars—but Huck has a low opinion of *everybody* in authority. Later, he says he likes the nigger Uncle Jake because he doesn't act 'above' him—

you know, like a king, right? Here—" He laid it open. "Tom's talking about 'that old humpbacked Richard' who's a king in Europe, and Huck asks what his full name is and Tom says kings only have one name. Then, Huck says he doesn't want to be a king if he only has one name, like a 'nigger.' Ergo, one name equals royalty."

"No." She shook her head gently. "'Niggers' didn't have surnames—like 'John *Doe*'—because their families were broken up. Folks who called 'em that *owned* 'em, bought and sold like cattle."

John was dumbstruck and Rosa saw it. "See, now— you're confused. Let's talk about *Tom Sawyer* later." She reached for the radio. "I'll put on some music." A compact disc spun up and a languid, throaty alto floated out in mid-song, seducing John's confusion away.

"Who's that?"

"That's 'Lady Day'—Billie Holiday."

"May I?" John reached into the space beneath the player and found the jewel case. He studied the woman on the cover, seeing an object in her hair, a comely sadness in her eyes, and a brilliant but tentative smile.

"What's that in her hair?"

Rosa squinted. "A flower—magnolia, I expect."

Turning the glassine wafer over, he ran down the song titles. "Hm."

"What?"

"Intriguing title: 'Strange Fruit.' What's it about?"

"Don't push so hard; just sit back and listen." She shifted in her seat. "When it comes on and you've heard it, we can talk about it."

He obeyed, with anticipation. The tune was two cuts away when he felt the car slowing. Rosa steered to a stop on the shoulder.

"Right about here. Take a look."

"This is where the accident was?"

"Pretty close, according to the accident report."

John powered the window down and stuck his face into the balmy air. "Pretty dark."

"Happened about this time; thought that might be helpful. Want to get out?"

John nodded and slid out. As he stood he caught the Milky Way at the horizon bisecting the night sky like a faceted bracelet on indigo velvet. He followed it upward and overhead until he was nearly dizzy. "Wow."

Rosa's chin rested atop the car, on her crossed arms. "Yes, sir."

Their distance from the city lights and a strong moon brought everything in front of him into sharper relief. "What am I looking at?"

"That's the Lake, itself—reservoir, really. Man-made, behind a dam."

"Huge."

"'Most 30 miles of shoreline, they say. Those lights you see are campgrounds. Folks come from all over to boat, hunt, and fish, too."

"Why?"

"Take in God's creation, I expect—same as you, right now."

John shoved his hands into his pockets and rocked onto his toes. Arching his shoulders, he inhaled. "What am I smelling?"

"Oh, probably southern magnolia and trumpet honeysuckle." She raised her nose. "Maybe a hint of piney woods in there."

Rosa saw John's head slip toward his chest and he fell silent and motionless. Concerned, she came around the car and touched his arm. He turned, his eyes shimmering.

"It's all so...beautiful."

She slipped her arm into his, gently. "Yes, it is."

He swallowed. "I wish—I wish I was part of it, that I *belonged* to it."

She watched her free hand push his hair behind his ear. "You will; I promise."

His look said he wanted to believe her but couldn't, yet. Rosa blinked the doubt away. "C'mon. Let's cross over to where it happened."

They hustled across the thoroughfare and stopped where the shoulder dropped away. Still clutching his arm, she turned south and strained to see as a pair of passing headlights bathed the ground ahead of them. Suddenly she pointed. "There!"

Rosa dragged him another 30 yards. Two elongated ruts appeared, cut into the rough grass and ironweed and snaking down into a cut. She stepped into one and guided him into the other; together they picked their way down deeper into taller grass and brambles. They came upon a flattened area that looked like an elephant had thrown itself into a thicket of holly, mountain laurel, and sassafras. Rosa stopped and dropped his arm. "Here. Close your eyes."

John did. A series of strobe flashes blew through his head at crazy angles in a fixed frame—crystal droplets darting into corners; a buckling yellow "Caution' sign; flying clumps of filamented matter; exploding glass. The frame bent in on itself and collapsed into darkness. Parts, but no sum.

"Anything?"

John shook his head fiercely, his white-knuckled fists at his chest.

She took him in hand again. "Well, let's go, then. No point in getting any more upset."

After she'd swung her sedan around and pointed it toward a faintly luminous Meridian, she monitored John in silence as, slumped against his door, he vacantly dragged a finger through the condensation on his window. Finally, she sighed.

"Time to get you home."

"HOME!" He lunged toward her, seizing her wrist. "YES! Take me there!"

She recoiled and tugged her forearm free. "I AM!"

"No—take me to *your* home!"

Rosa glowered, her eyes wide and her arm still elevated.

"I'm sorry, Rosa. I'm just so...*frustrated.* Alone in that prison cell for days on end, everyone tiptoeing around and looking sideways at the Mystery Man. Nobody around to tell me anything about myself. I need to *see* things until I can remember something— *anything*—that makes *sense* to me!"

Some of the iron came out of her eyes, but her jaw remained set.

John threw his arm over the back of the seat and moved his other hand deliberately toward her shoulder. Watching it make soft contact with the skin over her clavicle, much of the tension left her.

"I need to connect with people—like you. Kind people; patient people. I need to see where people are, and what they do." He made random circles with his nails. "Please, Rosa."

She drove, her eyes dead ahead. "If I do this, you cannot tell anyone at the center. Do you understand?"

"I really don't see—"

"D o—y o u—u n d e r s t a n d?"

He nodded and folded his hands in his lap and stayed that way until they hit town. Rosa didn't remain on 19 long, turning off into a neighborhood of nondescript tract homes. John calculated that they weren't all that far from Chaney. She pulled over and parked in the middle of a block, in front of an unpretentious single-story bungalow. It was faded but neat and the landscaping, though spare, was kept up. John tried the handle until he felt her hand on his.

"Just a minute; let me get the door." She gathered her things from behind the seat, digging her keys from her handbag as she arose. As she trotted up the walk on her toes to minimize heel noise, Rosa looked up and down the street. She fumbled the door open and motioned to him from just inside the door frame. His uncertain pace made her anxious. "Hurry!"

As soon as he hit the porch she reached out and jerked him inside, closing the door forcefully behind him and snapping the deadbolt. She busied herself with her parcels and mail. "Make yourself to home," she muttered.

He took it in. The living room suite was venerable—heavy on the brocade with those lacey, doily things favored by well-mannered but practical ladies pinned to the arms and headrests. He imagined that Rosa was not the first owner, and it nagged at him that at some point in his past he had dangled his bare legs and Buster Browns from furnishings very much like these. Threadbare spots in the aged wall-to-wall carpet peeked from under strategic and poorly matched remnants serving as runners. The old-fashioned rocker in the corner with the ruffled pastel cushions fairly beckoned, so John answered. Settling in, he closed his eyes and tried to imagine himself as Tom Sawyer in Becky Thatcher's parlor, in latter-day clothes; the thought and the sweet disorientation brought on by the slow rhythm nudged him toward giddiness. He came out of it and met the blank, glassy stare of an angular black box smack in front of him. He looked at Rosa quizzically.

"'Tee-Vee.'"

He scrambled out of the rocker to pursue the discovery but was drawn away by a pair of framed portraits hanging on the wall above the device.

"Who are they?"

"The one on the left is Jesus Christ. Bible say he the Son of God, sent by his Father to free mankind from his sinfulness by dying on the cross and rising up again." She leaned against a battered credenza while he ruminated, at once hoping for and fearing some sign of recognition. Nothing emerged.

John examined the broad, squarish head, slightly mustachioed and with close, tight curls, of a man with penetrating but comfortable brown eyes. "And this one?"

"Oh, he was a disciple of Jesus. Tried to lead his people to freedom using His teachings. He was murdered, too."

"Did he rise up again?"

"No; couldn't—just a man. What he said and did—what he stood for—will live within some of us forever."

Agitated by the whirling fragments in his head, John grasped at his hair and scalp with both hands. "Do you live here by yourself?"

"Yes. Didn't used to but I have, ever since—"

John followed her line of sight to an end table at the other corner, on which was a framed photograph of a dark-eyed younger man, beaming and confident. John was absorbed by it.

"My ex-husband." Rosa sounded far off.

"Where is he now?"

"State prison, in Jackson."

"What did he do?"

Rosa's voice grew wistful and weary. "Not so much what he did as what they said he did. In this place sometime it doesn't make a lick of difference."

"Did you—him and you...?"

"Kids? Naw—no time. He went up barely a year after we were married."

"Can he ever come out?"

"Not likely."

"What happened, I mean...?"

"He divorced me, if that's what you're asking. Told me it'd be better if I forgot all about him. Like that's natural, and easy." Her voice quavered. "Talking about it again makes me wish I was like you right now..."

John stood, feet apart, focused so hard on the manchild's image to find something in it for him that the sound of Rosa's collapse staggered him. She had drawn into a near fetal position and hit the back of the sofa with such force that its front legs left the floor momentarily. Half sitting and leaning, her hands were welded to her face and her torso shuddered under her sobs. Tears forced themselves through her taut fingers like thin pitch through pine bark. Wracked by uncertainty he went to her side. He lifted her cautiously, amazed that her upper arm and shoulder were so cool to the touch, until she rested heavily against him. Gently, he tipped her head over his clavicle and stroked her face and scalp until her racking subsided. The humid vapor from her breathing and secretions enveloped him and he drew it in headily, like a treatment. They sat, wordless and barely stirring, until calm came to them both. John felt for the first time since becoming conscious that he wasn't an unclassified oddity or merely invisible. By and by, the weight of her head came off him and he looked down into her face. He recognized himself in each of her dark irises and sepia pupils; refocusing, he lowered himself entirely into those unblinking wells. While nothing came clearer to him in their inky comfort, he found no barriers.

Sniffling, Rosa cleared her sinuses and throat and pushed herself away. John was transfixed by the resolve creeping into her softened face. She threw a leg over him until astride his thighs and drove him downward with both her hands, until his pelvis was buried where the cushions intersected. He felt paralyzed. Rosa unbuttoned her blouse and freed her breasts, which fell slightly and swayed as if stirred by an orchard breeze as she inched along closer. She ground her pubis into his and raised herself enough to work at his shirt placket. Her engorging nipples hung before him like ripened berries; he partook, and their acrid, salty sweetness nearly put himself outside his own skin. The sting of his teeth on her earned him a guttural yelp of surprise and pleasure. She watched him work, then arched her neck; her lips parted and acquired the sneer that meant good sense, tenderness, and anything else in the way had been overtaken by lust. Rosa crushed John's head into her bosom; he licked and kissed furiously, which fed the carnal hunger growing within him.

Strange fruit; strange fruit...

෫ℭ

Horses...Died on the cross...'Niggers'...Low-hanging fruit...crosses—

"Uhhh!" John sat bolt upright. His rousing faculties told him he was back in bed at the center, in sweat-soaked pajamas. His encrusted eyes and clammy skin felt the morning sun as he groped at the nightstand for the water carafe to chase his cottonmouth. Turning it to his lips, he caught sight of movement at his feet, in the shadow created by the one pulled drape; this distracted him enough to cause liquid to surge past his lips and rush down his face, pooling over the bed pad between his legs. He dabbed at the new reservoir helplessly with the sheet for a moment; he gave that up to scrub away the sediment compromising his vision, with better results.

The shadow stirred and a figure emerged. Here was Apparition Number One again; the face was unmistakable but the presentation was entirely new. The ratty flannel hunter's cap John had labored to classify was replaced by a small-brimmed Dobbs hat made of Panama straw, worn at a jaunty angle. Work shirt and coveralls gave way to a well-worn navy Polyester suit with high-contrast white stitching. A broad, paisley tie, thickly knotted at his wattled throat, stood out against a boiled and starched white shirt. A burgundy kerchief in the same pattern as the tie rode alongside in his breast pocket. There was the damned bag, front and center, slung between two gold and rhinestone cufflinks. The old, stooped gentleman shuffled a bowlegged step or two closer in his patent-leather, burgundy-and-cream Bostonians. He drew himself up and regarded John as dispassionately as his smoldering eyes would allow. John couldn't avoid the impression of a fierce predator high in a regal and distant oak, buffeted by time but deep-rooted.

John spoke first. "You're 'Freddy Dee?'"

The man swatted that away with a flick of his head. "That be Fred'rick Douglass DuBois." Doo-*Bwah*," he repeated.

"But I've seen you before, around here. Yes?"

"Cain't say."

"Anyway, you look different."

"H'it's Sundee; own muh way to choich. Lookahere, boy; Ah'm eighty-fi' yeahs ol', so le's git to it. You know who you is, yit?"

"Sorry. 'John Doe' is all I got, right now."

"'Spec' I kin show yuh who you wuz." Mr. DuBois flipped the gym bag at the patient and stood his ground. It landed in John's lap. He paused and glanced back at his visitor.

"Go 'hi'd, now."

John unzipped the tattered bag slowly. He could make out three larger objects with loose ones—coins; paper currency; keys; a knife; and such, he thought— around their amorphous edges. Parting the sides, he fished out a wallet. Through the plastic pane in the front pocket he spotted his likeness staring back at him, wide-eyed and tight-lipped. He acknowledged it with a slight nod and studied the data to its left, then raised his eyes and knitted brow. "'Custis Lee Davis?'"

"Yassuh," DuBois said coldly. "C. L. 'Duke' Davis— Junior."

"'Duke?' Who's 'Duke?'"

"He yo' hee-row—after yo' Grandaddy. Looka d' book."

"Duke" had already extracted the thin, hard-bound edition and was fixed on the image on the dust jacket's back side. It was a blue-eyed, fair-haired man, maybe 10-15 years older than him, judging from the jowly ruddiness. He turned it over. *My Awakening, by David L. Duke*. He opened to the Table of Contents and read the chapter titles; his receptors kicked into overdrive and his thoughts began to feel cyclonic.

"You been takin' keer bidness, too." DuBois pushed Duke back to the bag by flicking an inverted index finger.

Duke withdrew a three-ring executive planner and leafed through the calendar pages, reading their neatly-penned entries at random. As he went a vague foreboding and queasiness came to him, but he didn't know why.

DuBois' reserves were gone; he covered the remaining distance between them with one purposeful stride. Between his hands, raised reflexively, Duke saw the steel in the eyes bulging from DuBois' rigid face. He reached into an inside breast pocket and threw a distressed scrap of card stock onto the bed table. In the center of faded and blemished sepia, veined with cracks, Duke found a woman in a long print dress. Her feet were bare and stained; her head was splayed at a tortured angle by a taut rope attached to a swamp oak. The crowd of mostly men and boys in shirt sleeves, slouch hats, and boaters who surrounded her lifeless corpse in the dying light seemed cheerful and casual. She resembled DuBois; most everyone else looked like Duke. At the bottom was this scrawled legend:

Nigra gits hers.

Duke looked up, his mouth open, to see salty moats around his tormentor's swollen eyes turn into rivers. His face had eroded into a sagging softness.

"Thet's my Mama, Mistuh Davis: Mary Magdalene DuBois. Joo-ly Nineteenth, Nineteen 'n Twenty fo'. Ah wuz fi' yeahs ol'." Exhausted and solemn, he tapped on a tiny face to the body's left. Duke made out a grinning man in a fedora with a flash on his tweedy jacket. "Thet yo' Gran'Daddy: Hon'uble Rob'uht Jefferson Davis, Sher'ff a Neshoba County, Miss'ippi."

The dam broke in Duke's infernal, slack-jawed head. Tides and torrents of images crashed and splashed inside, drowning his cortex in a flood of abhorrence and paradox. A spastic abdomen was close behind.

"MIS-ter DuBois!"

Dr. Dunbar, flanked by Rosa, glided to the bedside. The octogenarian wiped at his eyes and nose while the physician ran through Duke's vitals, giving him the opportunity to come into control.

"Well—it appears our little experiment is at an end." Dunbar dropped the chart and pen with authority, folded his arms, and drummed one elbow point; presently, he took and released a long breath.

"Mr. Davis; there was no ambulance, no law, no emergency room. Frederick found you that night, bleeding and near unconscious. Knew who you were right off, even with your face all cut up. Swaddled you up as best he could and brought you here directly. We decided that night to keep you here, see what developed when you rejoined the living. They're still dragging the lake, looking for you."

Duke worked moisture back into his thick, parched tongue. "Why, in God's name? Who or what was...am I?"

Dunbar reached for his knees and stationed himself inches from Duke's face. "You, sir, are right now the new face of White supremacy in this state and—through the Internet—too many other places, as well. Two terms in the Legislature, candidate for Governor, you were doing right well at it, too, pulling at the frayed threads of the White Knights, the World Church, skinheads, and other parts of the old Alliance to try to weave them back into something powerful. We decided to show you the other side, while your ramparts were down. See if you could see." He straightened up and smiled.

Battered and bowed, Duke looked over at Rosa. "Were we...are you part of the plan, too?"

Rosa made her way to him with just a hint of hesitation. She bent and placed a kiss, light but complete, on his lips. She pulled away, her eyes shining. "How do you feel?"

Duke sensed that their calm, shared anticipation had him surrounded and he let it invade him.

"Different."

ಸುಡ

9 **Pallbearer**

ℰᎧᏳ

Harry clamped his arms around Hank's waist as much as their bulky clothing permitted and sucked in a breath. He buried his cheek in big brother's shoulder blade, knocking his leather visor askew and filling his inside eye with a damp lambs-wool earflap. He knew he'd be mocked, but it would be worth it. He liked the sensation of falling blind but was desperate for the closeness.

"Ready, 'Freddy?' Twenty-three skidoo!"

Hank jerked up his left galosh. The Flexible Flyer shot forward before he could plant the foot on the steering bar; his leg flailed upward, knocking his balance to starboard. They both heaved instinctively off their right buttocks. As they shuddered to the left, Hank saw the half-bare boulder, dead-legged on the right, and set his free boot into position. The left runner fell and bit into the snow and they regained the fall line. Down they hurtled, hitting successive ridges and getting more air with each one as their velocity increased. His legs pinned securely to the seat planks by his brother's rigid arms, Harry marveled in the weightless intervals and squealed at each impact. The angle started to come out of the hill. Harry grinned to himself in anticipation.

Here it comes!

Hank tapped out the first feint on the steering bar; the only remaining mystery was, *How many this time?* The answer? *One*—but on the same side. He punched his right leg out hard and buried their craft's front edge into a wet drift. The sled bucked and launched them into a crazy arc, like a collapsing seesaw. After a clinging aerial somersault they tumbled head over teakettle to a stop, just short of an icy stump. Hank rolled gingerly off his little brother and they lay on their backs, two heaps of sweaty flesh in sodden wool, framed by snow. They stared skyward through spindly aspen branches at the leaden sky as their heart rates subsided. Slowly, their heads rolled toward one another.

Harry's eyes shone. "Are we dead?"

Hank feigned seriousness. "Pert near."

They erupted, laughing like maniacs. *Perfect!* Harry basked in the unfettered affection, wishing it could endure. He stopped first to savor the sound of Hank's last few *huh-huh-huhs* until there was silence. Suddenly, there was his brother's ruddy face above him, at the other end of a dangling scarf and beyond his extended hand.

"Whaddya say, short-stuff? Once more—in front, this time?" Hank's eyes narrowed in mocking mirth. "Or..."

Harry stifled himself and reached for the hand. *Wait for it...*

Hank hoisted him until their faces were inches apart. "...Are you a 'FRAIDY-CAT?!'"

Giggling, Harry pushed at Hank's face and replied with equal force. "YESSS!"

"That's what I thought!" Hank really tried to force some contempt into it this time, but as always it didn't take. He brushed at the crystalline cakes clinging to his brother's back then stood apart to get his bearings. He arched his back and looked skyward, wiping clear mucous from his upper lip with a drenched mitten.

"Better get on home—light's goin'."

Harry looked down at steel buckles and black rubber. "Aw—What for?"

The elder Martz examined their "combined" Christmas present with satisfaction; it was his brother who wanted it more, but no chance with Ma that way. He took his case straight to the court of appeals and, in a rare published opinion, Pa took his side. He dug for the Flyer's rope and slung it over his shoulder as he groped for the seven-year-old's hand. They trudged out of the blanketed meadow and slipped into the carved ruts on the road downhill. As they crunched along, Hank's eyes wandered westward and up the silver and aquamarine shoulders of the peak named for Zebulon Pike that dominated their town. He stopped, nearly yanking Harry off his encumbered feet. He scowled.

"What are you doing?"

Hank's mouth hung slightly open; he shook his head slightly.

"Nothin'. Just thinkin'."

"'Bout what?"

"Drivin' up the Pike in an auto-mobile—goin' real fast. Thirty, maybe 40 miles to the hour."

"Aw, g'wan."

"Yes, sir—you'll see. Gonna be in Mr. Penrose's 'Hill Climb' one day." He put his hands on his knees and peered into Harry's face. "Got to dream, little brother. Don't you have a dream?"

Harry bit his lip and stared back. *Yes, big brother, I do. You can't understand.*

Hank shrugged. "Let's get crackin'."

Just behind twilight and barely ahead of curfew, the pair clambered onto the rough-sawn planks of the back porch and struggled with their overshoe clasps. They freed themselves by stomping on alternate heels and burst through the kitchen door. Dodging hips and elbows in the space between the wall and the glowing cast-iron stove, they doffed, unwound, and yanked until their outer garments dangled from pegs. Their order was as good as could be expected from hungry, exhausted males their age.

Mutter Florenz came out of the pantry into the spare electric light with two jars of spiced peaches. There they stood, their tousled sandy hair and crimson extremities each five points of contrast with their bleached, steaming long-handles. Her straight gash of a mouth lifted perceptibly at a corner.

"Heinrich!" She strode over and laid her fingers against her firstborn's cheek. "You must be frozen. Quickly—get your bath before you catch your death."

Hank turned his face upward. "Where's Pa?"

"He's in the parlor, reading his paper." She rubbed her upper arm absently. "He's upset about the War. Let's not bother him, all right?"

She smiled as he passed and watched him pad into the hallway. As she turned back her face fell and hardened.

"Pick up your hat, Harold," she said flatly. "And straighten up those clothes; they're a disgrace." She cuffed his ear sharply with her fingers. "*Schnell*! Quickly!"

Harry rubbed the sting out of his ear as he bent down, not daring to look at her standing over him, her hands on her hips.

ꟷ

Hank sat in his flannel nightshirt, aimlessly swinging his bare legs over the edge of the bed, when Harry came in from his tepid bath swaddled in Hank's too-big cast-off. He walked around to his side, pulled back the covers, and slid in. Hank swung himself onto the mattress.

"Ain't you goin' to say your prayers?"

Harry look at him askance. "To who?"

"God, stoopid."

"You know what I mean. Ma heard yours—I seen her in here."

Hank beckoned with his finger. "C'mon, get up. I'll hear 'em. C'mon. You don't want to go to Hell, do you?"

"Who says I ain't already there?" Harry muttered. He labored up to his knees, folded his hands, and began a dispirited recitation. Hank's hand rested on his shoulder. Harry finished, crossed himself, and sank back into bed. Sliding in behind him, Hank encircled his bony waist with his arm.

"She don't mean it, Harry. Not really."

Harry blinked at the frost-painted panes and waited for sleep to come.

A fog of perspiration and the odor of chipping varnish filled the nostrils of the spectators huddled in the frigid, poorly-lit gymnasium. After the referee raised and released his leaden arm, Harry used it to peel off his leather headgear and slogged off the mat. His coach clapped his shoulders as he threw the heavy gray warm-up over them. The warrior found the family in the bleachers and climbed wearily to them. Wilhelm Martz stood stiffly and extended his hand.

"Excellent..." He frowned a little, furrowing his brow.

Harry gulped a breath and gripped his father's palm. "Match, Pa."

"Yes—match. *Prima*." Wilhelm leaned away as his wife burst through and seized Hank's face with both hands.

"Heinrich!" She gave him the full once-over. "Are you all right?"

"'Course, Ma—I won!"

"It's just—I worry so that you will be hurt, *Mein liebschen*."

"Aw—it's real safe, Ma; and my third straight." Hank looked between them at Harry and winked. "Think I'm goin' to regionals this year! Well; gotta get back to the team, I guess." He peeled off, the slaps of his sneakers' rubber soles on the bleacher seats echoing off the enameled block walls. As his father sat, Harry jumped to the seat in front of him and bounced on his toes.

"Can I go out next year, Pa? Huh?"

Florenz pushed derisively at the boy's shoulder and spoke before her husband could. "Don't be silly. You're not as athletic as your brother and too small, anywayyou would just get hurt."

Wilhelm flicked his eyes at Harry, then quickly away. "We'll see, boy. Come—let's go to wait for Hank."

ℰᴏᴄℛ

Hank buttoned the dull, black gabardine gown to his neck. Turning to the bureau mirror, he set the mortarboard on his head at a jaunty angle. He whirled airily and thrust his arms out.

"Wottya think?"

Propped against the headboard, Harry peeped through his crossed shoes at the foot of the bed, folded his arms, and emitted a low wolf-whistle for effect. "Cat's meow, Mister Engineer. You decided where you're taking this degree yet?"

"Best response I've gotten so far is from the IRT back east."

"Where's that?"

"New York City — 'Interborough Rapid Transit Authority.' Imagine—me bein' a *NooYawkuh!*"

"Huh-huh. Doing what?"

"Cofferdams and subways, I think."

"Government job?"

"Well, yes—City and County of."

"It's 1929, brother. Capitalism and private enterprise are all the rage; haven't you heard? Jeez—didn't you ever take an economics class?"

"Wall Street itself's lookin' a little fragile these days,

'Frosh.'" Hank pointed, with playful purpose. "You might have taken a little more in civics and public affairs—you and your 'captains of industry' heroes."

Harry sniffed. "Oh, yeah; so I could carry on like you and your 'Red' pals."

"Hey—Russia wasn't the only country born out of revolution, you know."

Harry yawned, and scratched. "You can keep your *'Quo Vadis?'* Three more years of academic slavery and I'm on my way—finding my fortune in the big 'burg."

"Where's that?"

"Why—Denver, o' course!"

Hank chortled. "Ain't exactly New York, is it?"

"Big enough pond for this li'l fishie. Mark my words; land's the future. Downtown real estate—the cat's pajamas!"

"The 'Pope of Private Property,' eh?" Hank's glance was sideward and sly.

"Har-de-har-har. You'll see."

Hank looked at his wristwatch. "It's time, Ignatz. We should get downstairs—Ma's pert near out of things to find wrong about Pa by now."

A cloud passed over Harry's face. After willing it away, he sprang for the doorway. "Too old, too slow!" he bellowed as he slipped out of Hank's lunging grasp into the hallway. Laughing, they caromed off the hallway walls and galumphed down the stairwell.

৪০৫ৠ

Taking a last, nervous drag, Harry cracked the door and flicked his Lucky into the rain. He stepped back into the vestibule and resumed picking at himself.

"Cripes—help me with this thing, willya?" Carnation in hand, Hank nodded at the left lapel of his morning coat. "I'm an engineer, not a dandy like you."

Harry sighed and pinned the boutonniere on crisply, his eyes cast over the bridegroom's shoulder. "You can say that again, brother."

"Where are you today?" Hank said as he pulled Harry's gaze to his. "If you don't tend to business I'll have to hire me a new best man."

Harry squared Hank's jacket on his gaunt shoulders and brushed at them ceremoniously. "Just thinkin,' is all.

"What about?"

"Oh—stuff and nonsense."

"Come on..."

"How things have worked out in six years. Black Friday—"

"Told you about those Wall Street wizards—didn't I?"

Harry's eyes flashed. "Don't interrupt! Mr. Big-Time working for the State of Colorado, me marching in place, hustling a buck here and there. Dreams on hold..." The urgency in his voice relented a little. "Ask me, I think it was that engineer you voted into the White House who drove us into the ditch. And that 'pink' pal o' yours, Roosevelt, isn't doing so hot, either."

Hank crossed his arms. "Even though he seems to have a conscience, he's filthy-rich; that ought to make you happy."

"I don't care how bad things are—socialism isn't going to solve anything. It's—"

Hank's mouth went crooked. "The free market! Of course; how have we been so blind?"

Harry opened his mouth to retort but his brother's upraised hand silenced him. "Let's not argue; not today. Whatever else afflicts us, this is what's important."

Harry looked genuinely puzzled.

"Lottie and I are getting hitched—stoopid!" Hank opened his arms and welcomed his brother into a true but awkward embrace.

Harry sniffled a little. "If you say so. Give me the single life—no ball and chain for me!"

Random organ music rolled through the sacristy door. Hank clapped Harry's shoulders and adjusted his coat a little. "I'm goin' to the 50 yard line; see you in the end zone."

"Okey-dokey, Skeezix," Harry said, and watched him lope up the aisle.

℘ℂℜ

Harry answered the phone.

"You get in yet?" Hank sounded overwrought, which wasn't him at all and gave Harry pause.

"No. You?"

"I've been around to all the branches. None of them want me because I'm 34, with a wife and four kids."

"In six years," Harry clucked. "You and Lottie didn't have to be that Catholic; at least that was one thing the Old Battleaxe was right about—your marrying shanty Irish and having babies like kittens."

"Still denying that side of us, and pretending we're full-blooded colonists, are we? Let's not go down that road right now. Aren't you bothered in the least about what's happened, man? They attacked us!"

"Hey—I didn't say I wasn't going to serve, ever. I just don't see the point in breaking my neck to become cannon fodder. The smarter boys at the club are saying it never hurts to figure the angles first—make the circumstances work in your favor."

Harry sensed Hank's agitation now, even in the deliberate pause that was his conversational trademark; the longer it was, the more heartfelt the thought or sentiment to follow. "Suppose everyone thought that way? Where would we be then?"

"Fact is, everyone doesn't think that way; I do, and some others. We make our breaks; they don't. That's why I've got money in the bank and you've got mouths to feed on a federal check, Mister Full Scholarship."

Hank paused, longer this time, but only sighed. "You know, I wonder about you..."

"What's the big mystery? "I'm going somewhere and

you're—just you."

Harry's bitterness bit back into him instantly, and he hung up to avoid another pause.

ഇരു

Harry stamped his feet, his hands shoved deep into his topcoat's pockets, and looked up the tracks periodically into the dimness. He could see his breath but the late winter air was typically dry, so as an acclimated Denverite it wasn't the chill that animated him. It was—well, if he knew what it was, honestly, it didn't have a name. And he didn't.

The platform speakers crackled and blared. "Ladies and Gentlemen: your attention, please. Now arriving on Traaaack 22, the Union Pacific's Poooortland Rose. Please stand behind the yellow line." Complying, Harry stepped back as the engine chugged by; he began searching the coach windows. He didn't see his brother until he was halfway off the slowing step. Hank dropped his Gladstone at Harry's feet and embraced him that way he always had, causing the cold, stiffness, and intervening years to melt into simple boyhood. Harry hugged back, reflexively and hard.

Hank pushed back and touched the younger's face, as if to keep it from hardening into the defiant mask it had become. It didn't work.

"Good to see you, Harry. How are you?"

"As well as can be expected, I guess—given the circumstances. How was your train ride?"

Hank stretched upward and pressed his knuckles into the small of his back. "Uneventful—and long! Seemed odd not to have a lot of boys in uniform aboard."

Harry had retrieved the grip and started toward the depot lobby. He spoke over his shoulder. "Oughtta try out those civilian DC-3s; I use 'em whenever I can for business. United's come up your way with new routes, haven't they?"

Hank caught up. "Not all the way to Grant's Pass, they haven't. Anyway, it'd take just about as long and it's out of our reach just yet."

"I'm good for it. You know that."

"That's very generous; one day, maybe. All the arrangements must have put you out a tidy sum."

"It wasn't cheap. What the hey. Nothing but the best for the old bag: silk-lined mahogany box with solid brass appointments. Plant her right next to Kaiser Wilhelm, in that church plot in the shadow of the Peak. Just like they wanted."

To Hank, the lack of emotion and absence of irony seemed just about equal "So did you connect with the pastor at Redeemer and get the service set up?"

"You betcha."

"Full Mass and burial?"

"Yep; I'm not going to Hell on a technicality."

"When are they?"

"Tomorrow—11 AM.

"That quick? What time are we leaving in the morning?"

"Not 'we,' 'you.' I hired a car."

"You're not going?"

"No can do. Got business to attend to."

"But—it's Saturday."

"My sincerest apologies. I'm not a government clock-puncher, myself."

Angered, Hank thrust his arm out as a barricade to stop Harry. "That's not fair!"

Harry turned; his eyes were colder than the air. "As I recall, we grew up in the same house. You may have forgotten, but I haven't. Anything I owed her died when she did; once she's in the ground, the ledger's balanced, as far as I'm concerned."

Hank laid a hand gently on his brother's shoulder. "Harry, listen to me. I understand; I do. Lottie's had about as much use for "Ga-Ga" as you did, but it's not about her. You've got to go."

Harry knocked the hand away petulantly. "What—you're the keeper of the guilt, now?"

"Not for her sake, Harry—for yours."

Harry regarded him like he'd just arrived. "Let's get out of here. There's a great table waiting for us at the Brown Derby."

※※

It was clear and crisp in Boise on Christmas Eve — in fact, just the sort of typically arid, *après* snowfall evening that made the Bureau transfer palatable to Lottie. Cold, yes, but dry like her Denver, such that winter was less an unpleasant, squatting relative than an unpredictable transient who blew in and moved on. That, and no more of the fog, mildew, and other spawn of unrelenting moisture that had plagued their coastal Oregon existence.

Jimmy threw himself against the back of the corduroy sofa and, through cupped hands pressed against dewy glass, peered into the early dark. *C'mon — it's almost too late!* Two yellow headlight moons lurched from the street into the curb. Grinning, he made a beeline for the front door, arriving at about the same time as the heavy boots of the deliveryman made hollow thunder on the front porch's floorboards. Jimmy threw open the door as the man shifted the parcel to manage a clipboard. He saw Jimmy's eager face and scowled a little, mostly under the weight of the season.

"Need a grownup to sign for this, kid."

"Mom!" Jimmy bolted into the kitchen. "Unc's package is here!"

"Well, finally," Lottie sighed. "Maybe now you and the other six will shut up about it." She wiped her hands and followed the flapping flannel.

The man pointed, Lottie scribbled, and he laid the package onto Jimmy's outstretched forearms, which staggered him a little. The courier gave his cap a cursory touch — "Merry Christmas, Ma'am" — and as he turned fired an index-finger round and a wisp of a smile at the wide-eyed boy. "Kid."

Lottie pulled the door closed and trotted wearily after Jimmy, who already had the loot under the tree in the dining room, wrestling with the Kraft paper and twine. "For Pete's sake, Jimmy; can't you wait for the scissors?" She fished into her apron pocket and snipped through the bindings.

The cold air intrusion and tearing sounds were sufficient to trigger a full-on sibling alert. Six pairs of legs pumped downstairs and up from the basement, pounding toward ground zero.

"Is it — is it...?" Carly, the asthmatic, wheezed.

Jimmy beamed triumphantly over his exposed bounty. "It's the five-pounder!"

The Whitman's Sampler, with its contrasting stiff yellow cardboard exterior and gossamer tissues separating tiers of chocolates mapped precisely, layer-by-layer, on the underside of the lid, was as exotic as anything tangible that ever came into their household. It might as well have been marzipan from Tangiers.

"I hope you have the good grace to spare your Mother some nuts this time," Lottie said above the squealing, to no one in particular. She folded her arms and shook her head, slowly.

The blast of air came from the kitchen this time as Hank lurched through the back door, stamping and shaking off the flakes that he'd acquired on the regular trip from the detached garage. He unwound his scarf and flung his greatcoat and hat on the rack nearby. Lottie responded to his arms twining her waist from behind by reaching back and, without a glance, palming his cheekbone with precision.

"Well, looky here," Hank said. "Looks like Uncle Harry's come through in the clutch, yet again." He sank to his knees and lunged in mock desperation toward the candy, creating a tangle of limbs, laughter, and sticky faces.

"The Maple Nougat is mine!" he roared. The silent sweetness that followed magnified the glow from the bubbling electric candles nestled in the evergreen.

"All right." Lottie, ever the bad cop, began prying and lifting. "Wash up; dinner's almost ready and—don't forget—church's at 7:30."

There was a chorus of "Awwwww!" Jimmy lingered under his father's bent leg.

"Daddy?"

"Uh-huh?"

"Is Unca Harry rich?"

Hank sighed, a little. "Yup."

"Are we rich?"

Hank gently tousled Jimmy's umber hair. "Yes."

Jimmy turned his head and looked up with eyes soft but direct. "Then how come we don't buy Whitman's for ourselves?"

"Listen, James. There's rich and there's *rich*. Unca Harry is rich because he has lots of money. I'm rich because I have lots of..."—Hank tickled Jimmy until he squealed—"...you!"

Now astride his father, Jimmy clasped his neck and lay his head on his shoulder. "How come Unc buys us stuff?"

"Because he's..."—Hank was grateful his fifth-born couldn't see his slight frown—"...generous."

෴

Wow.

Jim sat stiffly in his jacket and slacks on the alabaster Tuxedo couch, taking in everything just beyond the enameled French doors. Pristine, cushioned furniture graced the aquamarine pool. Beyond were a massive brick barbecue and picture-book landscaping, framed by a fortress-like fence of dark cane. He compared this snapshot with the picture in his head of his own back yard — a careless, weathering swing set; a rideable "space coaster" shipped by Mom's Uncle Gene, from which vomit had to be hosed periodically; assorted pet graves; and patchy grass and scraggly, random shrubbery savaged by years of football, piracy, tag, and other childish abandon. Between what was in front of him now and yesterday's tour of their carefully-appointed rooms, he couldn't imagine what his cousins Forrest and Grace—not that much younger than he—did all day.

Aunt Judith materialized—Jim still hadn't adjusted to the lack of heralding footbeats he was used to all over his own, mostly carpetless house—with a generous Coke and crushed ice in a glass free of cartoons.

"Here you are, dear," she cooed.

"Thank you very much, Aunt Judith."

"Oooh—how very proper!" She bent at the knees slightly, closed her hands casually under her waist, and drew her crimson lips broadly off her tobacco-yellowed teeth. "You must call me 'Judy!'"

He gulped and stared at her magazine perfection over the rim. His face broadened. I got it! This is *"Leave it to Beaver" and I'm "Whitey!"*

Dad and Uncle Harry came out into the great room, faces ruddy from disagreement. Jim hadn't heard anything, adding to the mausoleum impression he was forming. He slid forward, extending his beverage toward the coffee table; unconsciously, Aunt Judith slid a coaster between it and the beveled glass. Harry came first, and cheek-pecked his much-younger wife. It struck Jim, who was barely hormonal, as less a transmission than a gesture, like waving to an acquaintance. Harry disengaged and rubbed his hands together.

"How 'bout a ride in the Shelby, sport—and maybe an afternoon with my Broncos?"

"Sure!" Jim was on his feet and startled by his own enthusiasm. He looked around Uncle Harry at his Dad with sober and cautious anticipation.

Hank smiled. "You bet; sounds like fun. I'll catch up with your Mom and the bunch at Jack and Mimi's. Unc can bring you along after." He turned to his hostess as his brother headed for the garage. "Thanks very much for having us, Judy."

She half-nodded and showed Hank and Jim to the foyer, her affixed smile decaying.

They walked around to the garage, where the overhead door glided up and the white-striped, cobalt machine roared to life. Harry slid into view, his lined gray face enlivened in the frame made by the windscreen, driver's door, and roll bar. He depressed the clutch and pumped the accelerator for effect. "One of the first 125," he shouted. "Whaddya think? Huh?"

Jim whistled. "'Bye, Dad—thanks!" He sprinted around as his uncle cracked the passenger door. Hank waved behind him on his way to his salmon-and-white Ford—always a Ford—wagon.

They wheeled away from the quiet East side and sped westward across town. Beneath the wind's and city's noise and above the throbbing power plant's, Harry chain-smoked unfiltered Camels and recited his chariot's specifications as though memorized from a manual.

ഇരു

Jim broke from his morose anger to fiddle with his tie and look around. The Cathedral was packed, the human heat and scents magnifying the blend of pressed linen, beeswax, and incense that had oppressed him all his young years as an acolyte and server. The atmosphere itself, it seemed, quavered and flickered like the platoons of candle flames before him. He leaned forward a little and looked at his mother on the aisle. Though obscured by black lace, she was the same grievous, detached mess she'd been since Dad was diagnosed. She was poorly equipped to accept and didn't deserve the role of young widow, but was too exhausted to resist when it was thrust upon her. Between them stretched his brothers and sisters, sharing their sense of numb disorientation. The elders dwelled in reflection of what had been, he thought, while the three younger ones were afflicted with the terror and yearning for what would never be. For him, a year into college, the six-week decline and loss of the distant, imposing authority figure who had become more a gentle friend to him at 15—when Mom's post-hysterectomy ambivalence drove his father to find emotional sustenance elsewhere—stoked Jim's ignorant, adolescent rage.

Uncle Harry clutched at Jim's left bicep. Jim saw that he'd been checking the house as well.

"How many you suppose are here?"

"Dunno, Unc." Jim tried not to sound irritated. "Place holds a couple thousand, and there are some standing."

Throaty sounds welled out of Harry, causing Jim to look him full in the face. His uncle's cloudy, sallow eyes brimmed with tears as he manfully stifled the rattle of the cigarette cough he'd had in common with his dead brother.

"They're going to have to recruit pallbearers for my funeral."

🙠🙡

Ernie clutched at Jim's arm against both the Denver winter and the unease extended family suffers, thrust into the complexity of unfamiliar loss. Too, she was unaccustomed to the thin cold that Jim had already known through four years of college that ended just before they met and married. Squinting into the sun barely 20 degrees above the leaden eastern horizon, they moved through the arid gusts and the iced grass toward the chrome quadrangle and mound marking the gravesite. He saw her clouds of labored breath and frosted heels and smiled weakly. "At least it's a dry cold."

"I'm okay."

He turned back and frowned. "Why do they do that?" She stopped him. "What?"

"Cover the dirt they've excavated with that cheap Astroturf. Who are they trying to fool — the grief-stricken loved ones? Do they think they truly notice anything beyond their own running noses?"

Ernie shrugged. "There must be some— "

Jim pushed away, throwing himself, arms out, into a disdainful pirouette. "The mind reels at the market research supporting that point!"

"Jim." She touched him tentatively. "What is it?"

He stopped and cocked his head, working his mouth as though trying to form words he'd never heard before. "Not sure. Memories. Dad. Rites. Complexity. Closure. Finality. This...this is just—sad. No vigil. No Mass—shit. No church! 'Graveside service." No eulogy—*nada*. Just a period on the last page of a tome of random prose."

"Why did you—we—come, then?"

"Because." Jim squeezed his hands together and pointed his index fingers at the hole. "Somebody should. Y'know—bear witness. 'Attention must be paid.'"

The crunch of tires called them back toward the road. They watched the distended Cadillac glide from the gravel into the muffling grass and discharge its beefy passengers, clad in black and sober indifference. *I wonder if the mob has its own witness protection program in the funeral industry,* Jim thought. He sensed Ernie looking up at him as he felt her arm tighten around his waist. He pressed his lips into her forehead for reassurance.

"'Scuse me; are you here for the Martz service?"

Jim looked into the doughy pink face, glanced quickly at the sod-green plastic nametag, and stuck out his gloved hand.

"Yeah-uh-Robert. Jim Martz. I'm the—Harry's nephew."

"Sorry for your loss. I hate to ask, but...can you give us a hand?"

"Um..." Jim glanced at the priest, Robert's pair of associates, and the lone, indistinct figure in the back of the sedan and his question expired, too. "Sure."

Robert had since gone into a quick huddle with the other two and they'd disappeared. They returned with two sweating, nonplussed groundsmen, kidnapped off a mower and backhoe. They all muttered awkward greetings and gathered behind the hearse, where Robert reached in to free the casket. Father Moran turned and offered Ernie his arm, gesturing toward the site.

Jim stepped back. "What about Aunt Judith?"

Harry's shepherd for the day looked baleful. "She's staying."

The sextet withdrew the box, hand-to-hand, until it was nearly free. Bracing, they overcompensated—the cancer had taken a third of Harry's bodyweight before losing its patience—and their load bobbed up as though levitated. On the front end, the conscripts raised eyebrows at each other to mark the pointlessness of their presence.

Jim and the diggers shuffled along self-consciously, trying in vain to match the professionals' practiced funereal gait. The slick leather soles of his Bass loafers against the hoarfrost made him concentrate on remaining vertical, so he had no thoughts to be alone with until Harry had been placed on the webbing over the void. After the half-hearted "Dearly Beloved" and not too far into the fill-in-the-blanks remembrance, that changed. Bound physically only to Ernie's hand, Jim transported himself through the whole of his Harry experience, direct and derivative. It saddened and shamed him that it all added up to so little.

"Would either of you care to say a few words?"

The vicar's rouge, earnest face broke Jim's reverie. He glanced at Ernie, who'd already shaken her head. He cleared his throat.

"Harold Friedrich Martz, son of Wilhelm and Florenz Martz. Brother to Heinrich Muenze Martz—my father. Loving husband to Judith and attentive stepfather to Forrest and Grace. An extraordinary success in business and finance. An agent for progress and development in his chosen city, its markets, and its sport. He was a man, of moment and consequence. Harry Martz was kind and generous to me and his other nephews and nieces. He will be missed."

It was as much of the Post obituary as he could remember to borrow.

The Rev wound things up as gracefully as he could, and Jim and Ernie stood by while the soldati morte cranked Harry into the hole. Jim stuck his hand under the plastic turf covering the mound and pitched down a handful of earth that rattled off the burnished coffin. *Ashes to ashes*—he smirked at the irony; tobacco had brought his uncle to this, just like his older brother before him—*Dust to dust...*

As they dispersed, the couple approached the glossy sedan. Jim peered at the heavily tinted rear window, pantomiming a knock until Judith lowered it.

"Aunt Judith, I'm—we're so very sorry for—"

"Thank you, dear; thank you both. You're very kind."

"If there's anything at all we can do — "

"We'll be just fine." Jim stared. Her coolness and purposefully neutral smile were unsettling. She fixed her eyes on his until the dark glass slid between them again.

ഇരുള

Jim watched Ernie settle in as he turned the key.

"What time's our flight, again?"

"Um—" She cracked her purse and peered. "Six-thirty."

He checked the dash clock. "Not quite 11:30." He stared out the windshield and tugged at his ear. "What say we lunch early and take a little detour?"

"Uh, sure."

"Do me a favor? Pull out the city map — "

She was already in the glove box and showed him Denver. He shook his head.

She fished. "Colorado Springs?"

"Yes. Look at the index and see if you can find 'Cemeteries.'"

Her finger glided to a stop. "Got 'em."

"'Evergreen?'"

"Uh-huh."

"Get us back to the Interstate, okay?"

ℂℂ

Following the caretaker's instructions, they found the Divine Redeemer parish section and began working their way through the older plots.

Ernie blew into her gloved fingers. "We're looking for a Martz plot, right?"

"Yeah—Wilhelm and Florenz."

"What's the date of death?"

"Him? No idea. I think Dad said once "Ga-Ga" died in the early Fifties. Can't be at all prominent—there's just the two of them and likely nobody's been here since she was planted. You take that corner; I'll take a right and we can meet in the middle."

They were 100 feet apart when Ernie stopped.

"Jim!"

He broke into a trot. "Did you find it?"

She pointed at a smaller, third headstone. "I thought your father was buried in Boise."

"He is." Jim squatted, yanked out obscuring weeds,

and brushed at the faded legend. "'In Memoriam. Heinrich Muenze Martz. Beloved Son of Wilhelm and Florenz. Born January 11, 1906. Died of Influenza February 22, 1906.'" He stood, staring.

"What's it mean?"

"Maybe nothing." Jim caught his breath and pressed his hands into his face. "No—no. Probably everything."

ℰℭ

10 Pipe Dream

೫೦೦ಚ

Jay Johanessen glanced at his diamond-inlaid Cartier. *C'mon, man—let's go! It's just a leaky trap!* He watched the gaunt haunches in Khaki coveralls jiggle from the torque being applied invisibly ahead. *Well, that's a plus, I guess—no butt crack.* The gyrations stopped and two oxblood Red Wings glided noiselessly backward, followed by an auburn ponytail that just cleared the sink cabinet's top frame.

David DuPriest squatted, storing his tools deliberately. He finished wiping his hands, stood, and pressed into a languid stretch. Out of the corner of his eye, he saw his retainer furiously drumming his fingertips against his face. "That ought to do it, Mr. Johanessen. Use it for a couple days and call me if there's any further trouble. Oh, and you should have a carpenter check the sink base's floor. That was a steady leak, so you're probably looking at dry rot. I can give you a couple references, if—"

Jay had seized his arm. "I have a major meeting in 15 minutes and it's a 20-minute drive!" David looked at Jay's hand until it fell off his bicep. "Give me a minute and I'll make out your bill." He fished into a hip pocket and produced a well-worn, triple carbon invoice pad.

Jay shifted on his feet. "Can't you just have your people bill me?"

David half smiled. "No 'people'—just me."

"You're kidding!"

"Nope. 'Sole proprietor.'" He toted up the charges with a flourish. "Here you are. A signature and a check would be appreciated."

Jay snatched the sheet away and peered at it. His mouth fell open. "Two hundred sixty-eight dollars? For a balky *trap*? *Jee*zus! What's that—20 minutes' work?"

David was stoic. "Plus the replacement J-bend."

"Some racket, man. God*damn*. That works out to more an hour than I billed out as a senior associate at my firm."

David turned half away, toolbox in hand. "That's more than *I* billed out as a senior associate, as well."

"Huh? Wait!" Jay lunged and caught David by the arm again, with the identical response.

"I assume you remember the hornbook definition of battery, from Torts class."

Jay looked down at his offending fingers. "Uh...oh. Sorry. You're a lawyer?"

"*Was.*" David set down his tools.

Jay brushed at his forelock. "And you gave it up to be up to your eyebrows in *shit* every day?"

David's cheeks dimpled ever so slightly. "I regarded it a lateral move."

"Why, for Christ's sake?"

"Stress, mostly. Failing marriage. Responsibility for another life."

"What do you mean?"

"Which part?"

"'Another life.' What? Somebody on the side?" Jay leered. A frosty stare obliterated his feeble attempt at camaraderie.

"A daughter."

The muffled pounding of footfalls on carpeted stair treads accelerated into the clatter of stilettos on Italian foyer marble. A mid-teen Britney Spears replica—abdominal baby fat straining over distressed, low-rise jeans, pushed-up caricature of a bustline, and calculated makeup—burst into the kitchen.

"Daddy! Did you transfer $500 into my checking account, like you promised? If I don't get that Moo Hoo bag by Friday night, I might as well die because I won't dare leave my bedroom this summer." She cocked an eyebrow, hands perched on her hip-folds; the sole of one of her expensive, impossibly pointed high heels marked time on the olive slate.

Jay had retreated to the counter and his knuckles grew whiter against the dark granite edge. "Why do you dress like that for a weekday? You look like a hooker."

Her eyes narrowed and her Lancōme-glossed lips parted. "I'm *15*. If you knew *anything*, you'd know that *everyone* dresses like this. Besides, I'm hanging with my friends at the Galleria today." She sneered. "You know? *Friends?* Like *clients*, except they actually *like* you?"

David could almost hear the bile and invective backing up behind her teeth. He cleared his throat.

They looked at him as if he'd just materialized. Jay extended an arm. "David DuPriest. Meet Skylar, my stepdaughter."

"Oh—the plumber guy." Dismissive filters slid through her eyes. "Nyztmeechoo." She bored back into her stepfather. "Well?"

Jay sighed. "The money will be on deposit by Noon."

"Cool. *Ciao*, everybody." She whirled into motion. *Clack-clack-clack-clack—*

"It's actually '*Addio'*—Italian for 'Good-bye.' '*Ciao*' is 'Hello.'" His pitch climbed. "We'll talk later!"

"What-EVER!" *Clack-clack-SLAM!*

Jay pulled at his face and regarded David wearily. "How old's yours?"

"Lizzie—for Elizabeth—is 16."

"She like...*that*?

David looked slightly out of Jay's gaze while he distilled the forming untruth. "Basically."

"What's she do?"

"Uh—student?"

"No. I mean, is she interested in anything?"

"Oh. She draws; dances; plays the piano." The image of her sunny face brought David a pleased smile. "Wants to be a fine artist. Or an astronaut."

"Huh." Jay searched for his reflections in his Allen Edmonds. "Mine's already a professional malcontent. Takes after her mother. Neither one hears a word I say; Skylar never did, and Carol just sort of stopped, after the lust wore off." Jay raised his eyes. "You happy?"

"I'm on the journey, yes—at least, since I took the other path." David picked up the invoice Jay had abandoned and offered it again. "Keep the yellow; the original and pink are mine."

"Two copies?" Jay cast into his breast pocket for his checkbook. "I thought it was just you."

"One's for the accountant—my wife, Sunny."

Jay filled in the date. "What's that short for?" He glanced at David's queue. "'Sunshine?'"

"No, actually. It's a corruption of 'Shuang.' She's Chinese; her name means 'bright, clear, and openhearted.' It's the best Lizzie could do when she was two—and she'd already mastered 'sun.'"

Jay raised his pen and peered at the ticket. "What's this, under your name?"

禅宗佛教

"Is that Chinese?"

"Yes. Those four characters are 'Chan Zong Fo Jīao'— for 'Zen Buddhism.'"

"So—you're a *Buddhist*?"

"Sunny teaches and Lizzie and I study; we all attend

temple. Yes."

"No shit! What does that involve?"

"Deepest understanding of self and the pursuit of true enlightenment."

"What else?"

"That's pretty much it."

Jay looked truly perplexed. "No, I mean, what's the payoff? You know, you're Jewish, you chair the Temple Building Fund and plant trees in Israel. Catholics keep the Archbishop in silk and marble; Mormons tithe 10 percent, minimum, and study their ancestors in caves. Protestants—well, protest, or whatever. What's your angle?"

David folded his hands before him. "How do I explain this? Zen worships everything, and nothing. It is the pursuit of the ultimate truth. Professor Suzuki calls it 'opening the mental eye to look into the very reason of existence.' Buddhism is a ladder useful to reaching that truth. Zen is the tong for grasping it."

"Wow." Jay scribbled, stopped, and began rolling the capped end of the pen between his lips. "Does it help?"

"Understanding can bring peace, yes."

Jay pointed the pen at David. "You think I could get some peace?"

"With total commitment, patience, and diligence? Of course."

"What are you doing Thursday?"

David blinked. "Um...I don't think I'm being clear, here..."

"I'll make you a deal." Jay shaped the offer with his hands. "Spend Thursday with me; audit a practice day, and show me some Zen techniques I can use to lower my emotional temperature. I'll pay you my hourly rate. What do you say?"

David half-shook his head. "Listen, Mr. Johanessen—"

"Jay."

"Jay. Zen isn't exactly like a day spa that takes drop-ins."

"How about this? We do a day together, as outlined. If within a week I feel like you've helped me lower my general level of stress at least 10 percent, I'll double the retainer as a bonus. C'mon—at 600 per, that works out to 9,600 bucks. That's a lot of backed-up toilets."

"In all honesty, Jay, I can't see how eight hours is going to help your situation that much." This time, it was David who reached out to clasp Jay's shoulder.

Jay smiled. "You really should have stuck with it, David, you know? With your negotiating skills, you'd be sitting where I am today. At least. Okay, final offer: six grand, flat, for eight hours, plus a match for the bonus. Twelve grand. Cash." Jay stuck out his hand.

David stroked his chin and reached into his back pocket. "Let me check on Thursday." He opened a small, spiral-bound notebook and flipped pages.

Jay guffawed. "God! Don't you even have a smartphone?"

"Oh, this model has all the latest features. Light; thin; indestructible. No batteries, never needs a 'hard reset,' and—" He tore out a page, crumpled it up, and shoved it into a front pocket. "—totally secure." He took a stubby pencil with an eraser out of the wire and pushed it at Jay. "Handsome stylus, with built-in 'Delete' key. Infinitely-variable font size and style..."

Jay opened his hands in surrender, then re-offered his right. "Thursday?"

David took Jay's hand. "Thursday's okay. I've got a Sub-Zero SZ90 filter replacement in Bel Air that I can move to Friday." He raised the other index finger. "One codicil."

"What's that?"

"No warranties, expressed or implied. Failure of consideration is not an option."

"Done. I'll drive us to the firm." Jay gave David a final once-over. "Dress appropriately."

David retrieved his toolbox and gestured amiably. "I

think I still have the Armani in the back of the closet. I hope the two-button front is acceptable; it's a little dated..."

"Go."

"Right." David pivoted. "See you bright and early Thursday."

"One last issue."

"What's that?"

"Don't call me 'Grasshopper.'"

"Amusing—but be warned. I know nothing about martial arts; if a fight breaks out, you're on your own."

ഔരു

Bing-BONG-Bing-BONG...Bing-BONG-Bing-BONG...

The cascading knell of Carol's prized Dorchester chimes meant either that Parliament was in session or someone was at the front door. Jay stirred and glanced at her, motionless. *Why does she never hear the goddamned things? Oh, yeah—earplugs.* He peered through the gauze of receding sleep at the clock radio. 5:30!? He snatched on a robe and staggered down the stairs.

"Good morning."

There stood David, just as advertised. Two-piece charcoal Armani with a two-button jacket and just a hint of a past season's flare at the wrists and cuffs. Blue Egyptian cotton button-down shirt with nondescript rep tie and unremarkable oxfords. A worn backpack dangled by his leg. He turned his head to show Jay that his hair was twisted and pinned into practical nothingness.

"Acceptable. Do you have any fuckin' idea what time it is?"

David looked skyward. "Is the sun up?"

"Yeah. So?"

"After his enlightenment, the Buddha was asked if he

was a god, a celestial being, or a man. He replied, 'I am awake.'"

"So, the first Zen lesson is 'The early bird gets the worm'? I'm not paying for that."

"No, not at all. 'Wakefulness is life.' It is the beginning of awareness."

Jay looked around and beyond his consultant. "How did you get here? Cab?"

"I walked."

"Walked!? Where do you live?"

"North of Topanga, just outside the park. Sunny's folks had a little truck patch up there decades ago."

"That's gotta be, what, nine miles?"

"By car; about half that using park trails."

"Even so, took you twice as long. What's the point?"

"Abandonment of hindrances—fear, control, and other distractions. Contemplation of the simple promotes clarity. May I come in?"

Jay scratched himself and stood aside. "Well, come in and contemplate away. I need to meditate on my pillow for another couple hours. I was up late, defending my inadequacy. Again. The *Times* should hit the driveway any minute and Consuéla should be up to put the coffee on by seven."

"Thanks. I brought my own reading material. Do you have any green tea?"

"Should be some in the kitchen, over the sink. Carol laid in a supply two diets ago. Help yourself."

"Words to live by," David muttered.

"Sorry?"

"Nothing. Enjoy your rest."

֍

Sipping tea, David pored over *The Teachings of Buddha, 115ᵗʰ Revised Edition,* cleansing his consciousness of the last round of shouting that had come from the master bedroom above him. Jay hit the back stairs' landing hard, shoving his French designer cravat into a loose double-Windsor. His jaw was set and Carol was right on his heels. Even in rollers and a dressing gown, she was a vision. Younger than Jay, bed-tanned, fit—and thus far holding off middle age with the alchemy of her class: Botox, laser dermatology, and disposable income.

"Honey, we've had the Getty thing scheduled for months—I'm chair of the planning committee, for God's sake. We can't just blow it off!"

Jay wheeled. "What's Friday, Carol?" he hissed.

Her eyes fell. "But—"

"First Friday of the month, Carol. *Poker Night*." He jabbed his index fingers at the corners of his mouth. "*PO-KER!*"

"Oh, yes. I forgot." She went icy. "The whisky warmup to Sunday's pageant: 'High-fashion Drunks in Golf Carts—Appearing Weekly at the Brentwood Country Club.'" Carol finally saw David at the island but Jay had already reloaded.

"Go for it, baby. That last little Nassau Barry and I cooked up more than paid for those implants. David, this is my second loving life partner, Carol."

Carol's eyes brimmed. "And you obviously already know my 'current' husband, Jay." David's mouth was half-open when she fled back up the stairs. Jay arched his back to allow some of the color leave his face.

"Any suggestions?"

"Am I on the clock yet?"

Jay smirked. "Not really—a deal's a deal. Let's go."

David had barely belted himself in before Jay sent the Beemer rocketing backward, tires singing, straight into the street. They slid diagonally to a stop. A minivan swept by to port in a honking swerve. David glared at Jay, who sneered back.

"What?"

He jammed down into "D" and they leapt down the hill and out the gate, ignoring the guard's cursory wave rendered from the safety of the shack—Jay out of habit and David out of fear. David swallowed and hung on as best he could as Jay bolted down to Chautauqua Boulevard, slid through the signal into the hairpin at Entrada Drive, and screamed north to Seventh. He turned and raced southwest the three miles to Fourth through a chorus of obscenities and reciprocated digital salutes. From Fourth he careened up the Olympic Boulevard on-ramp to the Santa Monica Freeway eastbound. Seeing the cars ahead crawling in queue up to the metered-access signals, Jay fishtailed onto the meager shoulder and sped around them toward the artery, still clogged near 10 A.M. He was bent on wedging himself into the merge lane when he heard the whoop and saw the blue lights behind him. He cursed and stomped the car to a stop. David exhaled. Jay seethed as he watched the Highway Patrolman's reflection set his kickstand, dismount, and stride toward his window.

"Good morning, sir. License and registration, please."

Jay released his grip on the wheel to get the documents and poked them disdainfully out the window. He peered at the officer's right breast. "Officer...Helmsin, is it?"

"That's correct, sir."

"I don't think you fully appreciate the type of trouble you're buying into, here. I'm an attorney—"

The cop raised a gloved left hand as he glanced at the license. "Tell you what, Mister Attorney...Johanessen; hold that thought while I do my radio check. Okay?" He disappeared before any further sound escaped Jay's parted lips.

"Mind a suggestion?"

Jay glowered at David. "Technically, you're still off the clock. I can handle this; I eat these guys for breakfast."

"Suit yourself. I enjoy walking—but not along

freeways."

Jay turned back to find a helmet framing sunglasses on a taut face. "Mr. Johanessen, I'm going to have to ask you to step out of the car."

"Why?" Jay demanded.

"Well, sir, leaving today aside, seems like there's a small matter of unresolved violations and a bench warrant or two. Your presence is required downtown, forthwith."

Jay crossed his arms and tossed his head. "That's impossible! There must be a mistake."

Officer Helmsin opened the door and jerked his thumb backward. "Step out, sir. Now."

Jay bounded onto the pavement, his fists clenched. The patrolman spun him efficiently into the door panel. "Place your hands on the roof of the vehicle and spread your feet." He proceeded to pat him down.

"This is an outrage! Now you listen to me; by the time my firm and I finish with you, you'll be washing cars in the Harbor Division. It won't take me 30 seconds—

"Hands behind you, sir, please." The cop slid the manacles onto Jay's wrists and snapped them into place. "Now, you just rest there, Mr. Johanessen, and I'll call a cruiser to take you in." He wheeled and Jay's face went from ruddy to crimson.

"Officer?" David's head and shoulders rose into view over the roofline.

Helmsin removed his sunglasses and squinted. "Yes?"

"A word, please?"

Helmsin palmed the grip of his sidearm. Jacketless, David revealed two empty hands.

Striding around the car, Officer Helmsin pointed at Jay. "Don't go anywhere, okay?" There was just a wisp of a smile. Jay's bulging eyes saw them join in close, indistinct conversation. David spoke calmly and Helmsin, arms folded, nodded gently. He broke away and headed back toward Jay. Before Jay could unleash another salvo, the cuffs were off.

"Your friend here has convinced me you're more trouble in custody than out. I still have to impound the vehicle, but I trust you'll take immediate steps to clear this all up. And—" He waved away Jay's incipient response. "—I strongly suggest you pay close attention to what Mr. DuPriest has to say."

David appeared at Jay's other elbow with their luggage and guided him toward the embankment while the policeman completed his duties. Jay wiped his brow. "What did you say to him?"

"Nothing special—that you were under a lot of pressure and hired me to help you overcome the self."

"Naw. That gun-toting pig is a Buddhist, *too*?"

"Well, monks do carry rifles on the lonely road but, no, not officially. He reads and meditates; says it keeps him from pulling his piece on the likes of you."

"Sonofabitch." Jay shook his head as if trying to expel something.

"What's our next move, boss?"

Jay fished into his briefcase for his Blackberry. "I'll call my secretary and have them send us a car." He speed-dialed. "Kat? It's Jay. Call ExecuTran and have them send a car out. Where? Uh, on the 10 about a mile east of Olympic—get on it, okay? Yes, again. No, the Beemer. What? Well, who gives a shit? I need a car *now*, Goddamnit." He rocked, kicked, and hurled the unit into the embankment.

David, watched, slack-jawed. "Um—do that often?"

"What?"

"Lose your—a phone."

"Once a month or so. Don't worry; I'm good for it."

Jay perched sidesaddle out an open rear door, produced a PDA, and stabbed at it while David faced front, focused on nothing, until the limo arrived. A tinted window slid down. "Executran. Mr. Johanessen?"

"About fucking time!" Jay bolted out and snatched

up his effects, jolting David out of his state. Over his shoulder, opening the rear door, Jay said, "Coming?"

"You're not going to wait for the tow truck?"

"At my hourly rate? Officer Friendly's already tagged it. Fuck it. It's the Chippers' problem now."

The broad-faced driver, hinting amusement, draped his arm along the bench seat at Jay as David slid in behind him. "Mornin', Mr. Johanessen. Bad day already, huh?"

Jay scowled. "Yeah, Kip—great so far. Your keen perception is dead-on, as usual. Too bad the Nobel committee doesn't have a category for livery drivers."

Kip's eyes shone. "Who's your wing man?"

David hesitated momentarily before extending his hand to blunt the discourtesy. "David. David DuPriest."

Kip twisted a little more and bent his elbow into an overhand shake. He eased the Town Car off the shoulder and accelerated. "You a lawyer, too?"

"Um—not really."

"Howzat, again?"

"Well, I mean, I used to be, but I'm not now. I'm a plu—"

Jay hissed.

"I guess, today, I'm an 'anti-stress advisor.'"

Kip nodded upward. "Specialize in the tougher cases, do yuh?"

David found the lilt in Kip's voice uncomfortably appealing until he noticed Jay's near-colorless hands clamped against his briefcase. He watched him meet the chauffeur's eyes in the rear-view mirror. "That's right, Kip. Two more sentences and you'll be back on the hack stand at LAX with the towel-heads."

Nice, Kip thought. He gazed back without quarter. "I don't know if he told yuh awready, Mister DuPriest, but I'm his third driver and the one outta three who puts up with his particular line of bull."

David saw that Kip's ears were getting redder, so he let the silence steep.

ഇരു

Jay strode across the concrete under Century City and assaulted the elevator button. Already half-way out his side, David circled to close the other door. He bent and bade Kip goodbye until the sound of the elevator's bell pulled him away in a trot. Inside, he braced as Jay hit "22" and punched the "Close Doors" button repeatedly. Outside, a woman struggling with a toddler and a stroller made for the still-open doors. David saw her and could see that Jay saw her. She lurched closer as the opening shrank. Jay relented and his expression went from trial to triumph—until he saw David's raised leg cross the lower sensor. The doors clanked and trundled backward; David blocked the beam with his hand while the overheated woman recovered and boarded. Regarding Jay contemptuously, she pushed the vehicle and her wide-eyed charge into the corner.

David raised his eyebrows. "Everybody in?"

She softened, and sighed. "Thank you, sir. Could you push 'four' for me, please?"

"With pleasure," David said, and obliged.

Everyone faced front for her leg of the journey. As she left, he gave her a cursory wave and wiggled his fingers at the little boy, who smiled shyly and sucked his fingers. David came to the elevator version of parade rest—hands crossed over groin, eyes focused on the floor indicators above the doorway. His peripheral vision caught Jay connecting with the "Close" button again. David didn't turn but spoke from the corner of his mouth. "Automatic."

Jay grimaced. "What?"

"The doors; they cycle automatically. Button really doesn't do anything."

Jay assumed the position coldly.

David tracked the lighted numbers' methodical creep rightward. When "20" glowed he cleared his throat. "It is as the Buddha's parable of the raft: the conveyance's value is for going, not for retaining—or, put another way, by absence of grasping one is made free."

Jay wiped his face with his palm. "Christ—speak English, willya?"

"I was." David sighed. "Consider it, will you?"

They arrived. Jay hit the opening like a tailback on a counter-trey. David followed, a distant but engaged official. The receptionist stiffened.

"Mr. Johanessen, your 10 o'clock—"

He wiped her away without looking at her.

"—Kat handed him off to the paralegals."

Jay whirled and rushed her station; he collided with the leather-covered carrel and trained an extended finger on her. "You let a client out of here billed at half my rate? Who authorized that, may I ask—" He peered at her nameplate. "—Miz Hudson?"

She lowered her chin with her eyes locked on him and pushed the boom on her headset down as if it really might prevent her from being understood clearly. "You weren't here, Sir. You couldn't be reached. She could have taken it to another partner." David glimpsed in her stare a flicker that acknowledged she'd crossed a line.

Jay's lip curled. "How long you been with us, Miz...Hudson?

"Ten months."

"Well, let's hope you make it to your first annual review." Jay steamed down the hallway, leaving them, a stray file clerk, and gawking clients in his wake.

David touched her left hand lightly. "That's a lovely stone; is it jade?"

She shifted her attention to her ring, then to David. Resentment yielded to warmth and a hint of color. "Yes—and diamonds. It's an engagement ring."

"Interesting. And your fiancée; is he—"

Rebecca Hudson gave her head a half-shake, which David took as a sign of her conviction that her bondage was temporary. "Oh, no—he's a fine artist; calligraphy and watercolor. He's Chinese."

David bowed. "Your children will be stunning. May your lives together be long and satisfying."

"Thanks." Her bodily tension drained away and her smile was pearls and pink. "Are you...Chinese?"

"I am and am not. I am open."

"That sounds like what Tsiu says." She understood.

David turned in where he found Jay's name etched in the opaque, frosted glass of a combination sconce. By stepping left, reflexively, he avoided colliding with Kathryn "Kat" Burns, Jay's indentured assistant. There she stood, weight slightly forward in cheap but fashionable tweed, her face blindly implacable. Framed by his open doorway, her arms clutched a clot of manila and bond. The cord from a headset dangled by her leg like an idle noose. Behind her a paper blizzard fell, punctuated by cursing. She bolted to a lateral file, dropped the mess on top, and glided back toward the vortex. "Be with you in just a moment..."

David caught her elbow. "It's okay; I'm with...him today. Kind of auditing."

Her eyes burned with sympathy. "I'm sorry." She went in and he followed.

Jay was sitting at his massive desk, smiling, his hands folded. Every available square inch of carpet seemed taken by sundered files. One folder remained before him. "Are we clear, Kat? There's only one case file I need for today, for the Van De Graaf conference at one?"

"Yes, Mr. Johanessen," she said meekly. "It's just that I had to handle your 10 o'clock myself and I didn't get to—" The drum of fingers cut her off. He pried her eyes up with his.

"What do we say, Kat?"

"'No excuses, Mr. Johanessen.'"

"That is correct. Kat Burns, say 'hello' to David DuPriest. He's going to make my life easier in one day—for a handsome sum, of course."

Turmoil boiled behind Kat's face as she uncrossed an

arm to greet David. "Pleeztomeechew." She disengaged and wobbled around, scooping up folders and contents.

Jay indicated a side chair. "Sit, swami." David did, and asked the obvious question in the manner of a dog, tilting his head sideways a bit.

"Oh—this?" Jay spread his hands, briefly, then angled his chair back and planted his feet on the desk. "See, Kat and I, we have this little ritual. Any day I have something big—key deposition; presettlement conference; trial; whatever—she's supposed to clear my desk of everything unrelated to that event." He ogled her backside, alongside the desk, indulging a fleeting carnal thought. "Sometimes, she doesn't get to it."

David saw her from the other end, on her hands and knees. They traded expressions; hers was solid scorn. "So, then, this was her doing?"

Jay dropped his feet to the floor and barked, "Kat? Leave us; you can finish this later."

Kat rose, smoothing her skirt and jerking down her suit jacket. She brushed at her hair and moved toward the door. "Yes, sir."

"Kat?"

She turned to see him holding out the one cogent folder. "Take your lunch hour to double-check everything's in order, okay? You brought something in, right?"

"As always, Mr. Johanessen." She took the file.

"Hey—hang on." He went into his briefcase at his feet, coming up with his PDA. He skipped it across the rosewood; it glanced into her thigh and landed at her feet. "Synch that up for me and get me a new Blackberry and set it up, too."

Kat bit her lip as she bent toward the device. She left, closing the door noiselessly.

Jay's upper eyelids were lowered. "Don't ever do that again."

"Do what?"

"Impugn my authority in this office."

David folded his hands. "You're serious, aren't you?" It wasn't really a question. "Don't be concerned; it's only a day. Anyway, that wasn't my intention. What I meant was, didn't your—the wasted two hours have something to do with it?"

"Doesn't matter."

"Certainly seemed to matter to her."

"Whoa! Is that advice I'm getting? Lead on, O Zen Master!"

David leaned in. "Don't you think your basic lack of respect for her and her feelings undermines your authority?"

"Not in this environment. Perceived weakness is the pathway to loss of power. Regardless, the relationship—Kat's and mine—it's what it is. Hey! That sounded pretty Zen, didn't it? She's her "self" and I'm my "self," right?"

"Look. Finding *satori*—'new viewpoint,' enlightenment—is grounded in personal experience. The contemplation and realization of self, yours and hers, must occur before self can be abandoned. What you just said was merely self-conscious."

"Sorry; I'm not following." Jay seemed sincerely perplexed.

"Let's back up. Do any reading outside the law?"

"You mean, now?"

David nodded.

"Oh, let's see. Popular beach trash; whatever my clients are into at the time, so I can stay a little ahead. The heavy stuff I kinda cull from *The New York Times Review of Books*. You know."

"So—your intellectual growth is based on 'hearsay?'" Jay blinked. David frowned when he saw that irony slide by. "How about college?"

"Just to nail the lower-division requirements for a business degree. Mostly American stuff."

"Any philosophy or theology in there? Comparative religion?"

"None to speak of."

"So," David grasped the chair arms, "when I say Aristotle; Plato; Aquinas; Rousseau; Descartes; Hobbs; Kierkegaard; Sartre—you would say?"

"Names. Of philosophers?"

"What about law school?"

"What about it?"

"Moses? Hammurabi? King John? Jefferson?"

"Names. Of 'lawgivers?'"

"What about concepts? Either category would do."

A glimmer. "Uh—'the meaning of life' and 'the rule of law'?"

David fought the images of Terry Jones's "Mr. Creosote" and Judge Judy out of his head. "Ah. Structure. Order out of chaos. Reason. Are we together on that?"

"I guess; wherever we're going, let's go."

"All right. Suzuki—I've mentioned him, right?— refers to all that—the body of Western existentialism— as the 'conceptual superstructure.'" The summary definitions that we're here. '*Cogito ergo sum*—I think, therefore I am.' Descartes. 'I am free and authentic; I exist.' Jean Paul Sartre."

"'I yam what I yam.' Popeye the Sailor Man."

"Funny. Zen is about piercing that superstructure to immerse oneself in everyday life. The goal is an inner spiritual experience that transforms and transcends. Here's the key, I think: the farther you are from your own experience, you are an equal distance from self-realization."

"If that's true, why all the emphasis on alone-in-the-temple, cross-legged meditation?"

"Let me make a distinction, if I'm able. As practiced in its various sects, Buddhism is a religion, with all the attendant emphasis on ritual; Zen is an antiritualistic set of disciplines. One is a football game, with all the trappings; the other is tossing a pig bladder around. In the former, *dhyana,* or *zazen*—meditation—is the end, the perfect contemplation of nothing; its mastery equals enlightenment. For Zen disciples, it is a means to an end—important but secondary to the primary exercise, which is the consideration of the *koan*, the kernel of truth, whose blossom is *satori*. Enlightenment." David slapped his thighs for emphasis. "Two doors to the same dwelling-place."

Jay rubbed his chin. "You mean, it's like in our culture, where some say that religion is essential to finding God and others say it's an obstacle?"

"Yeah, I suppose. I grew up a Catholic; when I was kid, it seemed like mere piety—mastering a strange, intricate ritual and memorizing a truckload of non-negotiable rules—was the definition of 'following Jesus,' even if it stopped at the Cathedral door. Of late, fortunately, it seems they're more dialed into following His teachings by daily example; you know, 'Do as I did,' as opposed to sitting around occasionally and talking about what somebody else said he did."

"As I recall from your invoice, you advertise yourself—"

"For the record, that's less an ad than a personal reminder."

"Whatever—'Zen Buddhism.' Isn't that self-contradictory?"

"I don't think so. Unless you're monastic or ascetic, some ritual is required to maintain focus; plus, we're social beings. I think of temple as both fellowship and continuing education."

Jay rose out of his chair, glancing at his watch. "This is all very interesting, but it's 11:45; we should wrap it up if we're going to grab lunch and make that conference by one." He rubbed his hands together. "So, take what you just said and put in the context of Kat and me."

"Here's the Rutter outline: contemplating the notion of existence—a life well-lived—is worthless unless you've *existed*. That's where *koans* come from; they're derived. Jesus, our Diety, was out there every day of his public life, down and dirty, drinking deeply from the cup of human existence. Whether he was defending whores from flying rocks or pushing Pilate, he was measuring every deed against his own *koan*—the Golden Rule."

"And, where Kat's concerned?" Jay churned the air with his hands.

David rose and hitched up his pants. He peered right into Jay. "Before you deal with Kat, or anyone else, try to see where you all are in the Big Picture. Reflect; anticipate the results of your actions. Act accordingly."

Jay paused at the window, hands on hips, to check on the skyline. "You know, Kat and I had it pretty good the first year or so. I helped her climb out of a bad marriage, got her full custody of Benjie. We actually had fun together, here."

"How long ago was that?"

"Five years. I got unhitched, remarried. Carol got jealous and froze her out. I've grown unhappier and Kat's borne the brunt of it. Being a single Mom and a solid Christmas bonus are probably the only reasons she's still here; she's that good."

They grabbed their jackets and walked out into the outer office. Kat swiveled in her chair and, eyes lowered, held out the Van De Graaf file. "Everything's there."

"Kat." Jay watched his finger draw a border around her stapler. "Sorry, uh, about this morning..."

"Oh, Mr. Johanessen, that's—"

"No." He raised the hand as if to swear and affirm, then went into his pocket and peeled off some twenties. "Grab some of the girls and take a regular lunch, on me, and buy Benjie a pizza with what's left. Take whatever time you need with the, uh, files. What's on for tomorrow?"

"Hm, Friday." She scrolled through Outlook. "Nothing major."

"Why don't you take off—on condition it's something fun. No housework. Promise?"

"Why—oh, sure, Mr. J—"

"Jay."

"Jay. Thanks!"

His jacket slung over his shoulder, Jay was on his way, shouting from the hallway. "We're going to grab a quick bite at Mario's; I'll get the file on my way to our conference room."

David watched a pleasantly flummoxed Kat from the doorway. Her mouth still hung open and her eyebrows were creeping slowly down from under her bangs. David grinned. "Path to enlightenment."

She laid the file down deliberately and tried to reflect. Moments passed; something seized her and she jumped up. "Wait! Shall I call for your table?"

The elevator doors closed.

℁ℂ

"Mr. Johanessen! Good morning! A little early for you today, yes?"

"Karl; what's up? Is my table open?"

Karl tugged at his cravat. "But you did not telephone for lunch today, my friend..."

Jay darkened. "Now, listen to me, Karl..." He felt David's fingers close on his tricep; he relaxed. "No big deal, Karl—whatever you got. Anything but the kitchen, okay?" David stepped from behind him, smiling.

"Very good, sir. That would be two, then?"

They were seated, ministered to, and suffered the litany of specials. Jay pointed to the menu on which David's hands rested. "You gonna check it out, or did you hear something you liked already? They do killer veal *Parmiagana* and clams Casino here."

"I'm a vegetarian. Thanks."

"The house Chianti's good. Do you drink wine?"

"Nope. Pellegrino will do nicely." David began to browse.

"Oh. Body's a temple; is that it?"

"Not really; I just prefer to keep the distractions to a

minimum. Cuts down on the psychological clutter."

"So—what does it for you? Brown rice? Lentils?" Jay was warming to his own wit. "I know! Bamboo shoots."

David snapped his menu shut. "I'm thinking hearts of Romaine with Balsamic vinegar and goat cheese ravioli with pesto sauce." He exaggerated an elevated sniff. "Is that sarcasm I smell?"

"No, not exactly. I'm just not tracking this, this belief system of yours."

David fixed on Jay. "It's not a system of beliefs."

"See?" Jay slapped the table. "That's my problem. All I've gotten from you so far is what it's *not*! What *is it*?"

"Relax. It's frustrating; Zen is by definition contradictory because it embraces both logic and illogic—thesis and antithesis."

"You *still* haven't answered my question."

"Fair enough. Ready?"

Hesitation. "Think so..."

"Pursuit of the highest affirmation, where *there are no antitheses*."

"How is that possible? Where there is good, there is evil; morality, immorality. God and Satan."

"To us in the West, that is logical. Theologically and philosophically sound."

"As I said..."

"To a follower of Zen, it is mere concept and convention; immaterial."

"Then, what decrees a moral life in Zen?"

"The core of Zen is the inner human spirit, pure and good. It is there; it transcends. Whatever burdens or diminishes it injures its wholesomeness. It cannot be chased, seized, or earned. It is found. It cannot be inflated, nourished, or defeated. It *is*."

"But, that doesn't *explain* anything."

"*Now* you've got it."

"Huh?"

"Maybe this will help." David rooted around in his

backpack and came up with a thin volume—*An Introduction to Zen Buddhism,* by D. T. Suzuki. "I know I've mentioned Suzuki. Here—" he thumbed to a dog-eared page "—listen to this: 'When Joshu was asked what the Tao'—truth—'was, he answered, "Your everyday life, that is the Tao." In other words, a quiet, self-confident, and trustful existence of your own—this is the truth of Zen, and what I mean when I say that Zen is pre-eminently practical. It appeals directly to life, not even making reference to a soul or to God, or to anything that interferes with or disturbs the ordinary course of living. The idea of Zen is to catch life as it flows. There is nothing extraordinary or mysterious about Zen.'"

"But, how—"

"Wait; listen. 'I raise my hand; I take a book from the other side of this desk; I hear boys playing ball outside my window; I see the clouds blown away beyond the neighboring woods—in all these I am practicing Zen. No wordy discussion is necessary, nor any explanation. I do not know why—and there is no need of explaining, but when the sun rises the whole world dances with joy and everybody's heart is filled with bliss. If Zen is at all conceivable, it must be taken hold of here.'"

David laid the book by his plate and searched for a tatter in Jay's shroud of confusion. The lawyer lifted his arms, grasping, and gave up; he smoothed his hair as the waiter glided over with the tray.

"Don't give up; there is no road to Damascus in Zen— Hell, for that matter, there's no road, nor destination. You're already there; you're just asleep. Take a break. Chew on it. And your food."

ᔕᔕᘉᖇ

At barely one o'clock, the pair flew toward Jay's office; anticipating, Kat extended the Van De Graaf file like a railside mail sack. Jay nabbed it and thundered by; David loped comfortably behind. She stuck her head into the slipstream. "They're in there."

Jay pulled up just short of the conference room's double doors and grinned at David. "Watch—and see what you've missed."

David folded his hands before his face. "Your obedient servant."

Bruce Greenbush, Esquire, pushed back and rose, checking his Movado Revi Museum. He charged around, smoothing his heavy silk Hermés, and clapped Jay on the upper arm. "Jay? Right on the button—almost."

"*Enchanté*, Bruce." They gripped and made a quarter-turn, wary primates without the overt sniffing. Counsel for respondent saw David and thrust his hand out. "Bruce Greenbush. And you are..."

"David DuPriest."

"Pleasure!" came from behind the plastic smile. He released and leaned into Jay. "What's this?" he said, not-so-*sotto voce*.

"David? He's...clerking with me, short-term."

Bruce eyed David with suspicion. "Kinda old—and irregular, to say the least."

"Take it easy; it's just a favor for a friend. Think of it as 'Career Day: Two Masters at Work.'"

"He understands the privilege, and so forth, I presume."

"Of course. Ready, I presume?"

"You'll know soon enough, pal."

They disengaged and took their respective sides. David settled into an armchair against the wall, at the end of the table nearest the door. Bruce placed his hand at the nape of his dyspeptic-looking retainee and whispered to him, pointing at David. He straightened. "Jay? My client, Norman Van De Graaf. You've received our offer of disposition and settlement, correct?"

Jay opened the folder deliberately and smoothed the top document. He stared hard at Norman. "Tara—Mrs. Van De Graaf—and I have reviewed it, yes." She sniffled and fumbled with the purse in her lap. Jay reached to the center for a tissue and delivered it with a flourish.

"I'm so sorry," she said, scouring her nostrils with scented cellulose. Jay patted her arm. Bruce rolled his eyes and Norman watched her reflection in the glass-topped, polyurethane gulf between them. His lip quivered imperceptibly.

Bruce moved to cut the drama short. "Well. Shall we review the terms for property division we've outlined?"

"Based on what you've proffered here, Bruce, I'd be inclined to advise Tara to file for an Order to Show Cause tomorrow. The shares of future business income are unrealistic and your inventory of noncommunity assets is a non-starter. If your client wants to fight this all the way down the line to trial, I think—" Jay lifted Tara's mucous-free left hand in his, lacing their fingers; she fidgeted. "—We have a lot to work with in the custody and support areas from an emotional standpoint." He transferred his attention from Norman to his counsel. "Bruce."

"Uh-huh." An earnest smirk appeared as he produced a fat accordion file. "Well, why don't we just take a few minutes to review the good work of our appraisers and accountants?"

Under the drone of the intensifying thrust-and-parry, David focused on the Van De Graafs. *Not your run-of-the-mill Bel Air bust-up,* he thought. *Nothing ostentatious about either of them. Well-dressed but conservative—certainly by L.A. standards. No obvious cosmetic enhancements; she might even do her own nails.* He was graying and thinning on top and she appeared her age—both of them upper forties, give or take. *No May-September trophy situation here.* If there were kids involved, they had to be at least high-school age. Early on, they stole glances at each other, flicking their eyes away quickly to avoid detection. As their advocates fenced, the pair's evasion slowed. They each looked, looked back, and seemed to grow indifferent as to whether the mouthpieces might notice. Bruce's and Jay's weren't the only pleadings in the room under review. David stood; the couple saw him.

"Is this truly what you want to do?"

Norman and Tara traded one more telegraph before they silently consulted counsel. Bruce was dumbstruck, in mid-sentence; Jay's chin slipped out of his hand.

Bruce leaped to his feet, flushed. *"ExCUSE ME?!"*

Jay was right behind. "What are you *DOING?!"*

"Norm?" Soft and expectant, Tara isolated on her husband.

Norman pushed his chair back, by gesture inviting Tara to do the same. Turning to Bruce, he said, "I'd like to give this a little more time, if you don't mind." Tara nodded, already moving toward the door. "Uh, thanks," she mumbled. Jay held up his hand; she ducked around it.

Unfrozen, Bruce shoveled paper into his catalog case, his laser-hot eyes beaming from David to Jay and back. "I do hope you can come up with some kind of explanation for this, Johanessen. Unprecedented!" He stormed out, running up on the Van De Graffs, strolling out arm-in-arm. Norman shielded his wife from the charge, collapsing them both gently against the open door. "I'll call you next week," he offered lamely. Bruce grunted and disappeared.

In the sudden silence, David waited, swaying a little. Jay slouched, his elbows propped on the chair's arms, tapping his pursed lips rhythmically with his interlaced hands and looking out the windows. "Sit down."

"I'd rather stand."

Jay swiveled toward him, sullen, and dropped his hands. "What the *fuck* was *that*?"

David set his bag on the table and worked a zipper. "May I read?"

Jay exhaled with force and abruptly turned up a palm. "Oh, why not? Please!"

David found his volume of choice and cleared his

throat. "'The venerable Shariputra asked the Buddha, "How am I to behave, O Lord, toward those in conflict?"'

"'Do not reprove them, Shariputra,' said the Blessed One, 'for harsh words do not serve as a remedy and are pleasant to no one. Assign them to separate dwelling-places and treat them with impartial justice. Listen with patience to both parties. Only the person who weighs both sides is called a sage. When both parties have presented their cases, let the community come to an agreement and declare the re-establishment of concord.'"

"Okay, okay," Jay interrupted. "We should have been nicer and gone to trial anyway. Doesn't explain why you just blew up the settlement conference."

"Please. Hear this out: 'There are two ways of re-establishing concord: one is in the letter, and the other is in the spirit and the letter. If the community declares the re-establishment of concord without having inquired into the matter, the peace is concluded in the letter only. But if the community, having inquired into the matter and having gone to the bottom of it, decides to declare the re-establishment of concord, the peace is concluded in the spirit and also in the letter.'"

"'The concord re-established in the spirit and in the letter is alone right and lawful.'" David closed the tome, silently expectant.

Jay was unmoved. "Don't see the connection. Bruce and I 'inquired into the matter' and counseled our clients accordingly. They're in control; we're just their instruments."

"That's not what I saw. I saw two people watching their lives unravel while they sat by, silent and powerless. This whole process is driven by the letter, not the spirit. To you, it's a construct, a game. 'Follow me, Point-A-to-Point-B. The-peace-is-concluded-in-the-letter; sign here. Pay me; thank-you-very-much. Good-bye-and-good-luck.' Remember what I said about the wholeness of spirit? To fail to even acknowledge it, let alone respect and try to understand it, is to do it the greatest harm."

"What are we supposed to do, then? Give it up and send everybody away to mediation?"

"That's a choice, a conceit—not a solution. The goal is affirmation; the *koan* is to 're-establish the concord in the spirit and in the letter.' Did you ever ask your client the question I asked in here today?"

Bruce was on his feet, shaking. "You know what? This is all very interesting but, at the end of the day, it's just so much *bullshit*. It's not my job to psychoanalyze these assholes. She got the counseling and mediation options laid out for her in the client materials. She was hurting, wanted the old man to pay, so she signed up and we went for it. Plus, there's a business side to all this and I've got obligations." His voice trembling, Jay leveled a finger. "Know what else? *You* were supposed to help me out here—simplify my life. Instead, I'm back to Square One with a client because of you—that is, *if* she's still even my client! The costs I've frontloaded on the firm on this one, I'm facing fee losses three times what I offered you—and Norm's good for it! That's a 50 grand turnaround; not bad for one afternoon. You're not getting a red cent from *me*, Krishna!"

Now perched on the edge of the table, his arms folded, David couldn't suppress a small smile.

Jay verged on apoplexy. "What? Is something *funny*?!"

"I was just thinking—*I* should pay *you*. I'm the one who got the affirmation."

"Which is...?"

"That I made the right choice, years ago. I was standing at the same fork in the road that you've already taken. Look, Jay—forget our little agreement. There's no magic bullet and I can't do anything for you in this environment—even if I felt you were willing. You're too close to it all when you're here, to see everything you need to see. Tell you what. My temple's having a social gathering in Griffith Park on Sunday at two o'clock—families. You, Carol, and Skylar are welcome to come. Maybe that's a sufficient distance."

"Don't do me any more favors, DuPriest. Speaking of distance: you know where the elevators are."

ℴℴ

The day was gloriously green and gold as the funereal Town Car wound its way toward the Pecan Grove picnic area inside Griffith Park. It was shortly before two; Jay hadn't spoken to David since Thursday afternoon but he'd had Kat call the temple and get directions.

Kip slowed near the head of the parking area. "What next, Mr. J.?"

"Slide down the back side toward the corner and park within sight of that closest group."

"You got it."

The car stopped and Jay spotted David's spare frame being pushed around by a bubbly, shrieking teenaged girl. *Must be Lizzie.* Her mother, Jay guessed, sat serenely by, shaking her head slowly as the pair toppled to the turf. Jay speed-dialed his new Blackberry.

"'Lo?"

"Were you asleep?"

"No. I'm drunk—if you care. Where're you?"

"Griffith Park."

"Golfing on a public course? Slumming, are we?"

"No golf. I'm meeting someone."

"She pretty?"

"Damn it, Carol. Where's Skylar?"

"God knows. Mall, if I had to wager. Why?"

"Can you come over?"

"In my condition? Bad idea..."

"Please. This is important."

"More important than '*PO-KER*?'" Her end clattered and went dead. Jay stared at the display in his hand until it fell into his lap.

Kip monitored the rear-view mirror, respecting the embarrassed quiet. Finally he gripped the front passenger's headrest and pulled himself around.
"Where to, Boss?"
Jay looked out at nothing. "Drive on, Kip. Drive on."

ഹരു

11 **Robbin' Hood**

ಬಾ

The furrows above Pettirosso "Petey" DiCappello's mono-brow plotted all his meager concentration, intent on the fiberboard tray between his porcine hands. His lips formed unuttered words as he left Italian People's to cross Butler.

Lemmesee—two milk, one sugar; one cream, no sugar; one double-mocha, half-caf... He blinked. *That Billy. What a* fessacchione—*coffee is coffee, right?*

BEEEEEEeeeeeep!

"Madre del Dio!"

The red SUV's glancing pass caused a comic bullfighter's pirouette. Panic forced Petey to collapse his grip, sandwiching the tray and crushing the bagged baked goods in the middle. Only one lid popped, but half that cup sloshed onto his left hand.

"OWWWW! Sonafa—"

He faltered in pain momentarily, but the insistent rush hour restored his grip and he waddled to safety through the remaining maelstrom of cars and curses. He laid the tray on a trash can, dug out his handkerchief, and pressed the throb out of his wet flesh. He picked the errant lid off a mummified rodent corpse in the gutter, cleaned it deliberately with his handkerchief, and replaced it. He mopped vainly at the cups, their ochre stains already preserved in the absorbent Styrofoam, and turned his attention to the crumpled bag. It was stained through and clung to its gelatinous inner mass like clothing to a burn victim. He tried a careful separation, tearing one seam top to bottom. He poked at the amorphous mess but only managed only to separate the Danish shale into an approximate number of indistinct units. Rearranging a few raisins and relocating some jelly at random helped, he thought.

Petey lifted his project, exhaled, and headed for the door of the *Ereditare di Italia* (Sons of Italy) Social Club, a storefront that grew more anachronistic daily as Butler Avenue and the rest of Chambersburg—known with affection to its denizens as "The 'Burg"—was dragged by gentrification toward that REALTOR® kind of respectability that typifies 21st-Century urban renewal. The Club's ugly, squat elevation could illustrate "eyesore" in Webster's on the natural; nearby pastel-oak-and-fern renovations and re-openings just made matters worse. It was anchored to the sidewalk by four courses of the blond brick last popular when Buicks were classified by their number of fender "holes." The shin-to-hairline plate glass and aluminum-frame door were all sheathed inside by vertically-applied rolls of contact vinyl that looked less like the intended stained glass than a blizzard of Technicolor confetti. One small corner offered the only promise of a glimpse inside but most of it was taken up by an old duochrome of John Paul II, which by now—being outside the beaten awning's daytime penumbra—looked more frail than its subject. Up above, the paint-starved basso-rilievo featuring Jupiter, Juno, and a gaggle of lesser deities might still have lent a modicum of dignity, had time and perching pigeons been kinder.

Petey put his beefy shoulder to the door and stumbled inside, underestimating as always the spring's degree of exhaustion. The Club's dim interior was consistent with its public face. Light came from sputtering fluorescence, beer signs, and the clanging glare of *macchine del pinball*. Sludge from generations of grease, grime, and tobacco smoke had paralyzed the beaten-tin *cherubim* in the ceiling tiles. Even a trained eye could produce at best a guess as to what color they— or the walls or the floor, for that matter—were. The kitchen, bar, and corner stage had long ago ceased to pique or satisfy gustatory and carnal appetites; about the only evidence they ever had were the odd bottle of Grappa or Galliano and the few remaining dingy portraits of regional headliners and ecdysiasts. The place's ambience had fallen so far below its own traditions or bare potential that it seemed to magnify the suffering of the occupant of the Crucifix in the far corner. A brand-new, imported brass espresso machine stood as sole evidence of the Club's present utility—a day room where mob *soldati* congregated for morning roll-call and family business assignments. Like its possible users, all it lacked for efficient performance was the proper connections—but who was to call the plumber was an assignment that always seemed to fall between the stools. So, after the ritual of accusations and throwing up of hands, Petey was pushed into traffic every morning to fetch breakfast for those without domestic resources.

The cascade of light punctured Giovanni Nonnula's concentration as he pounded his hip into the *Star Trek* machine, featuring a ridiculously top-heavy Lieutenant Uhuru. He turned, the ball dove between the flippers, and the machine mocked his latest failure to break into the top 10 scores with spiraling cartoon sounds. His bloodhound face fell further when he saw that Petey had muffed his simple task again. As his closest—well, only—friend, Giovanni broke noiselessly toward Biglietta "Billy" Scarlattino, who'd spotted the carnage and was halfway out of his chair with his mouth fully open.

"F'Chrissakes, Petey! Not again!"

Billy allowed Petey to set the goods down one-handed before he snagged his other arm above the elbow and spun him while hooking his foot behind Petey's nearer ankle. Petey hit hard on one buttock and splayed as far backward as Billy's grip permitted. Billy cocked his free fist and an eyebrow. "Sorry, Petey; you're outta luck. Maybe a simple beatin' makes an impression..."

Billy's focus was interrupted by the sudden ascension of a manicured right pinkie that he recognized as Giovanni's, which promptly disappeared up his right nostril, up to the gold-and-onyx Knights of Columbus ring. (It was merely a keepsake, a token from his *Zio* Sal—not a talisman. Giovanni owed his own fealty to but one liege.) Giovanni stepped into his swing and raised Billy, whose hands were now welded to the bigger man's forearms, to the balls of his feet. Petey slumped onto his back and covered his head. Billy remained on the hook while Giovanni paused to allow the rest of the fight to fall out of him and helped Petey up. After his center of gravity and breath came back, Billy crouched and tented his fingers over his nose, checking its integrity and position. He opened his hands as carefully as a missalette, relieved at the absence of tissue and non-mucosal fluid. Only then did something between a squeak and a nasal sigh find its way out of him, as prologue. "Jeezus Christ, Loot! Goddamn it! Fuck! OW!"

Giovanni's nickname had double significance. It referred, first, to his facility for keeping his assigned clients off the tab, making for a large and reliable weekly take. This, his other physical skills, and mute loyalty had put him on the fast track to being made among men. The moniker's other attribution was to his frequent and most favorite adverb.

Alain "Frankie" Valle, the club's self-anointed musician-historian, pitched a perfect low whistle. (His mother was a French war bride who'd extorted passage for herself and *le bébé* to Jersey out of the old man, then liberated herself. He hadn't had to wait for his own street christening; constant explanation drove him to it early on his own.)

"Holy shit, Loot! Where'd you learn that—Bruce Lee?"

"Naw—close, but no cheroot. Sun-Tzu. *Art of Warfare.*"

Ricky Necroforo weighed in. "Art's son—who?"

Frankie was annoyed but undeterred. "Who's he?"

"Chinese warlord and philosopher," said Loot.

"Where's he from? Upstate?"

Loot sighed. "It's a book, Frankie. Centuries old. About strategies—like surprise."

Shock and awe—brought on whenever it was suspected that someone had scratched into something more deeply literary than the *New York Post* ("Trick 'Em to Win!'/Says Gook Guru")—smothered that line of conversation.

"Still," Frankie managed, "That was fuckin' *impressive.*"

"Abs'loot'ly," said Loot.

Loot adjusted his hand slightly on the nape of Billy's neck. He'd raised him up by the collar originally to get him to stop shuddering and whimpering; now he was patting him gently, to relieve Billy's embarrassment and replace it with a little respect. Loot was that kind of leader. He kicked a chair out and pointed; Billy sat. Loot bent from the waist and rocked on his knuckles until there was regular order—which wasn't long. "Petey, give out what you got to those that ordered so's we can do some business."

Petey circled the table and did so as best he and they remembered, deflecting the sidelong glares of disappointment. There was no public protest, other than slightly nettled slurping and munching.

"Awright. Bobby, where are we?"

Roberto Tucca already had a sheaf of spreadsheets

out of his briefcase and on the table. He smoothed his retreating salt-and-pepper hair and adjusted his squarish reading glasses.   His devotion to dark semiformal attire alone—not to mention his canonical intonation and his ramrod posture—was enough to justify the honorific "Rev." As it was, his glancing affair with the seminary, with the unpleasantness about lending to classmates at usurious rates and his inscrutable accounts that lent little in the way of actual proof, justly earned it for him. Oh, he eschewed the title's use personally and discouraged it generally, remaining close enough to Holy Mother Church to fear the fires of Hell for such casual blasphemy. Nonetheless, he understood it was born out of admiration. His mastery of the entire Intuit suite and associated techno-jargon only reinforced his image in this subculture of the 'Burg as a mystic, a higher order of life.

"Right—third quarter results. We're 14 percent up on the pension fund skim, probably due to high-season day labor, and the take on the hockey and miscellaneous arena event tickets was up as well—even over better attendance numbers this summer—"

Loot dropped his hand on the ledger and pointed toward the corner. "Good job, Petey. Abs'loot'ly. You'll make it go on the baseball and the rock and highbrow stuff this season, too, right?"

Petey edged into the light a little and smiled. "Entertainment"—scalping and counterfeiting ducats— was his turf. Loot checked around for any sign of mockery. Satisfied, he lifted his hand.

"G'head, Rev."

"The construction and waste pads are holding their own. Documents are still depressed; the Chinese have really stepped it up, bringing the illegals in, in cans—

"Fuckin' Chinks," said Billy.

Rev cleared his throat.   "'Miscellaneous'—broads; booze; drugs; loans; simple protection—we're still losing ground to the Cubans and crackheads. That's the overview."

"Ain't like it was, is it?" asked Gil Manobianco, their armorer and enforcer. They all paused to reflect briefly on changing times and tides, each according to his ability. Gil stubbed out his Camel.

"Time was, anybody cut in on us like that, they got moved on—like, yesterday!"

Billy pounded down a fist. "AB-so-fuckin'—"

Loot's eyebrows twitched.

Billy caught himself in time. "—Ay!"

"What's the total, Rev?"

Rev flipped the page back and forth. "Goddamn it— I forgot to sum the last column! Little help, Petey?"

Petey slipped over and glanced at the pages. "Three million, six-ninety-nine, seven-forty-two—and change," he said casually.

"How much, EXACTLY?" demanded Billy, grinning like a yawning horse.

"Sixty-three cents." Petey smiled back. Loot blinked. Billy cursed.

It was Petey's only gift, other than his good and guileless heart. As Mama used to say, he was behind the door when God gave out everything else.

Loot banged his meat-and-bone gavel to adjourn. "Good—everybody outta this *merdiao* and on the street. Stay busy. *'A rubar poco si va in galera, a rubar tanto si fa cariera.'*" (It was his favorite proverb, with which he ended every meeting at the Sons': "Steal a little, go to jail; steal a lot, make a career.")

Petey hung back. "Can I take a little time to go check on Richey, Loot?"

"Abs'loot'ly. My best to Maria and her *giovane*. And, Petey—" Loot caught his arm, looking grave, but patted his cheek tenderly. "Don't get behind again. Yes?"

Petey turned the hand, kissed the ring, and disappeared.

ℬℛ

"Cap!"

Maria DiCorragio dragged her brother off the tired cement stoop and into her russet-brick rowhouse. (She'd never liked "Petey." It was too "little-boy" for the dimly earnest bodyguard who—though challenged himself—had seen her safely to womanhood, until she and Leon married. He was recalled to duty when his brother-in-law came back from the Gulf and took sick.) Petey widened his eyes to overcome the sudden gloom while she kissed his cheek.

"Hey, Sis." Petey's olfactory lobes came to life.

"*Specialità della casa—cannoli!*" she chirped. "Fifteen more minutes. Hope you're hungry." She poked at his girth. Petey smiled ruefully, cuffed the back of her neck like an overgrown lion cub, and dropped a letter-sized manila envelope on the kitchen table.

"It ain't as much as last month; times is gettin' tougher, I guess. Loot says—"

Maria shushed him with an index finger. "Cappy, you know I can't hear about it. You've been there for Richey and me since Leon died. I couldn't make it just on the pension and my job. I can never repay all your kindnesses, or your loyalty." She slid her arms around his waist and nestled her head under his chins. "*Come sei bella*," she whispered.

He kissed into her luxuriant Mediterranean hair. *Ti penso sempre,* he thought. "Even if I ain't the sharpest knife in the drawer?"

"Oh, Cap..." She tightened her grip.

"Richey in his room?"

"Yeah," she said. "Asthma's kicking up again."

Petey lumbered down the narrow hallway to the back bedroom. Richey sat on his bed, his bony knees drawn under his chin, picking intently at the laptop that had fallen off the truck right before last Christmas. He turned and most of the fatigue fell from his gaunt face.

"Unc!" he cried, springing onto Petey. They clapped each other and traded kisses. As he returned Richey to his perch, Petey noticed an imposing, hard-cover book next to the disk inhaler.

"Whatcha doin' over here?"

"Studying. I'm working on a paper on the legend of Robin of Locksley."

Petey picked up the violet volume and studied its gilded spine. *Robin Hood, by J.C. Holt.* Nothing registered. "Who's 'Robin Hood?'

Richey was incredulous but recovered quickly. "He's an outlaw, Uncle Cap. Like John Gotti—but nice."

"No kiddin'. Is he a made guy?"

"*Was.* He lived 800 years ago."

Petey squinted at the woodblock-printed frontspiece. "He's wearin' pantyhose—looks like a *frocio*!"

Being 11, Richey hadn't heard that term as yet—or, if so, hadn't owned up. "*Everybody* dressed like that then. For real—you don't know *anything* about Robin Hood?"

Petey brightened. "Oh, yeah. That thing that Mel Brooks did—about queer guys prancin' in the woods on the Home Box Office. Am I right?"

Richey laughed so hard he toppled onto his side and began coughing. Petey came for him, but Richey waved him off while deftly discharging the diskus and sucking down the medication. "I'm okay," he gasped. He focused until his breaths were regular. "Unc, Robin Hood was an outlaw because the law—weak Prince John and the Sheriff of Nottingham—was the enemy of the common people."

"Oh," Petey mused. "Kinda like the Justice Department?"

Richey stifled a giggle. "No—well, I dunno. I mean, they were cruel and overtaxed them and kept them down."

"I got it—the Legislature!"

Richey smacked his own forehead back onto his pillow. "Anyway, Robin Hood and his Merry Men stole from them and rich people who rode through Sherwood Forest and gave the money back to the poor." He hefted the book at his uncle. "Do you want to read about it when I'm done?"

Petey recoiled. "Richey, you know I'm a *babbo* when it comes to readin' and learnin' and stuff." He couldn't hide his disappointment.

"Wait!" Richey rolled to the far side of the bed and groped underneath. He dragged out a white cardboard carton, shifted the lid and came up with a glassine envelope. "Here—check it out!"

Petey was reluctant but Richey foisted it on him. "It's a Classics Illustrated Fourteenth Edition, Series Seven 'Robin Hood,' with the hand-painted cover. Got it for 28 bucks at Eastside Comix. 'Very Fine Condition.' Cool, huh?"

Petey sought permission with his eyes to remove it. Richey nodded, his lips parted in anticipation. Petey leafed through the pages as delicately as he could manage. "A fuckin' funny book! *Merda!*" Petey put his fist to his mouth and dipped his head, in fear that Maria had overheard. She tolerated profanity *in Italiano*; Anglo-Saxon was beyond the pale. Hearing nothing, he exhaled and resumed looking at the pictures. "Now, *this* is more my cuppa Joe!"

Richey spread his hands magnanimously. "Go on— take it with you." He turned serious. "Just don't mess it up, okay? That's a month's allowance right there, and part of the college fund," he said, gesturing at the box.

"You sure?"

"Absolutely!"

Petey rolled the document in half and placed it gingerly in an inside breast pocket, patting it through his gabardine jacket for good measure. He saw that Richey was peering at his machine again, so he half-knelt next to him and looked himself. On the screen was a sheet that looked like the ones the Rev carried around. "What's that?"

Richey shifted his eyes a little. "Keep a secret?"

"*Omertá*," Petey vowed, air-locking his lips with a flourish.

"My friend, Vigo, from school—his older brother's takin' computer science at the college. He's a *hacker*."

"I dunno what that is."

"It's a guy who uses a computer to break into other people's stuff—like bank accounts and whatnot."

Petey looked behind the screen. "What's he do—take off the back?"

"Jeez, Unc!" Richey punched Petey on his crossed forearm. "It's all done on-line, hooked up to the phone!"

"What's that, on there now?"

"It's the mid-term grades for my class."

Petey puffed himself up. "Young fella, do you know what the penalty is in the State of New Jersey for receiving stolen goods?"

Richey slapped his cheeks in mock horror, then thought a bit. "Hey! Do you think I could get made as an earner for a *borgata* by being a cyber-criminal?"

"*Figlio del Madonna!*" Petey threw an arm around his nephew and squeezed. "Don't let your Mama hear you talkin' like that! She married a legit guy so's you'd be legit, too."

"But—Grandpops was made, wasn't he?"

"Yeh, he was," Petey said pensively. "A lieutenant— God rest his soul." He crossed himself and kissed his thumbnail reflexively. "Only reason they still keep me around, outta his respect." *Still,* he thought, *it'd be nice to have another made guy before the line dies out. Aw, f'get aboudit.* He shook it off and pushed a finger at the boy. "You just work on getting' healthy so's you got a chance of catchin' them *donne giovani* when you start chasin' em. *Capisce?*"

"Unc?"

"What?"

"Are you gonna get married and have a kid someday?"

Petey laughed derisively. "Christ, kid, I can barely tie my own shoes. What's a nice girl gonna do with a *fannullone* like me? Besides—" he kissed the crown of Richey's towhead—"who needs a *figlio bastardo* around when I got a great kid like you to be pals with?"

ೕೲ

Loot wheeled his black Escalade into traffic toward their first stop on morning rounds. He looked over at Petey at the first red light.

"What're you readin' over there?"

"Funny book—about Robin Hood. Richey gave it to me; he's readin' the real book for school." The light changed and they continued in silence until Petey lowered the comic. "Loot, d'ya think we're like Robin Hood and his Merry Men?"

"Howzat?"

"I mean, like, we're stickin' up for the poor, takin' care of 'em and protectin' em from harm."

A distant look came over Loot. "Aw—maybe in times past, when life was simpler, it was like that. Honor-bound—noble, even. Now, we're just carryin' out orders and rollin' with the times. Nah, not Robin Hood; *Rashomon*, maybe."

Petey was lost. "Who?"

"Movie about the murder of an old-time Japanese mercenary—*samurai*." He glanced at Petey, still at sea. "Soldier for hire; you know, a button. Kinda like Gil."

"Was he a boss?"

"Naw, they were loners—didn't mob up, just wandered around lookin' for work. No *Cosa Nostra* for them. They carried their code inside—*hagakure*."

"Huh?"

"'The way of the samurai.'"

From the clouds over his face, Loot could tell Petey was intrigued. "So these Sammy guys—"

"*Samurai*."

"Yeh—so, they made up their own rules and did their own thing?"

"Not exactly; they did the jobs their masters hired 'em for—burn guys, guard the castle, and so forth—but everything they did was guided by their own, strict beliefs." Petey was still struggling, so Loot tapped his arm to get his attention and aimed his flat hand, fingers first, at his own sternum. "*Inside*, Petey. They took their orders from in here. They were loyal to their masters and did their work faithfully, as long as it didn't break the code. If it did, they whacked *themselves*."

"Now, *that* is fucked *up!*" Petey went quiet, already well past sensory overload. He mulled. He shifted. He looked out the window. "Is there a funny book I could look at about it, Loot?"

"Not that I know of—but, pretty good movie a couple years ago you could rent. *Ghost Dog*, starrin' Forest Whitaker as the warrior and a buncha *minchioni* playin' a *brugad*. Got that annoyin' hip-hop *merda* in it, instead of real music, but it gets the point across."

"Wait. Ain't that Forest Sherwood guy *uomo nero*?"

"'Whitaker'—Forest '*Whitaker*.' Yeah, he is. So?"

"I dunno, Loot. I got trouble with a Jap *or* a Blackamoor bein' a made guy."

Loot's jaw slackened. "'*Blackamoor*?!' Where the Hell did *that* come from, Petey?"

"Here," Petey said, raising the comic. "An African guy shows up on accounta some war or other—I didn't get it."

Loot whistled softly. "You're really somethin', Pettirosso DiCappello. A genu-wine piece of fuckin' work."

"Yeh?"

"Abs'loot'ly."

"Loot, I think I'm gonna stick with just Robin Hood right now, if that's okay." Petey returned to his literature without acknowledgement.

Loot checked his mirrors and signaled for a left. "You

do that, Petey. You do that."

℠ℛ

Petey had just turned in that Friday's receipts on hockey and Arena tickets to the Rev and was headed over to Sal DeForte's for lunch. *A nice Veal Capri and gnocchi—yeh, I earned it,* he thought. The late spring air was already delicious and the buttoned, heavy coats were giving way to light sweaters and open jackets. After four months of little more than big hair and lacquered nails on the streets to feed fantasies, the emergence from hibernation of the more stimulating attributes was turning conversation at the Club seasonally randy. Petey was oblivious, as always, they thought. A *chiavata* a couple times a month with his regular *battona* was as good as it got for him, they thought. What they didn't know was that the flowering freshness of even a Jersey girl stirred him more than hormonally. *All women should get respect,* he thought. *They could all be Maid Marian.* His cell phone went off. "H'lo? This is Petey speakin'."

It was Maria. "Cap, listen..." She sounded more urgent and tired than usual. "I gotta put Richey in the hospital."

"What's wrong?"

"His regular doctor at the V.A. Clinic wants to do some tests over at the Med Center in Lyons. He's been coughing up a lot more crud and the aerosols he's been using just don't seem to help him breathe anymore, and the cramps and diarrhea are getting worse."

"How's he doin', though?"

Maria knew what he meant. "Oh, you know Richey— 'Little Mario Sunshine.'"

"When does he gotta go?"

"Tomorrow." She faltered a little. "You'll drive over with me?"

"You know I will, Sis. What time?"

"Doc's gonna meet us up there; he wants to check him in right away. We should leave by seven."

"Pick me up at the apartment, okay? G'bye," Petey said and snapped his cell shut. He jammed his hands in his pockets and hunched his shoulders. It seemed colder.

ಐಎ

It could have been the comic sliding from his lap to the floor or Richey's latest coughing fit, but he was awake now. Petey sat up and was seized by the stiffness that comes from a fitful night in a hospital-issue side chair. As he flexed his joints and focused, he saw that the blanket on the other chair was thrown open and empty. He pushed to the edge of the chair. Backlit by filtered sunlight, Richey's filmy gown rippled on him as he shuddered forward to expel more goo into the basin between his knees. He wiped his mouth with a tissue and managed a thin smile.

"G'mornin', Unc. Did you enjoy the Jell-O?"

Petey glanced at the dinner tray he'd cleaned up last night after Richey finally nodded off, and flushed. "Sorry, Richey. I—"

Richey chortled. "'S okay, Unc. Woulda gone straight through me, anyway. 'Sides," he pointed at the glucose IV drip plugged into his arm, "I got the arm candy thing goin' on."

Petey gimped over, dragging a sleepy leg, and helped Richey untangle his oxygen line and guide it over his matted hair and into his nostrils. His sallow skin was glistening and clammy from sweats. Petey stared at his mottled, crimson hand against Richey's neck and wished he could inject about 30 or 40 of his auxiliary pounds straight through his fingertips into the kid. Conversation drifted into the room so Petey headed for the doorway. The white-coated guy with the stethoscope had just finished a sentence and, seemingly startled by

Petey's appearance, turned and fled briskly up the hallway. Maria was left standing there, head down, hugging her elbows. She unfolded her arms and turned to Petey, diverting the streams of tears with the back of one hand. She cleared her throat.

"Dr. Benetasso says Richey has cystic fibrosis. It's a disease you get from your parents"—she swallowed—"that affects breathing, digestion, and...making babies." While she steadied herself, she groped for some hook on which to hang her brother's limited understanding. "Cappy, you remember that guy with the funny name who used to play quarterback for the Jets? Oh, what's his name?"

"Vinny?" Petey frowned. "What's funny about Vinny?"

"No, no—way before Testaverde. Blond guy..."

"Boomer?"

"That's it! Boomer Esiason. His little boy was diagnosed with CF about 10 years ago."

"I seen him on TV. He looked okay, not like Richey."

"Well, Richey is a lot older than he was when they found out. There's no cure..." She took Petey's hand and pumped it up and down hopefully. "But—but there's a real good chance he could live into his thirties if he starts therapy right away. He says they can't do much for him here, but that there's a private hospital in Morristown that specializes in advance treatment. That's the good news." An anxious, guttural "HeHeh!" flew from her throat.

Petey's head spun. "What's the bad news?"

"The only benefits we got are military survivors'. I can't afford a private hospital." The tears came again and Petey felt so forlorn he could only think to turn away. There in the bed sat Richey, framed by the doorway, watching them worriedly. Petey turned back and clasped Maria's shoulders so fiercely she cried out.

"Don't you worry, Sis. I'm gonna take care o' this. Richey's gonna get everything he needs. Now, you go tell Richey so's he can be a man and you pray your rosary. I gotta walk and make a call." Petey kissed her and guided her gently toward the door. He strode toward the nurses' station, punching at his cell phone. "H'lo? Yeh, Loot? This is Petey speakin'—how you doin'? Loot, I gotta see the boss. Can you put in for me, please? Yeh—I'll tell you when I hit town. Okay? Yeh—g'bye."

ഇൗരു

Petey tugged at his collar, smoothed the jacket of his best dark suit, and sat. He looked around the dark, overappointed waiting area. The couple weeks since Loot confirmed the meet had been a blur. Maria had taken Richey to Morristown, checked him in, and plunked down the five grand Petey had in savings. She'd immersed herself in pulmonology; gastroenterology; respiratory therapy; pharmacy; nutrition; and social work. She'd exhausted herself with research, phone calls, and applications—federal; state; county; city; private foundations, with nothing to show for it so far but a litany of excuses. She made too much; Richey was too young; Richey was too old; demand was high; contributions were down; program cuts; politics as usual. Her frustration grew as her options shrank and stark fear gnawed relentlessly at her bravery. Richey's unwavering good cheer, even in the face of his steady physical erosion, and their blind adherence to the rites of Roman Catholicism kept the two of them somewhere near sanity.

"Petey! How's it hangin'?"

Petey hadn't heard that question much since Eighth Grade at Immaculate Conception, after which he and Augie Montagna went their separate ways. (Before that, he'd fielded it at least once a day—including Altar Boys and summers in Little League—since First Grade.)

"I'm good, Augie. You?" Petey stood and raised his

arms.

"Good, good." Augie rotated him full-circle while patting him up and down. (It was a compliment, really; not only was Petey not made, it was common knowledge he was denied sharp objects.) He concluded by placing his hand in the center of Petey's back and propelling him toward the door he'd left open slightly. "*Don* Anziano will see you now."

Petey marched in, stiffly, and tugged at his trousers. "Thank *you*, *Don* Anziano—"

Gaetano Anziano raised a skeletal hand to silence him and pointed at a chair. "Please," he said.

As soon as Petey's butt hit the chair, he understood Luca Brasi's plight completely. He, too, had rehearsed what Maria had written down for him half the night, and his own mind was a complete blank. And, in a way, he was already disappointed. He knew the *don* was in his seventies but he expected *venerable* to be more than pajamas, house slippers, and a ratty smoking jacket. Trenton's *capodecina* appeared small, tired, and distracted. Not even a cat!

"You know Lenny Casagrande over here and Cielo Manna, my *consiglieri*," he said, regarding his left and right. The administration nodded. He jerked his thumb behind him, toward a 20-something perched on the polished credenza. "My son, Giovane. He just got his M.B.A. from Rutgers." The kid bounded around the desk and stuck out his hand. He looked like he sold Kraut cars at some auto mall and had the teeth to prove it.

"Call me *Skip*. That's what all my Alpha Delta Gamma brothers call me."

Petey checked in with Lenny and Cielo, whose passivity he took for permission. He gripped the hand, which was flaccid and moist. *So,* Petey thought, *this is what came out of the* grilla *of the former Arlene Anziano's manicurist.*

Anziano the elder spoke. "May I offer you a beverage,

Mr. DiCappello? Green tea? Bottled water? No? Then, to business. Mr. Nonnulla tells me you have a request."

Petey found a piece of his mental script. "Godfather, my nephew, Richey DiCorragio, is very ill—"

Lenny tried not to make too much of a show of moving a piece of paper closer to the Chairman and tapping it at the top. The *don* stared there. "This is the child of your sister Maria and her late husband, the Army soldier?" he asked.

"Yes, Godfather."

"He is what, now—" Lenny held up his index fingers in parallel—"11 years old?"

"Yes, Godfather—12, this summer. He is in the hospital in Morristown—"

"Your late father, Nunzio, was a loyal friend and a great comfort to me for many years, may he rest with the angels," Anziano read. He settled back, tented his fingers and stared at the ceiling. Petey waited. After a time, Cielo cleared his throat. Slowly, Anziano's eyes returned from their astral place. He smiled at Petey. "Ah, yes." It took a few more moments for the rest of the bearings to fall into their races. "Continue."

"My nephew, Godfather, has cystic fib—"

"This is the child of your sister, Maria, and her late, uh, um—"

Skip had darted from the window to his father's side. He snatched up the sheet of paper, crumpled it, and threw it away. He took the old man's arms and pulled him out of the chair. "C'mon, Pops—it's time for your nap. Lenny, please?" He handed him off and Lenny squired him out a side door. Young Anziano took over the seat, whirled 90 degrees and glared at Petey. "What you've just witnessed, *Mister* DiCappello, is the end of a very long nightmare. Oh, the old fart still has his moments, but it's a real pain in the ass waiting around for them so he can sign papers."

"What about your mother?" Petey asked, befuddled.

Skip laughed. "Pleeeeeze! She did *nails*! She can be

bought off for lacquer, emery boards—and an occasional fur!" He flashed that white enamel soup filter. "Let's cut to the chase. What can I do for you today?"

"Uh, uh, *Principe* Anziano—"

Skip slapped his palm on the leather-covered desk pad. "For Chrissakes, can we just *drop* all the *la famiglia* crap? That is *so* last century! It's Skip! *SKIP!* We're all friends here; am I right?"

"Skip: my nephew Richey is real sick and my sister Maria and I need money to take care of him."

Skip folded his hands like a loan officer. "Don't you have any savings?"

"I did. We gave it to the hospital awready."

"How much was it?"

"Five grand."

"And how long did it take you to save it?"

"Oh, I dunno—10 years, give or take."

Skip cocked his head. "Why didn't you invest it?"

"I put it in the bank..."

"And how much do you think you'll need, before the kid croaks?"

Petey's face got hot.

"You did say *cystic fibrosis*, correct? That gives him, what, another deuce, if all the planets line up? How much, worst case?"

"I dunno; 100 large, maybe?"

Skip turned the desk calendar and jabbed a finger at it. "What year is it?"

Petey blinked. "Two-Oh-Oh-Five?"

"Exactly! New century, lab partner! If you'd put that money to work for you from the beginning, *Mister* DiCappello, you'd be a lot closer to your nut by now." The heir apparent stood and leaned on his palms. "See, this is what I have to contend with—*dinosaurs*! The rest of the world is jetting around in Gulfstreams and this collection of *losers* is still riding around on *garbage trucks*!" He pushed away, laced his fingers, and took a step to the right. "Lenny! Do you know what 'stuffing' is?"

"No, boss." *But I know what a turkey is,* he thought.

"'Stuffing,' friends, is placing paper assets in a captive insurer or fund that does no real business but is legally qualified in 47 states to pay out dividends that are fully deductible against taxable income. Counselor—quick! What's an 'R.E.I.T.?'"

Ciello Manna fiddled with his tie and coughed. In his head, he replied, *Arruso—quick! What's an I-N-D-I-C-T-M-E-N-T?*

"That would be 'Real Estate Investment Trust'—another serviceable way to inflate bogus investments and hide real income. How about a few more? Securities. Commodities. Energy contracts. IPOs and startups. Real investment funds, mutuals and broad pension funds—not your run-of-the-mill union skims. These are all bankable, high-yield fraud opportunities. See, your old, blood-and-muscle business plan no longer works because it's still focused on fear, lust, and withdrawal. Other than running numbers for butter-and-egg money—which the state lotteries have taken to a scale we could never equal—you've ignored the biggest target human nature has to offer—*greed.* Jeezus, even the goddamned *Indians* have figured that one out! Let me show you something, *Mister* DiCappello." He ducked around the chair, opened a credenza drawer, and produced a bundle of dot-matrix printouts bound in blue cardboard, which he threw in front of Petey and spun open. He riffled through a few pages for effect. "You see what these are? *Accounts.*"

Petey looked at the sheets, then at Anziano the Less. He was really warmed up now. He was on the move again.

"These represent our new centers of excellence—the reflection of our core values, our new parameters. The new, if you will, *La Cosa Nostra* paradigm."

Way more than a pair a dimes in there, thought Petey.

"I've liquidated everything I could lay my hands on and made it fungible. These deposits are the foundations on which we will build a brave new enterprise—paper wells from which rivers of cash will spring, to be diverted behind dams of paper and stored to generate yet more cash. This is our future, gentlemen—not as assassins, but *accountants.* Ken Lay had the right idea; up to a point; he merely flirted with fraud as a conceit to get him out of a jam. Means to an end—his, ultimately. We will make larceny our permanent address." He stopped behind the chair and rested his hands on it. "So, you see, *Mister* DiCappello, I'll need every dollar to launch this luxury liner. I'm going to have to take this labor-intensive square-rigger I've inherited into mothballs with a skeleton crew. A lot of you deck hands are going ashore—permanently."

Petey had no idea what young Anziano was talking about, but he had the basic sense not to interrupt the flow if he could avoid it. The eye-rolling he was picking up peripherally wasn't helping. Most of Maria's monologue had returned to him, so, at the first hint of a breach, he was ready.

"Our time together is about up, so let me break it down for you," Skip said. "Two words: You're fired.*"*

Petey was dumbfounded—even for him. *Get out,* he thought, *there's only one way outta the life and it ain't a pink slip—well, maybe two if you count Federal Witness Protection, which is more or less gettin' clipped on the layaway plan...*

"I'm not a heartless man, DiCappello. Cielo, see that our former employee gets another "five large"—as he puts it—as severance. Good day to you, Sir. Lenny will see you out. Oh—and good luck with the family." Skip rubbed his hands together and stalked out the same doorway the old man had disappeared into.

Lenny took Petey's arm delicately. "Sorry, Petey." He shifted into a stage whisper. "Wotta *gavone,* huh?"

Petey thought he got all of it, but the blood roaring

through his skull was making a racket in his ears. He nodded gamely, found his feet and tottered after Lenny, who handed the dazed Petey off. Augie bore him on his leg of the relay toward the outer door. Petey turned his head a little; Augie wasn't meeting his blank look. Petey stopped, tore his arm away, and stuck his face into Augie's.

"Augie. I'm knowin' you since First Grade. What inna name of Christ is goin' on over here?"

The bigger man still looked elsewhere as he nudged Petey into the hallway. "New day, Petey, new day. Go with God." The door closed.

༄༅

Petey trudged up the antiseptic hospital corridor in Morristown. It had been days since he was brushed off, but his head was still boiling. Try as he might, he hadn't come up with a way to break it to Maria what happened. He couldn't face Loot, either. His last hope was that Richey the lion-hearted would help him find the courage.

Three-Six-Oh-Four. He turned in and forced up some *entusiasmo.* "Hey, Champ! How's it goin'?" What he saw delivered an emotional rabbit punch.

There lay Richey, imprisoned like Gulliver in a Lilliputian tangle of glassine tubes. A vest like cop body armor, with two hoses running out to a boombox-looking machine, was draped loosely around his emaciated shoulders and chest—available for the next phlegmatic fit. He was breathing medicated mist through one of those fighter-pilot masks. His ever-bright eyes were glazed; in their sockets they resembled two agates that had fallen into bad custard. His breathing was shallow and labored; periodically, he would make a reflexive, *huck-huck* sound, like a small child does after the crying stops but before he feels fully redeemed. Richey rolled his face weakly toward Petey.

His pupils pierced the glaze and his hand came up. "Hey."

Petey's heart felt like a stone in his chest. He lurched to the bed, grasped the hand and wrung it hard enough that he could see it was hurting the boy. "How you doin', *Nipote*?"

"First-rate, *Zio* Petey." His wan smile knocked that stone into pieces.

"They feedin' you good, Richey? You getting' the calories you need?"

"Yeah—" His eyelids fluttered. "—When I can keep 'em down. And in." His eyes fell on the bulge under the covers that swaddled his loins. "But it's all good. The IVs pick up some of the slack."

Petey flirted with the notion of just scooping him into his arms and running away. A rustle breached his distress. He turned and found a boy Richey's age in the side chair, sitting on his hands and swinging his legs. Unlike Petey's, his moon face showed no trace of defeat, and studying it made the man-child a little stronger.

"Unc, this is my friend, Vigo. Mom brought him up for a sleep-over."

Only then did Petey notice all the prehormonal male debris around the room—a sleeping bag; video games; comics; action figures; and high-fructose corn syrup in various guises, both solid and liquid.

Richey arched his eyebrows. "You know—Vigo? 'Vigo-and-his-big-brother' Vigo?"

Petey stared back. Richey sighed and laid a finger on his lips. "'*Omertá*' Vigo?"

"Oh...OH! *Omertá*!" Petey shushed himself, took a half-step over and shook hands. "Pleeztameetcha. Howyez doin'?"

"A'ight," said Vigo.

"Lissen, Richey," Petey said. "I gotta step out an' talk to your Mama a minute. She at home?"

"Should be—it's after six," Richey said.

Petey fled the room and regrouped by leaning on the

wall and mopping his brow. He dialed Maria.

"Hello?"

"H'lo? Maria? This is Petey speakin."

"I know; I got your number on my screen." Caller ID was another technology that got completely by her brother. "How's Richey?"

"Sis," Petey hissed, cupping his mitt around the tiny mouthpiece, "the kid looks *terrible*."

"Has he coughed anything up since you've been there?"

"Naw"

"Is he sweaty or vomiting?"

Petey checked. "Uh, naw."

"Then, it's a good day, today." The flint in her voice made him edgy. "I'm sorry, Cappy. I'm exhausted. I forgot you haven't seem him in a while. By the way—how'd it go with the *Don*?"

"Uh, pretty good..." Petey's mind raced.

"Is he going to help us out?"

"Who?"

"*Don Anziano*, Cap!"

"Yeh—a little."

"How much?"

"I ain't ezzactly sure yet."

"Well. Money may not turn out to be a big issue—outside of what we've racked up already..." Her voice trailed off.

Petey strained to hear. He thought he heard sniffling, then...nothing.

"Sis? H'lo?"

Maria blew her nose. "I talked to the doctor this morning. He thinks Richey—" She swallowed a sob. "He thinks there might be bacteria there they didn't find before. Here, I wrote it down somewhere..." Petey detected the familiar sounds of an annoyed woman mining the contents of her purse, then the crackle of paper. "It's—it's called *Burkholderia cepacia*. It's a bug that in most cases resists any kind of antibiotic treatment and causes whoever's infected to go downhill really fast. It doesn't affect every patient the same way, so they think he might have picked it up from one of the other CF patients there. So—there's a good chance Richey may not get any better." She really broke down this time.

Petey was panicked now. "Don—Don't go nowhere, Sis—I'll get a ride and come right over, soon as I say g'bye to Richey. 'Kay? G'bye."

He rematerialized, it seemed, by the bed. Richey summoned him closer by curling his fingers. Petey leaned down and Richey touched his cheek; his hand was frigid.

"I want you to take real good care of Mom."

Petey feigned shock. "What're you talkin' about?" Richey's look said they both already knew.

"Oh, yeah..." Petey reached into his back pocket. "I brung your funny book back. I guess I'm done with it."

"You keep it, Unc. You're getting the whole collection, anyway. Read and enjoy!"

Richey's fragile image was awash in Petey's eyes. He blinked the excess out and stared at the four-color rendering of Sherwood's archer. A light came on—low-wattage, but adequate to chase his darkness away. He looked at Vigo, still sitting and swinging. "So, you gotta brother in college, right, Vigo?"

"Yup. Nunzio."

"Pretty good with computers?"

"Yup."

"Write his number down for me here, willya?"

Vigo did.

ℬℭ

The dumpy little lady all in black—including the *mantilla*—pinched Maria's cheek. "He was a good boy, a real *guerrierro*. Hold him in your heart forever, *il mio niece bello*. Be strong."

"*Grazie molto, Zia* Francesca," Maria said, kissing her leathery, powdered cheeks. "Thank you for coming. Carmine's got the car around. *Buona notte.*" She tried not to make it too obvious that she was prepared to use the front door to get her on her way, if necessary. She closed it deliberately and collapsed on her brother, on the sofa. She couldn't see it now, from sheer fatigue, but Maria would grow grateful for that thing that Italians and other immigrants bring in their luggage to America, to come together to encircle and bear up one of their troubled own. Musk oxen, blessed with speech, 24 centuries of culture, and culinary skills. She raised her eyes to the dining table. "Look at all that food! What am I going to do?"

They sat silently in the dwindling light, their fingers interlaced in Petey's lap.

"Wasn't it nice, what the kids did at Mass? That 'Memory Tree?' And the singing—like little angels!" She covered her mouth.

Petey slid his arm around her. "You okay?"

She rested on his ample bosom. "I'm dried out, Cappy. My Richey's in the ground, next to his father, and he suffers no more. That's a good thing. It's left to me, now. Once I figure out what to do about the doctors and hospital, it'll be on to the next thing—whatever that is."

Petey lifted her chin and looked more serious than she had ever seen him since Mama died. "You don't worry about nothin'. It's all taken care of; I fixed it. "Now..." He bit his lip, hard. "I just gotta go away."

Maria studied his eyes for clues but was too drained to press it any further. *Things'll be different tomorrow,* she thought.

⁎⁎⁎

In his undershirt, Loot stood before the stove and stirred the *Marinara.* The phone rang. He parked his cigar. "Yeah, this is Loot."

"H'lo, Loot? This is Petey speakin'."

"I know—gotcha on Caller ID." *Never mind.* "What's up?"

"I need you to do me a favor."

"*Certamente*, Petey—what?"

"I want you to take me out."

"Where?"

"Naw, Loot—*take me out.* You know. Burn. Clip. Whack."

"F'Chrissakes, Petey—*why*?" He pinched his sinuses. If it was anyone else, he'd be thinking, *This ain't funny, and I don't appreciate it.*

"I done somethin' bad, Loot. Real bad."

"What?"

"I stole from the *brugad*."

"Hah! What *brugad*? That little *cazzone*, Giovane Anziano—*scusilo,* I mean, *Skip*—stole the fuckin' *brugad* from *us*!"

"Whatever, Loot—I gotta make it right."

"Why's it gotta be me, Petey?"

"You're the only one I can count on. You're the only one ever treated me right, you know?"

"That's not what I meant. Why can't you—you know..."

"What, Loot?"

"Christ, Petey—I gotta spell everything out for you? You remember Frankie Pantangele?"

Petey concentrated; it came to him. "Aw—no can do, Loot. He was almost a *rat*, whereas I'm awready a *thief*. Besides, I'm thinkin' of Maria. They find out it was me and I checked myself out, they hurt her. I get fished outta the Delaware shot behind the ear, all nice and neat—different story. Last but not least—"

"What's that?"

Petey looked sheepish. "I don' wanna go to Hell."

Loot nodded. "Point taken. Just for the sake of argument, Petey—when?"

"Now. Tonight."

"*Jeez.*" Loot stroked his chin. "Can't I take some time to think it over?"

Petey shook his head, solemnly. "I got a schedule all set up. C'mon; won't take long. Put on a shirt; you'll be in bed by midnight." He headed for the exit. "Oh. I gotta swing by the apartment so's I can change and pick up my stuff. That okay?"

                        ഇൽൽ

Loot shifted from one foot to the other. "Petey! Whaddya doin' in there—sewin' a new suit?"

Petey's voice drifted out of the bedroom. "Don't rush me. Guy can't get pulled outta the river lookin' like a bum. Am I right?"

"It ain't a perp walk, Petey. C'mon!"

Petey finished up in front of the mirror and stepped ceremoniously into the living room. "Ta-DA!"

Loot had only one thought. *If Giorgio Armani was here, he'd stab his eyes out.*

"How'd I look?"

"A unique fashion statement, Petey."

"You think?"

"Abs'loot'ly."

Petey dropped the little gym bag he had, produced an envelope from inside his jacket, and pressed it into Loot's palms. "This here'll explain the whole thing. Don't open it yet. Pick up a copy of the *Times* a week from Friday and read the Business Section; then you can open it. You got that?"

"Yeah, Petey. I got the four-one-one."

Petey reached up and took Loot by the lapels. His eyes narrowed. "And, Giovanni: Do not fail me in this. *Capisce*?" He grinned.

Loot couldn't help himself. "*Si, Don* DiCappello."

On the way out, Petey reached into the closet and pulled out a ridiculous pork-pie hat and plopped it on his noggin.

Loot stopped. "Where'd you get *that*?

"It's my lucky hat."

Loot was perplexed. "Oh, yeah? It's so lucky, why've I never seen it before?"

Petey adjusted it to a jaunty angle. "Never needed it 'til now."

ஐcs

They drove around the 'Burg for awhile so Petey could take it all in one last time. They pulled over at the Sons' and just stared.

"I ain't been in, in six weeks," Loot said wistfully.

"Wonder what the crew's doin'."

"Nothin'—not a goddamned thing.   *That's* the problem. You wanna see anything else?"

"Naw."

"So. Where you wanna do this?"

"Ballpark, behind the right-field wall. I'll fall right in, and the river moves pretty good right there."

"You got it." Loot turned the wheel.

ஐcs

The Escalade glided left off Cass into Mercer County Waterfront Park. Loot hit the lights and guided it to the asphalt's southwest edge. *Good*, he thought. *Just enough moon to keep us from making a lot of noise.* He shut it off, killed the dome lights, and cracked his door. The ignition alarm went off; he jerked out the key. Petey seized Loot's arm.

"I was thinkin', Loot. Didja know that Robin Hood had a 'A.K.A'—y'know, uh...What's that other word?"

"*Alias*?"

"Yeh, that's the one. Anyhow, he was called 'Robin of Locksley.' Kinda like 'Petey of the 'Burg', I guess."

"Yeah? What's the diff'rence?"

"I'm just sayin'." Petey slid his bag from between his

feet and rolled out. Loot hung back. He reached behind the seat and retrieved a case. He lifted the .32 caliber Browning out. It was a gift, new, from his *padre ora defunto*, in 1968—rare, probably priceless by now. This was a special occasion. He loaded the magazine and chambered a round.

They stood by the hood for a moment, listening to the breeze off the Delaware animate the remaining dry leaves.

"Good thing it's October," Loot said.

"Yeh—no ball game. No waitin' around."

The pair picked their way to the water's edge. Loot braced Petey at the elbow so he wouldn't worry too much about his church shoes. Loot looked down at them. *I gotta admit,* he thought, *the old man's spats are a nice touch.* They stopped and, out of habit, Petey looked left and Loot, right.

"All clear," whispered Petey. "No traffic. Hey, Loot—"

"Yeah, Petey?"

"'Member when we was kids and would ride our bikes down here and skip rocks? 'Bout the only thing I ever beat you at, huh?"

"That's right. Good times."

Petey squatted and emptied the bag. He set out grubby, photos of Maria, Richey, and his parents, all smiling, and lit a small votive candle. He took the hat off and placed it on the bag.

"What about the hat?"

"Don't need it; I'll be safe in a second. It gets wet, won't be lucky no more." He knelt, facing the water, and wrapped his First Communion rosary around his hands. He folded them. "Okay, Loot—ready. 'Hail Mary, full of grace—'"

The report's echo raced up, down, and back. Petey pitched into the current without much of a splash. Loot watched him bob and recede until he was as indistinct as deadfall. He gazed over at the lights of Morrisville.

They danced—there was either something in the air, or in his eyes. He packed up Petey's relics, placed the hat carefully on his head, and left.

✄

Loot ducked out of rain through the back door, wiped his feet, and shook like a big dog. He hung up his jacket and was placing the hat over it when he reconsidered. He laid the lid and his fresh copy of the *Trenton Times* on the table, next to the envelope propped against the salt and pepper. He sat down and reflected. It had been a lousy 10 days since... Petey hadn't been found yet, which was a gift. There was already a family death watch on Maria, who was half-crazy when she wasn't sedated. The Avenue was busy with rumors that the *brugad* was bleeding cash under young Anziano—not so much a family any more as a dying factory. He pulled out the Business Section and scanned it. *NYSE, Dow-Jones, yada-yada...* His eyes fell on a four-column picture of a half-dozen *arrusi* in suits, holding giant scissors against a ribbon strung across a broad doorway. He read the caption:

> ...(l. to r.), members of the Governing Board of St. Francis Medical Center, reopen the wing that will house the Robin Locksley/Richard L. DiCorragio Cystic Fibrosis Research and Therapy Center...

Loot's eyes bolted to the story underneath:

> "Honestly, it's a gift from above," said the facility's Chief Operating Officer. "This unexpected endowment from an anonymous benefactor, supplemented by funds from the Boomer Esiason Foundation and in-kind assistance from the New Jersey State Organization of Cystic Fibrosis, will bring a state-of-the-art research and clinical therapy

facility to Central New Jersey. Our charter will be to help all those afflicted with CF, with emphasis on pediatric patients and those without means. With these resources, we expect to become a leader in finding a cure for this horrible disease."

Loot jettisoned the paper and seized the envelope. *Okay, Petey; spill it.* He inverted it; out fell a bankbook and a single piece of paper. He unfolded it and found, neatly printed by ink-jet:

```
Dear Loot:

How you doing?  I'm talking and Nunzio's
putting it in his computer.  He'll type it
up later or whatever.

I guess you seen the story about Richey's
new place at St. Francis by now.  I had to
put Robin Hood's real name in there, on
account of I got the idea from the funny
book.  I bet Boomer's happy; anyways, I hope
so.

Here's what went down.   I go to see Il
Compare to get some help for Richey being
sick.   That cacasotto of a kid dumps all
over me and tells me all about his plans to
wreck the brugad.   He waves a bunch of
papers like Rev's at me.   I see a lot of
numbers, which I remembered.   You know I
can't help it.

Anyhow, Richey tells me about Nunzio, who's
a champ with the computer and numbers and
the Whirlwind Web and whatnot.  He's a nice
kid.  (Look! He's blushing!)  He says he'll
work on a short vig so's he can finish
school.  His phone number is at the bottom.
He's got all the account numbers and
```

passwords and so forth, and he'll train up the Rev on the fine points. By now he should have moved pretty much everything that little *ceffo* stole.

Please give the bankbook to Maria. (She's allergic to computers, like me.) Nunzio's putting some by every month as long as she's around.

Well, that's about it. You're the *Capo di tutti Capi* now.

Your *fratello per eternity*,

Pettirosso DiCappello (a.k.a. Petey of the Burg)

P.S. Don't forget to burn this.

Loot went light in the head. He slid back, dropped his head between his knees, and made an effort to breathe. He labored to his feet and dialed his phone.

"Billy? Loot here. Get the crew together at the Sons' in an hour and have the Rev call me. Whaddya mean, whaddoo I mean? We're back in business! Am I serious? Am I *serious?*"

"Abs'loot'ly."

⁞⁞

12 Term Limit

ഔൠ

Recreational soul mates Zev Brannan and Barney Isleton bobbed and dozed in Zev's 18-foot Alumacraft northwest of the pier at Pinole Point, near where the Sacramento River empties into San Pablo Bay. As the silent November dawn cracked behind them, they shared the unspoken hope that not all the King salmon had found their way upriver, pursuing their evolutionary suicides. Sure, they'd settle for a trout or two; truth be told, they were grateful just to be out of the house—and on a Sunday morning to boot. Barney cradled his rod and fished a beer out of the cooler, opening it with some difficulty. "Durned arthur-itis." He neglected to rotate the EZ-open tab a quarter turn and it tore out a mustache hair at the first draught. "Gol-*DANG* it!"

Zev reeled in his bait, inspected it, and recast. "You rather be in church with the old lady this mornin'?"

"Point made," Barney said. He stood to stretch, and his eye caught a lumpy mass riding the current about 70 yards to starboard. "Hey! What you suppose that is?"

Zev peered through the mist layering the opaque olive waters. "Looks like deadfall to me."

"Let's check it out." They laid aside their gear and

Zev fired up the Evinrude while Barney hauled in the drift anchor. As they motored alongside, Barney hooked the shape's far edge with a gaff and rolled it over.

Zev flinched. "Mother a God!" A male face, handsome in spite of its pale bloat, surfaced, the well-dressed trunk and appendages below it sinking away from it. "What do you suppose—"

"Hold on a minute," Barney said. "I *know* this guy!"

℘℃ℛ

The Commissioner admired the sapphire blue California sky over Vallejo through the front passenger window. All the clouds, it seemed, were inside his head. He studied the pump-action shotgun bracket-mounted vertically above the transmission hump. At the wheel in plainclothes, California Highway Patrol Sergeant Ernesto Nuñez noticed, and prepared himself for the usual question—but with more steel. *Ernie: Don't laugh this time; it wouldn't be appropriate.*

"So, Ernie," Insurance Commissioner John Quincy "Jack" Quisenberry asked, "when are you going to let me break that bad boy out and squeeze off a few?"

Ernie checked his left outside mirror in case he softened prematurely. "No can do, Sir." He couldn't help himself; he cracked a smile and turned back. "When you going to stop asking me?"

Jack wasn't smiling this time. "Well, Ernie, my man—since the hearings start Monday, that may have been the last time."

Shit, Ernie thought. *Nice going,* pendéjo—*the only statewide elected official in memory who's treated his details as equals is going down, and you go and stick your foot in it!* He focused on his hands gripping the wheel and the horizon beyond them.

Jack read Sgt. Nuñez's discomfort; by reflex he came to his rescue. "Cheer up, Ernie. Maybe the next guy will drink *real* beer, instead of that Colorado Kool-Aid I like." Satisfied at seeing his driver's jaw and fingers relax, Jack resumed his dark reverie. *How did it come to this?* he wondered. *Military combat pilot. High-concept marriage. Business credentials. Three Assembly terms as a journeyman moderate. Elected and re-elected to a third-rail office, to which I brought management skills and, God forbid, results. Now I'm probably a fortnight away from being run out of Sacramento—and without benefit of electorate, unlike the other guy.* He came out of it when he saw the Maritime Academy exit sign.

"The Carquinez coming up, sir." Sgt. Nuñez eased the Dark Blue Pearl Crown Victoria over and onto the right shoulder, pulling in behind a white CalTrans pickup. A hard-hatted employee in engineer semi-formal and orange safety vest got out and presumed to guide him to a stop.

Jack produced a business card and scribbled on the back. He extended it to Sgt. Nuñez. "Here, Ernie. After you drop me, head into the City and pick up this guy at the *Chronicle*. He's expecting you; his office number is on here. Bring him here and call me when you arrive. You've got my cell number, right?"

The sergeant nodded. Jack stepped out and the sergeant pulled away. Jack had scarcely buttoned his topcoat before the excitable engineer was on him. "Good afternoon, Commissioner," he said. "Supervising Engineer Steve Soblett at your service." His fellow bureaucrat shook Jack's hand vigorously, telegraphing that he hadn't been this far above his station too many times. "Your driver radioed us you were coming by. To what do we owe this unexpected pleasure?"

"Call me Jack," the Commissioner said and clothed himself in amiable officiousness. "As you know, Engineer Soblett—"

"Call me Steve, sir?"

"—Of course...Steve it is. As you know, I'm a member of the Al Zampa Memorial Bridge Dedication Steering

Committee. I had business in the Bay Area," he lied, "and I wanted to take a minute to check on things before Saturday's ceremony. You know, before things get crazy here, generally and—well, for me, next week in the Capitol. You think that'd be okay, Steve?" He treated his conscripted host to a megawatt campaign smile.

"Uh, a bit irregular, sir—uh, Jack," Steve said, massaging his neck. "A little late in the day to get clearance from Sacramento...I don't suppose it would do any harm, though."

"That's great, Steve. I always appreciate initiative— never miss a chance to reward it in my own department. Walk me over to the South Tower?"

"Uh—the South Tower, Commissioner?"

"Well, yes, Steve. I can't see the 'big picture' from down here on the deck, now can I?"

"I don't know, sir; there's only temporary security before next week—us—and..."

Jack pulled out his cell phone for effect. "If it's too big a bother, Steve, just say the word and I'll get my ride back here."

"Oh, no, sir, I'm sure it'll be okay," the engineer said, yielding with a wave of his hands. He still seemed torn. "Commissioner, the South Tower is over a half-mile from here; I can drive you over if you like."

Jack shook his head. "It's a beautiful November afternoon and the walk will do me a world of good."

"Well, sir, it is a bit breezy today..."

"Steve, I'm a pilot. I know a little bit about moving air and turbulence."

"Sorry, sir—no disrespect. If you'll just follow me to the walkway, then."

The last exchange intimidated Steve for a couple hundred feet. Jack's finely tuned people skills detected the engineer's unease. "Tell me, Steve. How tall are the towers?"

Steve was eager to reconnect. "Oh, they're 410 feet, tip to ripple, sir."

"How do they stack up against the Golden Gate's?"

"Let's see—they're a little over 700 feet, so these guys are about 58 percent of the Golden Gate's suspension towers—give or take a tenth. It's also about 25 percent shorter than the Gate, but..." Steve's tongue was loose and rolling, and his hands and body language joined in as they walked. Jack smiled and nodded; they turned, and Steve carpeted the remaining distance with wall-to-wall factoids. They reached the tower on the Crockett side and paused under its western leg. At the door, Steve shut up long enough to draw his radio.

"Good stuff, Steve," Jack said. "Know what I like the most about the Al Zampa Memorial Bridge?" The receiver paused near the engineer's mouth. "It's named after a high-iron working man, who lived right over there, in Crockett." Jack winked. "Even if he was a life-long Democrat."

"Yes, SIR!" Steve pressed "Talk." "Mike. You read? It's Soblett. We have a guest. Open up."

The speaker crackled. "You got it, Steve." The metal-sheathed door opened a third and out leaned a head and upper torso. They belonged to a rougher copy of Steve, but older and more weathered. Mike pushed the door open and met Jack's gaze. "Regular security takes over after the celebration." Jack nodded an acknowledgement.

Steve beamed. "Mike Chyzhewski, meet Insurance Commissioner Jack Quisenberry!" They shook hands. "He wants to take a look around."

Mike peered under his glasses and flipped at the top page on his clipboard. "Don't see it on the schedule—and it's already quittin' time."

Deliver me from state employees, thought Jack.

Steve sighed. "It's a *drop-in*, Mike."

"Yeah, okay. Whatever. C'mon in."

"I'm going to hand you off now, Commissioner; Mike will show you around." Steve put a hand on Jack's shoulder, tentatively. "I just wanted to say, sir—I'm a

Democrat, too, but you give 'em Hell next week, okay? I think you've done a great job up there. My sister down South had a pipe break in her house a couple years ago— got nowhere with her insurance company. Your Consumer Services people straightened it out in less than a week."

Another satisfied taxpayer, Jack thought. *Wonder if he'd mind making a few calls?* "Thanks, Steve. I appreciate it. And you keep this magnificent structure up and open. Deal?"

"You betcha, Commissioner!" He hustled off toward the north side shack.

Mike gave ground, allowing Jack to get fully inside. Jack looked up through the gloom. T2's interior shaft fell away into darkness like a vertical subway tunnel. The elevator's disappearing, ladder-like track and the long aluminum string of receding points of light enhanced the impression. His new guide pushed a helmet at him. "Here, you'll need this. Regulations, you know." Jack warmed at the irony and treated it as the customary signal for casual *bonhomie* to follow. It didn't come.

"Want to leave your lid here?" Mike asked gruffly, motioning toward Jack's forest green *Loden Heute*, complete with Grandl mixed feathers.

"This? I'll just carry it along, if you don't mind. A gift from the old man, when I was first elected. I'm kind of attached to it."

"Suit yourself. Long drop over water, mostly."

Mike directed Jack toward the fragile-looking metal elevator and guided him inside. He shut them in and hit the switch. The lift lurched into its rickety ascent. Jack checked his surroundings. "Roomy."

"Holds four, maximum." Mike stared ahead, hands clasped in front of his spread legs and planted feet. They herked and jerked in unison as the tiny carriage jostled them. Mike finally glanced at Jack. "Kinda got you by the short ones over there in Sacramento, huh?"

Jack held it in for a moment. "You don't like me much, do you, Mike?"

"Don't have a lot of use for politicians."

You mean, the lazy, greedy bastards who buy into the vision and round up the bucks to make things like this happen? Jack smirked. "I think you need to spend a little more time with Steve."

They continued in silence until the car reached the top. Its gear teeth ground to the top of the ratchet, which noisily brought it to a stop. Mike pushed the door open and Jack looked around. "What now?"

"We climb that ladder 15 feet to the inside of the crossbeam, then another 10 up to the deck, topside."

"Well, let's go!"

Mike inventoried Jack's attire—hat in hand; suit; tie; overcoat; and dress shoes. "You sure?" Jack responded by mounting the ladder and climbing. Mike shrugged and followed. They reached the crossbeam's interior and Jack wheeled onto the last ladder without hesitation and made for the manhole. *Well,* Mike thought. *At least he's not a complete pussy.* Jack pushed the cover over and stuck his head up. He felt the hint of wind gusts but wasn't compelled to hold down his hard hat because the westward stub of the leg was a serviceable windbreak for the deck. He pulled himself up and bent to offer Mike a hand. Mike regarded it like it was radioactive. Jack shrugged, came to his full height, and stepped to the northern handrail. A bluster opened his topcoat tails and forced him to clamp a hand on his hard hat. He let out a low, sustained whistle of appreciation.

"Oh, *Man!*"

With the fading light, the bracing sky bled from horizon to horizon in progressive layers, from values of indigo to cobalt to royal. The stringy, scudding fibers of high *Cirrostrati* were tinged with vermilion, almost matching the massive cables that fell away from their enormous saddles on either side, toward Pier 1 to the south and T3 to the north. The geometric grace and simple power of the span's cable-suspender-deck design was even more breathtaking from this, its top elevation. Interstate 80 snaked up and emptied onto the span, the westbound Travis-to-Emeryville leg already sluggish with rush hour. The company town of Crockett lay at the three bridges' southeast quarter. A massive, block cutout sign at the campus's west edge announced in red and white neon the silos, rectangles, piers, and semi-trailer tangles of the anchor of the burg's economy:

C & H
PURE CANE SUGAR

Jack flashed on the television commercials he'd seen as a kid, featuring perfect, brown *menehune* training their enormous dark eyes on the camera and gaily chirping, around baton-sized stalks of sugar cane:

> *"See-N-Aytch, See-N-Aytch, Mama uses it to bake her cakes,*
> *She bakes the sweetest cookies, snacks, and candy—They're Dan-Dan-DANDY!*
>
> *See-N-Aytch—The pure cane sugar from Hawai'i.*
> *WHEEEE—SEE-N-AYTCH!"*

Chorus over, they all—he couldn't remember how many—alternated between grinning massively and gnawing busily on their individual servings of freshly-machetéd cane. It was one of those epiphanies of youth—*sugar* comes from *Hawaiian sticks*? He had turned and related his boyish amazement to the Old Man, who put down his paper, stubbed out his Winston, and described at length the vast fields of agriculture and streams of commerce that lay behind the sugar bowl. Oh—and, by the way, sugar also came from Louisiana and beets. Jack had checked out mentally when his Dad was warming to farm subsidies, but—still. Lesson taken. Life is complicated.

To the South, Jack's eyes fell on the two nearest of the receding chain of transmission towers that also telegraphed the scope of the human congestion that lay beyond. Turning northwest, Jack could still just trace the tip of Mare Island, the U.S. Navy's first Pacific installation that built 500 warships through five wars, a mile away. *Farragut took command in 1854, four years before Mobile Bay and immortality*, Jack thought. *I wonder—would 'Damn the torpedoes—full speed ahead!" work for me next week? Or should I take advantage of these waters, tonight, to make myself less immortal?* Finally, he caught sight of the particolored coils and spires of Six Flags Marine World, behind the Solano County Fairgrounds. Its pennants and brilliance were missing, because it was off-season. *God, how Johnny and Abbie love that place,* he recalled. Just last summer they blew through Looney Tunes Seaport. Even Trish got into it, granting a brief parole to her inner child. She rode Monkey Business and screamed for and applauded the bottlenose stars of the Dolphin Harbor Show. *Screw political correctness! Flipper was Lassie with fins.* Then they pigged out on junk food. *Trish had a friggin' corn dog!* Johnnie was in fourth grade now— by next summer he'd be "at least this tall"—ready to step up to the big kids' coaster—Zonga! *Will I be there?*

"Hey." Jack snapped out of it. Mike's hands were on his hips. "You about done?"

"Do you need to go?"

"Yeah—wife's waiting dinner."

"Why don't you go on ahead? I'll be fine."

"Anything happens, I ain't responsible."

"I wouldn't worry about that, Mike. Anything happens, it'll be on me—believe me."

"Just one thing." Mike pointed purposefully. "Pull the door shut behind you and let the shack know you're gone."

"Will do."

Mike slid into the manhole as Jack watched. He stopped at his shoulders and threw a mock salute. "See you on the news," Mike said, grinning balefully.

Jack smiled back and nodded. *Go fuck yourself.* "Be careful going down, Mike," he replied. His latest tormentor disappeared, leaving the hatch ajar. Jack heard his feet hit the ladder rungs and the elevator start. He listened to the fading rattle while he gripped the safety rail and the darkness closed in. The descending blackness made the winking red warning beacons at the tip of each tower leg that much more evident. In examining them, he caught the yellow bill of the hard hat in his line of sight. He doffed it, exchanging it for his soft woolen headgear. He considered its glossy rigidity while tossing it between his fingers and catching it every couple inches or so. *Won't be needing this anymore,* he thought. He flexed his knees and, crossing his arm to the offside hip, flung the lid out, hard. The wind caught it in various swirls as it fell, ceasing its rotation. It shuddered and jerked as if attached to a string controlled by a bored child. Jack watched it arc through the girders and hit the windshield of a car inching along the eastbound span. *Well—that wasn't very smart.* His breast pocket vibrated. He fished out his cell phone and read the flashing screen. *Shit. Trish.* "Hello?"

"Where are you?"

"Out of town."

"Really? Visiting your little 'friend?'"

Jack clenched his free hand. "You want to start right in on that again; is that it?"

"What are you getting all exercised about? I'm not the one who slept with a Goddamned *intern.*"

"Trish, for Christ's sake. I've told you a thousand times—I didn't *sleep* with her."

"That's not what *she* says—all over the papers and television! I can't leave the kids unsupervised in front of the set for a second."

Jack pressed at his temple. "You don't think the 30 grand from the tabloid and the appearance deals had anything to do with that? We didn't have sex; at least, not the way people who care for each other do."

"Oh, I forgot—the Clinton corollary. Dropping your pants and getting sucked off in the office doesn't count. Right?"

Maybe the occasional blow job at home... Jack held it in with a quick breath, then slowly exhaled. "Look, Trish, can we not do this now? I'm sorry it happened. I'm sorry I hurt you. I'm sorry it made everything that much worse. I don't know what else to say. I've apologized to you so many times I feel as hollow as 'I'm sorry' must sound to you by now." He teetered at the edge of the pause for what seemed an eternity.

Finally, Trish spoke. "I know, love. I just want it all to stop—" Her voice cracked and faded as she held out the handset and lost control. He wanted to jump, right then, but his feelings for her and his accursed *noblesse oblige* wouldn't allow him to yield to his weakness. He just cradled the cell helplessly with both hands until she seemed to recover. "The kids okay?"

Trish sniffled and dabbed at her eyes. "Homework."

"How was school today? Did they say?"

"The usual—name-calling, kids repeating the slander and threats they've heard at home. Even their friends are shunning them, for their own sakes." She sighed. "Johnny got detention for pushing another boy down at recess today. He says he doesn't want to go back, or keep playing soccer, or anything else."

"Abby?"

"Your little princess?" She hadn't said that to make him feel guiltier, but she realized that it would anyway. "She feels the same way. We talked a little this afternoon; turns out she's worried about me. Thinks I might run away."

"Jesus," Jack said. "It's so unfair, for them. I wish I

could just make it all go away."

"Well, you can—sort of..."

"Baby, we've talked about this. I can't resign without negotiating an orderly exit strategy first. I—we—need some assurance that there won't be civil or criminal liability. I mean, I can't just turn tail and run without defending the office. I'm the only Republican elected to statewide office before the recall. I have to think about the party..."

Trish laughed bitterly. "The party. That's rich! You know as well as I do that there are at least a half-dozen termed-out legislators who are falling all over themselves to be appointed to replace you."

"Now, that's not fair, Trish. A lot of them have reached out, and gone to bat for me these last weeks..."

"Sometimes your naiveté is breathtaking. You were practically the only moderate left in the California Republican Party before Schwarzenegger came along. You were elected and re-elected from the center—by Reagan Democrats, independents, and 'declined to states.' Your 'friends' in the caucuses who don't hate you outright are jealous and, in either case, they'll be happy to have you out of the way."

Jack knew he'd suffered a takedown; now he was just trying to wriggle out of the pin. "Well—what *about* Schwarzenegger?"

Her trademark musical laugh, untinged by anything, came out of Trish. She was genuinely amused. "Arnold? He's not a *Republican*! He's the standard bearer for the new, dominant ruling class: 'Media Celebrities.' Then there's Westly, 'Dot-Com Tycoons,' and Bloomberg, 'Sage Investors'—all sanctified as purer and holier than 'politicians' by your friendly, neighborhood media outlets!"

Her mirth and sarcasm re-energized him, as it always did. "Don't forget Nader, Rosenfield, and Court—'Consumer Advocates!'"

Trish let the moment die in silence. "So—back to the

original question." She felt him tensing. *Men—can retain only one thing for more than five minutes!* "I mean, where are you?"

"Oh," Jack said, relieved. "Vallejo."

"Vallejo! What's in Vallejo? Six Flags is closed." She ignored the warm rush of positive memories to focus on immediate answers. *He's being evasive; he thinks he's protecting me from something too unpleasant to talk about. Do they always have to be so obvious? What is it? Vallejo, Vallejo...the Carquinez...new bridge committee.* Cold fear took her over. Her mind raced as Jack continued.

"I'm getting together with Craig. Ernie's bringing him here—'meeting halfway,' I guess you'd say."

"Why Craig? You two haven't spoken at any length in years." She bought time, still casting about for a way to articulate the obvious.

"I just want to talk to somebody I trust about all this."

"Well, thanks a lot!"

"No! No. Please don't misunderstand. He's flesh and blood, but distant enough to have nothing to protect. He knows who I really am but is enough of a trained and principled journalist to see things at arm's length. He—"

"Jackie," she said resolutely. "Come home. You haven't faced it, yet—maybe Craig will help, I don't know—but it's over. It's already decided. Everything that really still matters—us, Johnny, Abigail—is here. That's all that's left to fight for. We'll start tomorrow. I love you very much." She hung up, fighting her rescue instinct. *I'd rather flee that fight—he needs to sort this out for himself.* Tears sprang to her eyes and her deep frustration bent her in two.

Jack's shock was short-lived. His phone's immediate, urgent palsy startled him. It was Ernie, presumably with his passenger. "Sergeant Nuñez. Where are you?"

"At the south end of the bridge, Commissioner. Are

you coming down or do you want us to come to you?"

"Meet me at the span-level door in the western leg of T2. I've got to come down to get the door anyway."

"Ten-four, ten-four." Ernie did a passable Broderick Crawford, when he felt like it—another shared joke; this edition sounded forced, at best.

Jack stroked his chin absently as the descent began. *This is going to be awkward—at least, at first. Absurd way to get reacquainted, really. I'll just have to bluff or charm my way through the tail-sniffing part and hope for the best.* He leaned into the door and met moving air that was a little less hostile. There they stood, the patrolman and Craig Quisenberry, both mute in troubled anticipation. *Falstaff and Iago! Good sirs!* Craig seemed bigger than he remembered, though he'd had a couple inches on Jack in every measure, most of their lives. They'd been thick as thieves since sandbox, which was more or less foreordained. Their fathers, Mickey and Roger, were and remained as close as brothers could be, given the times and the circumstances. They played sandlot ball, slogged out of the South Pacific alive, and settled into sturdy and respectable marriages within hailing distance of one another. Oh, they couldn't finish sentences like their brides Judy and Eliza could; it never really came up, because at any given moment one knew exactly what the other was thinking. Moving inside that circle, it would have been remarkable if Craig and Jack *hadn't* been close since boyhood. Craig's mottled, doughy features and hulking bearing had always complemented Jack's clean, spare "pretty-boy" looks and angular gait. His cousin's thick, russet ringlets, full beard, and silver ear stud completed the contrast. *Maybe it's more like Ishmael and Ahab, him and me*, Jack thought. *But who's chasing the whale?* They hugged easily and genuinely—not that "good game," male thing with the forearm in front, eyes to the side, and an off-handed clap or two to the back. Jack pushed Craig back a little at the elbows and met his eyes. "How long's it been, buddy?"

"Six years, plus—since you first dragged yourself out of the primordial slime of the 'Lower House' and got elected Grand Poobah of Protection." Craig sighed theatrically. "Ah, the conundrum of the ethical journalist in the post-modern age..."

"And the cowardly editor-publisher who would otherwise refuse to sign your paychecks," Jack added.

"Out, out, Moral Relativist!"

They all laughed heartily. Jack took advantage of the weightless interlude. "I'm sorry, Ernie—we tend to get carried away and there's obviously a lot of pent-up demand. You can take off. You've beaten me out of all the overtime you're going to get today, *compadré*."

Ernie was more sober that he wanted to be. "You sure you're going to be okay, sir? How'll you get back to town?"

"Oh, we'll be fine. We'll do about an hour's worth of witty reparteé, then grab a bite and a cab. Seriously—go home to Estrélla and that *jai alai* team you're creating."

Jack's wheel and sometime wing man looked to be as offended as his inchoate playfulness permitted. "*Gringo estúpido! Hispanics* play *jai alai*. We are *Latinos!*"

Jack was obeisant. "*Sí, Señor; soy un cerdo. Me disculpo lo más sinceramente posible.*"

"Hey, *mi amigo!* That Mexican immersion thing really paid off! Who *says* tax dollars aren't well-spent?" Ernie was crestfallen when he realized an instant later that Jack would likely never have the chance again to reach out to California's 13 million *Latinos*. It was a sorrow to him because he felt they, as he, would admire his *sinceridad y compasión*. They clasped hands and parted in reluctance. Jack and Craig watched him melt into the deepened night.

"Okay, now. Seriously..." Craig was somewhere between puzzled and put out, his hands on his hips. "What in *God's* name are we doing here?"

Sheepish and vulnerable, Jack pursed his lips. "I—I

just needed to talk to somebody before—" He glanced at Craig, whose arms had fallen to his sides. "—before next week."

"About what?"

"God*damn* it, Craig! *Everything!*"

"Okay, okay. Take it easy. Jesus. Why me?"

Jack looked wounded. "You're just about the only person left whose confidence I can count on."

"What—you mean, 'off the record?' Craig brimmed with irritation. "I won't write about it because I *can't*? Is that it?"

"No, Craig, not that. You and I both know that 'off the record' is meaningless any more, even in the most benign of circumstances. I mean, I trust you to not *repeat* it. You're the only person I can think of who will be honest with me without some other agenda getting in the way."

"Okay." Craig backed off. "Conceit accepted."

"Well, let's go up, then."

"Huh?"

"Up. The tower. To the top."

"*Why*? We can *talk* down here." Craig's eyes darted at the rail edging the pedestrian walkway. That side of his body seemed rigid to Jack.

"I don't know—*because*. Come on, man. It's the first uncalculated thing I've done since high school."

Craig swallowed and avoided Jack's eyes. "I—I can't."

"Why? What do you mean?"

"I'm afraid of heights."

Jack started a smile but the narrowing in his cousin's eyes stopped it. Craig jerked his hands out of his pockets and spread his arms in frustration. "I have *vertigo*, man. I get dizzy and disoriented."

"Oh..." A pulse of recognition came over Jack. "The *tree house*. I always thought you were just—you know..."

Craig rolled his eyes. "Yeah, I know—'chicken.'"

Jack touched Craig's upper arm gently. "I'm sorry; it's a lot to ask. I just wanted to go where there's a decent chance we won't be interrupted." He affixed that face that had always managed to get Craig to do something in the range of unreasonable to dangerous. "Do it for me? I promise I won't do anything rash and I won't let any harm come to you. Please?" The face began sliding into a juvenile pout. "Pretty please?"

Once more, Craig yielded. "As long as you don't resort to the 'double-dog-dare...'"

"Okay. Good." Jack guided Craig into T2's chunk of a leg. He felt him tense as he looked around and up, so he braced him at his back and took his arm for reassurance. "You're not going to tell me you're *claustrophobic*, too, are you?"

"No, but don't rush me, okay? David Blaine I ain't."

"No problem." Jack went into the elevator and waited. "Whenever you're ready."

Craig took a deep breath and blew it out. "All right. Let's do it. And—" he raised an index finger into Jack's face. "I know. 'Don't look down.'"

Jack laughed and closed the door. He started the car and hung on Craig's shoulder to occupy him. "So—how's Michaela?"

"Fine." Craig's eyes darted in Jack's direction and returned. "We're separated."

"No shit! How long?"

"Six months."

"How's Sammy taking it?"

Craig's head fell toward his chest and bobbed slightly. "He's 15. How do you think he's taking it?"

"Let me guess—too old to just assume that it's his fault, so he blames *both* of you. Close?"

"Bingo. Could be worse; we're making the effort to be grown up about it. 'Amicable' is the preferred usage, I think."

"So he's spared the headache of taking sides. I wish my kids were old enough to escape that part."

"Has Trish pulled the plug, too?"

"No—not yet. She's been incredibly brave but I'd be a complete fool to expect her to ride out what's ahead, even though she'd try to if I asked her. Where are you two now?"

"She's in the house in San Rafael. I moved into an apartment near the 'Chron' four months ago. Sam stays with Mike during the week—school."

"What is he now—freshman?"

"Sophomore. Early birthday—remember? He's playing Jay-Vee basketball this year. Pretty good, too. Six-one already."

Jack whistled softly. "Is he a hulk, like the old man?"

"Naw, thin as a reed right now. Pediatrician says he should top out at six-six or seven, 225, maybe. Already quicker than I ever was."

"Cleaner living, no doubt." Jack's eyes danced.

"Hah! That's pretty funny, coming from the Collegiate King of Controlled Substances!"

Jack feigned concern. "Pipe down, willya? There might be a 'most likely to vote' within earshot."

Craig smirked. "*That* may not be a problem you'll have for much longer."

Jack reddened. His arm slipped back to his side. Craig rebuilt the bridge with his own arm. "I'm sorry, Jackie. Really. That was meant to be funny, not cheap. I guess I've been a little raw myself, lately. I picked up the phone to call you not long after Mike dropped the bomb. I didn't know who else to call."

"You should have—fuck 'em if they can't take a joke." Jack massaged his scalp. "Damaged goods, ain't we? Everybody knows why *my* marriage is in the shitter. What's your story?"

"Nothing as melodramatic as—" Craig checked himself. "—a personal tragedy or terminal disease. Sixteen years of trying to fashion lust, two disparate careers, and a kid into a deeper, coherent whole. When routine cooled things down, it seemed too much like work—for both of us, I guess. She—being the maven of cyber-content—insists that print journalism's days are numbered and resents me for loving it too much to admit it and move on to something 'more productive.'"

"Wow. I'm really sorry, Craig."

"Yeah, well..."

They lurched to a halt. Jack sped Craig out of the car and toward the ladders; his steps, though quick, were leaden. "After you," Jack said, electing to block the downward view. Craig ascended with the *élan* of a condemned prisoner. Jack followed patiently, marking his cousin's hesitations as generously as he could. Half out the manhole, Craig turned and sat on its edge. With his eyes fixed on Jack, who was head-high like a prairie dog, Craig crabbed backward until his back touched the east leg's inside surface. There, he sat. "If you don't mind, I prefer the cheap seats to the front row."

"Not a problem," said Jack, now fully erect and at the safety rail. It was completely black and a steady easterly had replaced the earlier gusts. *About 22 knots*, he guessed. Waterborne reflections of ship and shore lights showed a discernible rippling in the slow-moving surface. Jack pulled his hat tighter and clapped his hands against his upper arms. "Odd, isn't it?"

"What's that?" Craig asked miserably.

"That we're capable of piling mundane details of math and engineering one on top of the other to make a structure like this, that—standing on it—puts practically everything human into pitiful perspective. *Deus ex machina*."

"Great," sniffed Craig. "I'm stuck on a windy handball court 400 feet up, over very cold water, with Jean-Paul-fuckin'-Sartre."

"That's 430 feet, to be exact."

"Oh. Sorry. Joseph-fuckin'-Strauss."

"Who's he?"

"Designed the Golden Gate. Listen, Jack: conceding that I'm the turd in the punch bowl, can we get on with it and get down from here? Please?"

Pensive, Jack braced his elbows on the safety rail and tented his fingers. "Hm. Where to begin?"

"When do the hearings start?"

"Monday."

"You ready?"

Jack turned, casting his arm in an arc. "For what? The latest installment of the Salem witch trials?"

"Well—that's a constructive approach..."

"I'm not accepting any blame for *that*. This has dragged on for months and I've gotten exactly no traction for my side of the story. It's been an endless barrage of accusations, 'swirling rumors,' and speculation fed by 'unnamed sources.' They've dragged my staff up there, piecemeal, surprised them by swearing them in, and carpet-bombed them with *non sequiturs*. All to make them—and, by inference, me— look guilty on television!"

Craig saw his cousin's color changing, even in the dim, red winking glow from 10 feet above them. "Jack, I know you're frustrated. Calm down. If I'm going to be any help at all, we've got to break this thing down and examine the parts. Deal?"

Jack stood down, came to Craig and leaned against the wall over him. "Yeah; okay. Deal."

Craig drew up his knees, enfolding his shins. "Let's start with the settlements. What happened there?"

Instantly, Jack's back came up. "Look, if you're buying into the premise that I'm the only elected official who's ever used his enforcement authority to solidify his position—"

"Relax," Craig said sharply. "You're not listening. What I meant was, how did all that happen, and were you involved?"

"Willie handled all that stuff. His theory was we'd have to match the Attorney General dollar-for-dollar to compete for earned media, if we were going to have a decent shot at him for Governor."

"Yeah, but, did anybody bullet-proof it up front? Like, test the underlying legality? Monitor the negotiations? Dot the 'eyes' and cross the 'tees?'"

"Christ. *He* was the lawyer; I'm not a lawyer."

"But you brought him to the Department, right? Did any of the career insurance attorneys sign off on the idea or the details? Christ, I'm not a lawyer, either, but it stinks that those deals weren't taken into Superior Court to get blessed."

Jack's irritation was crowded by mystification. "Like I said, I left all that to him. He was there for me from Day One of the first campaign. Completely loyal. He was my *friend*, for God's sake."

"Was he?"

"Of course."

"Why'd he resign at the first hint of headlines, then?"

Jack was fully irritated again. "Haven't you ever trusted anybody implicitly?"

"If you mean professionally, probably not—but that's not my point. Seems to me that anyone who placed your relationship and your future ahead of all else would have been more forthcoming, for your sake. And, would have stuck around."

Jack looked like he'd turned something attractive and familiar over for the first time and discovered an unexpectedly ugly side. He couldn't think of anything to throw up in defense. Nonetheless, Craig pressed the point. "I wasn't on the story, but everything I've read suggests that the companies who ponied up were deeply resentful of the whole exercise."

"So? Who'd expect them to be happy about it? Willie said they were just sore losers."

"Think about it. They were your *allies*. Sure, you were a politician running for Commissioner, but you built the bridges. You weren't just another hack with higher ambitions; you had business credentials and actually cared about rebuilding the market—and you did it, in your first term. Do you think anybody who put you first would risk wasting that kind of capital?"

Jack's sense of reality teetered on its shaking foundation. "What are you getting at?"

"Do you really think one Senate select committee that couldn't lay a glove on you for three and a half years suddenly got that much better at ferreting out details?"

Jack nodded ruefully. "That bitch and her staff have seized every excuse to get something on me; that's obvious. But, come on—it's the flood of leaks from my Legal Division that are keeping them afloat."

"Well, they do have something in common. They all had cause to *hate* your guy—your *friend*—and he's gone. So, they're getting even—with *you*—by talking to legislators and reporters. It's an harmonic convergence of political enmity and personal resentment."

Jack gnawed on his fists for a long moment, looking away. "Do you really believe that?"

"From where I sit? I do."

Jack pivoted and slid down the wall, slumping into a crouch near Craig. The reporter could see he was chafed by the raw logic of this realization, so he elected to break the line of inquiry. Jack was about to speak when their attention was grabbed by the increasingly insistent drumbeat of blades against air. Jack jumped to his feet. A helicopter appeared above the northern horizon, gaining size and altitude. Its resolute beeline toward the Zampa's towers eased into a slower, upward climb, which became a lazy, hovering circle when the craft reached mid-span. The searchlight suspended below its nose snapped on. Its harsh halogen shaft thrust at the towers as the chopper swiveled on its rotor's axis. Craig came to his feet unsteadily as its stark beam fell upon them, blinding them. They shaded their light-singed eyes with crossed forearms, trying to find sight. Noise and turbulence fell on them as the pilot descended toward them. "Who do you think it is?" Jack shouted.

"Dunno. Highway Patrol, maybe?"

"Don't think so," said Jack, preferring to believe that

Ernie's loyalty was still stronger than his doubt. The increasing violence of the downdraft mixed with the steady easterly, causing them to grasp at each other unsteadily. The light went dark as the machine came abreast of them, separated from the tower's carapace by little more than the radius of its blades. Craig spied the legend emblazoned in white on the metallic crimson skin:

He cursed.

"What?" cried Jack.

Craig put his lips near Jack's ear. "It's those pirates from *News9atNight*. Typical."

The door slid open and the dark was sundered again by searing light—this time, the *klieg* atop a camcorder. Craig raised his palm against his forehead; he recognized the small red LED and caught the lens reflection. He clenched Jack's topcoat against the gale and engaged his eyes.

"I'll get rid of 'em."

The combination of the interruption and his general distrust of broadcast journalists made Craig forget himself. He released Jack and lurched toward the 'copter, waving it off wildly. The ship shifted away slightly. As Craig reached the safety rail, spread-eagled, he looked out and down. His equilibrium vanished, he wheeled and staggered clumsily, and Jack saw both his eyes fill with a queasy terror. Craig fell hard against the rail and his arms began to windmill as his back arched. Jack was frozen in horror until he saw Craig's feet leave the concrete. He lunged forward, seized handfuls of Craig's jacket, and reversed his momentum. Craig clamped onto Jack's lapels and followed. Their redirected momentum carried them backward into a heap in the center of the deck. Jack pushed his clammy, gasping cousin onto his side and raised himself to an elbow. The light disappeared, the door closed, and the helicopter rolled out of sight like an airborne pinniped. Jack leaped up to the rail and scoured the dark. Though he could hear a faint *thrum-thrum-thrum*, he couldn't get a fix on the intruder. "Do you think they'll be back?"

Craig was seated, his hands clamped to his head to steady his malfunctioning gyroscope. "You can count on it," he croaked. He crawled over the manhole to the western side and wedged himself into the right angle between wall and deck. Jack knelt in front, stroking Craig's head and neck until his eyes cleared and color returned to his face.

"You okay, now?

"Yeah, I guess." Craig shook his head violently. "Where were we?"

Jack was relieved. "You'd just ripped me a new one about how I didn't handle the settlements."

"Right. Well, let's not lose the thread. What are you going to tell them about the foundations?"

Jack deliberated, anticipating another unvarnished opinion. "The truth. That I didn't know where the money was going."

Craig bored deep with his eyes. "I believe you, because I know you. You've got to know that there are those who've already decided not to, no matter what— which leaves those who can't, and those who won't."

"Wow—that's awfully cynical, even for you."

"It's problematic, Jack. You let a campaign consultant who was carrying your last election debt send a guy from his shop to yours to handle the money. Turns out he wasn't the brightest bulb in the array and, on top of that, weak—a small man tryin' to live large. Human nature. Case closed. That's the perception you're working against."

The slack in Jack's jaw said it all—Craig's words were a punch to his psychological solar plexus. He struggled to his feet and paced while whole sentences fought with each other to get out. "God*damn* it, Craig! The thing that always paid off for me as a leader was to hire the best people I could find and *trust* them. I just don't understand how that failed me so completely this time."

"'Trust—*and* verify.' I think it was one of your major Republican deities who said that. Why didn't you get out front with an investigation when Nimrod quit? You know—'no stone unturned,' 'let the chips fall where they may.'"

"Departmental staff advised me to do that, but the political team quashed it."

"Why, in God's name?"

"Felt like weakness to them—a concession. They wanted to test it first."

"Un-fucking-believable. You're flirting with a jury because they wasted six weeks on focus groups? I suppose stonewalling the Assembly committee was their idea, too?"

Jack's silence was assent. Craig poured it on. "Jesus, Jack! Why do you think Davis got recalled? The guy wouldn't make a decision unless he had proof it tested in the high sixties! Crises don't wait around for poll results. Let me ask you this. Did any of this feel *right* to you? What happened to the killer political instincts that got you through two elections and a term-and-a-half of dedicated controversy?"

"I—I don't know," Jack stammered. "Until this started, the enemies and the challenges seemed familiar. It's hard to divine what really matters any more. Nobody seems to care what we've accomplished in six years. Personal policy rates came down 14 points since I took office and that market's still robust—even after Nine-Eleven!"

Craig glared. "Don't tell me—tell *them*!"

"It's all been so dirty—sordid, "Jack said. "Stolen documents. Wholesale violations of confidentiality laws. Forged signatures on Senate Rules letters demanding documents. Subpoenaing my deputies on Friday afternoon for a Monday morning hearing so they can't find lawyers. Hell, I stand accused of political featherbedding by a legislative majority that spends millions on staff whose sole purpose is to get them re-elected. It's all there!"

"Jack, listen to me." Craig studied the backs of his hands and folded them. "They will win, as long as they can get away with trying you *in absentia*. They will also win if you persist in getting down and dirty with them. They've already defined the issue: 'Ambitious Republican spends quake victim dollars to advance career.' They've been as relentless as you've been reticent. What is it you flesh-pressers are fond of saying? 'On message.'"

"What *should* I do? What *can* I do?"

"You don't have the time or field position to mount a counter-attack—you're too deep in 'confirm or deny' territory. You have to take the high ground."

"How?"

"Call a press conference in the Capitol a half-hour before the gavel falls. Just you—no bureaucrats, no counsel, no political phalanx. Announce three things. One, you've asked the Department's cleanest, purest career lawyer of rank in your Legal Division—Democrat, if possible—to petition the Superior Court for a special master to take control of the foundations—segregate all the records and freeze the assets and accounts—and produce a complete audit and recommendations as soon as possible. Two, you've asked the Highway Patrol to investigate, top to bottom, and take the results to the Attorney General. Three, apologize."

"Apologize? To whom?"

"Everyone. The Legislature, for appearing to be less

than forthcoming—which you're going to fix in 30 minutes. Insurers, for allowing your staff to run roughshod over them. Your electorate, for forgetting where the buck stops. And, finally, to all the folks who buy insurance, for getting distracted from Job One—keeping their insurance rates low." Craig folded his arms and watched Jack's dying emotional embers burn a little hotter.

"'The best defense is a good offense.' Is that it?"

"More like, 'Nothing ventured, nothing gained.'"

"Still, sounds pretty risky."

Craig sighed. "What have you got left to protect, Jack? At this moment, your political future is in free-fall, there's nowhere for your family to hide, and the Dems are braiding rope. The whole of the Capital press corps is on death watch; all that's left undecided is when and where you stumble and whether you're too wounded to get up again. This, I know: as cynical as all those bastards are, there remains a small, cowering part in each and every one that hopes against hope that, one time, one of you will step out from behind the curtain, admit you're not the Wizard, and beg forgiveness. We get paid to make you gladiators but, at heart, we want Mr. Smith."

"You know that, for certain?"

"Christ, Jack, I *am* one of those cynical bastards. Have been for 20-odd years. Hanging around, clinging to the slender hope that one of you will have the guts to break the cycle."

"What cycle? What do you mean?"

"This *danse macabre* that politicians and the print media have been involved in for the last generation. 'Scratch my back and I'll scratch yours—give me something first and your agenda moves to the top.'"

"You don't think television has anything to do with it?"

"That's the irony. Better than 80 percent of the electorate get their 'news' from TV, but what scant attention the networks and affiliates pay to government—after murders, fires, celebrities, and ratings tie-ins—they get from our headlines. So, they mirror the prevalent trends in the dailies. One side feeds the beast and the other doesn't—presto. 'Prevailing opinion.'"

Jack put his hands on his hips. "Whatever happened to balance?"

Craig guffawed. "Why do you think we scribblers are cynics? All editors demand any more is a rough proportion of adversarial quotes—and the sooner, the better. There's no fact checking or rewrite; too expensive. So, three 'liberal' quotes plus three 'conservative' quotes equals 'balance.' Talk radio and TV have upped the ante—it's all about conflict. More, bigger, and faster fights mean higher profits. There's no time to sift the evidence, let alone reflect on it. Gather, record, and publish; make a buck, stay alive. It's a business—first, last, and always."

"So, you think the print media are dying?"

"That's beside the point. You can't die when you're working for the same shareholders, up the chain. The workings of government are like anything else that doesn't produce good pictures. If the story is too complicated to be told in less than three minutes at 11, it won't be. We're supposed to dig out the stories to make it appear corporate is meeting its 'public' obligations. The system's about quotas, more or less, and your side hasn't been making its deposits. You can't catch up conventionally. Your only option is to go for it."

Jack faced Craig and concentrated himself into a crouch. "I go up there and let it all hang out, like you said. Will it work?"

"If by that, you mean: 'Will it rescue my tenure and revive my future?' I can't answer that. Here's the absolute novelty of it, Jack." Craig made a small megaphone of his hands. "It's *the right thing to do*. The rest is up to the reader and the viewer."

"God, if there was just some way I could *measure* it, or puzzle it out..."

Craig worked his jaws, searching for another way to provoke the insight. "Remember Watergate?"

"Of course."

"Somebody at the time—I forget who—wrote that, by the time the House hearings started, at least 70 percent of the American people had made up their minds Nixon was guilty. They could see it in him; they were just waiting around to see if their elected representatives would step up and make the decision. They fought; they stalled; they agonized—hoping for intervention or deliverance.   Death, clever legal advice—anything. Then, they stepped off into that century-old void and did it. There was no other way." Craig could see the gears engaging behind Jack's eyes. "Fast-forward to Clinton. Invoke a remedy used twice in over 200 years to give the boot to a twice-elected President—for a *blow job*? The only reason it went to trial was because he lied, he parsed, and he had an ironclad majority of the other party in the House. Would it have made a difference if another Senator had stood up or sat down? I don't think so. I think the public wrote it off as a political exercise before the trial, because that's how the *intelligentsia* drew it up.   They turned their backs and said, 'Got nothing to do with us.' It'd never have gotten out of the box if ol' Bill had said, '*Yes.* I *did* have sex with that woman. I'm sorry, Hillary and my fellow Americans; I let you down. I was weak. Won't happen again. Now, can we get on with it?'"

"His Vice President lost the White House," Jack insisted.

"Well—yes and no," Craig said. "What put it in doubt for him was not taking the risk of saying, early and often, 'Hey—*I* ain't *Bill!*'"

Jack wanted to say something, but he was too close to the edge of the precipice he had been warned all his political life to avoid to come up with anything that wasn't merely rhetorical. "'Damn the torpedoes...?'"

"Exactly. *Trust* it, Jack. They *like* you because you're *real*—not a cold, poll-driven weasel. Use it. They sense you're a leader; don't disappoint them. Put it in your own words. The worst that could happen is the other guys win anyway, but you walk away with your integrity. Otherwise, you'd better get used to the adjective 'disgraced.'"

"Wow."

Craig scooted a little to allow Jack to slide down beside him. They stared at the other wall for a time, both sensing that the Rubicon had been crossed. Finally, Jack spoke. "Do you remember how all this got started?"

Craig knew what he meant, but toyed with him anyway. "Easy. The Dems took every statewide office but yours in '98?"

"No—"

"Apollo 11."

"What were we—11?"

"Summer, Sixty-nine—going on seventh grade. I was, anyway. You were a lot older—11 and a half." Craig flashed the Cheshire grin, forcing Jack to smile at last. "Who was who? I forget."

Jack glared, still smiling. "A President named Jack had said eight years before, *We're gonna be on the moon in 10 years.* After he got killed, it seemed like everything went to Hell. My folks—it was like they'd died, inside. Then, suddenly, *there we were—ahead* of schedule! Slipped the surly bonds of Earth for another world for the first time in human history, just because *he said so.* I thought, *Man. Could I do that?*

"Yeah." Craig rubbed the back of his neck deliberately. "And there was Uncle Walter, the solemn guy who told us how it was every night, the picture of professional detachment, wiping his eyes and saying, 'Oh, boy. Oh, boy.'" That's when I made my mind up who I wanted to be."

"Wait." It was Jack's turn. "Didn't you make noises about being *Armstrong*?"

"Uh—maybe. But..." A chagrined Craig rolled his eyes toward the edge.

"Ohhhhhhhh," Jack said decorously. "Riiiiight." He punched Craig's shoulder, playfully.

Craig's smile faded. "Where are we, cuz?" He made an elevated fist and pointed his knuckles at Jack. "Truth or dare?"

Jack met this reporter's fist with his own. "Truth. *And* dare."

"Right on."

The opposite hatch cover flew open. Even in the dark, Craig recognized that particular pile of horsehair and cheesecloth that emerged. "Aw, Christ." He leaped up, still slightly unsteady.

Shit! thought Jack. *The maintenance stairway!* "Who is it?" Jack asked.

"Dick Feingold."

"*NewsNine*?"

"Yeah. Got to be a camera up his ass."

The hairpiece was followed by a bloodhound's face, a microphone, and a trench coat. The broadcast journalist struggled onto the deck and extended a hand down toward another, larger head with natural foliage that had appeared behind him. "Hurry up, Butch—*goddamnit!*"

"Why don't you ever carry any of this shit—*Dick*?"

"I got the tripod last time, didn't I? Quit whining."

Butch was out and bent over, hauling up his sound belt and camcorder, when Craig took a few Frankenstein steps over and planted himself in front of Feingold. "What are you doing up here, Dick?"

"That's a pretty stupid question—even for an occasional columnist."

"At least people know I can actually write. How did you get up here?"

"Well," Feingold looked around Craig at Jack, "some

of us don't have influential relatives, so a boat and my good friend Benjamin Franklin got us in at the water line. As they say, 'Money talks and bullshit walks.' Now, if you'll excuse me, I have a story to do. Commissioner—" Feingold took a jab step around Craig and darted toward Jack. "Why are you up here at night, Commissioner? Are you planning something drastic? Butch, get the Hell over here!!"

Butch finished buckling his belt and shouldered his camera. He hit the light switch as he strode toward his partner. Craig pivoted and cut him off. "I really don't think this is a good idea..." He placed his hand over the lens and pulled the apparatus toward him.

Butch jerked the Sony away. "Don't touch the equipment, asshole!" He swiped at Craig with his free hand. Craig knocked his arm away and closed in on his chest. Glowering, Butch swung the camcorder down into his right hand, gripping it by its handle. He stepped into Craig and pushed him backward, hard. Craig caught his leading heel on the instep of his trailing foot and forfeited his balance. He careened backwards toward the rail on sickly little steps. Jack saw him slipping away and ejected Feingold away from him. He bounded toward the rail and lunged at Craig, intending to take him down. Craig fell more directly into his path than Jack had judged. He hit him at his collarbones and reflexively threw his arms around his neck. The force of their combined momentum lifted them aloft. All Jack could see was his cousin's wide eyes under his as he heard and felt the small of Craig's back hit horizontal steel. They cartwheeled into space.

Butch remounted the recorder and rushed toward the rail. Feingold caught him by his shirt and dug in his heels. "Are you insane?" he hissed. "Do you want to create proof we were *actually* up here? Let's go!"

෨ල

Trish leaned heavily against the kitchen island, swirling and staring vacantly into her Chardonnay. Sergeant Nuñez collected his radio and pointed his low quarters toward the back door. "You going to be okay, Trish? Estrélla's got dinner on by now..."

"I'm fine, Ernie—really. You go along now..."

He paused in the open door, digging for a smile.

"...And a hug for her and kisses for the *niños!*" Trish's *gusto* was as half-hearted as his cheer. The door closed. She massaged a temple with her free hand. The muffled, melodramatic drone of a familiar broadcast voice-over reached her ears. She bolted toward the family room.

"*...And so, in a dramatic turn of events, 72 hours before he was due to face his accusers, scandal-plagued Insurance Commissioner Jack Quisenberry scaled the new Al Zampas Memorial Bridge, apparently intent on taking his own life. As this exclusive NewsNine atNight footage shows, his cousin, journalist Craig Quisenberry, attempted to intervene. A struggle ensued—*"

From the door, Trish recognized the ubiquitous helicopter footage, showing Jack and Craig staggering around each others' grips on Tower 2's deck, ending with Craig's back arched over the safety rail with Jack attached to his lapels.

"*—after which both plunged to their deaths in the chill waters of the Sacramento River. This is Dick Feingold, Channel Nine News...*"

Trish jabbed the set's power button and wheeled, looking down into the dazed faces of her children. "I thought I told you—no more watching television without Mommy!"

Johnny started pounding his head with his fists, savagely. "That man said Daddy killed Uncle Craig!"

Trish was immobile. She looked at Abby, whose moist eyes were submerged in shock. Trish gathered her up, took her brother by the arm, and pulled them with her toward the sectional. She sat and pulled Abby to her bosom, clutching the back of her head and kissing her curls. Johnny knelt at her feet, hugging her leg and sobbing. "Ssshh," she cracked, trying to coo. "It's all right. It'll be all right. You'll see."

Abby pushed back at her mother's hand and looked resolutely into her face. "Was Daddy a bad man?"

Trish's heart fled. *Our life is over. How will I ever explain any of this before the hatred blinds them?*

෨෬

ABOUT THE AUTHOR

E. G. Fabricant

writes and lives in San Jose, California. This is his first
collection of short stories.

Connect to E.G. online at:

EGFabricant.com